IF SHE COULD

ALLIE MCDERMID

ALSO BY ALLIE MCDERMID

Love Charade

Love Detour

Love Magnet

Long Time Coming

1

Hazel Paterson blinked awake, her friend Yaz's flat a hazy apparition as she came to. Sunlight flooded through the bay windows in foggy beams, forcing her to screw her eyes tight. It was far too early for this. Granted, she had no clue what time it actually was, but regardless of the hour, she'd rather not be awake.

The distant roar of a kettle hinted Yaz was up and getting ready for their job at Galloway Insurance. Which meant it was eight-ish. Hazel rolled over, pulling the duvet close to her face. Yep, way too early to be awake.

'Rise and shine, motherfucker,' Yaz chirped, padding into the living room. The smell of fresh coffee assaulted Hazel's nostrils. 'Move your feet, I need my sofa,' they said, giving Hazel's ankles a not-so-gentle whack.

Hazel groaned in response, shifting her legs out of the way while trying her level best to go back to sleep.

She should have known better.

Yaz clicked the TV on, slumping onto the sofa with a thud, and slurped their coffee.

Sometimes Hazel wondered if they did it on purpose.

She let out a wavering breath into her pillowcase, not caring if Yaz heard her annoyance. This was Yaz's world: Hazel was just a temporary fixture.

Reluctantly, she turned onto her back, letting her eyes adjust as she stared at the ornate ceiling rose circling Yaz's light fitting. It was a nice gaff, typical of the west end, with high ceilings, big windows, and well-proportioned rooms. Just a shame the mortgage bill was big, too.

The west end was never for her anyway. Glasgow could well be divided into quarters and a person's heart always lay with one, never them all. For Hazel it was the south: it was more homely than the posh west end, more scruffy, a little raw around the edges, while still being up-and-coming. It suited Hazel just fine.

'So,' Yaz said, the word as loaded as a freshly pulled grenade.

Hazel fought the urge to roll over and go back to sleep.

Yaz continued. 'Think we can have a chat tonight?'

Hazel's stomach lurched, a vice-like grip tightening round her organs. She took a moment to compose herself and rubbed the sleep from her eyes. 'Or, we could talk now? Otherwise I'll be worrying all day.'

It was true. Nothing good ever started with *can we have a chat?*

Yaz shifted to face Hazel. Despite their job, Yaz was always well-dressed. Today they had on a crisp white shirt with a gold chain looped under the collar. Hazel would bet her final pennies (which admittedly wasn't much these days) that if she bothered her arse to crane her neck she'd see her enby friend was sporting ironed trousers and newly polished shoes. Didn't matter that they'd spend the day faceless behind a phone: Yaz always brought it.

Hazel scowled at her own bleach-stained T-shirt.

'What was that face for?' Yaz asked with a quiet laugh.

'Nothing, nothing. What do you want to talk about?' Hazel replied, pushing herself up on her elbows.

Yaz took a deep breath. It wasn't often Yaz was lost for words, or stalling them at least. 'I know things were tough after . . .' they began, trailing off.

'Ashley. You can say her name,' Hazel grunted, her muscles stiffening at the mention of her ex-fiancée.

'Ashley,' Yaz repeated, gently. 'And I know I said no rush, but it's been a while and, like, do you think, maybe I could get my space back soon?'

Hazel's stomach dropped. She'd known this day would come but she wasn't prepared. To be fair, if she was Yaz, she would have asked weeks ago.

After she'd broken up with Ashley and been forced to move, Yaz had kindly offered their sofa. A week or two at most. Well. That was the plan. A week became a month, and a month became nearer three. It was inevitable, really.

'I can help,' Yaz offered, their eyes gleaming with the possibility of being useful. 'I can loan you money for a deposit, or whatever.'

It was a kind offer but a deposit wasn't what worried Hazel. The break-up was tough. Catastrophic, even. What had meant to be a hiatus from work had been as successful as her temporary camp-out on Yaz's sofa. And when you're a self-employed personal trainer, taking time off really wasn't an option. Not to mention the fact that drink and bad food had become Hazel's two new besties. Her clients wanted results straight away: most of them had soon found someone else that offered stability and practised what they preached.

'Appreciate that, thank you,' was all Hazel could muster.

It wasn't Yaz's fault Hazel's life was as stable as a game of Jenga on a choppy cruise.

Yaz's eyes grew sympathetic, their brow furrowing with concern. 'You'll be fine. I know you and you've got this.' They gave Hazel's leg a jiggle through the thick duvet before turning back to face the TV and the morning news.

Hazel slumped back into her pillow. Her head ached, the memory of a bottle of red wine coming back full force. Her stomach flipped for a whole new reason. Booze on an empty belly had been a bad idea. *Story of my life.*

'So, when?'

'Huh?' Yaz asked, coffee mug paused at their lips.

'When do you want me out by?'

'Oh, just as soon as.'

Hazel nodded, her lips pursed. There was nothing to say to that. *Thank you*?! *Sure, no problem*?

There was no one else to stay with. Well, no one she'd wanted to stay with. Everyone else had flatmates, or partners, or worse still, *children*. Yaz was asexual and a chronic lone wolf. Hazel would feel like she was stepping on anyone else's toes, no matter where she went, but at least here the damage was minimal.

'I'll make some calls today, see where I can go,' Hazel said, her eyes on the TV even though she wasn't watching in the slightest.

Yaz grunted in acknowledgement.

She'd planned to call in at the gym last week but when working on the courage to actually go in, she'd made the mistake of taking a walk in the local park, only to see Ashley's friends Kirsty and Rhona, arm in arm, annoyingly in love and happiness personified. Her mood didn't so much spiral these days, more helter-skelter from one emotion to another: a bad game of snakes and ladders where she never actually made any progress.

She'd turned around, got the bus straight to the supermarket, and filled up on booze.

Yaz's once sympathetic ear was wearing thin.

Hazel was sick of herself, she got it. There were no hard feelings.

Maybe Shelly could take her in? Just until she got a few PT jobs, enough to please the letting agents and prove that she had an income.

Yaz straightened themselves, ready to rise. 'You good? I need to get going.'

'Aye, yeah, I'm fine.'

'Bullshit, but I appreciate the effort,' Yaz said with a smile as they stood. 'I'll cook dinner tonight. We can get a game plan together.'

Hazel nodded. 'I'd like that. Thank you.'

'Right, best be off,' Yaz said with a final, pity-fuelled smile.

IT TOOK until nearly noon for Hazel to finally get up. She didn't sleep; instead she lay, cocooned on the sofa, tossing and turning, alone with her thoughts and the ever-growing rock in the pit of her stomach, pinning her in place.

She ran a hand through her short brown hair as she waited for the kettle to boil. It was feeling fluffy. She'd not been to a hairdresser in ages. Maybe that was where to start. A little self-care to get the ball going.

There was no way she was going south again but she could take a walk this afternoon, find a new place to trim her top and shave her sides. The fresh air would do her good, blow the dust balls from her mind.

She'd browsed on her phone for a bit before getting up. She had enough savings to pay for a few months' rent but convincing letting agents she was a safe bet wasn't going to be easy. No job meant no income: with so many hoops to jump through when renting she was liable to fall at the first hurdle. No sense starting off on a bad foot. She would talk to Yaz tonight, plead for another week or two. A retail job wouldn't be so bad. Time to pull her socks up.

She paused the spoon stirring her teabag.

The idea of a nine-to-five job made her head swim, her stomach knot. It was one thing to want to move on but actually doing it required willpower and mental gymnastics Hazel simply didn't possess the energy to perform.

She shook her head, snapping herself out of her mental fervour. This was a cycle she couldn't afford to repeat. Yaz wouldn't see her homeless, but she was running dangerously close to pissing off the only true friend she had.

Change needed to happen today.

She chucked the spoon into the sink with a loud clatter and supped on the scalding hot liquid.

If she at least applied for a job, Yaz could see she was serious. It might buy another week.

A melody floated through the walls, one she'd not heard in a long time, and it took a hot second for Hazel to clock it was her phone ringing.

She walked through to the living room with so little urgency she might as well have not bothered at all. No one ever called her. Not any more.

She sipped her tea once more, staring at the now-black screen of her phone.

Maybe it was Ashley.

Her heart sank when she clicked the home button to see it was Dad.

However, Hazel couldn't even remember the last time he called. Her heart tripped over itself, fresh worry clawing at her throat.

She hit call and the ringtone went on forever.

Finally: 'Hello?'

'Dad, it's me, Hazel. You okay?'

There was a pause and Hazel didn't like it one bit.

'It's your mum—'

Hazel's stomach dropped.

——————

2

Louise King thundered into her living room, only half-remembering why she'd come through.

'Mum, where's my other sock?' she asked, flapping the twin-less clothing in the air.

Mum glanced up from her book, barely taking in the colour, never mind the make or style. 'No idea, darling. Sorry.'

Louise grunted, the coil of frustration in her belly tightening further. She did all the washing in this house, Louise should know where the bloody sock was, but right now, a lost sock was close to being what finally tipped her over the edge. Toddlers had the right idea: sometimes all you needed was a good old-fashioned temper tantrum. If only she could thrash her feelings out on the floor.

'It's fine, I'll find it,' she grunted, turning on her heel to leave. Mum went back to her book without another word.

Upstairs, Louise swung her head into Cameron's bedroom door as she stomped down the hall. 'Bag packed?' He didn't even look up from his video game, headphones clamped around his ears and his half-empty holdall on the bed. She huffed loudly. The game's blaring gunfire was drowning her out, so she ruffled the bag, shouting so he might finally realise someone was behind him and, truthfully, to release a little of the pent-up energy fizzing through her. 'PACK. NOW.'

His eyes grew wide as he snapped the headphones around his neck. 'Huh?'

'PACK.'

'Chill, it's not until tomorrow,' he groaned.

She left before the teenager could piss her off any more.

She inhaled slowly, tamping her mood. He'd be fine this weekend. They'd probably just do exactly what he was doing now. Play games, harmless stupid games.

She reached her bedroom, her own half-packed rucksack laying abandoned on the bed. New socks. She could buy new walking socks. There, one problem solved.

If only she could help Marie so easily.

It was a shock to get the call this afternoon saying that a member of her walking club had broken her ankle. A silly accident in the garden, nothing crazy, but bad nonetheless. Tom didn't drive. How were they going to do anything?

She'd pop round this evening, bring some flowers, see if they need anything.

'Find it?'

Louise jumped at the sound of Mum's voice. She turned to find her leaning in the doorway, arms folded across her chest.

'Not looked yet,' she said with a defeated sigh as she dropped to perch on the edge of the bed.

Mum ambled over, pulling Louise into a hug. She pressed her face into the chunky knit of Mum's jumper, inhaling her floral perfume.

'It'll be fine,' she reassured, running a hand over Louise's unruly blonde waves. They were frizzier than usual today, as if her bad mood was seeping out of her follicles.

'I know. It's just socks.'

'I wasn't talking about the socks.'

Louise smiled against Mum's chest. 'It's just . . .' She steadied herself, knowing emotion already nipped at her words. 'What if he gets a tummy ache or has a bad dream?'

Mum jiggled as she laughed silently. 'Lou, he doesn't even come to you now and he's next door.' She pulled back, searching her daughter's eyes. 'He'll be fine. It's one night, and yes, you're further away from him than usual but he's in good hands. He's going to have a blast.'

Louise pulled her lips tight, knowing fine well Mum was right. But logic wasn't going to win this internal battle. She'd even considered making Cameron come on the trip. He'd hate it though. Trekking with a bunch of middle-aged women wasn't exactly how a seventeen-year-old boy wanted to spend his weekend. Especially if the other option was a night at his mate's.

Time to change the subject, before Mum talked any more sense into her. 'I'm going to see Marie later, do you want to come?'

Mum stepped back, her hands falling to her sides as she considered the offer. 'Hmm, no. I'll go after the trip. I want to conserve my energy.'

'You nervous?'

'Never.'

Louise simply raised her eyebrows in response.

This trip was a big deal. She'd started the walking group a few years ago, having seen how desperately the women of Perth needed a new social outlet.

Working at the sports centre as a community liaison officer was more than just organising sports and jumble sales. Most of it was *watching* – finding the gaps that needed filled and fixed. She'd seen the huddles of women after yoga, the ones who stayed back a little longer, dying for a natter but not having the time – not now the class had taken up the spare hour they had.

So, she launched Walkie Talkie. A weekly meetup where women could have a chat and wander around the local park, or The North Inch as it was really called. (Insch in Gaelic, a level area or piece of dry land in a swamp. Tasha had taught her that pub quiz-worthy fact.)

It started small, a few women every week, but over time it had grown to nearly twenty regulars.

Now six of them were going on a ten-mile walk to raise money for Breast Cancer Awareness. Never in a million years did Louise see it becoming what it was. Seeing the impact it made was euphoric; it made her soul light up.

That being said, if she didn't get her sock situation sorted it might all end in tears.

Tyndrum to Inveroran was no small beans. Granted, it was the easiest section of the West Highland Way, Scotland's most famous and lucrative walk, but it was still nearly ten miles and would take the best part of the day.

'I'll be going to the shops first, get some socks. You sure you don't want to come?' Louise offered again.

'Nah, me and Cameron will stay here. He'll keep me out of trouble.'

Louise ignored the joke. 'I might put a thing in our group chat, see if anyone else needs stuff from the shop since I'm going.'

'Do you want me to do anything for tea?' Mum asked, now hovering in the doorway.

'Nah, I'll grab us a pizza on the way home. Save on the washing up.'

'You sure?' Mum arched her eyebrow, emphasising the silent point she was making: Louise was taking on too much, forgetting she could delegate. Why put other people out when she could just crack on, though?

'Totally. I can get it on the way home.'

Mum turned to leave, calling over her shoulder: 'Packed your boots?'

'Not yet. I was just going to wear them, no sense taking up space with big boots.'

'Uh-huh.' Louise was sure she could hear a smile in her mother's words as she wandered off.

She rounded the bed and pulled the sliding mirror door to her wardrobe open, dropping to squat.

Boots. Where were her boots? *Christ, I better not have lost them too.*

They were up the back, where she'd left them from their last practice walk. She pulled them out, setting them by the bed, ready for tomorrow.

There, poking out the top of her left boot: her lost sock.

If you didn't laugh, you'd cry.

3

Broxden roundabout came into view as Hazel followed the motorway from Glasgow. Usually the sight made her skin tingle with excitement: she was nearly home. But today, coming back to Perth felt like the searing cattle brand of failure on her flesh.

Since Dad's call, explaining that Mum had fallen in the garden and broken her ankle, Hazel had found herself at a crossroads. Packing up her stuff from Yaz's had taken moments but deciding what to do had taken a lifetime. Finally, hours later, she'd hopped in the car and given in to the fact she was destined to be a deadbeat nobody.

This was it. The final nail in the coffin.

She was being dramatic. But sometimes you needed to exaggerate to work through stuff.

At least, that's why she told herself it was absolutely necessary to be belting out Carrie Underwood as she slowed to match the pace of the upcoming traffic.

Mum was fine, her dignity was more damaged than her leg, but she and Dad needed help. Which meant moving back to Perth. Which solved so many problems. The universe had basically handed her a solution on a silver platter. She could have done without it slapping her in the face with said platter afterwards, though.

In any other circumstances, she'd have no qualms about going home. Since Dad lost his driving licence to diabetes-induced vision loss Mum had driven them everywhere, so they needed her, initially at least.

But like this? No job, no home, no fiancée? Returning to her childhood bed was like zipping back in time, all her achievements wiped from reality.

She crawled round the roundabout, feeling like the massive metal grouse in its centre was taunting her. Its wings were spread but it was going nowhere. Just like her.

Of course, moving back presented a new problem: how honest should she be? They knew Ashley had left her, of course. But the lack of flat, the failure of her business: Hazel had kept all that under wraps. Life was bad enough living in the shadow of her little sister, Charlotte. High flyer Charlotte, who had the common sense to bugger off to Australia with her charming boyfriend and never look back.

Maybe she could bend the truth a little, make her seem like the selfless hero for once.

She rounded the corner into the sleepy suburb of Oakbank, with its picture-perfect bungalows, and steeled herself: time to put on a show.

'Mum? Dad?' Hazel called as she shuffled into the house, duffel bag on her shoulder. No response from Dad but that was par for the course: he was deaf as a post these days.

She dumped her bag in the hall, by the telephone table, and made her way to the living room.

If there was one comfort in life, it was that her parents' house never changed. Not once in the thirty-seven years Hazel had walked the earth. It always smelled the same, of washing powder and potpourri; the lights were always at a minimum; and the place was never less than a sweltering 22 degrees.

Hazel let her eyes wander to the photos on the wall as she trailed down the hall. Her and Charlotte as kids, complete with questionable matching outfits. Diplomas and university certificates. Charlotte smiling broadly with her university degree. Hazel with a gold medal for swimming – she must have been eight? Nine? – also sporting a smile a mile wide.

It was a hall of highlights, the crème de la crème of Paterson life. Hazel sure as hell wouldn't be adding to it any time soon.

She poked her head into the living room and found her parents asleep on the big sofa. It was just after teatime and the sun cast hazy strips of light into the room, like dancing beams of gold. This room hadn't changed either. Down to the electric fire being on. So much for summer.

She plonked herself on the small sofa perpendicular to theirs, a little heavier than usual, in the hope it might wake them up. Nothing.

Next plan of attack: she reached over, hoping to shimmy the remote free from Dad's grasp as he held it loosely to his chest, on top of his admittedly decreasingly round belly.

She'd made it an inch when he sprung to life.

'Hey, whoa, who's there?' he yelped.

Hazel snapped her hand back with a chuckle. 'Just me. You were out for the count.'

Mum stirred next, forgetting her injury and wincing in pain when she moved her leg.

Hazel scooted round to her side. 'Hold up, you okay? Can I get you anything?'

Mum scrunched her eyes up again, still coming round. 'Hazel, you're here.'

'Of course.'

She leaned forward to hug her daughter but pain contorted her features again. Hazel closed the gap, helping her relax. 'It's so good to have you home.'

'Now, what can I get you?'

'Nothing, nothing, just sit,' she replied, patting the small space in front of an embroidered robin cushion.

Hazel cooried in, leaning against Mum's arm as Dad changed the channel to a fresh quiz show. Maybe being back wouldn't be too bad.

~

'You alright?' Dad asked, keeping to the threshold of Hazel's room.

It had changed over time: it was no longer *hers*, but it was nice enough. A few hints at the past remained, things she didn't want to take into adulthood and her parents probably didn't know a better place to put: medals, awards, posters and pictures. The double mattress was the same, and even though her childhood stripy wallpaper wasn't to her taste it wasn't offensive. They'd laid a new carpet and changed the position of the radiator, making the room familiar and foreign all at once.

'Yeah, just unpacking.' She had been, then social media had gotten the better of her and cut the job short.

'Your mum would like a chat. She's in the living room still.'

Ominous. 'Okay, one min.'

Dad was off before she could ask further questions. Today had started with a terrible chat and it was going to end with one. What would it be now? The ankle break was worse than they thought? Hazel couldn't stay here? They knew she didn't have a job?

She was going to put a ban on anyone ever using that phrase again. No more 'chats'.

Hazel took her time going to the living room, hoping that if she prolonged this long enough, Mum might forget what she was going to say. It had happened before.

Unfortunately Mum was more alert than ever when Hazel found her propped up on the sofa, just where she'd left her before. Her eyes shone with excitement but the way she was subtly wringing her hands together made Hazel's palms sweat.

'Everything okay?' Hazel asked, not hiding the uncertainty in her voice.

'I think so. I have a favour to ask, though.'

The second worst phrase you can hear, fantastic. 'Uh-huh. What's that?'

Mum patted the space Dad usually occupied. 'Sit.'

Hazel perched on the sofa, her back straight, braced for whatever was coming.

'Do you remember me mentioning a walking group to you?'

Hazel wracked her memory. 'Vaguely, how come?'

'Well, we're raising money for breast cancer. Carole had it last year and now, touch wood,' she said, tapping her head, 'is finally clear. It's our way of giving back for saving our friend.'

'Okay.'

'To fundraise, we're going on a walk.'

Hazel arched her brows. Was Mum asking for sponsorship money? 'Uh-huh.'

'Well, I was going on a walk.' She motioned to the cast around her lower leg, her face dripping with disappointment.

'When was it meant to be?'

'Tomorrow.'

'Yikes.'

'I know. Such a stupid thing to do, just a silly accident though. But now,' she shrugged, her gaze still fixed on the cast. 'I feel I've let everyone down.'

'Don't be silly,' Hazel reassured, giving the thigh on Mum's good leg a wee jiggle. 'People will understand.'

'I know but the girls—' Mum paused and Hazel smiled at the use of girls: the youngest was sixty at best, if she was remembering Mum's pals correctly. 'I just, I don't want to risk the sponsorship, and I know how much it meant to Carole that we were all together. I was wondering, I know it's not quite the same, but—'

Hazel cocked her head to the side, a good idea of where this was going forming in her mind's eye.

'—would you do it for me?'

'Me?'

Mum laughed under her breath. 'Yes, you! My superstar personal trainer daughter. It will be nothing to you.'

'How far is it?'

'Just ten miles. Give or take.'

'Ten miles?' Hazel repeated, almost choking on the words. She'd be lucky if she'd even walked that distance in the last three months combined.

'You can borrow my equipment, if you don't already have it, and I know you already have walking boots.'

'I, er—'

'It would mean a lot to your Mum, love,' Dad said from the doorway and Hazel nearly jumped out of her skin. Seems he could be as sneaky as her when he wanted.

'Consider it,' Mum said, pleading with her eyes.

'Ten miles? Easy terrain?'

'Of course. We're hardly experienced; it will be a walk in the park for you.'

Hazel turned the idea over in her head. A ten-mile walk with a bunch of nearly pensioners? It would be easy: this time last year she could have done it in her sleep. Plus, it would gain her some serious plus points to soften the blow of telling her parents about her lack of job or housing.

'Just to get this straight: it's tomorrow, yeah? One day? And that's it?'

'Well, there's a hotel booked at the finish line. We're not the fastest of walkers. It seemed the sensible thing to do. Make a weekend of it.'

Hazel gulped. That made things a little more complicated. Although, Mum spoke fondly of these women – if Mum rated them then surely one night with a gaggle of easy-going women would be a breeze?

'So, a walk and a night in the hotel? I don't need to drive them all there or anything?'

'No, no. That's all sorted. We've booked a minibus.' Mum puffed her chest out, proud as punch, as if that was the achievement of the century.

'Right, yeah, sure,' Hazel said, her voice giving away the fact she still had a sinking feeling in her gut. There had to be a catch.

Mum's eyes lit up as she pulled Hazel in for a hug. 'You're a star. I knew I could count on you.'

The quiet sound of Dad's footsteps leaving the room suggested he approved of Hazel's decision.

'Anything for you, Mum,' Hazel replied, still squeezing her mother tightly.

Mum pulled back, a smile twinkling in her eyes. 'Now, my bag's packed. You'd better check everything is okay for you. Otherwise Louise can pick stuff up for you. She posted in the group chat she was going to the shop.'

Since when did Mum do group chats?! 'Louise – she's one of the women doing the walk?'

'Yep, she's pretty much organised the whole thing. I think you'll get on.'

The hairs on the back of Hazel's neck prickled, her brain slowly catching up with what she'd agreed to do. She'd gone from living the life of a near recluse to being front and centre, having to make a good impression, put her PR face on for a full twenty-four hours. It would be tiring but she could do it. For Mum.

'Right, well, I guess I'd better check your bag,' Hazel said, standing. Nothing felt real: even walking to her parent's bedroom was like being on autopilot.

This was good though. She was helping. As soon she got back she'd broach the issue of being jobless. Mum and Dad would be on such a high from her doing the walk, she'd be fine.

The doorbell chimed, making her pause in the hall and double back.

No doubt it was one of Mum's pals, bringing flowers round or just wishing her well. Although, now Mum was in the world of group chats maybe it was all digital. Next thing she'd be saying she had a Facebook.

Hazel smiled at the thought, but it was short-lived. Her features flipped to a scowl after seeing who now stood at the door.

'Louise,' Hazel growled.

4

'Hazel,' Louise squeaked.

Silence hung in the air as Louise's brain shut down. Somewhere at the back of her mind sparks of reasoning were firing, but nothing was making sense. This was Hazel's parents' house; it was perfectly normal that she would be here. But after nearly eighteen years Louise might as well be face to face with a ghost.

Hazel's face was like thunder.

Louise chewed on her cheek, nothing sensible coming to mind, no way to break the ice. Then her hands had the bright idea to extend on their own accord, holding out a bag of shopping and cellophane-wrapped flowers without any explanation.

Hazel didn't move.

Her arms wouldn't go down, though. Instead they did a little gesture, as if encouraging Hazel to take the blasted things. Which would be great, but words would be even better.

'Marie,' was all she could manage.

Right on cue, Hazel's mum cut through the void, a bodiless voice that Louise could hug the life out of.

'Who is it, love?'

'It's Louise,' Hazel called over her shoulder, saying her name like it was dirty.

'Ohh, bring her through!'

Hazel stepped aside, still brooding in silence.

Louise gulped. Things had always been rocky between them, but she'd not expected this. So much water had passed under the bridge; this level of malice was a little extreme.

She'd been here a million times, so she didn't need to ask Hazel for directions, thank God. She switched into friend-mode, a smile now plastering her face as she entered the hall. She was here to see Marie, not her moody daughter.

'Where are you?' she called, sounding more like herself.

'In the living room,' Marie replied, surprisingly upbeat for someone who had been through so much today.

Louise rounded the corner into the sage-green room to see her friend propped up on the sofa, her cast-laden leg resting on the edge of coffee table. 'Oh, Marie, are you okay?'

She sighed. 'Been better.'

'What's happened?' Louise asked, putting the bags by the table and sitting by Marie in one seamless motion, flowers now resting in her lap. She'd only been given a brief explanation on the phone. Marie wasn't the type to be doing anything dangerous, hopefully nothing too severe had been the cause.

'I was repotting some plants, misjudged my footing, tumbled right over the pots and into the verge. Silly, really.'

'That must have hurt. Are you okay now? Need me to get you painkillers?'

'You're always looking out for me. No, no. I just had some, thank you.' Her eyes drifted to the flowers.

Louise's mind was so focused on Hazel that she'd almost forgotten she was holding them. 'Oh, yeah,' Louise gushed, her cheeks flushing crimson. 'These are for you.'

Marie accepted the humble bouquet, turning it in her hands as she admired the red and white chrysanthemums. 'They're beautiful. Thank you.'

'Hazel's home?' It was more of a question than a statement, her brain refusing to accept the awkward encounter was real.

Marie's smile enveloped her entire face. 'Yes! She came home as soon as she heard what a silly idiot I'd been.'

'That's good. I'm glad you and Tom will have an extra pair of hands.'

She arched her eyebrows in response. 'I know, it was such a relief when she said she was coming through. She's so busy with work, you have no idea. But of course, I do all the driving so we'd be pretty sunk without her.'

'Is she staying a while?' It was an innocent question and yet her throat contracted a little at the thought.

They'd never been friends. Not even acquaintances, really. Hazel ran in different circles to Louise. That was high school, though: in the Venn diagram of life there was often a party or event to cross everyone together.

Louise's cheeks grew hot at the memory. She wasn't exactly the best version of herself at that age. It was no wonder Hazel wasn't happy to see her.

'Not sure,' Marie answered, her eyes now wistful. 'Depends how much time she can take off work, but I'll be in this cast for at least six weeks according to the hospital.'

Louise placed her hand on Marie's and gave it a reassuring pump. 'Well, you've got me if you're ever in need.'

'You're a star.'

'Any time. Now, obviously we're away tomorrow, but is there anything else you need? I've updated our accommodation about the change and you'll have seen me let the group chat know.'

'Actually,' Marie said, drawing the word out like it was loaded. The glint in her eyes said it was a good addendum, though. 'Hazel is going to take my place. I wouldn't want to jeopardise the sponsorship and she is more than happy to be part of something so special.'

'Don't be silly, we'd still get the fundraising money. Wait —' Louise said, her brain finally processing Marie's words. 'Hazel is coming on the trip? With us?'

Marie chuckled. 'Yes! She seems quite excited, I think. Is that okay?'

'Yeah. Sure.' Louise's stomach tied itself into a knot.

'Yass, I'm starving,' Cameron said as Louise passed by the living room door. He snapped his headphones off and sprung to his feet, soon hot on her heels as she went through to the kitchen.

She leaned her hips against the counter, her gaze fixed on the empty space in front of her.

'Pizza?' Mum asked, her voice a thousand miles away.

Louise snapped back to life. 'Shit. Don't,' she added, before Cameron could scold her for swearing.

'Did you leave it in the car?' he asked, looking around like it might be on the floor or hidden in his mum's hair.

'No, no. I forgot to get one.'

'Forgot?' he whined.

Louise scrunched her face up. This was not good.

Her mind was on a spin cycle.

She'd stayed with Marie for another twenty minutes and Hazel hadn't even come to wish her goodbye. Tom had popped his head in to say hello: he was always lovely. But Hazel? She was nowhere to be seen. Probably off throwing darts at pictures of Louise, if her earlier greeting was anything to go by. And now they had to travel to Tyndrum together. Walk a trail. Stay overnight.

It was going to be so awkward. Just the thought made Louise's neck itch. She scratched at the ever-growing heat spot below her ear.

'You okay?' Mum asked, her brow furrowed.

'Yeah, yeah. Just got lots to do.'

There was no point talking to Mum about Hazel. There was so much going on around that period of her life—Dad, school, *herself*—she'd never once mentioned Hazel to family. Apart from to gossip and moan about her, Louise never even spoke the truth about Hazel to her friends.

'What we gonna eat then?' Cameron was already on the way to the fridge but Louise had purposely let supplies run low, knowing they were to be away for a weekend. Cameron was no small guy: at just past seventeen he already towered over her and had a muscle mass that could easily eat her out of house and home on a good day.

'I'll phone for a pizza,' Louise announced with a sigh, fishing her phone out of her back pocket. Mum snatched it away.

'*I'll* phone for a pizza. You take a seat. I'll pour you a wine. A *small* one, before you say you're up early,' she added before Louise could protest. 'As usual, you've done too much. You need to rest.'

'You packed?' Louise asked Cameron, ignoring Mum.

'Of course,' he mumbled, head still in the fridge.

'Really?'

'Mostly,' he replied, closing the fridge now his pillaging was complete. A goofy smile was half-obscured by a flapping piece of string cheese that hung from his mouth.

'That means not at all.' Louise huffed and rested her head on her arms, choosing the countertop over the sofa. If she could just stay here forever, it would all be okay.

'Now, look. Listen to your mother,' Mum jested, pulling at Louise's elbow. 'Get to that sofa.'

Louise grunted. She didn't need to relax, she needed sedated. There was no point arguing with Mum though. She shuffled through and flopped onto the sofa.

'Call me when the pizza comes,' Cameron called, already halfway up the stairs.

Mum poured two wines, one eye on the door. Satisfied Cameron was out of earshot, she spoke. 'You still worrying about him?'

'A bit.' It was easier to lie. The truth would need a PowerPoint presentation to explain. Besides, it was only a half lie.

Mum passed Louise a glass and got comfy in the armchair. 'He'll be fine. He's a good lad.'

Louise took a slow sip of wine, the heat from the alcohol silencing some of her thoughts. Not all of them. But she'd take what she could. 'I know. I must have driven you potty at that age.'

Mum pulled a face. 'A little. You turned out okay.'

'Eventually. Bit of a wobbly middle.' That was an understatement. And that *wobbly middle* was who Hazel knew. It was no wonder she was so stand-offish. If Louise encountered her younger self she'd be appalled.

'A wee bit. But no one's perfect. Now, pizza before your poor son resorts to eating that yoghurt we've had for months?'

'Go for it,' Louise said, wavering a hand between them as she leaned her head into the squishy back of the sofa and closed her eyes.

Everything would be fine. She was no longer a teenager. She was a grown-ass woman who had her shit together.

So why did her heart still trip when she thought of Hazel Paterson?

5

Hazel looked at her phone, half hoping for another family emergency so she could tell the taxi to turn around and take her home.

It was a short journey to the car park of the sports centre but it felt like they were hitting every red light imaginable.

Thank God.

On the one hand she wanted this over as quickly as possible. On the other, she was nowhere ready to see Louise Menzies. Or King. Whatever she was now.

When she'd moaned to Mum about her lack of information she'd been quickly corrected over Louise's name. So the woman was married now, what difference did it make?

Hazel puffed her cheeks out, exhaling slowly, hoping to defuse some of the nervous energy jangling her muscles.

Of course Louise would be married now. She probably had the perfect husband, two kids, a picturesque house, a dog or two as well.

She'd always been the opposite of Hazel: why not carry on the tradition?

Would she be the same bratty woman Hazel remembered? Whispers behind hands, calculated conversation, and laughter cut short when Hazel entered a room?

How much could a leopard change its spots?

'Top car park or bottom, love?' the taxi driver asked.

The campus hadn't seen much renovation over the years but it was still impressive. A large grey dome made up most of the sports centre with two rectangular buildings at the rear, with a series of sloped car parks surrounding the three sides that didn't flank the Inch. Inside lay squash courts, indoor football pitches, meeting rooms, and a state-of-the-art gym. Just to name a few of its assets.

'Here's fine,' Hazel said despite not seeing the minibus. If she got dropped off at the top she could walk down, *slowly*. Give herself time to adjust.

The sun licked her skin as the taxi drove away, even though it was the wee small hours of the morning. It was going to be another hot summer's day. She yawned as she crossed the empty car park. Sleep hadn't come easily last night – once the wheels of her head were spinning it was too late. She was awake, stoking her anger with the past: stuck in a loop of terrible home movies. She would finish replaying one scenario only to start again. Analyse. Remember. Pick apart. Over and over and over.

Some people get under your skin and no matter how hard you scratch you're stuck with them for life.

She'd not thought about Louise for years but now she was all Hazel could focus on. She was right back to being seventeen – dreading every day at school, every party that was meant to be fun, all soon turned upside down by Louise Fucking Menzies.

Even before she'd rounded the back of the centre Hazel could hear the chatter of excited women.

She hauled her bag up, adjusting where it sat on her back. Everything felt off, like she'd put her shoes on the wrong feet and her T-shirt on backwards. Her skin hummed with anxious anticipation.

At the bottom of the car park her trail buddies lingered around the minivan, Louise at the edge of the group, glowing with happiness. If only people came with a dimmer switch.

She raised her hand to Hazel, waving like they'd been friends their whole lives, with a grin to match.

Hazel didn't return it.

This wasn't the time to hold grudges, though. This was the first time meeting Mum's best friends. First impressions were important.

She boxed up her emotions to deal with another day. It was a skill she wished she hadn't had to perfect in the last few months, but beggars can't be choosers. If only she'd become a dab hand quick enough to save her business.

'Hey,' she said to the group, mustering the best smile she could.

Louise hoofed to her side, smile still on full beam. 'Hazel, hey! So glad you could make it. You okay? Warm, isn't it?' The words spilled out in a torrent. Was Louise nervous? Probably just the hike, not Hazel's presence.

'Yeah, it is.' Hazel said, her tone flat. She surveyed the group. 'Is that us all here?'

Louise's eyes scanned the women around her. 'Yep. Jerry, the driver, is just inside. He'll be out soon. Want to get on?'

'Sure.'

Without another word Hazel boarded the bus and headed straight to the back, plonking her rucksack on the seat beside her, lest Louise get any ideas about striking up conversation.

She shoved in her EarPods and turned up her music.

Today was going to be long.

THE BUS JOURNEY hadn't been bad. The majesty of the Scottish Highlands had done wonders to calm her nerves. By the time they arrived, Hazel was in a decent mood. She'd chipped into polite conversation when needed and all in all, time and music had done wonders for getting in the zone, ready to make a great impression on Mum's friends.

This section of the West Highland Way was deemed the easiest but it was still a challenge at just under ten miles long.

The walk started in the village of Tyndrum, which seemed a hive of activity with walkers intent on doing the same journey as Hazel and the Walkie Talkie crew. The place was tiny. If Hazel lived here the constant throng of visitors would drive her potty. There was no way they did *that* much for the local economy. Perhaps the locals knew what they were getting into though, living on such an iconic route.

Not long after leaving the village the path spilled into glorious glens. Greenery surrounded them and Hazel could feel her bad mood slipping further, like the fresh air was carrying it away.

As the valley widened they followed the railway and the gaps between themselves and other groups created a comfortable distance. In parts, it was easy to believe it was just them and the sheep.

Now more relaxed than ever, it was easier to strike up

conversation. Plus, if Hazel kept busy with other members of the group, there was less chance of Louise getting her one-on-one. A few times she'd tried to engage, inserting herself into chats, only to quickly fall back as if Hazel was oozing a physical repellent. She still lingered though, and Hazel caught her looking a few times like she was just itching to talk. Hazel hardened her defences. There was no chance she was weaselling her way in.

The rest of the group were lovely. Carole, the reason for the walk, was a retired headmistress. There was Donna, Louise's mum, who in fairness seemed lovely. Jodie was a retired bank clerk. Eunice wasn't quite retired but she was bloody well looking forward to it – *just three years to go!* – and was a nurse. She had two boys. And two cats. She seemed to talk about both interchangeably, which was confusing at first, but after explaining how she had to shave Colin's rear end Hazel soon twigged he was a ragdoll cat and not her police officer son.

Finally, there was Barb, who was the youngest of the group at a sprightly fifty-two and who currently worked in the accounts department for a company selling prosthetic limbs.

'So, people go round selling legs?' Hazel asked, a weird mental image taking over as they travelled the second stage of the route near the bottom of Beinn Dòrain, the impressive mountain having towered over them for the last few miles.

Barb chuckled. 'I guess when you boil things down, yes.'

'But only to surgeons and specialists, yeah?' Louise asked, falling into step with the two women at the back of the group.

'Oh gosh, yes. They have to be specially fitted.'

Louise smiled at Hazel, as if she'd made a monumental contribution to the conversation.

Hazel's chest tightened. Louise's hair was different and crow's feet bookended her eyes, but it didn't matter. She was still the girl looking at her across the room, her friends whispering and laughing, making tears threaten.

'Need to tie my lace,' Hazel mumbled, dropping to kneel.

She fumbled with the already secure laces, trying to look busy. It wasn't long before a shadow loomed over her.

Louise extended her hand to help Hazel up.

She hesitated for a second but it was no use: there was being stubborn and there was being straight-up rude. Hazel slapped her palm into Louise's and she hauled her upright.

'You doing okay?' Louise asked, setting off to catch up with the group.

Hazel matched her stride. 'Yeah, fine.'

'Everyone is doing really well. We've done a few trial walks of the same length but you never know until you're actually here, what with the different terrain and stuff. Sun's a bit hot though, innit?'

'I've got plenty sunscreen on. It's not too bad.'

Hazel looked around, only finding sheep and bracken. Nothing that could end this torture.

'Me too. I mean, look at me, I burn in the winter.' Louise laughed under her breath, her steam running out with the lack of response from Hazel. 'Still, the river running down my back isn't really helping my morale.'

'No doubt.' Finally, they were close enough to the other women that Hazel could slip back beside Eunice. 'So, tell me more about Colin's blood pressure?'

She bit back a smile at the huff Louise expelled.

6

The day might have been blistering hot but Hazel was as cold as ice.

It didn't matter how hard Louise tried, there was no penetrating Hazel's hard shell. Even just looking at Hazel made the brunette's brow furrow and her features set. The air around Hazel was heavy, an almost palpable forcefield announcing how much she hated Louise.

Louise kept to the back of the group, purposely a few steps behind as she gathered her thoughts.

Speaking to Eunice you'd never know Hazel was annoyed: she was smiley and pleasant, asking questions and listening intently to her walking partner.

A few steps closer though and her Louise-field would activate and all comms would shut down.

It made Louise's tummy flip and her skin itch.

How to fix this?

'You alright?' Jodie asked, waiting trackside for Louise to catch up. 'You were in your own wee world there.'

'Just thinking,' Louise replied, dialling her smile back up to a more acceptable level.

'We're doing well, aren't we?'

'God, yeah! Do you not think so?' They were making good time and so far there had been no mishaps. *Touch wood.*

'We're smashing it.' Jodie smiled, her eyes on the women ahead. 'Carole is in her element.'

It was true. She was spearheading the group, thundering on like there was no tomorrow. Louise had been sceptical that she could keep the pace, but nearly six miles in Carole showed no sign of slowing down.

'She is. It's so good to see her back to her old self.'

Jodie's gaze flicked to another member of the crew. 'It's a shame Marie couldn't join us. Hazel seems lovely, though.'

'She is.' It would seem even Louise was shutting down when it came to Hazel. She quickly tacked on: 'We went to school together.'

'Oh really? Small world! I guess that's Perth for you, though.'

'Don't I know it.'

'Will we stop for food soon?'

'I thought you'd never ask,' Louise replied with a smile.

They found a spot, not far off the trail, and got comfy on the mats they'd brought. Sandwiches and refreshments distributed, Louise felt her shoulders relax a little. She'd been tightly wound all day, the muscles in her back as tense as a fully stretched rubber band.

She bit into her cheese sandwich, taking in the view as her friends chattered around her. It was beautiful here. The cone-shaped mountain, Beinn Dòrain, had been their constant companion on the walk. At first it had looked scarily steep but now they were rounding its other side she could see how it was one of the easier Munros to conquer.

Still, she wouldn't be climbing it any time soon. She was much better suited to level terrain.

The group were doing well: a few sore feet and inevitable blisters, but nothing serious.

Louise pulled her phone from her gilet's pocket. No service. The way she scrunched her face up didn't go unnoticed by Mum, who quickly shot her a wink. She'd known the signal would be patchy here but it didn't stop her worrying. What if it never came back? She'd need to call Cameron when they got to the hotel. Would there be a phone in the room? Or a payphone near? Shit, did payphones still exist? She didn't have any change. Someone else would probably have some on them. What if Cameron didn't answer—

'You okay?' Mum asked, cutting through her thoughts like a hot knife through butter.

'Yeah, just enjoying the views.'

'Something else here, isn't it?'

Louise offered a thin-lipped smile in response. It really was, though. Times like these, she was thankful to live in Scotland and have scenery like this on her doorstep.

Another group of walkers passed, waving hello and calling friendly greetings.

'We've made good time; we can stay here a while,' Carole said, her gaze following the other group, a hand over her eyes to shield her from the sun.

'Why not?' Mum agreed before taking a huge bite of her corned beef sandwich.

'You doing okay, Hazel?' Louise asked. The fact she'd chosen to sit as far away as possible from Louise hadn't gone unnoted. Any further and she might as well be on Beinn Dòrain.

'Great.'

This was worse than talking to a moody Cameron.

She couldn't push it, though, not in front of everyone else.

As if picking up on the atmosphere, quiet descended over the gang as they munched on their food.

'We should take a group picture soon, for Marie,' Louise said, hoping it would draw conversation out of Hazel.

'Do you want me to take it?' Hazel asked, getting to her feet.

'We can set a timer,' Louise replied, bouncing to Hazel's side and finding a rock to balance her phone on.

Hazel's lip twitched with the hint of a smile and Louise couldn't help but lock eyes with her, returning her own uneasy grin.

By now, Hazel couldn't hide her smirk.

Louise's brow knitted together, confused by the sudden change of reception. 'What's up?' she asked with a nervous giggle.

Hazel sucked on her bottom lip before answering, her smile threatening to widen even further. 'I think you just stood in sheep poo,' Hazel said, only just keeping herself together.

Louise looked at her boot. Sure enough, a huge bulge of brown poked out.

'Ew, yuck,' Louise yelped, scraping her boot in the long grass.

'Unlucky, Lou,' Hazel chuckled as she walked back to the group.

Maybe, just maybe, Hazel was finally softening.

~

IT TOOK NEARLY five and half hours but they finally made it to Inveroran. Louise's legs ached and her back was soaked. But the group and herself were still in good spirits. A rest and a large glass of wine would be heaven. Louise imagined the taste of a chilled Pinot Grigio on her tongue and smiled.

They'd done it.

All the planning and training had paid off. Not a hitch to be had.

As they descended the path, leaving Loch Tulla behind, Louise pulled her phone out for the umpteenth time. After what felt like an age a single bar appeared in the top right of her screen.

She stared, expecting messages to flood in, a few missed calls.

Nothing.

She fired off a text to Cameron, just asking how he was doing, but it was taking forever to send. She stuffed the phone back in her pocket.

'Will we have a wash and meet downstairs for a drink?' Barb suggested to a chorus of approval as the hotel came into view.

The cream-painted hotel was the only building on the thin tarmacked road, making it a hive of activity with walkers. Silver tables and chairs lined its outside and every one was filled with walkers enjoying hard-earned refreshments. A few toasted them as they walked by.

Inside was dark and traditional with a wooden bar greeting them on entry. Carole took the lead and got the attention of a lingering barmaid. 'We're here to check in.'

'Of course,' she replied, all smiles. 'Come round to this side and I'll get the sign-in book.'

Carole followed her directions and the group

congregated around the far side of the bar, away from thirsty patrons.

The barmaid had just started her spiel about the rooms, peppered with chitchat about the walk, when Louise's phone rumbled in her pocket. She pulled it out, one eye on the barmaid, the other on the phone's screen. A flurry of texts from Cameron and a missed call.

The top one: *MUM CALL ME NOW. URGENT.*

'Back in a minute,' she said to no one in particular, thankful the group paid her little attention as she snuck off because her voice was already sporting a slight wobble.

The fresh air hit her like a slap in the face as she exited the bar. She took in an unsteady breath, her legs already threatening to shake as she made her way to a quieter side of the building, away from the cheery outside patrons. Safely tucked away by some discarded beer kegs and in the path of a shadow, Louise hit the call button.

It rang for forever, making her heart swoop to her belly with a thump that reverberated to her knees.

Finally he answered. 'Mum!' he chirped, sounding decidedly cheerful for someone who surely was at death's door, had been kidnapped, or was critically ill.

'Cameron, you okay?' She fought to keep her voice steady.

'Yeah, grand. Listen, I forgot to pack fresh boxers.'

Louise cocked her head to the side, her heart bouncing back to her chest like it had been bungee jumping. 'Is that why you messaged?'

'Yeahhh?' he replied, drawing the word out like she was crazy.

She could swear, her emotions trapped between frustration and relief. She swallowed hard and wiped the back of her hand across her damp brow. *This boy will be the death of me.*

'You've got some on though, yeah?' she asked, grinning like a maniac at the absurdity of it all. She'd spent the day, nay prevailing weeks, fretting that something bad would happen, only for him to shoot her nerves to death over some underwear.

'Course I've got some on.'

'Right, well, it's only one day. You'll be fine. You having a good time?'

He huffed, unhappy with the answer, but didn't fight it. 'Amazing. Darren's dad is taking us to Wolfhill tomorrow to fire air rifles.' There was a pause, like he was wondering if he should have disclosed that information. Too late: he carried on. 'Which should be fun.'

Louise bit her bottom lip, holding back the words she really wanted to say. There'd been no mention of air rifles when she asked Ru if he could stay over. But Alan was a sensible guy, otherwise she wouldn't have trusted them in the first place.

It would be fine.

Probably.

She'd text Ru once this call was over.

'I'm jealous,' she lied. What he got up to these days was out of her control, but she was just grateful Cameron still told her everything. Well, at least she hoped he did. They'd always been tight but age was coming between them now: no matter how close they were, a teenager was never going to be besties with their mum.

They had a code word – BANANAS – that he could text if he ever felt unsafe and she'd made the promise to drop everything and come to his aid no matter what. Thankfully, it had never come into practice.

She'd lain awake last night, certain today would be the day it pinged through on her phone. He'd had plenty sleepovers and adventures in the past and she'd been away herself a few times, but there had never been an instance when both her *and* Mum were away.

Inveroran wasn't far away, so she'd considered bailing, bringing her own car and driving home to leave the other group members to enjoy a night alone, but Mum had talked her round.

Cameron wasn't a wee kid any more. He was more than capable of looking after himself.

But he'd always be her baby. Just the thought of him possibly going off to university made her eyes sting.

She'd have to get him plenty of boxers, since that was obviously an issue.

'You still there?' he asked.

'Yeah, sorry, what did you say? Signal is bad,' she lied, again.

'I said I need to go, Darren and I are playing FIFA.'

Louise shook her head, a fresh grin spreading across her face. Typical – she was losing her mind and he was having the time of his life. 'Yeah, sure. Have fun. Love you.'

'You too,' he mumbled and hung up.

Too cool to say in front of his pal. This time tomorrow she could give him a big hug and all would be fine.

She put her phone away and took a minute to compose herself, her heart rate having not quite received the memo that everything was okay. It jingled against her ribs, making her want to shake her arms and legs out like a scarecrow, get rid of the nervous energy. Realising she was alone and out of sight she did just that, relief washing over her instantly.

Louise let out a long, breathy sigh.

Wine. Whatever the question was, wine was the answer.

She'd phone Ru after taking a breather in her room, composing herself before finding out what this whole air rifle thing was.

She rounded the corner, making her way back towards the rabble of the pub.

Living with Mum and Cameron she barely ever got time to herself. Would the room have a bath? Now that would be a luxury. Would the pub let her take a glass of wine back to the room? *Please God, let there be bubble bath.*

Pushing open the heavy oak door she was met by Mum, leaning against the bar with a rueful grin playing on her lips.

'Everything okay?' Louise asked, returning an uneasy smile.

'Good, yeah. Got the room keys.' She swung a key with a chunky leather keyring from her finger, her smile not budging.

Louise held her hand out, expecting her own.

'About that. You might have a little issue . . .'

7

'So, this is a fucking shambles,' is what Hazel wanted to say. Instead, she said, 'Hey, in you come,' when Louise knocked on the door.

Of all the people.

The only blessing was Louise looked as pissed off as Hazel felt.

'Not ideal, eh?' Louise said she shuffled into the room, slinging her bag by the dark wood wardrobe.

This was the first time she'd not seen Louise as the poster child for a dental practice: her grin was nowhere to be found. Although, she'd noticed her face drop at reception, something on her phone taking her attention outside. Maybe something else had happened and it had nothing to do with sharing a room.

They'd booked single rooms but somehow one had become a double, and although Hazel had tried her best to argue that Louise should share with her mum, the idea had been shot down: Donna was a terrible snorer who suffered from restless leg syndrome and wouldn't wish that on anybody.

With everyone else declining to take one for the team, quickly claiming their room keys and scuttling off, Hazel soon found herself with a bunk mate. It was over in a second: a whirlwind of misdirection and suddenly she was dropped into her worst nightmare.

A double bed with Louise. If she'd told teenage Hazel of her fate she would have baulked.

Hazel wandered to the other side of the room and leaned against the windowsill, the bed a literal barrier between them. If only she could create something as solid tonight.

Louise went to sit on the edge of the bed, only to be stopped by Hazel's voice, causing her to hover for a second.

'You sure your boots are safe to wear in here?'

'Huh?'

'Your boots? *Sheep poo*,' Hazel tacked on when the penny didn't drop.

She'd wiped them pretty well on the long grass and stomped about in a rogue puddle but still, shit was shit. Hazel didn't want it tracked through the room.

'Crap, you're right, sorry,' Louise grumbled and disappeared into the en-suite bathroom.

Under any other circumstances this would be a nice place to stay. The room was small but cosy and its mix of old-fashioned wooden furniture made it feel like a cottage, one that perfectly suited the rolling landscape spilling in front of their window. Come night-time the place would be a dot in a sea of darkness, no other signs of life to be seen for miles.

Hazel looked at the faded lampshade hanging from the ceiling. Tonight, she'd be stuck with Louise. Little Miss Rainbows was probably plotting her next scathing remark right now. Although, she'd been far more palatable this time around. Less giggling and snide remarks than teenage Louise. Leopards were spotty, though, and that was that.

'How's Marie?' Louise asked, appearing from the bathroom, now bootless. Hazel noted the bright red nail polish on her toes. Of course Louise had time for pedicures.

'Good. Shaken up but good.'

'Will your dad be okay taking charge until her cast comes off?' She looked genuinely concerned, which made Hazel's insides churn. What right did Louise have to worry about her mum and dad?

'Guess he'll have to cope.'

Silence descended over the room like a fire blanket on a flame: heavy, thick, suffocating.

Louise chewed on her bottom lip.

Hazel kept her gaze straight ahead.

She could quite happily get through the evening without uttering another word. It would be easier that way. No expectations, no awkwardness. *You keep to your side of the room, I'll keep to mine.*

But Louise wasn't going to make life easy. It was never her style.

'They've got my number – I don't live far. So you don't need to worry when they're on their own.'

'I wasn't worried.'

Louise's eyebrow quirked, a comeback sitting on the tip of the tongue.

'Wha—' was all she managed before there was a sharp knock at the door.

'Girls, we're going for a drink, coming?' the disembodied voice asked. It sounded like Donna.

'Just need to shove my trainers on, Mum,' Louise replied, her eyes not leaving Hazel's as if this was just a pause in the conversation she was playing out in her head. Whatever she intended to say, Hazel didn't want to hear.

'I'll join you now,' Hazel called, grabbing her hoodie off the chair on the way to the door.

～

AFTER THE FIRST PINT HAD WOUND ITS way into Hazel's bloodstream the evening became a little easier. Conversation flowed as effortlessly as it had on the walk, and the universe had finally thrown her a lifeline and made the only available seat for Louise at the opposite end of the table.

It hadn't stopped the stolen glances Hazel kept inadvertently catching.

Now full of steak pie and chips, Hazel was content in her own wee bubble as the bar's patrons thinned around her. There wasn't a hope in hell she was going upstairs a second before she had to, though. Louise was liable to follow.

It looked like the other ladies were as intent on staying downstairs as she was, so they weren't likely to be left alone any time soon.

'It's so nice to get a rest from John,' Eunice said, her wine-flushed cheeks growing darker as she giggled guiltily. 'That sounds terrible, but you know what I mean, God forgive me.'

A chorus of approval rippled through the group, stopping at Louise who stayed silent, her arms crossed in quiet contemplation as she listened. She'd probably be rushing home into the arms of her doting husband tomorrow, to a cacophony of stories about how much he and the children had missed her. Even the dog would be howling in delight.

'His gout still causing trouble?' Louise asked, now cupping her hand to her chin, creating her own headrest.

'When is it ever not?' Eunice replied with a sigh. 'You lot are a tonic, though. Always are.'

Louise smiled warmly in return. 'Always happy to help how I can.'

Hazel mumbled into her beer. When did this sweetheart persona start? Was she like this all the time or did it switch off the minute she crossed the threshold of her house? Did her husband even know the real her? It was easy to live with someone and not know the real them, not until it truly mattered.

'A little pause from real life is always welcomed,' Louise's mum said with a roll of her neck. Now they were sitting, muscles were starting to ache and stiffen, the exertion of today catching up with them.

'I'll drink to that,' Louise beamed, jumping to her feet, quickly en route to the bar. 'Another round?'

Hazel watched as she leaned against the bar, tapping the phone she'd pulled from her pocket and checking for messages as she waited.

There was a haze to Louise this evening, a damper muting her mood. Like she wasn't on full sparkle. It was Hazel's right to be angry about the room though, not Louise's.

She should have been grateful Hazel had even opened the door to her and wasn't simply running off with the room key, leaving her to fend for herself.

Not that the idea hadn't crossed her mind.

But it would have made the journey back home awkward and Hazel didn't want to risk being stranded.

Beer was definitely clouding her thoughts but her initial anger was now reduced to a low simmer, a diluted acid coursing through her veins compared to the jagged vitriol that had flowed earlier.

She'd sleep tonight, avoid conversation, and come downstairs as early as possible for breakfast.

She could survive this.

She'd been through much worse in the last year.

Hazel continued to watch Louise, hoping to catch a glimpse of her mask slipping. She was scrolling on her phone now, one foot resting on the gold pole that ran the length of the bar. It was a nice hotel. Much like the room, it was dated and worn around the edges, but that was all part of the charm. Its low ceiling with original beams and plastering made it cosy, as if it was holding in the atmosphere, hyping it up in a small space: laughter was etched into its walls, good times into its tables, and happiness in its fittings. People came here to be joyful and the mood stuck.

If only Hazel could extract a dose herself.

She didn't like being grumpy all the time. A year ago she would have given herself a good shake. Fair enough, Louise was heightening her feelings, but she couldn't deny she'd been in a slump for a while. Since her engagement ended, Hazel's inner compass had shifted south and suddenly a good day was marked by not being crabby or having an afternoon cry.

Sadness was a growth in her chest, its thorns snagging her and its roots snaking around her bones as it made itself a permanent home in her heart. The longer she felt like this the harder it was to remember who the old Hazel was.

Didn't matter, though.

She didn't exist any more.

Louise gripped three tumblers in her hands, walking to the table with careful precision, as if she was on a tightrope.

She placed them down with a smile. 'I'll just grab the rest,' she said and was off before anyone could offer a hand.

The second trip was harder, with a mix of beer and wine glasses. Only Hazel seemed to notice. Louise took it in her stride, like nothing was too much of a bother. Hazel's gut twisted with annoyance that no one had offered to help, but they were all so engrossed in conversation they'd not even glanced Louise's way.

Like hell would she offer a hand, though.

Finally, Louise reached the table. Not a drop spilled.

She pumped her eyebrows and smiled as she passed the drinks to the right people.

Hazel could box her right now, just for having the audacity to be so bloody cheery.

She swallowed the notion down with a gulp of beer.

Louise had barely sat down when Carole cleared her throat. 'You know I'm not one for speeches,' she said, raising her glass, clearly about to prove herself completely wrong. 'But I'd like to give a few words.'

The group fell silent and Carole continued. 'You all know my history, so I don't need to tell you why we're doing this, but I just wanted to say thank you again. Not just for fundraising but for the support you've given me.'

A warmth descended over the table, so hot Hazel could swear she felt it on her cheeks.

Carole turned to Louise. 'And an extra special thank you to you, Louise. I don't know what any of us would do without you.'

'Hear, hear,' Barb boomed with a raise of her wine.

Louise's cheeks blushed red but she didn't protest.

'Modest,' Hazel mumbled into her beer and was sure Louise's mum gave her a quick sideways glance.

Maybe Louise heard too because she cleared her throat. 'You'd cope,' she said, mainly to the rim of her wine glass.

'Nonsense,' Carole scolded. 'If I'd not had this group during my treatment I would have been lost and I'm sure everyone else here has their own version of that too. Without our Walkie Talkies Lord knows what would have happened.'

Louise shrugged, struggling to respond.

Barb filled the silence. 'To Louise.'

Louise's cheeks went the colour of Carole's red wine and she scrunched her face, as if wincing.

The rest of the gang raised their glasses, echoing Barb's toast. The heavy weight of peer pressure jolted Hazel's arm to move too but she couldn't bring herself to speak. Some things were a bridge too far.

8

Louise was tempted to crank the heating up, anything to ease the chill in the bedroom. Hazel's steely demeanour could freeze Perth's River Tay in July.

They'd trudged upstairs in a group, the good mood of their company instantly vanishing as the door closed. This place was like an airlock.

Hazel was gone in a jiffy, locking the bathroom door before Louise had a chance to talk.

Which was probably a good thing because Louise had no idea how to broach the subject.

She got her stuff ready and waited on the edge of the bed, intent on getting changed as fast as possible, so she and Hazel could clear the air.

Hazel didn't even make eye contact with Louise as she left the bathroom and went to her side of the bed.

Louise flew into action and got changed as quickly as she could, surprised not to bash any limbs in the small bathroom after three glasses of wine. Their big dinner had sobered her, thank God. Otherwise, who knows what she would say to Hazel.

Hey, did you know I had a massive crush on you in high school?

The idea spread a smile over Louise's face as she brushed her teeth. She shook her head, silently scolding herself in the mirror.

It was true. But some secrets were best kept.

There weren't many girls that Louise could remember crushing on in high school. Caitlyn, the heavenly hockey player from a few years above, and Mrs Lockheart, the HE teacher, had a special place in her heart but Hazel, she was the real deal.

Back then, when Hazel had long hair and clear skin, the notion was absurd. She was forbidden fruit. Out of bounds. But now, with her styled short hair and snaking tattoos, Louise wondered if things would be different if they'd only just met.

Although, Louise had heard murmurs of an engagement one one walk, but it was when Cameron was struggling with his Nat 4 maths and Louise was fully absorbed in emailing tutors and not really listening.

Sometimes on Walkies Talkies she hung back and let the gang get on with it. Company was nice, but with so much going on it was quite often her only real alone time. Fresh air did wonders for her soul.

A name? Did Marie ever mention a name for Hazel's fiancée? It hadn't stuck if she did.

Yikes. She really had to pay more attention. It was a start though, a segue into softening Hazel, a strong topic of conversation showing her that she was different now. Louise wasn't who Hazel once knew. She spat foamy toothpaste into the sink as she thought. She couldn't just climb into bed and start a game of twenty questions about her fiancée. She'd need an opener first.

She wiped her face on the towel and steeled her nerves.

The thought of someone hating her made all her muscles tighten. Why waste an opportunity to right a wrong? It was now or never.

Hazel was on her side, facing the wall, when Louise exited the bathroom.

Louise cleared her throat, knowing fine well Hazel wasn't asleep.

She perched on the edge of the bed, as if there was still a chance she might not sleep here. 'Can we talk?'

No response.

'Hazel.'

With a sigh, Louise climbed into bed, clicking the lamp off to plunge the room into a hazy glow. The curtains weren't blackout blinds, that was for sure.

She turned to face Hazel, propping herself up on her elbow. She wasn't asleep. No way. And if she was? What was the harm?

'I'm sorry.' The silence was more comfortable now, giving Louise permission to continue. The feeling was one-sided for sure, but that was irrelevant. 'I was a real shithead in school. But I had . . . stuff going on. I know it's not an excuse.' She shrugged, feeling silly because Hazel wouldn't have seen the gesture. 'Anyway, I just wanted to say, cause I've obviously hurt you.'

She watched the gentle rise and fall of the cover over Hazel. Still asleep. Cool.

Louise slumped down, intent on getting comfy, but knowing sleep wasn't on the agenda just yet.

The floodgates were open now, offering catharsis. Time to extend an olive branch of peace. 'If it helps, I screwed myself over as much as I did everyone else.'

There was a shift on the mattress, like Hazel had moved.

Louise held her breath, not wanting to mask any signs of life. Nothing.

How much to share? Maybe the point was to move forward now, not dwell on the past. New bridges were stronger than trying to repair broken ones.

'Your mum said you were engaged. Congratulations.'

There was a definite bounce in the bed now and Hazel huffed so loudly that somewhere in the Scottish countryside, a little piggy's house flew away. 'Are you ever going to be quiet? I'm trying to sleep,' she grunted.

'Sorry, it's just . . .' Louise pushed herself on to her elbow again. 'Can we talk?'

'About what?'

'The fact that I'm sorry.'

'Okay. Good. Now can we sleep?' Hazel groaned, still facing the wall.

The tug of annoyance pulled at Louise's chest. They were adults, only one of them wasn't acting like one. 'Is that it?' She tried to keep her voice level but agitation hid itself between the words.

Hazel spun to face her, brow furrowed and jaw set. 'I hereby forgive you and all your sins. You are excused,' she mocked, rolling a hand towards Louise like she was a royal courtier.

'I'm trying to be nice.'

'There's a fucking first.'

Louise wanted to fling the covers back, steal a car and go home there and then. She was fizzing. Cartoon Louise would have smoke coming out her nostrils in great plumes. She took a few deep breaths, dulling her emotions.

Suddenly the double bed felt tinier than ever, despite the huge cavern of anger forging a divide between them.

'Look, it doesn't matter if you like me or not, but I

wanted to acknowledge I was a bit shitty towards you in school. I probably could have been nicer and for that I'm sorry.'

'Probably could have been nicer?' Hazel scoffed.

'Yes,' was all Louise could manage. A cold sweat bloomed on the back of her neck.

Hazel chewed on her cheek, her dark eyes boring into Louise's even in the darkness, stealing the air from her lungs. 'You outed me to my sister,' Hazel finally said, her tone flat.

Louise's stomach flipped. No, she hadn't. There was no way. 'No I didn't.' Only a slight shake to her voice suggested there was any doubt.

Hazel nodded, making them bounce on the old mattress. 'Uh-huh. Giana Peters' party, you asked my sister if I was a raging lezzer cause I'd set my Myspace to liking guys and girls.'

Louise opened her mouth, letting it hang when the words refused to come. She had no recollection of that but also no memory of *not* doing it. She snapped her mouth shut.

Hazel continued, 'Next morning she flew into my room to quote you verbatim. What was I meant to do? She'd already found my Myspace.'

Louise cracked her jaw from side to side and narrowed her eyes, her gaze set just above Hazel's shoulder. Why would Hazel lie about that? It had to be true. 'That's really shitty.'

'Yep.' Hazel pulled her lips together, as if holding the rage in.

'I don't remember, but who I was then isn't who I am now. That was inexcusable and I wish I could make it up to you, but I can't.' Louise slammed her head down on the pillow. It was easier to talk to the ceiling than make eye contact with Hazel. 'I was a real dickhead then.'

'No kidding. That was just the tip of the iceberg with you.'

Louise covered her eyes with the palms of her hands. 'I don't need to hear the rest. If you could pay for amnesia for chunks of your life, believe me, no price would be too big to block those years out.'

'Yeah, well, sorry to shit on your little trip of repentance, but despite this sunshine-and-rainbows persona you've developed, this' — she said, wagging a finger between them —'is never going to happen. You might have everyone else fooled but not me.'

Louise shot upright faster than a peppermint dropped in a can of Coke. 'Excuse me?'

'This.' Hazel repeated, still wiggling a hand in the air. 'A leopard doesn't change its spots.'

'That's hardly fair,' Louise snapped. 'You have no idea what I was going through then.'

'Go on then.'

'What?'

'Tell me what was so bloody awful that you had to make my life a living hell?'

Every muscle in Louise's body stiffened. She didn't talk about Mark. Dealing with him at the time had been torture enough.

'Come on, Lou. What ailed little Louise Menzies so badly that she had to take it out on everyone else? Grades not high enough? Not enough boys after you? Daddy only bought you one pony for Christmas?' Her eyes shone in the moonlight, enjoying every moment of twisting the knife.

'Enough.' Louise turned onto her side, tears rimming her eyes. Silence bathed the room as she fought to keep composure. Saliva flooded her mouth and soon her nose was blocked. She couldn't cry. This wasn't how this conversation could end. She swallowed hard and took a deep breath. 'It's not Menzies any more, it's King,' she managed, her voice like a timid schoolgirl's.

A bounce of the mattress told her Hazel had slammed herself against the pillows. 'Right, sorry, you got married. Whoop-de-do.'

'No,' she replied, her voice still shaky. 'My dad, Mark, was an asshole, so I changed it to my mum's name.'

There was a beat, where things could have gone either way, before Hazel answered. 'Must run in the family, then.'

There was no point arguing. Louise scrunched her eyes shut, ignoring the tear running down her cheek.

9

Hazel stared out of the window at the back of the bus. The chatter of the other women had died down to quiet conversation, most tired from yesterday's hard work.

Louise wasn't herself, though.

A small part of Hazel felt bad. Not enough to apologise, but big enough for her to register the heavy feeling in the pit of her stomach.

She hit skip on her phone as Adele started, not wanting to listen to anything sad. Her mood was bad enough without filling her ears with heartbreak.

Louise's quietness had been picked up on, but she'd passed it off as tiredness. Had Hazel pushed too far? Said too much? Compared to what Louise had said and done to her, it was mild.

It didn't ease the rocky atmosphere strung between them.

They'd woken and dressed in silence, sat at either end of the breakfast table, and boarded the bus without a single word. That had to be a new record for Hazel. Even at the worst points of her break-up with Ashley, they'd spoken.

Louise didn't deserve her time, though, and after today she would never have to devote another second to her.

Hazel watched the Perthshire countryside roll past the window. The route home took the back roads and it was a welcome change to the usual motorway she'd endured for years when travelling back from Glasgow. Maybe she'd take this way from now on, make a point of going out of her way to search out a little slice of beauty.

If the last year had taught her anything, it was that you had to look out for yourself. Numero uno. *Please put your mask on before helping others.*

If that meant driving a different route or giving bullies like Louise what was due, then so be it. Self-care was paramount.

If she was going to get out of this slump, she needed to get her priorities straight.

An issue that had been hovering at the back of her mind scooted to the forefront: where next?

She'd texted a few friends, who had all done a wonderful job of coming up with excuses as to why she couldn't crash with them. Which was fair enough but there was no way she was about to spill the truth to Mum and Dad. They had enough on their plates right now.

Yaz had enquired about her new set-up but it was obvious they didn't want to host her again.

As Perth trundled closer, worry made Hazel's palms sticky. They passed Castlehill Farm: a Perth institution with a thriving coffee shop beside their livestock farm. Not long to go now; they'd be back at the sports centre in ten minutes.

Maybe that was the answer. The same way Castlehill Farm had diversified, maybe she could too? All she needed was money, a little something to get her back on level land.

Barb turned her way and reached a hand out, wanting Hazel's attention. She pulled an earbud out. 'Huh? Sorry.'

'Donna is asking if you'd like a lift home?'

Even as a repeated question Louise was shooting her mum daggers. God knows what deathly stare had gone her way in the first place.

10 in a taxi or an awkward drive home? Hazel looked at the sunshine bathing the green fields flanking the road, deciding on a third option.

'Thanks but I'm going to walk home,' she replied, mustering a polite smile.

'Someone's keen after yesterday,' Eunice quipped.

'It's only four miles.'

'Only!' Barb boomed.

'It's a nice day,' Hazel said, already looking forward to feeling the sun on her skin. Today was the start of positive change.

SWEAT DRIPPED down Hazel's back as walked the final hundred yards to Mum and Dad's house.

It had been a nice walk home despite the heavy bag on her back. Without the distraction of the rest of the gang she was free to think, turnover possible solutions, let her mind wander. It was amazing what could be achieved on a sunny day.

Nothing concrete had come to mind but she had thawed a little, hope acting as a hot water bottle on her ice-encased heart.

The power of the walking group played in her mind, as if the universe had dropped her into the scenario with purpose. Ashley's friend Rhona always said there was a plan bigger than ourselves at foot. Maybe she was finally being led in the right direction.

There was no denying the good that Louise was doing. She's heard the stories first hand from the other women in the group. Could Hazel spearhead something similar in Glasgow? Or create a wellness centre?

Pound signs fluttered through her head. These things took money. No sense getting ahead of herself just yet.

She stopped at the top of Mum and Dad's steps, under the rickety arch swathed in sweet peas, and texted Yaz: *hey! I know it's a big ask but can I crash at yours for just a few more days? I have a plan.*

She stuffed her phone away. This would work.

She bounded down the stairs with a fresh spring in her step.

She rang the doorbell to Mum and Dad's house. She'd left her house key at home yesterday. Good job they couldn't go anywhere unexpectedly.

After a while movement appeared in the doorway, a shadowy figure through the frosted glass.

'Hazel!' Dad exclaimed as he opened the door, stepping aside to let her in.

'Mum okay?' she asked as she hauled her bag to the floor in the hall.

'Really good actually, won't stay still though,' he said with a smile and a roll of his eyes.

Hazel hadn't expected anything less.

～

THE CEILING HADN'T CHANGED a jot since she moved out. Which wasn't surprising, really. She couldn't remember the last time anyone, let alone her parents, had confessed to painting a ceiling.

Hazel traced the lines of the coving circling the room. Getting up from her childhood bed was proving an issue. And it wasn't just because of her aching limbs.

Yaz had replied to her text late afternoon – *Pal, look, I'm sorry but I just can't. Hope you understand* – and she'd been spiralling ever since. The only thing keeping her sane was the straight, predictable lines on the wall.

Where the heck was she meant to stay?

A knock at the door made her flinch.

'Hazel, you got a moment?' Mum asked, peeking into the room. 'Oh, you sleeping? Sorry.'

Hazel perched herself upright on her elbow. 'Mum, what are you doing up?'

She waved a crutch quickly towards her daughter and almost lost her balance. 'Got to get used to these sooner or later.'

'Still,' Hazel said, rushing to her feet to guide Mum into the room and to her bed. 'What's up?' she asked, supporting Mum by the elbow until she was sitting.

She looked at the flimsy bit of paper in her hand, crushed from holding onto the crutch. 'I know you're back to Glasgow tonight cause of your clients, but could you nip to the shop for us before you head? Just a few things to keep us going until I'm better adjusted.'

'Course! You don't need to worry about that. Did you not like the idea of online?' Hazel had gone over online shopping with them the day she arrived home and even set up an account with their favourite supermarket.

Mum took a deep breath, the beginning of a huge sigh. 'Your dad says he'd prefer to see what he's buying. Something about bruised apples.'

'He can't see the bruises anyway,' Hazel joked. Dad had been known to eat mouldy bread and pass it off as medicinal instead of admitting he just couldn't see it.

'You know what he's like,' Mum replied, finally letting the sigh escape.

Hazel nodded. 'No probs. I can get you some stuff. What about after, though?'

Mum's face remained stoic. 'Louise has offered to help.'

Louise. The golden girl, at it again. 'Look, I can come back every weekend. It won't be a hassle.' It would be a fair whack of money on petrol, but they were worth it: that's what credit cards were for.

'No, no, you're busy,' Mum soothed, giving Hazel's leg a jiggle.

'Never too busy for you.' An idea pinged in her head, a 100-watt lightbulb of a zinger. 'You know, I could juggle some stuff around, get Anita to take a client or two, do my other classes online. How about I stay a few more days?'

Mum's eyes lit up. 'Are you sure? I don't want you to lose business for me.'

'Nonsense. If they can't understand my mum needs me, they're not clients I want anyway.'

'Then it's a deal.'

What was a little white lie when it made her mum so happy?

10

L ouise held her breath, waiting for Tom to open the door. She guessed it wouldn't be Hazel. Not if her mum had told her who was visiting.

It was great news that Hazel was staying to help out, but it certainly made visiting her friend more complicated. Hopefully Marie would be up for a coffee next week, take things out of the house and away from her daughter.

A week had passed since their spat at the hotel but the idea of seeing her still made Louise's stomach queasy. She scrunched her face up at the thought. In an ideal world she would never see Hazel ever again.

As if she would be so lucky. Hazel greeted her at the door. 'Greet' was maybe the wrong word. That would involve speaking. Open the door and step aside, while staring at the far wall. That was more accurate.

Louise could play that game too. She waltzed past her and down the hall, ignoring the way her heart thrummed against her ribs. Confrontation was not in her repertoire. It was done now. No casualties.

She entered the living room to find it empty.

'Marie?' she called.

'She's not here,' Hazel said, appearing behind Louise and making her jump.

'As in at all?'

'Huh?'

'Is she in the house?'

'I should hope so. Hardly going to make a run for it, is she?'

Louise waited for further explanation, suddenly aware how close Hazel was to her. With anyone else it would feel a normal distance, but the air between them was so heavy Louise was liable to crumple under the weight of it. She took a step back. 'Any idea where she might be?'

For a second it looked like Hazel might simply shrug and have Louise search every room like a privacy-invasive game of hide and seek. This wasn't her house; she couldn't just be going in every room.

'She's in the garden,' Hazel said with the tiniest flicker of a smile. 'Through the conservatory and onto the patio.'

With that, she was gone as quickly as she'd appeared.

Marie was in a recliner, enjoying the sun. No sign of Tom.

'Marie,' Louise called quietly, aware her friend had her eyes closed and wouldn't appreciate a jump scare. Not that she'd be doing much jumping with the massive cast she had on.

Marie slowly opened one eye, shielding her face with a hand as she adjusted to the light. 'Oh, Louise! Hello!'

'Hey,' Louise said, looking for somewhere to sit. Her eyes settled on the metal chairs around the small al fresco table.

'Pull one of those out, we can chat properly then.'

She did as told, carefully taking a chair and positioning it near to Marie. 'No Tom today?'

She tilted her head to the left. 'In his greenhouse.'

Louise nodded. She always fancied a greenhouse. Never enough hours in the day, though. Not to mention the fact Louise was crap with plants. 'You getting on okay?'

'So-so,' Marie replied with a tight smile. 'I'm determined to master these crutches so I can get a little independence back.'

'Great you've got Hazel to help for a bit, though.'

Marie grinned. 'I don't know what we'd do without her. She's so good for organising her sessions to be online; means she can stay as long as we need her.'

'Oh really?' Hazel was a PT: surely she couldn't do this indefinitely. 'She'll be here for a while longer, then?'

'Oh yes, she's even said she'll push my chair on the next Walkie Talkie. How good is that? I was worried I would miss out until this stupid cast was off.'

'That's wonderful,' Louise said, teeth gritted.

'SHE'S TAKING THE PISS NOW,' Jordan said before gulping the last of her pint.

'I would hardly say staying in Perth to help her parents is *taking the piss*,' Louise replied, twiddling the stem of her wine glass between thumb and forefinger.

'Yeah, but, Walkie Talkie is your thing. She can't do that.'

Jordan James, barely a jot over five foot, and full to the brim of undiluted wisdom. Or so she liked to think.

'She can do what she likes. And I'm going to have to put up with it,' Louise said with a sigh. 'I can hardly stop going to my own gatherings.'

Jordan's eyes trained on her empty glass, as if telepathically alerting Louise to her need for another. She would, as soon as she was done moping. Which might be a while.

Deep down, she knew the only option was to be civil, but Hazel made her insides feel like someone had tipped her out, put her contents in a blender, then shoved it all back in. Walkie Talkie was her safe space. Good vibes only, kinda thing. She couldn't relax if Hazel was there, plotting her demise with every step.

Jordan leaned back, the collar of her shirt touching the back of her neck as she stretched out. 'I just can't imagine you being an arsehole.'

Louise's cheeks reddened. She'd done so well boxing those years up, and now Hazel was ripping everything to pieces and scattering the memories like a sugar-high toddler on Christmas Day.

'Well, I was. So, can't change that.'

'Definitely no way to make it up to her?'

'Like what?'

'Buy her a drink?' Jordan looked at her empty pint glass again. 'You can practise now, if you'd like?'

Louise bit the corner of her lip, suppressing a chuckle. 'Always so subtle.' She downed the rest of her wine as she stood. 'Same again?'

'If you'd be so kind.'

She scooped the empty glasses up and walked to the bar. The Queen's Head was quiet tonight. Not surprising, since it was a Monday. She wouldn't usually drink on a school night –heck, she wouldn't usually drink full stop – but she needed to offload and when she'd texted Jordan only to discover she was in town, it felt rude to knock back a gift from the great beyond. A little negotiation with Mum to watch Cameron and hey presto, her evening was sorted.

Once she'd ordered, Louise watched Jordan sort through

the stack of mail she'd brought for her. Sometimes it really sucked having a nomadic best friend. Other times, when things just seemed to align, like today, it was the best thing ever. The joy of seeing her always trumped whatever shit was going on.

They'd met when Louise started an LGBTQ+ book group at work. Jordan had never read a book in her life before joining (and Louise guessed that still held true, given some of the *alternative* observations she'd made about their monthly books) but wanted somewhere to meet like-minded women. Perth might be the only city in Scotland to not have an official gay bar. The fact irked Louise. Unless she wanted to broach changing the canteen at work into a speakeasy there was nothing she could do, though. And it had been hard enough to get management to stock milk alternatives. Running a somewhat illegal lesbian bar was *probably* a step too far.

Now Jordan got her mail delivered to Louise's house and popped up when work allowed. The rest of the time she travelled the length and breadth of the country in her caravan, working in the construction industry.

Louise was an anchor, but she sometimes wished Jordan came with a rope, so she could reel her back in when she really needed her.

At least she was here today.

She carried their fresh drinks over to find Jordan's brow furrowed in confusion as she stared at a letter.

'What is it?' Louise asked, placing Jordan's beer down. Without taking her eyes off the letter she picked it up and took a long sip.

'Some eejit wants me to take out a credit card with them. Pre-approved for 20k.'

'Tempted?' Louise joked, raising an eyebrow as she drank her wine.

'I mean, that's a lot of cups of tea.'

'Even you'd have trouble drinking that much.'

'Me? Nah. There's more tea in my veins than blood these days.' She stuffed the letter back into its envelope. 'Heap of shite as always.' She pushed a pile towards Louise, keeping two envelopes back for herself. 'For your shredder.'

'*Gracias*. Wish I could go in after them.'

'Now, enough of that. Hazel will come round, if you want her to.'

'What do you mean?'

'If you're not fussed, just leave her be. She'll scurry back to Glasgow soon enough.'

'Not fussed?'

'Yeah, just let her hate you.'

Louise winced: going by the way her stomach swooped to her knees at the thought of it, that wasn't an option.

Jordan leaned closer, moving her pint to the side so she could gain another few inches. 'Look, you've said sorry. Unfortunately the ball's in her court now.'

'So, that's it? That's your advice?'

'Aren't you pleased I called by Perth?' Jordan joked.

Louise ignored her question. 'So, that's your advice? Don't speak to her on the walk?'

'Give her space,' Jordan replied with the sage nod of someone who professed to know things. 'Or, if it's really bugging you, find a way to show her you've changed.'

'Easier said than done.'

'You've worked bigger miracles.'

'Still haven't figured out how to get you to buy a pint.'

11

Hazel watched as a blue tit skipped along the branches of Mum and Dad's cherry tree, finally hopping onto the feeder and merrily scooping seed into its mouth, not caring that more was falling to the ground than actually being consumed.

Mum was making her do the Walkie Talkie this evening. They'd decided it would be too much on crutches, so they'd hired a wheelchair. It would be handy to have anyway: crutches were proving trickier than expected.

Which begged the question: why couldn't one of her pals push her after Hazel dropped her off?

Mum was adamant, though. Something about spending time together.

It was warm this evening, so Hazel had opted for a sleeveless T-shirt and joggers. Mum's lingering gaze this morning told Hazel all she needed to know about her tattoos being so exposed. The only one she'd *really* disapproved of was the one wrapped around her neck: she'd questioned Hazel's sanity and future job prospects for that. But when you were a self-employed PT, tats were nothing. The opposite, maybe. Some clients definitely came for Hazel and not the fitness. And where was the harm, when they got fit and had a nice view away from their husbands for an hour? Hazel's bank balance never minded.

Hazel loved her tattoos. They were a badge of honour, a timeline of her history – each one had a story. The single letter A over her heart burned hot. She'd got it for her ex-fiancée. The sooner it was covered the better. If only she could afford rent: then luxuries like banishing the permanent memory of her dickhead ex could be indulged too.

'You ready, Hazel?' Dad called from the conservatory door.

Hazel adjusted her sunglasses as she sat up on the recliner. 'Yep, Mum good to go?'

'Raring!'

She'd already loaded Mum's chair into the boot, so it was just a case of loading Mum now.

With a heavy sigh, Hazel stood. Helping her parents was no problem but having to slot into their routine was tedious.

They'd had her out to three different coffee shops this week. Which wasn't awful but they were so slow (crutches notwithstanding) that Hazel quickly found her patience waning and the urge to do a runner growing. Once in a while was fine. Enduring life at a snail's pace 24/7 was something else.

Then there was the constant need to repeat everything. Since when did they get so deaf? She was sick of her own voice.

Hazel took the steps at the side of the house up to the driveway, deciding not to bother going back inside.

Whenever she felt like this, she reminded herself she

was lucky to have her parents at all. Some people weren't so fortunate.

Didn't stop her wanting to launch a plated cream scone like a frisbee after she'd asked Dad if he wanted a knife or fork eighty-nine times, though.

Deep breaths.

Dad was helping Mum along the front of the house when Hazel met them at the corner. 'You going to be alright on your own?' she asked Dad.

He bounced on the balls of his feet, holding back excitement. 'Got a Saints match to watch on TV.'

If only they could swap places. It had been ages since Hazel had been to a football match *or* watched one on TV. Better still, it would be good to play. Maybe there was a local five-a-side she could get involved in. She made a mental note to google it later.

She hovered her hands behind Mum as she ascended the four small steps to the driveway.

'Like climbing Everest, they are,' Mum said with a huff, one hand on the back of the car to steady herself as she caught her breath.

'You don't think this is too much, too soon?' Hazel asked, hopeful she could get out of this charade yet. She'd missed last week's: what harm would another do?

'Nonsense; do me good to get fresh air.' Mum turned to Hazel. 'Be a dear and get the door, will you?'

Mum safely in the car, crutches stowed on the back seat, they were off. There had never been any trouble finding conversation but suddenly Hazel felt like the unspoken was suffocating the words between them.

Nearly two weeks had passed since Mum's accident and pretending to have online client sessions was getting harder to fake. It wasn't the physical complexities of it – go to her room, shout and jump about a bit – but more the heavy weight of lying.

White lies were one thing, but keeping a pretence going for this long was borderline wackadoodle.

Sooner or later she had to tell them the truth.

Now though, as they whizzed down the Glasgow Road into town, was not the time nor the place.

'Looking forward to seeing your friends?' Hazel asked.

'Oh yes, although, I've been keeping up to date with them online so I'm not totally out of the loop.'

She still couldn't get her head around Mum and Dad's sudden launch into the 21st century.

'Yvonne's got chickens now.'

'Chickens?' Wait, which one was Yvonne again? She'd soon find out.

It wasn't long before they were at the sports centre and Hazel was surprised to find a group of at least twenty women lingering near the entrance. Some were huddled in small groups, others had broken off into pairs, and some stood on their own.

In the centre of the mass was Louise. Her baggy bright blue polo neck, complete with council logo and lanyard, set her apart from the group.

She broke into a grin at the sight of Mum and strode to the car to help, parting the group like she had a staff and they were the Red Sea.

'Marie! You made it.' She beamed, opening Mum's door before Hazel had time to get round to her side. She focused on the chair instead, yanking it out of the boot and locking it into position.

She pushed it round to Louise as she held Mum's elbow, helping her out of the car.

As Mum plonked into the seat, Louise's gaze snagged Hazel's and stayed for a second, as if literally caught.

Hazel tensed her jaw.

Those mahogany-brown doe eyes weren't going to work.

She looked away, breaking the connection, and Louise returned her attention to Marie. Hazel was just here to push, nothing else. Everyone could ignore her for all she cared. In fact, that would be the best scenario.

With Louise at Mum's side, Hazel pushed her towards the crowd, cheers and murmurs of excitement filtered through, filling her heart with pride. Mum was a popular lady.

HAZEL'S PLAN TO blend in as part of Mum's mobility equipment was working a treat. She pushed, Mum chattered. In a gang of at least thirty women when they finally set off, it was easy to become part of the furniture. Literally, if you counted the way Hazel's sweaty palms gripped the handles of Mum's chair.

Mum was currently in discussion with Barb about a new bus route.

'I don't get why they couldn't just add the stop to the original route instead of making a duplicate. It's literally just the same with *fewer* stops.'

Hazel zoned out. They'd been going just over twenty minutes and were about to loop past the sports centre. It wasn't a bad route: level, tarmacked, and a nice view of the river for nearly half of it.

She used to run here. Her main circuit had been the path behind Mum and Dad's, cutting through the rest of Oakbank, but every now and again, when the weather was good, teenage Hazel would come down to the Inch and pound the path here. Running was great for clearing her head. Why she'd not done it recently was a mystery.

She added running to the list along with five-a-side football. She'd start both ASAP.

Glancing upward to check she wasn't about to career into anyone as the path curved, she caught Louise's eye. She'd been on her phone, keeping to herself, but at that very moment she'd looked up, locking her gaze with Hazel's. She smiled weakly before going back to her phone, a frown dominating her features.

Hazel snapped her attention to the path ahead.

Smiles and sad eyes weren't going to shift Hazel's perception.

'How many times do we go round?' Hazel asked as they passed the sports centre and Mum's conversation lulled.

'Usually twice. Am I getting heavy?' she joked.

'Never.'

It was true. Well, not somewhere so flat. Hazel's muscles were grateful for the workout too. It had been a while.

If money hadn't been an issue, she would have been tempted to join a local gym. She was close to running on fumes though, her overdraft scarily close. If Dad hadn't been giving her petrol money for all their excursions, she'd be well and truly sunk.

A lady Hazel didn't recognise, wearing colourful glasses, came level with her and Mum.

'Marie!' she exclaimed. 'How are you?' Pleasantries exchanged, she turned her attention to Hazel. 'And I hear you're engaged. Congratulations! Big day must be coming up soon?'

Hazel's muscles stiffened. It wasn't her fault: how was she to know? The question still made Hazel queasy, though. What was the correct answer in this situation?

It was one of the reasons she'd stopped training. Thinking of her client's questions, or having to randomly tell them, was panic attack-inducing. She'd made the mistake of being happy and wanting to shout her news from the rooftops when they'd first got engaged. She'd never share personal stuff again if she got back to one-on-ones. It wasn't worth the aggro.

She opened her mouth to speak but the words were missing in action. Mum twisted to look at her.

Unnamed lady cocked her head, confused by her lack of response.

It should have been next month. Tears threatened. She gulped them down.

'I—' she croaked.

'Yo, Judy,' Louise said to the woman with colourful glasses. 'Could you push Marie for a teeny tiny moment? I need to borrow Hazel for a sec.'

After a moment of hesitation she obliged, taking over from Hazel.

Louise gently led her away by the elbow over to the far side of the group, away from the bustle and chatter.

She checked Judy wasn't looking before pulling her phone from her back pocket. 'You don't have to talk to me. I just figured you would appreciate a breather from the questions.'

'Were you listening?' Hazel asked, accidentally sounding snippy.

'No. I just happened to be near,' Louise replied, matter-of-factly. 'Go back and answer if you want.'

Hazel rocked her jaw from side to side while she thought. 'No. You did me a favour. Thank you.'

Louise wasn't fazed. She offered a thin-lipped smile with a shrug before slowing her pace, leaving Hazel to herself.

Hazel clicked her tongue to the roof of her mouth. Thankful for the help of Louise King. Whatever next?

She watched Mum and Judy. She'd probably filled her in by now, giving Hazel the pleasure of returning to pitiful smiles and awkward condolences.

She should be used to it by now.

After what felt like nudging the appropriate amount of time to be away, Hazel returned. 'I can take back over,' she said to Judy, holding her hands out to take Mum's chair.

Judy didn't argue. 'There you go,' she said, her smile dripping with sympathy. It sure as heck wasn't to do with pushing Mum, either.

Without another word Hazel picked up the pace, pushing Mum with gusto and leaving Judy behind. Time to move conversation on.

'How many biscuits do you think Dad will have scoffed by the time we get back?' Hazel asked. He was terrible for snacking when Mum was away. Like a naughty child, he took his chances when the responsible adult was out. Problem was, his diabetes didn't take breaks.

'He should be so lucky,' Mum replied with a chuckle. 'I hid them.'

Hazel laughed under her breath. 'You'll be for it when we get home.'

'It's a chance I'm glad to take.'

Hazel looked to the side, another sharp corner coming up. Louise was still lingering near the edge, engaged in conversation with a young woman in her twenties. She caught Hazel's eye and smiled.

This time, Hazel returned it.

12

L ouise looked at her phone as she walked along Cedar Drive. Nothing.

She'd been surprised when Cameron had told her he'd applied for a job at McDonald's, but nothing had prepared her for how she'd feel when he went to the actual interview.

He'd not even wanted her to drive him and she was under strict instructions not to pick him up, either. She'd joked about having a craving for a burger and been snappily shut down.

It was only a ten-minute walk from their house but it might as well have been the moon.

The distance between them was growing, no matter what she did. It felt like she'd gone to sleep with an infant son and woken up with a fully grown man in the bedroom next to hers.

He'd even grown a bizarre attempt at facial hair.

Surrendering to the fact she wasn't to go within a hundred yards of the burger joint, they'd agreed he would text when he was done. Just to let her know how it went.

Nearly forty-five minutes had passed and still nothing.

Nerves twisted her insides into new, impossible shapes.

He'd get the job, no doubt about it: that wasn't her worry. What was niggling was – what if he *did* get it? Another check on the lifelong list of firsts. If she blinked he'd be at university, just her and Mum left in the house.

She stuffed her phone into her gilet pocket with a huff, her face set in lines of disdain.

Living with Mum wasn't the worst, but Cameron's super-speed sprint to adulthood had highlighted another issue: Louise would soon be in her forties with only her mother for company.

Being single had never been an issue but suddenly it felt like she'd failed at something, something huge, and she'd done it all without trying.

With everything going on with her dad, her parent's messy divorce, building a new life with Mum, her more-than-*questionable* coping mechanisms, and finally the arrival of Cameron, dating was so far off the list it had its own time zone.

She'd dallied in her twenties, racking up one long-term relationship to prove she wasn't a complete failure at human interaction. But the break-up had been so harsh on Cameron that she'd sworn off seeing anyone new, only for time to slip through her fingers like water through a sieve.

One minute you're twenty-three, thinking you've got a lifetime to figure shit out. Next moment you're mid-thirties, stomping about the neighbourhood cause you can't catch a fecking break.

She reached the top of Marie and Tom's road and slowed her pace. Wouldn't hurt to call in and see if they needed anything.

Jordan's advice was tough to swallow, but maybe there was no other option but to leave Hazel alone.

Not that she was heeding it as she pressed the doorbell to number eight.

Hazel's car was in the drive but a minute passed without any activity. She was just about to leave when shadows skirted the frosted inner door, hinting someone was about to appear.

A blurry figure loomed closer to the door. Hazel.

'Hey,' she said as she opened the door, her face emotionless. 'What's up?'

Louise balled her hands in her gilet pockets, sweat suddenly blooming on her palms. 'Was just out for a walk, off to the shop, I guess, and I wondered if you guys needed anything?'

Hazel studied her with quiet scepticism. Okay, her reasoning sounded flimsy, but it was the truth. She could hardly launch into a tirade about a possible impending midlife crisis. It was only Tuesday, after all.

'I don't think we need anything, but come in, I'll ask Mum and Dad.'

Louise followed her in, feeling like a massive wally. She should have kept walking.

Marie and Tom were on the patio, each enjoying a cold beverage, complete with lemon slices.

She gave a little wave. 'Hey.'

'Louise is wondering if we need anything from the shop?' Hazel asked with the ghosting of a smirk.

Marie scrunched her mouth in thought.

'Mum wanted tonic water and I needed peace, so I thought I'd take the scenic route,' Louise informed.

Hazel's side-eye didn't go unnoticed.

Going one and half miles in the opposite direction of her house was a little more scenic than normal, but why not? It was a nice evening.

'I could do with a fresh iceberg lettuce, actually,' Marie replied.

'No problem!' Louise exclaimed, standing a little straighter at the thought of being helpful.

'Hazel, you can grab some money out my bag before you go.'

'Go?' Hazel repeated, her mouth frozen open on the vowel.

'Saves Louise coming back and company is always safer.'

Hazel chewed her cheek.

'Really, Marie, it's no problem. I'm enjoying the walk. I can bring a lettuce back no bother.'

'Nonsense. It'll only take a minute. Hazel doesn't mind.'

Louise didn't need to look at her to know Hazel ruddy did mind.

'Right, okay, fine,' Hazel conceded, scratching the back of her head to avoid eye contact. 'Gimme a min and I'll grab my trainers.'

This was going to be fun. Too late now.

'You getting on okay?' Louise asked Marie.

'Brilliant. And it's so good having Hazel; she really has been a godsend.'

'I bet,' Louise replied, and really meant it.

Speak of the devil: Hazel reappeared, shoving her pre-tied trainers on, jabbing her feet against the paving to force them in. Louise often shouted at Cameron for doing exactly that. It was a sure-fire way to ruin a good pair of shoes.

Quick goodbyes exchanged, they left the house.

Louise led, aware Hazel was silently seething.

She waited until they were nearly at the top of the road before speaking. 'You don't need to walk with me,' she said, not even turning around. 'We can go our separate ways.'

'Going to the same place though. Be a bit weird if I just followed you.'

'What's new?' Louise mumbled under her breath. Weird *was* the word when it came to her and Hazel. The air hissed and cracked around them with their own personal thunderstorm, ready to explode at any moment.

'Excuse me?'

Oops. She hadn't meant for Hazel to hear that. She stopped. 'Look, I know you hate me. And I can't change that, so whatever. I'd love for you to know the real me, but . . .' She waved a hand between them before walking off and cutting up the steps to a small area of parkland. It was a shortcut every Oakbanker knew, and the shorter this excursion was, the better.

'Why are you so desperate for me to like you?' Hazel asked without malice as she came level with Louise.

It was a question she'd been asking herself. She took a deep breath. 'Because when I see you, and the way you look at me, I feel like old Louise. And I hate it.'

'Well, if you were less of a dick maybe fewer people would look at you like this.'

'You don't get it. It's fine.' She picked up pace.

'Tell me what I don't get.'

'It doesn't matter. It's just if you're going to be sticking around I'd like to agree to a truce or something. You have every right to hate me, but if you could just give me a chance, if we could start over, maybe we can be amicable around each other.'

'Then tell me what I don't get,' Hazel repeated.

'My dad—' Louise started, but it was too big. The words were mountains she wasn't prepared to scale. 'I had family stuff going on. Dark stuff. And on top of that I was suppressing my sexuality and, well, I might have taken the latter out on you. I was angry and mad at the world and when things were bad at home, I found power elsewhere. Sorry.' She kept walking, eyes straight ahead, unable to meet Hazel's gaze. Maybe she'd never be able to look her in the eye again, not with the way her heart was thundering against her ribs, her throat tightening with every breath.

'You're gay?' Hazel asked, a strange lilt to her voice as if the wind had been knocked from her.

The absurdity erupted from Louise in a bark of laughter. 'That's your takeaway from all that?' she asked, suddenly filled with enough courage to look at Hazel.

'I just . . . you?'

'Sorry, was being a member of the gang subject to a certain look?'

'No, no.' Hazel backtracked, waving her hands like she was putting out a fire. 'It's just, I went to school with you. You had boyfriends. You made fun of me in the locker room. Made snide remarks. I remember it all, Louise.'

'I know. Like I said, misguided inner homophobia or something.' It was her turn to wave her hands as they resumed their climb up the hill. 'Well, not homophobia. I just, I didn't want to cause more issues for my parents.'

'More issues?' Hazel was starting to sound like a parrot.

'It's complicated. But it's water under the bridge.'

'But that's why you changed your name?'

'Yep.'

They walked in silence for a few beats, only the sound of a car door slamming in the distance reminding them they were in the middle of suburbia.

'You still live round the corner?' Hazel asked, her voice more level now.

'Nope. Mum and I moved after she divorced Mark.'

'That's your dad?'

'Yeah.'

'So where do you live now?' People usually asked why she called her dad by his first name. Louise was glad of the reprieve.

'Western Edge. Right in the thick of it.'

Hazel nodded, mentally doing the maths on Louise's evening walk. 'Why did you come to this shop? You're miles away.'

'Needed a walk. Mum's doing my nut in.'

Hazel smiled, *actually smiled*. 'Living with your parents is shite at our age, eh?'

Louise tamped down the excitement fizzing in her veins and stifled the need to text Jordan to let her know: she was having a conversation with Hazel. A normal, adult, conversation. *Yippee ki-yay.*

'It has its moments, but yeah. Real pain in the tits sometimes.'

Conversation dulled again but Hazel kept pace. This time their silence wasn't awkward or heavy; it was verging on natural.

'I'm sorry about the divorce and stuff.'

Louise smiled weakly. 'Thanks.'

It wasn't something she spoke about. New friends knew it was just her and Mum. And friends from school were no more: she didn't even have them on Facebook.

Sometimes the best way to deal with pain is to distance yourself, create barriers, and hope to fuck it doesn't catch back up with you.

The shop loomed. She'd been here a thousand times when she was younger. It was a tiny little place – like, really tiny – in the middle of the bungalows and semi-detached houses, but as a kid it was ice poles, morning rolls, and 10p sweets.

It had felt massive then, but now Louise was spoiled with a mini-market near her house and the realisation this place was no bigger than a large living room.

Still. All she needed was tonic water. It could be a guy with a cool box for all she cared. Going out of her way was more than worth it to make headway with Hazel.

'Better get this lettuce,' Hazel said, with a friendly smile, and her eyes shone in a way Louise hadn't seen before: it was genuine.

Fresh guilt clenched her stomach. She'd make it up to her. Past Louise was a dick, but she wasn't.

'And I'd better get tonic water for my mum.'

'I forgot you were on an errand for yours too,' Hazel said, stepping aside so Louise could go into the shop first. 'Check us out. Living at home *and* our parents' personal skivvies. They've got it made.'

'I'll say.' Louise paused, making sure Hazel was still with her and hadn't disappeared up one of the three slim aisles. She could swear the walls closed in a little further every time she visited here. 'You enjoying being back in Perth?'

'It has its moments. It's kinda the lesser of two evils just now.'

'How so?'

Hazel turned a crisp lettuce in her hands, inspecting it before deciding it was the one. 'Long story. She said iceberg, yeah?'

'Yeah.' Louise replayed the conversation in her head. 'I think.'

'She'll get what she's given.' Hazel raised the lettuce slightly and shot Louise a quick smile that made her dimples pop. 'Lettuce secured. I better be off.'

Best to quit when she was winning. 'Yeah, course. See you around.'

'Yeah, maybe.'

With that she was off, at the till in two seconds flat. Louise rounded the aisle, taking her time to get to the fizzy drinks, but really just wanting to hide the grin that was on her face.

Things could work out yet.

13

'What's this for again?' Hazel asked, eyeing the contents of Mum's mixing bowl. She knew fine well where it was intended for; she just wanted to wind Mum up.

Another week had passed and somehow 'sous chef' had now been added to her parental CV.

'Remember, it's Helen's birthday and I promised everyone some pavlova.'

To be fair, Mum's pavs were a thing of legend. She'd made one every Christmas for as long as Hazel could remember. They were worth ruining her macros for.

'So, I'm helping, and I get none of the end result?' Hazel joked and got a swift whack in the arm with Mum's ancient hand mixer.

'I'll make you a wee mini one, how about that?'

Hazel smiled sweetly. 'You're the best.'

She was prepping fruit – cutting strawberries, dicing raspberries, and washing berries – so Mum could quickly assemble the pavlova tomorrow. It would need to sit in the oven tonight and cool off before anything could be added, but with other things to do and Helen's birthday bash starting at eleven, preparing them now saved precious time.

'You okay with me just dropping you off?' Hazel asked, stealing half a strawberry and popping it in her mouth when Mum wasn't looking.

'Of course. I'll take my crutches, but Helen's bungalow and garden is nice and level. I'll be fine.'

Hazel had lied about having a PT sesh tomorrow, but now the thought of Mum being on her own was making her skin prickly. 'Will Louise be there?' she asked, just as Mum turned the noisy mixer on.

She turned it off, the beaters clattering against the bowl as it slowed. 'Huh?'

'Will Louise be there?'

'Louise?' Mum repeated like she might never have heard of the woman. She carried on regardless. 'No, definitely not. She'll be working. How so?'

'Just, she could help you if you needed anything.'

Mum pursed her lips. 'Cause she's more young and nimble than us old codgers?' She did a wee shimmy in Hazel's direction: well, what her ankle would allow. It was tough with her leg bent on a chair, but she still showed Hazel what for.

Hazel giggled. 'No, because . . . well, actually yes. You've hit the nail on the head.' She bumped her hip into Mum's. Regardless of what hung between them, Louise was good to Mum. Hazel knew her. Trusted her. She would have felt safer if Louise had been there to look out for her.

Mum turned the mixer back on and got to work whipping the egg whites and sugar together.

Hazel bit down a smile. If she closed her eyes she could be eight on Christmas Eve, getting ready for their influx of visitors the next day. Charlotte would be in the living room with Dad, reading a Christmas book together. Those were the days. Cousins, uncles, aunties, grandparents muddled together in a hug of laughter. She'd spent last Christmas alone, hoping Ashley would come back to the flat, even though she'd lied and said she'd come back to Perth. Life really did spin on a penny sometimes.

Mum switched the beaters off. 'Now for the big test.'

Hazel grinned, knowing what was coming.

Mum held the bowl over her head, the stiff peaks of mixture holding their shape. When she was little, a piece of her secretly wanted it to drop, especially if it was done over Charlotte's head.

'Perfect, as always,' Hazel congratulated.

Bowl back safely on the table, Mum's eyes grew wistful. 'It's so nice having you home.'

'It's good being home,' Hazel replied, her eyes set firm on the raspberries she was chopping. She set her jaw and took a deep breath. 'I—work—it's—' She'd rehearsed this a thousand times but nothing was going to plan.

Mum was on pause, her hand resting beside the spatula she'd meant to pick up two seconds ago. 'What's wrong?'

'I don't feel happy at work. I dunno, something just feels wrong,' she lied. She'd weighed it up over many sleepless nights: it was better to ease out of it rather than jump in the deep end of failure. 'I was wondering, would you and Dad mind if I stayed here a bit longer, just while I transition to something else?'

'Of course, darling.' Her eyes were misty as she turned to Hazel and gripped her forearm. 'You've not been yourself for a long time, and whatever you decide to do, your dad and I will support you.'

'Thanks,' was all Hazel could manage. She didn't do tears in front of other people.

'What will you do about your flat?' Mum asked, spooning the pavlova mix onto a baking tray.

'Yaz is fine with me moving out.' She's told her parents Yaz had a two-bed flat, not that she was couch surfing. 'They prefer being on their own, anyway.'

Mum nodded, smoothing the mixture into a circle with a dip in the middle. 'Oops, almost forgot!' she exclaimed, stealing a dollop to place at the side. 'Your mini nest.'

Hazel smiled. 'Thanks.' She chopped a few more strawberries before speaking again. 'You're really fine with me staying, even if I don't have a job?'

'Of course. We love having you home.' She picked up the tray, but Hazel batted her arm.

'You put that down. I'll put it in the oven. Bad enough you're standing,' she scolded with a cheeky wink.

It took seconds to bung it in the oven and return to her chopping board. In that time Mum had taken over and messed up the system.

Hazel stood, hands on hips, jokingly agitated. 'You doing this or am I?' she jested.

Mum leaned back to her side. 'Sorry, sorry. Old habits die hard. I'm not used to having any help,' she said with a smile.

Even before Dad's eyesight started failing Mum was the house's jack of all trades. Hazel and Charlotte were expected to keep their rooms tidy but it took longer than Hazel would like to admit for her to notice that Mum did everything else. From cooking to cleaning to managing appointments and the garden: Mum did it all. It wasn't that Dad was lazy, it was just the roles they'd slipped into and, like Mum said, once you started, you soon found yourself stuck in the habit.

Hazel never wanted to get like that.

Before Ashley, Hazel had been single for a long time, choosing instead to focus on growing her business. Glasgow was a sea of personal trainers and it had taken a while to lock in the right clients and get momentum going. She gave it her all and her personal life suffered.

Everything was so easy with Ashley. They'd hit things off straight away. Before her, Hazel didn't know she was missing anything. Work was all-consuming; it masked the gaping hole in her social life.

Now it was all she could see, big and black, growing wider by the day.

Whoever said mistakes made you stronger was full of shit. She wished every day she'd never met Ashley. Given a time machine, she'd skip the dating event where they'd met and stay in, do some crunches.

Not that she could blame Ashley for everything; some fuck-ups were all her own. But she was the catalyst that ignited the spark which eventually led to Hazel's life burning to a cinder.

Being back home was working wonders, though. She was drinking less and thinking a little clearer. It was hard to live in a pit of despair when your mum expected you to get dressed and drive her to get her nails manicured.

Hazel scooped up the remaining strawberries into the glass bowl Mum had placed by the chopping board. This was going to be one mean pavlova.

'Anything you want me and Dad to do while you're out tomorrow?' Hazel asked, eager to lighten Mum's load where she could.

'You've got a PT sesh – just focus on that.' Mum's brow furrowed. 'If you're not doing PT sessions any more, what do you think you'll do?'

Hazel scrunched her face. She'd run in so many circles with her indecision, she'd literally made herself dizzy one day. 'Haven't quite figured that out yet.'

Mum placed a hand on Hazel's forearm. 'Well, whatever you do. We'll support you. And you can stay here as long as you need. Don't give it a second thought.'

'Thanks.'

Mum's eyes darkened as she lost herself in deep thought. 'I don't think we've said it often but me and your dad, we're proud of you. Really proud. And I mean it: whatever you do next, we'll be proud of that too.'

Hazel finished chopping the final strawberries as she spoke, hoping to God she didn't lop a finger off through the mist clouding her vision. This was more like prepping onions than berries. 'Thanks. That means a lot.'

Mum straightened, a new lease of life zapping through her. 'It's going to be so good to have my girls back. All of us together again!'

'Huh? When?'

'Did she not tell you?'

Hazel rolled her eyes. She and Charlotte spoke three times a year: birthdays and Christmas. Mum still had it in her head they could be the Waltons, with a little effort. 'I've not heard from her for months.'

Mum batted the air, physically getting rid of such a silly notion. 'She's back this weekend.'

'This weekend?' Hazel repeated, mouth agape.

'I know! It's going to be great.'

'Why's she coming back?' Charlotte hadn't been home in years. There was no way she had heard about Mum's leg and booked a flight. Something was up.

'Erm, well, you know,' Mum replied, trailing off.

'Why?' Hazel repeated, drawing the word out.

'She'd already booked it for, well, your, anyway, she'd booked it and couldn't cancel, so now we're all going to be together. It's that fab?'

Hazel didn't share the sentiment. She racked her brains for what the hell Mum was on about. This was worse than trying to guess what actor she was on about. *You know, that man, in the film with her, from that film in the 90s! Has a beard!*

The penny dropped. 'My wedding,' Hazel said, the words like acid in her mouth. 'You can say it, you know. I am aware of it.' She tried to add a chuckle to make it light-hearted, but it came out strangled and odd.

'Alright, yes. That's why she was coming back. The flight was non-refundable, so she's still coming over.'

'And Jimmy? Is he coming too?'

Mum wiggled her mouth from side to side. 'She said he's been called into something important with work.'

'Doesn't he sell cars or something?' Jimmy was Charlotte's long-term boyfriend and one of the big reasons why they moved to Oz in the first place. He was a little too preppy for Hazel's taste, but he always tried, and Mum and Dad liked him. She couldn't really fault the guy.

'I have no idea these days. You know Charlotte is never very good at keeping us in the loop.'

Charlotte was flaky at best, downright rude at worst. Not that Mum would have a bad word said against her.

'Am I to pick her up?' Hazel asked. Any more penny-drops and she was at risk of becoming a coin-pushing machine at the arcade.

It was Mum's turn to set her eyes on the fruit. 'If you could, I know it would mean a lot to her after a long flight. We'll all go. Make a day of it.'

Hazel huffed and instantly felt Mum's steely gaze. 'Right. Fine. Jeezo.'

'You're a star.'

Hazel bit down a comeback. Out of the frying pan and into the fire.

14

'And how's your new bird?' Jordan asked with a devilish grin.

'Shut your face,' Louise jested as she sat on the far-side sofa of Jordan's caravan. 'It's not like that. And I've not seen hide nor hair of her since we went to the shop.'

'Sounds like she's done a runner. Wise woman.' Jordan stood in the tiny kitchen area and stirred the mugs of tea, leaving the bags in to settle.

Jordan's newest job had been postponed for a few days, so Louise was relishing the fact her bestie was still pitched in Scone caravan park, just outside the little town not far from Perth.

Her caravan was looking top notch, as always. She'd bought it off eBay for a tiny sum and done it up herself. She wasn't just an electrician; she was a good craftswoman too, nimble with tools and a sharp eye for design. It wouldn't be to everyone's taste but Jordan had it decorated just as she liked: a variety of greys and blacks, a huge picture of New York above her bed, and a few dashes of personality in the form of cuddly sheep toys. She'd pass them off as the dog's, but Louise knew better.

Her dog, Hux, a wiry wee beagle-griffon-Lord knows cross, lay outside, enjoying the evening sun. Jordan had suggested they join him but Louise needed a break. She'd spent most of the day outside with a mother and toddler group. Her head throbbed and it definitely wasn't just from an excess of sun. Toddlers could be feral wee beasts.

Finally, Jordan placed their mugs of tea on the small table between them.

'Happier, then?' she asked, giving the tea a blow before taking a swig.

'I guess. I'd need to see her again to be certain.'

Jordan narrowed her eyes. 'You're sure there's not more to this than you're letting on?'

'What more could there be?'

'A new gay in the village and you're telling me it's not crossed your mind?'

Louise shook her head before putting a hand over her heart. 'Nuh-uh, promise. Scout's honour.'

'Mhmm. You know, it wouldn't be a bad thing.'

'What would?'

'If you liked her. In all these years I've never known you to have a woman.'

Louise shrugged. 'Jordan, I've had one not-so-awful conversation, half-conversation at that, with the woman. I think you're jumping a little ahead of things there.'

'Yeah well, you know yourself. Just keep an open mind.'

'And what about you?' Louise asked, desperate to change the conversation.

'Me? Too busy for that rubbish.'

'Aye, right. You've got a different girl in every postcode you've visited,' Louise joked.

Jordan shifted in her seat. 'Nah. Hux keeps me company enough. I've even deleted Tinder.'

Louise pulled a face. 'Really? Though, to be fair, I don't know how you did it in the first place.' She'd met Sally on OkCupid all those years ago, but online dating was even more cut-throat now. She and Jordan had drunkenly swiped through matches and messages one night with their friend Bex. Even between the three of them they couldn't squeeze any chat from prospective partners. Most of them ghosted. It was no place for the weak and Louise knew her ego could never take it. Can't get hurt if you never try.

'It was boring. I'd rather spend my time with Hux, or learning my guitar.' Her eyes drifted to the acoustic guitar in the corner of the caravan. She'd still not treated any of the gang to a song, which was unusual for Jordan: usually confidence reigned supreme.

'And what about Eleanor Oliphant?'

'Who?'

'The book we're meant to be reading for the next book club meeting, which is—' she made a show of looking at her watch even though it didn't show the date, '—next week.'

'Oh, that! Finished it. Ages ago.'

'Really?' The smirk on Jordan's face confirmed the opposite but Louise wasn't here to rock the boat. 'That's good. I'm looking forward to hearing your thoughts on it.'

'Oh, and don't I have some of them! Why don't you bring her?'

'Who?'

'Hazel? Why not invite her to book club?'

'You think?'

'Yeah, why not? Does she read?'

'No idea?' Louise's cheeks were growing hot at the

thought. It was one thing to walk to the shop together but to ask her to come to book club felt a step too far.

'You don't think she'd come?'

Louise shrugged. 'Probably not.'

'Why you all red?'

'Am not.'

'Are so.' Jordan chuckled. 'Why not text her?'

'Don't have her number.'

Jordan reclined, arms crossed, hands tucked into her armpits. 'Socials?'

'She's blocked me on Facebook. I know that much.' Years ago she'd seen Hazel pop up as *someone you might know*. Her friend request was swiftly rejected and she'd not been able to search for her since. Not that she'd done much sleuthing. Okay, maybe a little.

'Well, when's the next Walkie Talkie?'

'Next one is Thursday.'

Jordan rubbed her hands together with glee, giddy joy making her sit back up. 'That's the ticket. Right, well, invite her then.'

'I dunno. You, in a room with her. I feel trouble will go down.'

'Me! When have I ever been trouble? What do you think I'll do?'

'It's what you won't do that worries me.'

'Huh?'

Louise didn't know either but the sentiment was the same. 'You'll be sizing her up. Making a match or something.'

'Oh, you think I'll fancy her?' Jordan said with a lopsided grin.

'No, no, course not. She's way too masc for you. I mean

you'll be thinking of matching me. Us. *Accidentally* letting something slip.'

'I would never.'

Louise noted the glint in Jordan's eye. 'Swear on Hux's life.'

'Now, don't be getting carried away.'

'Exactly.' She took a gulp of her tea. Jordan didn't know it, but she was doing a grand job of distracting Louise from the real issue at the helm of her brain: Cameron was starting his new job this evening. She'd not been happy with a midweek shift but he assured her it was only to accommodate training and once he was back at school it would be weekends only. She knew how shift work went, though – soon he'd be covering sickness, picking up hours, enjoying an ever-growing pay packet – but school was never his forte anyway. He was a good kid; he just lacked direction. When it came to selecting his Highers Louise practically had to pick them for him. A job would do him good, give him focus. He could leave after this year if he really wanted, but Louise didn't see the sense in squandering a chance at good grades for a few months' work.

He would have started before she got home from work, so it was either pace the living room and potentially be snippy with Mum *or* come and see Jordan. It was safe to say she'd made the right decision.

'How about I swear to be on my best behaviour? Will you invite her then?' Jordan asked, tea now half-finished.

'Your best behaviour looks a lot like most people's worst, but okay. It's a deal.' Agreeing and doing were wildly different things. Book group consisted of her four closest friends. Putting Hazel into the mix was all kinds of wrong.

～

THURSDAY CAME AROUND IN A FLASH.

Not surprising, since she'd visited Jordan on Tuesday. But still. Suddenly she was standing on the edge of the Walkie Talkie huddle and Hazel was pushing Marie towards the group.

Louise's heart thrummed against her ribs.

She didn't have to ask her. Only she and Jordan knew her intentions.

But the words were stuck in her craw.

It was like she'd only just learned to walk and now Jordan wanted her to run a marathon. Baby steps. There was no sense in overwhelming herself.

'Louise! How are you?' Marie asked as Hazel drew her level.

'Good – clouds are looking a little suspicious but we'll be fine,' she replied, crossing her fingers.

It was a good crowd today, nearly back to normal numbers. They always tailed off at the start of the school summer holidays as people went on vacation or battled with childcare. Now August was nearly on the horizon, schedules were evening back out.

There were even a few new faces.

'My phone says rain in thirty minutes,' Hazel said with a wry grin.

'Ever the optimist,' Louise shot back with a smile, but quickly worried she'd already overstepped. She was being too familiar. 'Although, phones are annoyingly correct these days, aren't they?' Her cheeks burned, despite the lack of sun.

A smile pulled on Hazel's lips but Louise couldn't place its intention.

'I'm sure we'll be fine,' Marie chipped in with a wave of

her hand. 'If we can walk in the winter we can cope with a little summer rain.'

THE DRIZZLE STARTED twenty-five minutes later. Louise pulled her cagoule hood tighter. Hopefully it wouldn't amount to much.

A few women had turned up jacketless, but it was the kind of rain that made the air lighter and smelled like hot tarmac.

'I used to love running in weather like this,' Hazel said and Louise nearly jumped. She'd been so lost in thought she hadn't even noticed who she was walking beside.

'Used to? So you don't run any more?' Louise asked, ignoring the way her stomach was lurching back into its correct position.

'Not so much. I've kinda fallen out the loop with a few things.'

'How so?'

Marie chatted to the lady beside them as Hazel pushed, her face furrowed in thought. Finally, she spoke. 'I went through a bad break-up. It threw my routine out of whack.'

Louise nodded. She'd never been through a real break-up. She and Sally had split amicably. But she knew how heartache could break you so badly it was impossible to know how the pieces could ever fit back together. 'I've always fancied running, but I get tired just walking,' she said with a chuckle, trying to lighten the mood again. 'Getting back to old habits now?'

'Slowly. You don't know if there's a five-a-side or anything here, do you? I'm keen to join a club if I can.'

It was like she was being handed this conversation on a plate. Jordan's voice filled Louise's head. *Ask her to book club!*

But she couldn't. Her mouth had the words locked away, forbidden from being used. 'Five-a-side?' she repeated, getting her thoughts in order. 'Women or mixed?'

'Probably just women, if I'm honest.'

'They're on a break just now but I think they start back up again in a week or two. I can check my calendar later, give your mum a text with the details.'

Hazel looked at the top of her mum's head as she animatedly talked about the hardships of growing aubergines. She turned back to Louise. 'Or I could just give you my number. Cut out the middleman.'

'Yeah, sure,' Louise replied as she fished her phone from her back pocket. She was pleased her voice only cracked a little.

She passed it to Hazel, who stabbed her number in before passing it back with a small smile. 'No prankies.'

'Never.' A grin spread onto her face as a memory flooded back. 'Although, one time me and Gill – you remember her? – we pranked Mrs Vincent, the French teacher. We put something in her juice.'

Hazel's eyes grew wide. 'That was you? Oh my God, that was the talk of the school for weeks.'

Mrs Vincent was notoriously horrible. And not just in the usual, too-much-homework, bit-too-strict way. No. She would pull people in front of class to make fun of their clothes, make comments about people's hair, single out particular pupils and make their life a misery. She'd even hit someone on the back of the head with a heavy French dictionary.

She had a penchant for drinking copious amounts of orange squash from a water bottle on her desk. So, for leaver's day, Louise had stolen chilli powder from Mum's pantry. One glug and she'd never seen someone go so red.

To be fair, it was Gill who'd put the powder in, but Louise had played her part in distracting her. Sometimes she felt guilty about the whole thing but remembering how Mrs Vincent had once made snide remarks about her pal Toni's ginger hair levelled things out. It was a little coughing, nothing bad.

'I still feel bad about it,' Louise confessed. 'So don't tell a soul.'

'You shouldn't feel bad. You're a legend.'

Silence fell between them, as if Hazel had suddenly realised how absurd it was to be having this conversation, and for her to give Louise a compliment.

No matter how much Louise wanted them to be friends, would their past always hang over them? A dangling anvil threatening to fall at any moment and snuff the whole thing out?

Maybe she was asking too much. Sometimes you had to cut your losses and keep facing forward, leave the past where it belonged.

15

Hazel slammed the pillow over her face, knowing complete isolation was too much to hope for, but without a mute button for her sister she'd take what she was given.

Charlotte had been home for just over an hour. Meaning . . . she'd been getting on Hazel's nerves for around fifty-nine minutes.

As requested, they'd had a *fun* family excursion to collect her from Edinburgh Airport. She was pleased to see her little sister, no denying it, but a car trip filled with incessant chatter had Hazel's hands aching from gripping the steering wheel so tight.

Despite moaning about how jetlagged she was, Charlotte had parked herself in the living room and had been yabbering non-stop ever since. Mum and Dad were lapping it up.

They were having a barbeque this afternoon, just the four of them, to celebrate her return. Hazel was sure as hell nipping to the shop before that.

She might have sworn off booze the last few weeks, but

today was filled with problems only beer could answer.

Charlotte had barely changed. Bright, bubbly, with impossibly white teeth, her sister was her opposite in looks and personality. She might have been on a plane for the last twenty-four hours but her long blonde hair was still wavy and bouncy. She could have had the best night's sleep and just done her make-up, if you didn't know better.

Hazel wanted to throttle her.

There was a baseline level of acceptable happiness and Charlotte was so far off it, she probably didn't even know the line existed. The line was a dot to her.

Hazel growled into her pillow as laughter rippled through the house.

It was good to hear her parents happy.

But.

Surely there had to be other ways.

God, did this mean Stacey and Nina would be around? The trio were inseparable in secondary school and Hazel knew from Facebook that they'd kept in touch. Mum had better start chilling the prosecco now. Get the strawberry martinis on ice. Start soundproofing the garden in preparation for all the squealing.

'Hazel!' Mum called.

'Yeah?' Hazel replied, lifting the pillow just enough to be heard but refusing to leave the safety of her bed.

A few beats passed before she heard: 'Hazel!'

'Yeah?' Hazel screamed.

'Hazel!'

Oh for fuck's sake. Even if Mum didn't hear her, Charlotte certainly had. Hazel threw the pillow against the wall and stomped through to the living room.

'Yes?' she huffed.

Mum acted affronted. 'No need to be so moody,' she said

with a chuckle. 'Could you run to the shop for me? The big one, not up the road. I forgot Charlotte had gone veggie.'

Charlotte rolled her eyes in Hazel's direction, as if inciting some form of sibling connection. Hazel ignored her. 'Yeah, sure. Anything in particular?'

'Sausages. Burgers. Whatever. But not Quorn. Hate that stuff. Get the good brands,' Charlotte replied.

Hazel clapped her fingers to her open palm, in Charlotte's direction.

'What's that for?' she asked, side-eying to Mum.

'Money. You want all that, I need money,' Hazel said, snippily.

Dad pulled a twenty from his wallet. 'Alright, girls. Look, here's some money. Charlotte, why don't you go with Hazel? Make sure she gets what you like?'

Hazel opened her mouth to speak, hoping to make up an excuse on the spot, but Charlotte was already talking.

'Actually, I'm bushed. Is it okay if I sleep?'

Mum melted with sympathy, leaning into her daughter as she held her forearm. 'Of course, you'll be tired. Hazel can get the food and everything will be ready when you wake up.'

Hazel mustered her best smile, only just keeping her sarcasm to a level which wouldn't result in a telling-off from Mum.

Without another word, she padded back to her room to grab her trainers. The sooner she was out of the house, the better. She was throwing her jacket over her shoulders when her phone vibrated on her bedside table.

Louise.

Hazel cocked an eyebrow as she read the text.

Just in case, here's the link to a local volleyball team as well.

She'd texted yesterday about the five-a-side in the sports

centre and Hazel had already completed the sign-up forms. Volleyball, though. That was a new one. Didn't they have to wear skimpy outfits? Hazel smiled at the thought. Going into a sport where you were already ogling your imaginary team mates probably wasn't the best idea.

Still, she fired off a reply, intent on lightening her sour mood.

Anything to get out this house.

The reply was almost instant:

Your mum still doing your head in?

Worse. Little sister is here now.

No way! I thought she was in Australia?

She was. Sadly not any more.

She stuffed her phone away, despite its vibrating. Louise could wait until she was out of the house. Charlotte's voice still drifted down the hall like a woodpecker drumming against Hazel's skull.

The week had been centred on Charlotte's arrival and Hazel had spent a few evenings helping Mum prep her room, washing towels and bedding, and cleaning the house.

Maybe Mum was just too focused on seeing Charlotte – it had been a few years, this was a big deal, no denying it – but Hazel's skin stung with the fact that no one had checked in on her.

Somewhere, in an alternate galaxy or a magic mirror, Hazel would be getting married in seven days.

She kidded herself they just didn't know how to approach it, or that they were protecting her, not wanting to bring something so painful up. But, deep down, she knew they just hadn't given it a second thought.

If Charlotte had descended last year she would be texting Ashley for support. That was the hardest part, the piece of her that hadn't recovered. She was regretting her past, suffering her present, and mourning her future: with absolutely no one to talk to about it. Yaz wasn't the *emotions* type and none of her other friends were close enough to offload on.

So much pain and the only person she could have trusted was the one who'd held the mallet, smashing her to pieces.

If only there was a pause button she could hit, give herself a break.

'Hazel!' Charlotte called. 'Think you could get me some chocolate as well?'

'Sure,' Hazel growled back.

HAZEL PUT the bag full of shopping on the passenger seat as she got in the car. She'd ignored the devil on her shoulder and used Dad's money to get Charlotte the food she wanted, not the Quorn. Plus a six-pack of beer for herself.

She leaned her head against the headrest and sighed. Today was too much. It was clawing at her insides, frustration swelling in her chest and coiling her muscles, making them tighter with every passing minute.

After letting out a ragged sigh she pulled her phone from her pocket. Louise's name sat on her lock screen, her earlier message still unread.

It wouldn't kill Charlotte to wait another half hour for her stupid sausages.

Louise: *time to nip to the shop for another lettuce?*

Hazel couldn't help but smile. Louise was surprisingly funny. Her muscles loosened a little. She snapped a photo of the sagging bag on her seat and added: *Charlotte's already got me running her errands.*

It was a surprise to see three bouncing dots quickly appear, considering Hazel had left her hanging for over half an hour.

Ooft. She didn't hang about. I hope that beer is for you.

You've already got me pegged. Figured I deserved it.

Too right. Question is: where you going to drink it?

Think I could get away with it in the car? Hazel backspaced. She didn't want Louise to think she had a problem. And drink driving was no laughing matter. *Don't think I can go solo tonight but I'm hoping it will numb Charlotte's voice a little.*

Hazel watched her phone but no dots came. She placed it on her lap and looked out of the window.

It was a nice evening and the supermarket's car park was packed. Charlotte had been lucky to get anything – the good weather had obviously sparked a wave of barbeques across Perth and now the aisles were cleared of produce. If Charlotte had been a meat eater she would have been lucky to get a chipolata.

Her eyes darted to her phone as it vibrated against her thigh.

What about going for a run?

Huh?

Tonight?

Not necessarily. But you said the other day you missed it. Might be a good way to get some peace.

Hazel pushed her bottom lip out as she thought. It wasn't a bad idea, especially while the nights were still long and the weather decent.

Her fingers were typing of their own accord, her brain on autopilot before she had a chance to talk herself out of it: *Maybe tomorrow. Fancy joining me?*

16

L ouise pulled her foot to her bum and stretched her
quad. She lasted two seconds before wobbling and
completely losing her balance.

Hazel, bless her heart, said nothing.

Louise couldn't remember the last time she went
running. In fact, she wasn't sure she'd ever run while
sober.

She'd warned Hazel of this fact but apparently it wasn't a
problem. She was a PT: it was what she did best.

Louise couldn't help but imagine a tortoise trying to
keep up with a whippet.

'You ready?' Hazel asked, clapping her hands together.

'More like, are *you* ready? You're about to go so slow
you'll be going backwards.'

'I've seen you walk, you've got stamina. Just need to up
the pace a little.' She smiled and Louise calmed a little.
'Slow and steady. This isn't a race.'

It wasn't racing that worried her. It was not making a
bloody fool of herself.

'Right, let's do this,' Louise exclaimed, doing a wee jump

to prove she was fully up for it. Her calf twinged as she landed. *Off to a good start.*

'Any injuries I should know of before we start?'

Louise thought. 'None that I can remember. Had a clean sheet during my days as a pro athlete.'

'Alright, alright,' Hazel said, jesting. 'I just wanted to know in case you had dodgy knees or anything.'

'I might do. But I've never ran. Guess we'll find out today.' The only body part she was worried about was her pelvic floor. All she could do was cross her fingers and hope for the best. She'd switch to crossing her legs if that method failed.

'Okay, match my pace. You'll be fine.' With that, Hazel was off.

They'd met behind Hazel's house, down by the little stream that ran the length of the path flanking the houses in Oakbank, affectionately known as The Burn. Thankfully, the path by The Burn was flat. That was, at least until they got to Louise's neck of the woods, Western Edge: from there it was all uphill. At least she was heading towards home, though – if she needed to duck out she didn't have far to hobble.

This wasn't bad. She jogged level with Hazel, her heart rate only rising a fraction.

'This wasn't how I expected to be spending a Sunday,' Louise said, her voice jolting with each pound of her feet.

'What do you usually do?' Hazel's voice was perfectly level.

There was no mistaking who the personal trainer was. Hazel's toned physique was highlighted by her aerodynamic sleeveless tee and well-fitting shorts. Louise had scrabbled to find the only shorts she owned that could possibly pass as running attire (bought for lounging by the pool in

Lanzarote) and a T-shirt she usually wore to garden. Thankfully, she had a sports bra for walking, or she'd be liable to give herself a black eye.

Sundays. What did she usually do on Sundays?

'Sundays,' she repeated to herself, still ruminating on an answer. 'Depends. Sometimes I'll just chill. Other days I might garden. Go a walk. Dunno. We always do the big shop on a Saturday so I can stay in if I want.'

Hazel bit back a smile. 'Living with your mum has done a number on you,' she joked, her voice still annoyingly unaffected by their ever-increasing pace.

'What do you mean?' she chuckled.

They'd reached the wooded area that passed the local play park now. Louise tried in earnest to forget how much her legs already burned. They weren't even within sniffing distance of the incline.

'You're in your mid-thirties. Single. No one depending on you. You should be out, enjoying yourself.'

This would be the moment she corrected Hazel, dropped Cameron into the conversation, but her mouth went dry. She cleared her throat, hoping it would dislodge the truth.

Only, it wasn't the truth she'd wished for that floated to the forefront of her mind.

Her brain whirled into action. *It's not a lie, just an omission.* She'd been on dating sites long enough to know how women reacted when you said you were a single mother. They either ghosted or bowed out respectfully. Most people Louise's age either didn't want the responsibility, or didn't fancy a ready-made family. At least, that was true for the women she'd met so far.

The way Hazel's triceps flexed in the light, the curve of her top as it clung to her abdomen – there was no way

Louise's brain was going to shut up any time soon. *Keep your cards to your chest. Figure these feelings out before you blow it.*

'I'm always so tired from work,' she said, breathless for so many reasons.

Fuck. She hated when Jordan was right.

'Fresh air is always a good idea,' Hazel said, leading them through the woods.

The sunlight split the trees, washing Hazel's features with dappled shadow. Louise slowed her breathing. She couldn't have feelings for Hazel. How stupid was that?

But, if she dug deep enough, that had been a huge part of teenage Louise's problem.

Louise was struggling to keep her own sexuality hidden; her feelings for Hazel had been dangerous. It was easier to mask them in venom than confront the issue head on.

More than once, after a few drinks, she'd considered how it would feel to kiss Hazel.

A memory played in a loop, crystal clear: she'd been watching her at Christopher Mercy's birthday party. Hazel was across the room, a bottle of alcopop cradled to her chest, hair in a ponytail and a tight polo shirt on. Even then she had a cracking body. Louise had lingered her eyes too long, got lost in her thoughts, and before she knew it Leonie was asking what the hell she was staring at. She'd made some snide remark about how gay Hazel looked and tacked on something else stupidly homophobic, and they'd laughed. Gazes pinned in Hazel's direction as their eyes met. Hazel had turned bright red and left the room.

Shit.

Louise felt a bit sick and it wasn't just from the running.

'You okay?' Hazel asked, slowing to a fast walk. 'You've gone pale.'

'I'm good,' Louise snapped back, as cheery as she could.

She picked up the pace, determined to show Hazel what she was capable of. 'Will we just go straight over?'

The path exited the woods and crossed a main road, otherwise you had to pound the pavements with no option but to tackle a hill. At least if they stuck to the path she would be out of public view. Sweat was already dripping.

She checked both ways and crossed before Hazel could protest.

'Yo, speedy Jo, slow down a little.'

'Nah, I've got this.'

Now she'd started, she couldn't stop: the same way her head was going a thousand miles an hour, flooding her with intrusive thoughts.

They followed the path that passed the back of some flats and Louise realised, despite living in this area for her entire life, she'd never actually come this way.

They turned a corner and a steep hill almost stopped her in her tracks.

Her legs wished it actually had, Christ they were burning. Not half as much as her chest though.

She smiled despite the pain, thinking about how she was literally running from her problems, and yet her number one problem was keeping pace as easily as if she was walking to the shops.

'You're a mad woman,' Hazel jested.

Louise didn't answer. She couldn't. Her mouth was filled with a metallic taste and her lungs ached for air.

It was like someone had lassoed her with a rubber band and was pulling her backwards, but she wasn't about to give up.

'Peching a little?' Hazel asked with a wry laugh.

'Nope.' The word came out a grunt.

With every step she slowed a little until eventually they

were at the top of the hill and Louise allowed herself to stop. She held her side, wincing with every breath.

'Jesus Christ,' she wheezed.

Up here they were level with the motorway. She faced away from Hazel and watched the cars whizzing past as she tried to catch her breath.

Please don't pass out.

'You good?' Hazel asked, putting a hand on her shoulder.

That put her back to square one and her breath hitched.

'Got a stitch,' she lied, certain Hazel must have felt how her muscles had stiffened.

The heat of her face was no match for the lingering warmth where Hazel's hand had been. She may as well have branded her with a searing hot iron.

'Skipped a few steps there,' Hazel said, still sizing her up.

How had she not even broken a sweat? Louise dragged the back of her hand over her sopping brow. She dreaded to think what her fizzy mane looked like, despite being tied up.

'My house isn't far, if you want a break,' she suggested, her voice ragged.

Hazel considered the offer. She looked at her sports watch, checking the mileage. 'That you done?'

'How far have I gone? Miles, I bet.'

'Zero point eight miles.' The corner of her lip twitched.

Louise cocked her head, hands now on her hips. She angled herself to see Hazel's watch. 'Zero point – you sure?'

'Watch never lies.' Hazel's smile was full beam now and Louise could help but return it.

'The hill,' she said, waving her hand in the direction they'd come. 'Must count for something.'

'A bit. C'mon, let's take it slow, we can go further. I know you've got another mile in you.'

'So, you and Charlotte don't exactly get on?' Louise asked, happier now they were going at an acceptable pace. Hazel was right; at this speed it wasn't bad.

Hazel waggled her head. 'It's hard to explain. We're just totally different people. When she's in the house it's like the whole vibe changes.'

'You mean she gets all the attention?' Louise joked. Her breath was more level now but could already tell by the ache in her thighs that stairs would be an issue tomorrow.

Hazel laughed under her breath. 'Not so much. Well, she does, but I don't mind that. It's like, I dunno.' She turned the right words over in her head before committing. 'It's like I'm quite content in my wee bubble, then she rocks up and the whole house is flipped upside down. It's the same house but suddenly it's heavy and horrid, like it's not my home any more.'

'That must be horrible.' Louise's eyes wandered to a wild rabbit nibbling the grass as they passed the park at the top of the Western Edge. It looked like Hazel was going to loop them through the suburb of Burghmuir, then back to where they started in Oakbank. Louise's legs twinged with relief: one more tiny hill, then level land would soon become downhill. *Hallelujah.* 'Has it always been like that?' she asked Hazel.

'The same but different. If that makes sense.'

Louise nodded. 'Being related doesn't mean you have to get on.'

'Blood is thicker than water,' Hazel recited with a roll of her eyes.

'But blood can go bad. Being related isn't a free pass to be a dick.'

Hazel worried her bottom lip between her teeth. 'She's not so much a dick. She just really gets my tits in a twist.'

Louise couldn't help but laugh, but it soon turned to a wheezing cough. Her body wasn't equipped for hilarity *and* running. She slowed to a standstill, hands on her knees as she caught her breath.

Hazel stood over her, a smile dancing on her lips. 'You know what I mean, don't you?'

Louise straightened herself. 'Oh yeah, some people just have the power to do that. All they have to do is breathe.'

'Exactly.'

'A few weeks ago you thought the same of me, though.'

Hazel broke into a jog, shooting Louise a wink as she pushed off. 'Who said I still don't?'

'You don't though, do you?' This time she managed to laugh without buckling over; she was level with Hazel now, enjoying the smirk on her face.

'You really want me to answer that?'

A week ago the answer might have been no, but the smile Hazel was battling told Louise she'd like the reply now.

'Of course.'

'You'll need to catch me first.' Hazel was off, shifting to sixth gear and leaving Louise in a trail of metaphorical dust.

'Oi!' Louise giggled, trying in earnest to catch up. Her feet pounded the pavement, the small incline feeling like she was scaling a mountain. She wasn't about to let Hazel win, though.

They rounded the corner onto the busier main road but Hazel wasn't perturbed by the passing cars. She carried on at speed, all the while shooting backwards glances to Louise, checking her competition with a grin on her face.

She was going to keep going, wasn't she? This was a piece of piss to her.

Louise willed her legs to go faster but the burning in her calves was ramping up with every kick. She lunged at Hazel, hoping to grab her T-shirt. 'Hey! Come on,' she wheezed.

Hazel giggled. 'Flagging?'

'A bit.' She sounded like a broken kazoo.

Hazel slowed, jumping back when Louise made another playful grab for her. 'Too slow.'

Louise slowed to a stop, hands grasping at her side, pressing down on the most painful point. 'Truce, please. I'm dying.'

'Okay, okay, can't have the head of the Walkie Talkies' blood on my hands. Half of Perth would come for me.'

'As if,' she said with a smile, tipping her head back and puffing her cheeks out before letting out a long, rough, breath. 'Christ on a bike. How are you not sweating?'

'I will, once I get a few more miles in.'

'More?' Louise scrunched her face up. 'I really would die.'

'Don't worry, I'll let you off this time.' Hazel wandered off, leading them past the ambulance station that was nestled between the bungalows of Burghmuir.

'And to think you do this for fun,' Louise joked. A river of sweat flowed down her spine. She dreaded to think what her face was like.

'Sometimes for fun; most of the time just to clear my head, get the endorphins flowing.'

'I'm certainly flowing,' Louise said, running a hand down her sweaty upper lip. 'That'll be my pooch shifted. Surely I've lost pounds after that.'

'You don't have a pooch. And you definitely don't need to lose weight.'

Louise was thankful her cheeks were already burning red.

'Not that I've been looking,' Hazel quickly added.

'No, course not.'

They exchanged a quiet laugh teamed with a stolen glance. She was definitely reading too much into it, though.

Weeks ago this woman would have happily shoved her in a ditch. Much like her running, she needed to go slowly before breaking into a sprint.

'I'll probably head home once we get to the junction,' Louise said, pointing ahead in case Hazel had suddenly gone blind or developed amnesia.

'That's cool, I can take the long way home without any slow coaches.' The dimple popped on Hazel's cheek and Louise wondered if her lungs would ever hold air again.

'Cheeky wee sod, aren't you?' Louise jibed.

'That's only the start of it.' Another wink and Hazel was off, full speed, leaving Louise to admire the view.

17

'This feels so surreal,' Charlotte gushed.

If her sister said that phrase one more time, Hazel was going to lose her mind.

Days had passed but Charlotte's enthusiasm showed no signs of dying down. In fact, Hazel could swear she was getting more peppy. Or maybe Hazel was just low on caffeine: she was choosing to spend more time in her room just now, instead of hanging out in the kitchen and conservatory like she'd enjoyed before the Foghorn from Down Under descended.

Charlotte carried on, despite the lack of encouragement from anyone at the table. 'This time last week I was in Melbourne. Now I'm here, with you.'

Mum smiled sweetly. 'And aren't we lucky?'

Hazel played with the cutlery on her now empty plate. Her taxi duty for the day was taking the family out to the local farm shop and café, Castlehill Farm. It was packed, even though it was a Wednesday. Hazel wasn't sure she'd ever visited the place and it *hadn't* been packed. She could remember being a teenager when the farm's tiny animal shed was converted to hold a half dozen tables. Now the café dwarfed the farm in terms of revenue and was a Perth staple. The place was huge, with a log burning stove in the middle of the newly erected conservatory, doubling their capacity again from the extension they'd added a few years ago. Paintings of chickens and cows adorned the walls alongside chic cottage-core furniture, just in case you ignored the panoramic views and forgot you were on a farm.

Hazel envied their business acumen. They even had a massive shop to further tempt punters to part with their cash. No doubt Mum would have Hazel carrying a basket for her shortly.

'What's Jimmy doing today?' Dad asked, wiping at his mouth with a paper napkin.

Hazel stopped poking at her fork as Charlotte leaned closer to Dad; a screaming child at the next table had obviously drowned him out.

'What was that?' Charlotte asked.

'Jimmy, what's he up to this week?' Dad repeated.

'Oh, Jimmy.' Charlotte beamed, returning to a more relaxed position. 'He's just working, nothing exciting.'

'Shame he couldn't be here,' Mum fawned.

'I know, he's super gutted too, but he just couldn't get out of work.' Charlotte flashed a smile: up, down, and away again like she was a wooden puppet.

'Next time,' Mum suggested.

'Better not take you so long to visit again, though!' Dad joked. 'I'll have popped off by then.'

Charlotte batted his arm. 'Dad! No! Don't say that.' She gripped her hands round Dad's bicep and cosied in.

She'd always been a daddy's girl. Hazel couldn't remember the last time she'd hugged Dad. They just didn't have that kind of relationship.

'Do they still do those amazing strawberry milkshakes?' Charlotte asked, pulling at the sleeves of her jumper so they covered her hands. She'd mentioned at least a thousand times how the opposite seasons were messing with her head. *Back home it's winter!* Hazel had noted the way Mum winced at the word home.

'I certainly think they do,' Mum replied, twisting in her chair to catch the eye of a waitress. 'Hazel, do you want one?'

She shook her head. It was tempting, but there were more nutritious things she could fuel her body with. She'd wrecked her physique enough recently; it felt good to be looking after herself again.

'I'm good just now.'

'Oh go on, Hazey!' Charlotte oozed.

Hazel bit down the twisting in her gut from her sister's terrible nickname. Charlotte's friends all called her Charlie but with family she was always Charlotte; anything else felt wrong in Hazel's mouth and Mum said, 'I called you Charlotte, nothing else!'. Still, her sister persisted with *Hazey*. Thankfully, it had never caught on. Just another ill-fated attempt to pull Hazel down to Charlotte's level.

She seemed out of place in Perth. A sun-kissed star, with freckles splattered over her nose, perfectly tousled blonde hair, and now a nose ring, giving Mum palpitations. Even her clothes shouted *stranger*: she'd be better suited to a surf shop than a wee Scottish farm.

Maybe if she'd moved to Australia *Hazey* would blend in with the beach too. It was easy to become one with where you lived.

It was a surprise to Hazel how little she missed Shawlands. Glasgow had been her home for so long she'd expected a period of mourning for what she was missing out on. But the thing was: she wasn't really missing anything.

Apart from Yaz, everyone was coupled up. The glory days of going out or impromptu house parties were long gone.

She had as much of a social life in Perth as she did Glasgow. No man's an island, but break up with your fiancée and you can sure as hell find yourself marooned.

'I might have a wander round the shop,' Hazel said, pushing her seat out and standing before anyone could protest.

Mum put a hand on her arm, stopping her from moving. 'Now hold on, I'd love a look round too. Let your sister have a milkshake, then we can all go round together.'

Hazel sat back down with a huff.

As PREDICTED, Hazel was the pack horse carrying the basket. Charlotte was free to roam.

Mum was doing well on her crutches; she could get a good pace going when she wanted. Which was exactly what happened when she spotted a blackcurrant gin.

Hazel ambled behind, in much less of a rush than her mother.

'Do you think Charlotte still drinks this?'

Hazel looked at her sister, who was examining a jar of chutney on the other side of the shop. 'Dunno. Probably. Or was that Jimmy?'

Mum scrunched her face. 'Was it Jimmy? Bit girly, isn't it?'

Hazel chuckled while bumping her hip into Mum's. 'Twenty-first century, guys can drink purple stuff.'

'Is it actually purple?' she asked, tipping the bottle from side to side to see if the glass was clear or coloured.

'I think so. Isn't it? Anyway, either way. I've seen them

both drink it, so worst case scenario, she can take it back to him.'

'Good plan, Batman.'

Hazel smiled. Mum had never changed her phrases in all her life.

'Whatcha doing?' Charlotte asked, trotting over with a jar of artisan piccalilli. She placed the bright yellow chutney in the basket without a second thought. Her eyes caught the booze Mum had just put inside. 'I didn't know you drank gin?'

'It's for you. Or Jimmy,' Hazel corrected.

'Jimmy?'

'Hazel thought if you didn't like it, he would have it. You were drinking it the last time you were in Perth.'

'Were we?'

'Definitely. I remember you split some on the outdoor cushions. Stain's still there.'

Charlotte shot her daggers before relaxing her features back to a faint smile. 'Oh, yeah, I remember. Was Jimmy's drink more than mine.'

'You can take it back, a wee treat from me,' Mum said.

'Actually, he's totes off gin, if I'm honest.' She took the bottle from the basket and put it back on the shelf. 'But, if you're dying to buy something, what about this whisky?'

'If that's what he likes, you get it for him,' Mum reassured her.

It was nearly double the cost of the gin. Not that Charlotte noticed.

She put it in the basket. 'Thank you! We both like that, so it works out better for me.' She giggled. 'We can have one tonight, Hazey? Together.'

'Can't tonight – busy, sorry.'

'Oh really?' Mum asked with more surprise than Hazel

thought necessary. She *could* have a social life. It was a total lie, but that wasn't the point. There was no way she was spending an evening with Charlotte.

'Yeah, meeting a friend for a drink.'

'On a Wednesday?' Charlotte queried.

'The joys of self-employment, Charlotte. Yes, today, which is Wednesday, I am going for a drink.'

Charlotte pulled a face while sticking out her tongue. 'Alright for some. Maybe I'll see if Nina and Stacey are free. We could get a lift into town together.'

'Yeah, whatever,' Hazel replied, suddenly becoming fascinated by a chorizo sausage ten paces away.

Shit. Going out on her own was one thing, but with Charlotte and her motley crew on the prowl she couldn't be caught solo. All she wanted was some peace. After a day of family, an evening drinking whisky with Charlotte wasn't on the cards. Now she was in too deep.

Maybe she could let Charlotte arrange a night with her pals, then say she got cancelled on last minute.

Another one of Mum's famous phrases rang in her head: *liars always get caught.*

Too late now. The lie was out there.

'Who you meeting?' Mum asked, coming level with Hazel at the meat fridge.

Hazel shook her thoughts free, aware she'd been holding a sausage for an extraordinarily long while. First time for everything. 'Meeting?' she repeated, stalling for time.

'Yes, tonight.'

'Ah, yeah. Sorry. Erm—' *Fuck.* Who did she know in Perth? 'Just someone from school.'

'I thought everyone moved away?'

'From my friend group, yeah. This is someone else. More of an acquaintance, really.'

Mum narrowed her eyes. 'You're being awful shifty. Is there something you're not telling me?'

This woman, forever reading her like a book. Hazel scratched the back of her neck. 'No, course not.'

Mum's eyes remained slits. 'Is it Louise?'

'Louise?' Hazel blurted, so loudly the woman beside them tutted as she reached for a packet of beef mince.

'You've been hanging out quite a bit recently.' Mum smiled shrewdly. 'It wouldn't harm you to make a new friend.'

'I'm not meeting Louise.' Hazel's cheeks burned hot at Mum's phrasing. She'd enjoyed running with Louise. She was easy to talk to and it was nice to have someone to vent about Charlotte with. But: *one text doth not a "new friendship" make.* Or multiple texts, for that matter.

'Mum, can I get this tempeh?' Charlotte asked, bounding over like a dog off the leash.

'Sure, darling.' Her eyes hadn't left Hazel's, though. It was like she was looking into her very soul, racking through the index cards of her subconscious, and cross-referencing all her secrets. Hazel shivered.

'Right, fine, yes,' Hazel huffed, collapsing like a house of cards under Mum's glare. 'I'm meeting Louise.' It was either admit to whatever Mum thought she saw, or invent someone new. The latter would only lead to more questions.

They'd only hung out once. Mum was totally overreacting. Although, they had been messaging every day. *Were* they friends now?

Recently, something had just clicked. Hazel was fed up using all her energy on being angry. After the last year, she was all out of hatred. She was enjoying Louise's company –

so what? She could never move forward if she kept her hands gripped around the past. Hazel wasn't who she was back then; it would seem Louise wasn't either.

Mum smiled, smug that she'd apparently figured out whatever the heck she'd figured out.

'Who's Louise?' Charlotte asked, her brow creased.

'From school – you'd know her if you saw her,' Hazel replied. Her heart was ticking at an awkward pace, thinking about how she was going to wiggle out of this later. Did this place sell shovels? She'd be better to invest in one now; would make digging this gigantic hole a damn sight easier.

'Louise,' Charlotte repeated, thinking so hard her eyebrows nearly touched.

'Blonde hair, brown eyes, this tall,' Hazel said, waving a hand just below her own eyes to indicate height.

Charlotte shook her head with a pout. 'No clue. I can see her when we head out; where you meeting her?'

Hazel wanted to growl with frustration. Instead she gave the steak pie on the adjacent shelf a quick prod. 'We've not decided yet.'

'How about I say to the girls we'll meet at Melrose's, go somewhere together?'

A little growl escaped before Hazel could bite it down. 'It's just the two of us, sorry.' Hazel's brain was going haywire. Inside her head, red lights flashed. The gremlins that ran her thoughts were running in circles. MAYDAY, MAYDAY! The longer this conversation went on, the worse it got. She turned to leave but Charlotte stood her ground: she was boxed in.

She cocked her head, a wry smile forming. 'Is it a date, Hazey?' Her eyes lit up, thinking she'd realised something spectacular.

'No, it's not a date,' Hazel moaned. She looked at Mum.

'Honestly, it's not. Louise said she needed to talk to me about something.'

Hazel's brain gremlins high-fived each other, pleased with fabricating such a good lie on the spot. The warning lights still flashed but she ignored them, in too deep to back down.

Mum nodded. 'She okay? Nothing serious?'

'No, I think it's to do with me wanting a new job.'

The gremlins looked at each other. That was maybe a step too far. There would be follow-up questions now. Too late. Hazel forced them to sit down and shut up.

'That's brilliant,' Mum gushed.

'You want a new job?' Charlotte asked.

This was too much for the meat section of a farm shop. 'Look, can we talk about this later? This basket's heavy.'

'Course, yes. Sounds like we have lots to catch up on,' Mum replied, looking pleased as punch.

'Actually, I might get some pickle too,' Hazel lied, looking at the contents of the basket for inspiration.

Family dispersed, Hazel sauntered off to the pickle shelves. This couldn't wait: God knew where she'd be made to drive to next and with the day wearing on, she needed to intercept Louise now. This lie had so many arms and legs she was going to at least have to bring some of it to fruition.

She whipped her phone out.

Fancy going for a drink tonight?

18

'How does this look?' Louise asked, arms out to show off her full outfit as she entered the living room.

Cameron and Mum studied her, eyes flicking from head to toe and back again.

She'd changed a few times before settling on a loose denim shirt and grey jeans. She felt good, but was it too mumsy?

This was all so last minute. It was making her insides fizz.

She'd never been so indecisive before meeting a friend.

But this was Hazel. Completely new territory from the likes of Jordan or Bex.

'Why are you so dressed up?' Cameron asked, chewing on his cheek as he picked apart what all this might mean.

'I am not,' Louise snapped back. 'Am I? This isn't too dressy. Is it?' She pawed at her shirt.

Mum shook her head. 'No, it's fine.' Her words said nonchalant, her face said suspicious.

Louise ran a hand over her hair. She'd opted for a messy

bun. There was no time for showers and straightening it took a frickin' age.

When Hazel had texted this afternoon, she'd just about dropped her phone in a puddle as she coordinated the safety cycle round the Inch. It was one thing to go running, but a text out of the blue wanting to go for a drink was something else.

She was more than pleased with the progress they'd made, and if Hazel had kept things at that, happy days. But this? This was bigger. Maybe Louise had built a bridge and now she actually wanted to be friends. Not just old school pals with plasters over gaping wounds, playing nice.

'You think I look okay then?' she asked again.

'Yeah good,' Cameron said, eyes fixed on the TV.

'Very nice,' Mum chipped in. Her gaze hadn't left Louise's.

'Good, right. Well, I'll go pick a bag now.'

It wasn't a surprise when Mum appeared in her bedroom door two seconds after Louise entered the room.

'What's going on?' She crossed her arms and leaned against the door frame, her face spelling optimistic concern.

'Going on? I'm looking for a bag.' Louise grabbed her two favourites from the shelf in the wardrobe. 'Brown or black?'

'Brown. No, I mean what's going on? Is this a date?'

Louise's brow furrowed as she gulped. It wasn't, but she'd be a liar if she said she'd not considered how would feel if it was. *Over the bloody moon* was the answer to that.

'A date?' Louise repeated, spluttering to add to how preposterous the notion was.

'You just seem awfully nervous?'

'Me?' Louise scrunched her face so hard her cheeks nearly swallowed her eyes. 'I'm not nervous.'

'Why do you have different shoes on, then?'

'Huh?' She looked at her feet. 'Hmm.' Sure enough, she had on two different white trainers.

'So?'

Louise kicked one shoe off and ducked to her wardrobe, looking for the abandoned companion to the one she'd kept on. 'I'm tired. Just a mistake.'

'Do you like her?'

Louise froze, not because she'd been rumbled, but because Mum had some brass balls on her. She never had been one for hanging about. 'Hazel? No. No more than as a friend, anyway.'

'Uh-huh. She's nice; you could do worse.'

Louise stood, awkwardly because of her lack of shoe. 'Mum. Hazel and I are just mates. I'm just my usual, doing-too-much-at-once-self.'

'You know she's single? She and her fiancée broke up.'

'Well, that's a shame for her.'

Mum pursed her lips, thinking. 'Okay, fine. You need a lift into town?'

'I was just going to get the eight.'

'The bus takes ages – let me run you. Cam will be fine for twenty minutes.'

'You just want to see Hazel, don't you? Be nosy?' Louise replied, only half-joking.

'Doesn't sound like me,' Mum said with a smirk.

MUM WAS TALKING but Louise wasn't really listening. She fought the urge to jiggle her leg as nervous energy flowed through her like a thousand angry bees.

It was purely because of the situation, not the person. Or so she kept repeating to herself.

Just two people who knew each other at school, catching up. Nothing else.

So why did her stomach drop, disappointment hitting her like a whack to the chest, when she spied Hazel with her sister and two others?

'Anywhere here is fine,' Louise prompted, aware she'd just cut Mum off mid-sentence. *Oops.*

They'd arranged to meet outside Melrose's, one of Perth's biggest and oldest establishments, although the name had changed more times than Louise had changed her outfit this evening.

Mum pulled in by the opticians. 'You going to text me when you want home?'

'Nice try,' Louise replied with a chuckle. 'I'll get a taxi; in fact we'll probably share one since we're all so close together.'

'Sounds like you've got this evening all mapped out.' The glint in Mum's eye showed what she was really thinking.

'Hilarious. Now, don't wait up.'

'Remember you're working tomorrow,' Mum said as Louise got out the car, it was said as a joke, but Louise knew better. Her teenage reputation would never be forgotten.

'I know. Bye, Mum.'

She'd say it felt like old times, but teen Louise was more likely to be sneaking out and drinking vodka on the bus with her mates. There were no maternal taxis in those days.

Finding a break in the traffic, Louise bounded over to the group. Her nerves were still getting the better of her, so it was good to expel some with a gentle jog.

Hazel was off to the side, attention fully on her phone, when Louise came level.

'Hey,' Louise said, feeling like she should hug her or do something. She stuffed her hands in her pockets instead.

'Hey,' Hazel replied, eyes snapping up from her device.

'Hey! Louise! Oh my God, what a blast from the past. Jeezo!' Hazel's sister boomed. Charlotte? That was her name, wasn't it? She'd been filed away in the recesses of Louise's mind for the last twenty-odd years, and Hazel had only mentioned her by name once when they were out together.

Best not to say it in case she was wrong. 'Hey,' Louise replied, vaguely recognising the other two women as well. Their names were truly lost to the ether, though. 'Where we heading?'

'Oh, they're going to The Mill,' Hazel quickly informed, 'Too busy for me. I thought we'd go to The Nook?'

The Mill was a pub just around the corner; on a Wednesday it was unlikely to be rammed but Louise didn't protest, not if it meant ditching Charlotte et al.

Plus, The Nook was nice enough and *would* be quieter. Easier to chat. She'd been there on a staff night out years ago, and knowing Perth, it wouldn't have changed much since.

'Just text us if you want to meet up, Hazey,' her sister called over her shoulder as they parted ways.

'Hazey?' Louise asked once they were out of earshot.

Hazel rolled her eyes. 'Don't.'

'Not quite besties yet?'

'Honestly, she's been doing my nut in today. I asked Mum when she was leaving and she said Charlotte's not mentioned it. Which is weird.'

So it *was* Charlotte. 'That is weird. Surely she must have booked a return flight?'

They wandered down the High Street, cutting up the

vennel by the theatre. This was definitely the scenic route to The Nook but going the other way would have meant walking half the distance with Charlotte.

'She will have. Most likely Mum's just forgotten or not asked, hoping the golden child will be here indefinitely.'

Louise overlooked the jibe. Some fires roared boldly enough on their own; she didn't need to stoke it. 'She'll have work, though – she can't be here too long.'

They were back on the right road now, quiet Mill Street that ran parallel with the once bustling High Street. The buildings were old and industrial, hangovers from Perth's heyday when mills processed oats and barley. Hence the name of the pub Charlotte was visiting, on the corner of the street.

Right now they were walking past the impressive structure of Pullar House, once a dye merchants' who eventually became the pioneers of dry cleaning. It was hard to imagine this street as anything else: a cluster of car parks and delivery doors for the retail units.

Hazel sighed. 'Hopefully. I mean, she was only meant to be here for my wedding; she can't have booked that much time off.' Everything but Hazel's feet froze: she was still walking but Louise could tell by the chill in the air that she was wishing life came with a rewind button.

This wasn't a conversation for the loading bay of Boots the Chemist. 'She'll just be enjoying being home. No one wants to think about the end of their holiday when they've only just started it.'

Hazel's shoulders relaxed. 'I guess. I just wish she'd be a bit quieter about it, though.'

∾

THE NOOK WAS DEAD TONIGHT; it was like having the place to themselves. Hidden under one of Perth's most popular restaurants, The Nook's aesthetic was somewhere between a cottage and a cave. With no natural light, its ambiance came from carefully strung fairy lights and candles. Its exposed, original grey stone walls only added to its cosiness. Down here you never knew what time it was or whether it was blowing a gale outside, making it perfect for parties and times you just wanted to forget the world beyond its sturdy walls.

'It's not that I'm jealous of her. It's just . . .' Hazel said, rolling her beer between her palms as she tried to find the words. 'With Charlotte here, all eyes are on her, and for once I could do with a little attention. No one's even asked how I am.'

Two glasses of wine in, Louise was feeling brave. Conversation was flowing. Hazel clearly needing to get a lot off her chest about her sister, but Louise could feel the weight of the unsaid settled between them as physically as the dripping dinner candle in the middle of the table.

'So, your wedding was meant to be this weekend?' she asked tentatively, partially regretting the question as Hazel subtly flinched. She'd asked her out for a reason, though, and if the reason was to offload, Louise needed to know the big picture, warts and all.

Things had started out slowly at first: how was your day, what did you get up to? Then formalities had relaxed; they'd found a rhythm. Jokes started and Louise got to enjoy those dimples that appeared every time Hazel *really* smiled. Soon though, Charlotte had come up and Hazel was off, no punches spared. It made sense now, why she'd asked Louise out. She needed someone to talk to and Louise was a friendly ear.

Hazel, nodded gently. 'Yeah, Saturday.'

Louise mirrored her with a little nod, letting the new information sink in. Her knowledge of Hazel was spotty at best, completely blank for most. It was like putting together a jigsaw puzzle but you only got one piece a week by post.

'I know it's a silly question, but are you okay?'

Hazel's eyes locked with the dregs of her beer as she thought. 'Yeah, I guess.'

'You guess?' Louise added a quiet laugh, hoping not to drag the conversation so low it couldn't be recovered.

'It's just weird, isn't it? You know things can't happen as you planned, but it doesn't stop your brain turning over and over what you're missing out on.'

Louise knew that feeling all too well. When she'd got pregnant with Cameron she'd spent a good chunk of her early twenties wondering if she'd messed up. That was different, though. She had no regrets about Cameron, just a serious case of FOMO when looking at social media and all the adventures her peers were able to indulge in.

'She obviously wasn't right for you though, so you're not missing out. But I know thinking of it that way will feel impossible just now.'

Jordan wouldn't rate that reply, but sometimes support could only be pulled out your arse, on the spot. After all, there were no correct answers.

She'd always been a good listener but more often than not people came to Louise with problems she'd never experienced, so she never truly knew what to say. Mostly, all they needed though was a comfortable shoulder with *okay*s and *uh-huh*s peppered in the right places. A lot of the time people just needed their voice to be heard – they didn't actually care what your advice was.

Hazel shook her head, lost in thought. She huffed

through her nostrils before answering, frustration showing in the whites of her knuckles as she clutched her now empty glass. 'That's the thing, though. I'm sloppy seconds. I wasn't good enough then, why would I be good enough for anyone else?'

Louise drained the last of her booze. She hadn't expected things to get personal so quickly.

This was the problem with new friendships; it was impossible to know how the land lay. If this was Jordan she would be brutally honest and say it was time to move on, stop dwelling on the past, and get a grip.

But this was Hazel. One wrong move and she'd be back to stage one, labelled the angry, hurtful Louise of the past.

Time to tread carefully.

'What do you mean sloppy seconds?' She could hazard a guess but needed to know more before committing.

Hazel sucked on her bottom lip. This wasn't going to be a quick fire convo, but Louise had the time if Hazel had the words. 'She—' Hazel cut herself off with a sigh. 'She didn't exactly cheat on me. Well, maybe. She did and she didn't.'

Louise unpicked the sentence, turning every word over with careful precision, as if they were ancient fossils that needed a full examination before leaving her hands. 'If you have enough doubt to use the word "exactly", that says it all. No wonder you're hurt.'

'I think that's it, though. Maybe it would have been easier if she did sleep with her. Then I'd be able to be mad. Right now, I'm just the one who wasn't quite enough. A better offer came along and she took it. So, I'm constantly wondering what's wrong with me.'

If they were closer, Louise would pull her in for a hug. She barely knew Hazel, but no one deserved to feel like shit. Her hand twitched, used to delivering comfort physically.

Hazel didn't seem the touchy-feely type, though: reaching over, even just to touch her hand, was too much.

'There's nothing wrong with you. She just didn't appreciate you. One day the right person will come along and treat you how you deserve to be treated: like the sun shines out your arse.' That got a smile from Hazel. Louise continued: 'Because that's how a partner should treat you. And if they don't give you their all, they're not the one.'

'So, is that why you're single? Cause no one's seen the light shining out of your backside?' Hazel asked with a laugh.

'Not quite. It's complicated, I guess.'

'Can't imagine Perth is bursting with eligible lezzers, either.'

Louise pulled a face. 'There's no point going on dating apps if you're not willing to travel, put it that way.'

'Never want to leave?'

Louise shook her head. 'Home is home. It's not everyone's cup of tea but I like it here.'

'So, no dating apps. How do you meet women?'

Louise could tell Hazel was wanting to change the subject, shift the focus away from her. Which was fair enough, she'd just shared something major. 'I don't,' she replied with a hearty laugh.

'Oh come on, surely there must be somewhere?'

'You after a date?'

Hazel's cheeks turned red. 'Definitely not. Just making conversation, curious I guess. It would be nice to make some queer friends if I'm having to stick about.'

'You're not going back to Glasgow then?'

'Seems I'm stuck here for a while.'

Louise's heart boomed for a single beat before returning to normal, as if someone had struck it like a gong. The notion that Hazel would only be here until Marie's leg healed had occurred to her, but after she asked about joining local clubs Louise had grown hopeful it was more permanent.

'Do you read?' Louise asked, unable to look a gift horse in the mouth for a second time.

Hazel pursed her lips in thought, taken aback by the sudden shift in conversation. 'A bit, why?'

'Sorry, it's relevant, promise. I hold a LGBTQ+ book group every month in the centre. Well, that's what it's marketed as. No one new's joined in yonks. It's just me and my pals, really.'

'Oh, yeah. When's it on?'

'Friday.'

'This Friday? I don't think I can read that quick. Thanks for the offer, though.'

'Honestly, Jordan's never read a book in her life. It's fun, promise.'

Hazel screwed up her face. 'Maybe next month, but I'm not sure a book group is really my thing, to be honest.'

'No bother. I'll text you the details, just in case.' Hopefully Louise didn't look too disappointed, but inside she was deflating, fast. 'One more for the road?' she asked, wanting a quick break from speaking, lest her real emotions seep onto her face.

'Yeah, why not?'

Louise composed herself, managing a smile as she got up from the table. At least she could tell Jordan that she tried.

19

Hazel took a seat on the free recliner by Mum. 'How you doing today?' she asked, a hand over her eyes to shield her from the sun. Summer was tailing off but today was another scorcher.

'Good. Your dad's still in the greenhouse.'

Hazel swiped her gaze to the little greenhouse at the bottom of the garden. For someone with reduced vision, Dad did a grand job cultivating a crop on his own. He'd put a whole variety of fruit and veg on their plates since Hazel had returned home. The latest bounty was a host of chunky courgettes. He'd tried sweetcorn, but it just hadn't been hot enough. Maybe next year.

Conversation fell silent. It would have been comfortable had Hazel not still been focused on the date. One day to go until her proposed wedding and still not a peep out of the Patersons.

She wasn't going to be the one to break, though. Petulance was Charlotte's speciality, not hers.

Well, not to her sister's degree.

'Got any plans this weekend?' Hazel asked, secretly hoping Mum would bite.

'Not much. There's a farmer's market on the Inch tomorrow. Fancy going to that?'

Wandering rows of stalls when she should be walking down the aisle. What a swap.

Still, if the weather was good it would be nice. There were usually amazing artisan soaps and other knick-knacks as well as food. Not a bad way to spend a Saturday.

It wasn't that she was still deep in mourning. Yes, her ego hadn't quite recovered, but the main point was everyone's reluctance to care. So, she wasn't the centre of their universe? They could still have an ounce of decency and recognise it might be a difficult weekend for her.

She'd messaged Yaz this morning. But, as of today, not a word all week. It wasn't like they had the Save The Date pinned to the fridge still, but it didn't take a lot to know August held some significance. It was like they'd all raced forward, too busy to hold onto Hazel, who was standing still, tethered to what could have been.

Mum was still looking for an answer. 'That would be nice,' Hazel finally replied, gulping her annoyance away. If they'd all moved on, she should too.

What did she want? A cake? A day of pampering for little jilted Hazel? Everyone to hug her and hold her and say it would be okay?

What was the point in being so bitter? Ashley probably hadn't given tomorrow a second thought. She would spend the day with Dani in their loved-up bubble, with their annoying friends, in that stupid pub they all loved. If they did acknowledge the day, it would probably be to say 'thank God you dodged that bullet!'.

'What's up?' Mum asked and Hazel jumped a little.

'Huh?'

'You looked very deep in thought. You okay? Something must be bothering you.'

Hazel shook her head. 'It's nothing.'

Mum turned as best she could. 'Now, you tell your old mum what's up.'

Hazel took a deep breath. Now the opportunity was here it was all so redundant. Why was she bothering about something that couldn't and wouldn't ever happen? She'd had enough of pitiful faces and comments. No need to dredge up more. 'Nothing, just tired,' she lied.

Mum didn't buy it. 'Is it work? No luck on the job hunt yet?'

She wasn't aware she was *meant* to be hunting just yet. She'd been focused on taxi duties, not killing Charlotte duties, and trying not to lose her mind duties.

The topic of work was a good distraction though, and there was no need to worry Mum by blurting her inner dialogue out. She'd embarrassed herself enough by telling Louise so much.

'I just don't know what to look for.'

Mum pepped up a little, seeing how she could be handy. 'Okay, well. You don't want to PT any more, correct?'

Hazel waggled her head from side to side. She'd really enjoyed her run with Louise. She'd forgotten how rewarding one-on-one work could be.

The thought of returning to Glasgow made her want to boke. There she was, a failure, her reputation tarnished by the last year, another cog in Glasgow's gossip machine. She would have to move mountains to regain trust.

The other option was staying in Perth. Which wasn't the end of the world in terms of her social life, but starting from scratch was tough; it took her years to get a financially sustainable level of clients in Glasgow.

That would probably mean living at home for a while.

'I dunno. I do and I don't.'

Mum pursed her lips. 'What's putting you off?'

'I don't know where to start.'

Mum chuckled. 'As in, with everything that's putting you off? Are there a lot of things bothering you?'

'No, no.' Hazel corrected her with a smile. 'Physically. Physically I don't know where to start.'

Glasgow was permanently stuck on rainy days, a black cloud filled with Ashley and constant reminders of Hazel's past hanging heavy overhead. Perth was spring air, daffodils pushing through the soil, promising a new start.

The more she thought about it, the more tempting Perth was. When she'd moved away, aged nineteen, she'd barely looked back. The world lay before her and Perth was a tiny speck. Especially when it came to the possibility of a love life. There weren't even dating apps back then. Perth held no prospects. Work, friends, partners: all of it was possible outside the city gates. How could somewhere so small compete?

That was the thing, though: there was comfort in the familiar. She knew here. She had family. As far as fresh starts went, it was a safer bet than most.

But it would mean taking a giant leap back and living with her parents.

Her mind rushed forward then zig-zagged back to where it had been five minutes ago.

Alternate Reality Hazel was getting married tomorrow. Her business was booming. In a year or so she'd have started a family. The rest was blissful.

Current Hazel, sitting in the sun with her mum, deep in

thought as she tried to wade through her worries, was back to where she was at nineteen. Except now time was ticking and if she hung about too long she'd have missed the boat: jobs could be manifested, she'd meet a partner surely, but a family? She'd probably never get that.

Christ. This was too much. Time to curl up in bed.

'Physically start? With your PT job? Or with changing careers?' Mum asked, seeking clarity.

'It's a bit complicated.' Hazel stood. 'I just need to loo. Back in a bit.'

She left before Mum could argue.

She'd barely made it to her room when her phone rang.

Yaz.

Maybe they had remembered after all.

She took a deep breath, hoping to steady herself and sound normal.

'Hey,' she said.

'Hey, Hazel! Just wanted to check in, see how your little vacay to the east coast was going.' Sounds of the city enveloped Yaz's words; they must be walking from work to the underground.

'Less of a *vacay*, more of a stay-stay.' She slumped onto her bed, legs dangling over the edge as she lay back.

'Oh really?' Yaz sounded genuinely shocked.

'Nowhere else to go, do I?' It came out snippier than intended. 'Sorry. I'm just not having the best day.'

'How come?'

So they didn't remember. 'Nothing, just the usual.'

'Charlotte.'

'You bet.' She actually hadn't been too bad today. But it was only early evening. She still had plenty of time to get Hazel's tits in a twist. 'So, what are you up to this weekend?'

'Not much. Going with Nora and her kids to Kelvingrove

tomorrow. So probably just chilling tonight, charge the old batteries.'

The museum would be a good distraction. Current funds wouldn't stretch to a Glasgow jaunt, though. 'I hear you – those kids are something else.'

'Not to mention Nora,' Yaz replied with a chuckle. 'What about you?'

The need to mention the wedding twisted Hazel's stomach into a tangled knot. No sense causing a scene though. So, Yaz didn't remember? They didn't owe Hazel an apology or explanation. They had a life, people forgot stuff.

'Dunno. Mum wants to go to the farmer's market.'

'Sounds okay. Charlotte going?'

'Of course.'

'Take headphones, you'll be fine. Listen, I'm at the underground, better go or I'll miss the train. Catch you later!'

They were off. Hazel threw her phone onto the bed.

She wanted to scream, throw a tantrum. Anything to get rid of the sinking feeling in her chest. If she didn't do something she was going to pop. Anger and frustration were her new best friends. Even the thought of going for a run was too much.

She got under the covers and cocooned herself. In here it was just her. No one to annoy her. No one to hurt her. She wished she could be as blasé as everyone else instead of fixating on the date. She took a deep breath. Tomorrow was just another day: if everyone else could carry on regardless, so could she. Just another Saturday.

What did normal people do on Saturdays?

She could text Louise, go for another drink. Or would that be weird? She didn't want to bother her.

Nah, she'd go to this stupid farmer's market, then see

where else Mum fancied. If her parents called the shots, she could spend less time in her head, more time being distracted.

Just another Saturday . . .

~

A KNOCK at her bedroom door woke Hazel up. She hadn't realised she'd dozed off.

She opened a bleary eye to her empty room.

Another knock. 'Hazel, you okay?'

Mum.

'What? Yeah, sorry, I was asleep.'

'Sorry!' Mum blurted, still just a voice in the hall. 'I'll come back.'

'No, no. Come in. I'm awake now,' Hazel replied, her voice croaky. She pushed herself onto her forearms.

Mum gently opened the door, her smiling face appearing a second later. 'You okay?'

'Yeah, why?'

She hobbled to the bed, and Hazel fought to wake up as Mum lowered herself on the edge of the mattress, crutches now resting against her thigh.

She rubbed sleep from her eyes as Mum spoke: 'I was worried I'd upset you earlier.'

'Me?'

'You left very quickly.'

'Just a bit overwhelmed, that's all.'

Mum nodded, silence falling between them as she thought. 'You don't want to go back to Glasgow? Is that it?'

'Part of it.'

'Well, why not stay here?'

Hazel let out a quick breath. There were so many layers

to this, it was more complex than even she could handle, never mind explaining it to someone else. 'Everything just feels a bit much, if I'm honest.'

Another silent nod. 'Well, what can I do to help?'

Hazel shrugged. Tears nipped at her eyes and the sudden urge to cry choked her. Ashley had cut her ties with the land and now Hazel was floating free, only Mum's guiding hand to stop her from sinking under. The trouble was, she didn't think she was strong enough to pull herself out, no matter how long Mum waited on her.

'Ever wish life came with a reset button?' Hazel asked, trying in vain to laugh but emotion strangled any chance.

'I know, love.' Mum put a hand on the nearest lump in the covers: Hazel's knee. 'If I could take the pain for you, I would. I'd do anything for you, you know that.'

'I know.'

'How's it hanging, saddo?' Charlotte asked, wandering in without knocking.

'Charlotte,' Mum scolded.

'Whoa, what's going on?' The chocolate bar she'd been scoffing was paused by her mouth. She chomped down on it as she crossed the room to Hazel's bed. 'You okay, Hazey?'

Hazel rolled her eyes. Any emotion she'd felt was dissipated: Charlotte acting like an atomic bomb, clearing the area of any sentiment or fragility.

'I'm good. Just having a chat.'

'Anything I can help with?'

'Grown-up stuff, sis.' She'd hoped to sound sarcastic but it came out sincere, Mum was halfway through shooting her a side-eye when Charlotte playfully swiped at Hazel, proving her right.

'Hey! I can do big stuff,' she huffed. With half a chocolate bar hanging out her mouth, Hazel doubted it.

'Now, now, you two. Come on.' Mum turned to Hazel. 'You tell me if I can help.'

Charlotte looked, searching Hazel's face for what the conversation might be about.

Time to be the bigger person. 'I'm having work issues.'

'Oh yeah?' Charlotte replied, straightening herself. 'Client acting up?'

'More like I'm acting up.' Hazel wasn't sure she'd ever had a conversation in bed with Mum and Charlotte. All she needed was Dad to slot in beside her at the pillow end and Julie Andrews could star in a musical about them.

'You been chucking your dumb-bells out the pram?' Charlotte asked with a grin.

'Just at a crossroad and not sure which way I want to go.'

'I get ya.' Charlotte's eyes brightened. 'Why don't we go to the pub tonight – we can have a chat?'

She was persistent, Hazel would give her that. 'Not tonight, sorry.'

'Oh, come on, please. I'm going crazy being stuck inside.' She flicked her eyes to Mum – 'No offence.' – and back to Hazel. 'Come on let's do *something*.'

The thought of being solo with Charlotte at the pub was nauseating. They'd never done anything just the two of them. There was no way Hazel was hanging out with the Brat Pack though: Charlotte was enough, never mind Nina and Stacey too.

'What about your friends?' Hazel asked, hoping to pass the buck.

'Busy. Jobs and boyfriends.'

'Well, can you not FaceTime Jimmy then?'

Charlotte set her face. 'Not unless I get up at stupid o'clock.'

'There must be something you girls can do,' Mum

chipped in. 'No sports? I don't think I can lay my paws on your bikes very easily. You enjoyed the Walkie Talkie yesterday, didn't you, Charlotte? Nothing like that for you youngsters?'

'There's a book group you could go to but you'd need to be LGBTQ+,' Hazel said, her brain lurching into autopilot to offer an option before she could take it back.

Charlotte sat up, enthusiasm dialled to the max. 'I can be lez for lit.'

Hazel cocked her head to the side. 'You can't just pretend.'

'How? What they going to do? Quiz me? They can't say no based on looks. I could be bi, or pan, or demisexual, aromantic, asexual, le—'

'—right, calm it, Merriam-Webster. It's tonight and you've not read the book.'

'So? We're new. We'll go and see if we like it, what the people are like. Then we can read the right one for next time.'

'One: there is no we. And, two: you won't have a next time. You're back to Australia soon enough.'

Charlotte pulled a face. 'Always such a stick in the mud. This is what you need. A change in routine. Come on, it'll be a laugh.' Charlotte's face grew serious. 'If it's shit, we never have to go back.'

'Language,' Mum said with a tut.

Both daughters ignored her. Hazel sighed. 'That's easy for you to say. Louise will be there. You might be fleeing the country, but I'll have to see her again.'

Charlotte pouted, putting on her best puppy-dog eyes. 'Please. Do this and I'll never ask you to do anything again.'

～

THE SPORTS CENTRE was stuffy tonight, like the air con was broken. Or maybe it was just the fact that Hazel had never done anything so spur of the moment before. Turning up to a book group without a clue what the book was. This was radical.

She took a deep breath. Yaz was going to lose it when she told them what she did tonight.

'It'll be fine, Hazey,' Charlotte reassured, swanning through the foyer like she'd been here a thousand times. Thankfully, there was an A-board directing the way or Charlotte was liable to have them walking into a squash court or staffroom, the way she was brashly thundering on.

So far, Hazel had only experienced the outside of the centre while waiting on the Walkie Talkies to start. Inside was a lot more sterile than the modern architecture would have you guess.

The walls were exposed brick, giving it a funky edge, but the worn green linoleum and matching plastic seats suggested hospital at best. Hazel took another breath. The comforting smell of rubber and hard work filled her lungs: the smell of gyms the world over.

Charlotte led them down a long corridor with a low ceiling, strip lights and noticeboards like checkpoints on the way.

Finally, chatter spilled into the corridor as they reached an open door .

Hazel gulped.

This was it.

Charlotte wasted no time. 'Hey,' she said, her usual smile unwavering.

Hazel gave a meek wave, peeking out behind her sister. 'Hey.'

The group chorused their hellos in return: four faces staring back at them, seated in an open circle.

They were a mixed bunch. Most were about ages with Hazel, but in looks, they couldn't have been more diverse.

Louise stood by a desk and flip chart; maybe the room had been used for training at some point in the day. A steaming mug of tea or coffee was poised at her lips, only just hiding a smile. 'Hazel, you made it!'

Hazel relaxed a little at seeing how excited Louise was. She seemed absolutely over the moon that they'd come.

To Louise's right sat a woman dressed in black, wearing workies' trousers and boots. Her eyes trailed the sisters, taking them in with no remorse.

Beside her, the red-haired woman in a sensible blouse pumped her eyebrows with a grin, as if to say *welcome to the madhouse.*

Then came a much older woman, dressed like she'd come from an office and totally engrossed by her phone, and finally a woman with mad black curls and a tatty band T-shirt, who patted the seat beside her, a friendly smile directed their way, 'Lou, you never said we were getting fresh blood.'

'Ladies, this is Bex. Gail—' The woman on her phone looked up momentarily. 'Tasha, and finally Jordan.'

Jordan's eyes fixed on Charlotte. 'Pleasure to meet you both.'

Hazel watched as her sister held her own. 'And you,' she answered, still holding Jordan's gaze as if they were hooked together.

'Alright,' Louise bellowed, making a show of sitting down. Jordan turned her attention away from Charlotte, the smile creeping onto her lips suggesting it had been a ruse to annoy her friend. 'Well, welcome to book club. Guys, this is Hazel and Charlotte.'

They took a seat and Hazel had no clue what to do with her hands. Everyone else had books. Or phones. Well, apart from Jordan. She had nothing: she wasn't fazed, though. She sat, ankle to knee, arms crossed across her chest.

Hazel tucked her hands under her thighs. It was better than wringing them.

She tried to look at the cover of the books but they were at awkward angles; it was no use. Tasha's book bulged with slim sticky notes. Hazel gulped.

'Who wants to start us off?' Louise asked, taking another sip of her drink. The group exchanged looks. Nada. Louise shook her head, as if she'd just remembered something important and was telling herself off internally. 'Hazel, Charlotte, we've read *Eleanor Oliphant is Completely Fine* this month. Sorry, I didn't think you were coming or I would have told you.'

'That's fine,' Charlotte chirped. 'I read that a while ago and I think I remember it. I loved the twist at the end.'

Murmurs of agreement rippled through the women.

'Personally,' Jordan announced, and Gail groaned. 'I think it could have done with more lesbians in it.'

Bex sighed. 'She says that about everything,' she said, leaning towards Hazel and Charlotte.

'She even said it about *The Book Thief*,' Tasha moaned, pronouncing the title with a stab of frustration.

'Well, tell me any book, actually no, *situation*, that can't be improved with more lesbians,' Jordan ventured, reclining further back against her chair.

'Definitely not *The Handmaid's Tale*, which is what you said the other month,' Gail said with another groan.

'Actually,' Jordan quipped. 'I stand by that one. Same goes for the TV show.'

'So, you finally watched it? Bet you've still not read the book though,' Bex batted back.

The playful exchange was like watching a tennis match as the comments flitted from woman to woman. Hazel had expected a stuffy discussion, not this light-hearted banter.

Tasha cleared her throat, stopping Jordan from issuing a comeback. 'Well,' she declared, fanning her book out to a page marked by a green Post-It note. 'I would like to discuss whether the author intended Eleanor to be seen as having ASD.'

'ASD?' Gail asked.

'It stands for Autism Spectrum Disorder. It's an umbrella term that covers the different levels of autism.' She ran a finger down the page she'd marked, settling on a paragraph underlined with pencil. 'For example, Honeyman writes—'

'I need more tea,' Jordan said, getting to her feet and cutting Tasha off. 'You guys want one?' she asked Hazel and Charlotte.

'I can help,' Hazel said, grateful for an excuse to take a breather. She'd never read this book and it sounded heavy – she'd have nothing to add to the discussion if she stayed sitting.

Hazel was sure Louise squeaked as Jordan crossed the circle of seats to lead her to a table at the back of the room.

'Cheers,' Jordan said, looking back to the circle.

Louise spluttered, choking on her drink while Tasha continued quoting the book.

Unperturbed, Jordan aimed for the refreshments.

A huge silver tea caddy sat at one end, a smaller, more modern caddy to its side, presumably with coffee. A jug of milk and a few white cups were spread over the rest of the table. A plate with a few crumbs sat sadly in the middle.

'I scoffed the last biscuit earlier, sorry. Didn't know we were entertaining tonight,' Jordan said, keeping her voice low so the discussion could carry on, uninterrupted, behind them. Louise had finally stopped coughing.

'No bother,' Hazel assured, reaching for a cup.

Jordan looked over her shoulder. 'Don't worry, once Tasha gets the deep stuff off her chest it gets fun again. She's a proper bookworm, gets really into these things. Classic teacher's pet.' She bit her bottom lip to suppress a smile.

Hazel pushed the button on top of the coffee caddy, releasing a stream of steaming coffee into her cup. 'I'm enjoying it so far, don't worry.'

'You don't need to lie to me,' Jordan replied with a grin. 'Gail's usually a good laugh but she's got some heavy work shit going on. And Bex is always up for a spirited discussion, shall we say.' She punctuated her words with a quick wink.

'Good to know,' Hazel said, getting another cup to fill with coffee for Charlotte.

'Then there's Louise. But you know all about her.'

'I'm not sure I do,' Hazel replied, completely focused on not spilling coffee as she wrangled the remaining dregs from the caddy. The group must have nearly finished it before they arrived.

'Huh?'

Hazel snapped back to reality. 'We went to school together. She's changed a lot since then. I don't know anything about her, really.'

'Consider this the perfect opportunity to get reacquainted then,' Jordan said, touching her cup to Hazel's as if cheers-ing. 'Louise could take you—'She paused to sip her tea and behind them, Louise choked again. 'To one of your old stomping grounds.'

'Really, we just used to see each other at parties.'

'Yeah I've heard she was pretty wild in her teenage years. I mean, she's pretty wild now if yo—'

'Jordan, can I get a top-up?' Louise called, her voice clipped.

'Sure thing, dearest,' she answered over her shoulder. She leaned closer to Hazel. 'Just, go easy on her. I hate to have the good intent—'

'JORDAN.'

'Sorry, Her Highness calls. Oh look,' she said, seeing a broken chocolate finger poking out from under a saucer. 'Finger?'

'Nah, I'm good, thanks.'

'I'm lucky to have found that. Louise can be awful greedy when it comes to fingers,' she said, before popping the biscuit shard between her teeth.

'I'll bear that in mind,' Hazel replied with a smirk, well aware of what Jordan was doing. Winding up Louise was obviously her favourite form of entertainment at their gatherings, which accounted for the lack of book.

Jordan bit through the biscuit as Louise's chair squeaked. She hid a grin with over-exaggerated chewing as she finished off the biscuit. 'Good. Saves any future disappointment.'

'Jordan, you'll never get a job in hospitality,' Louise huffed.

'Thought you could do with getting your step count up.'

Hazel smiled. Jordan was an expert at pushing Louise's buttons. It was funny seeing her so flustered, revealing a new side to Louise, trying desperately to be professional while no doubt wanting to clobber Jordan around the head.

The word *cute* momentarily popped into Hazel's head before vanishing in a puff of smoke.

'I'm sorry, we've tried getting rid of her but she keeps coming back,' Louise grumpily joked to Hazel as she jostled into the space by Jordan, a hand briefly on Hazel's back for leverage as she squeezed in, ready to fill her cup despite it being half full.

Her touch lingered on Hazel's skin, so she subtly wiggled the unexpected feeling away.

'It's these biscuits you keep leaving out. How's a girl to resist?'

'I wouldn't know, you've scoffed them all,' Hazel jibed back, matching Jordan's energy.

Jordan grinned. 'Can't hold Louise back from a Hobnob.'

'Ladies, will we get back to discussing books?' she retaliated, sounding like a disgruntled teacher.

'Only if you insist,' Jordan groaned.

Hazel smiled: she was going to enjoy book club. She could already tell.

20

Saturdays usually started with running Cameron into town but now he was a man (urgh, that felt weird to say) of employment, Louise was at a loose end.

Mum had requested they visit the local garden centre, with no intention of buying plants; she just wanted a cream scone.

However, they were now wandering through the bedding plants with Mum picking up cartons of begonias and pansies, occasionally cooing over the pretty colours before putting them back.

'Is it not a bit late for planting stuff?' Louise asked, quickly checking her phone in case she'd missed a message.

'A little. Just looking for now.'

Likely story. They both knew fine well they'd be leaving with at least one armful of vegetation.

Sure she felt a vibration in her pocket, she looked at her phone again. Nothing. This must be the start of insanity.

She'd messaged Hazel this morning, just to see how she was, given the date and all.

A reply had come quickly and Louise was soon

surprised to find herself in a constant back and forth with Hazel. She'd just messaged her about the next book the club intended to read –*The Seven Husbands of Evelyn Hugo* – and was eagerly awaiting her thoughts on the choice.

Louise still couldn't quite believe Hazel had come to book group. Charlotte had commandeered most of the talking, but together they'd made a good first impression. Going by Hazel's enthusiasm today, she was keen to come again too.

Happy days.

Jordan had, somehow, behaved as well. She'd messaged late last night, after Hux's final walk of the day, to joke about why Louise was so keen to get on Hazel's good side and spark a friendship, given Hazel's good looks.

Louise had kept her mouth shut. If Jordan knew she was right about her feelings for Hazel she would never bloody shut up.

'What do you think of these dahlias?' Mum asked, just as Louise's phone drummed against her hip bone.

She fished it out. Hazel: *Well, at least it *does* have lesbians in it. I bet Jordan still doesn't read it though.*

'Well?' Mum prompted.

'Huh? Oh, yeah,' Louise grunted, looking up from her phone. 'Not sure about pink though.'

Mum tutted. 'Mmhmm. Who's got you smiling like that?'

Louise snapped to attention, the grin plastered on her face refusing to fade despite being caught. 'No one, I mean someone, but . . .' she trailed off.

'Uh-huh.' Mum pumped her eyebrows. 'A mother always knows.'

'I'm sure you do,' Louise jested, stuffing her phone away now she'd replied.

'How's she keeping?'

'Who?'

'Hazel?'

Louise held the corner of her bottom lip between her teeth, stopping another smile adding to the blush on her cheeks. No point denying it any longer. 'She's good. She was meant to be getting married today, so I thought I'd better text her, see how she is.'

'Why not take her for a drink? Take her mind off things.'

The thought had crossed her mind but it felt like too much. Although, Louise's scales of decision were tipping back and forth on another issue, one she needed to address with Hazel no matter what route their relationship took: Cameron. It was only a matter of time before he came up in conversation. In fact, it was a wonder he hadn't already.

It was a big deal and Louise needed Hazel to hear it from her.

'She has enough on today without seeing me.'

'Oh yeah? What's she up to?'

Louise actually had no clue. In all the chatter they'd not shared plans. That could be her next text.

'Just family stuff. Probably.'

'So you don't really know.' Mum handed Louise a pot with a white dahlia in it. 'Here, hold this.'

'I don't but why does it matter?' she asked with a shrug.

'Because, it would do you good to get out. Even if it is just as friends. Cameron's busy with his job now; you should be enjoying your freedom.'

'I'd rather not be *free*.'

Mum's eyes turned sympathetic before growing wide with excitement as she spotted a violet dahlia at the back of the display. 'Look at that one, Louise! Can you grab it for me?'

Louise handed the white flower back before going on tiptoe to try and reach the beautifully coloured plant.

Mum continued: 'I know you're not happy about Cameron having a job, but that's my point exactly. A little distraction will do you good.'

Louise huffed as she pulled herself up and closer to the shelf. 'Does it have to be this one?' she grunted.

'Yes.'

'Jeezo.' Her finger tips grazed the plastic plant pot, edging it closer. 'I'm perfectly fine about Cameron having a job,' she managed.

'What a twisted web you weave,' Mum chuckled.

Finally, the pot was close enough to grasp. Louise grabbed it and dropped to the ground with a loud huff. She winced, a muscle in her side contracting. 'Ouch. What do you mean by that?' she said, laughing through the pain.

'So, you've no qualms about your son having a job and Hazel isn't even on your radar?'

'Exactly.' Louise closed one eye. The pain was subsiding but, Lordy, getting older was no joke. These days she was liable to pull a muscle putting on her shoes.

'You've always been a terrible liar.'

'That's because you brought me up so well.'

'There you go again.'

They both laughed at that.

'It's not lying,' Louise countered when they'd both recovered from Mum's joke. Now Mum was looking at marigolds. If she wanted another from the back, she could get it herself. 'It's just deflecting the truth.'

'Meaning?'

'That it's easier to say what I say than say what I mean.'

'I have no idea what you're on about.' Mum offered a

thin-lipped smile, then placed a carton of flowers into Louise's hands.

She shook her head. Louise got it, that was all that mattered.

Louise watched as Mum admired a display of ready-made hanging baskets. To be fair, Mum's green thumb kept the house looking superb. Between the three of them they did okay. The only thing Louise didn't trust Cameron with was the hedge trimmer. She didn't even trust herself, having cut through the wire a grand total of thr—

She jumped a mile, throwing the carton of marigolds into the air, as two fingers poked into her side, a stranger now standing behind her.

Laughter erupted from her mystery assailant, echoing through the once-quiet outbuilding.

'Oh my God, I'm so sorry!'

She turned to find Hazel, doubled over in hysterics.

Louise brushed herself down, buying time while her heart rate levelled from thundering to a capable trot.

Fear had kick-started its jangling pace, now nerves stopped it from returning to normal.

'Hazel, what are you doing here?' she asked, picking the carton off the floor. Mum had wandered off, not before shooting her some serious side-eye and a knowing smile.

Hazel's laughter subsided. 'Sorry, again. Didn't expect you to jump like that. I'm here with Mum and Dad. And Charlotte, of course.' She threw a thumb over her shoulder, towards the alpine section through the glass double doors.

'I'm here with Mum.' She scolded herself internally; that felt like a weird thing to say. Was it weird?

'So I saw. She keeping okay?'

'Yeah, yeah. So-so. How's Marie?' Inside, Louise was

shaking, a combination of adrenaline and shock making her feel like she was standing on a vibrating pad.

'She's good. Cast comes off soon – she'll still need to take it easy but it will make things a damn sight easier.'

'I'll say. But no more taxi duties. You'll be gutted.' Her insides calmed slightly: this was flowing better.

'I'm sure they'll find new ways to keep me busy.' Hazel looked over her shoulder. 'Best be off, although, not like they can leave without me.'

Mum's voice cut over Louise's shoulder, making her jump again, although this time it was far less noticeable. 'Hazel, wait. You busy?'

'Now?'

'Well, now, later, tomorrow?'

Louise turned to glare at Mum. Where the hell was this going?

'I'm free tomorrow if you need my help with something?'

Was it too much to kick her mother in the shin? Whack her over the head with a plant pot? Louise didn't like this one bit.

'Not me, but Louise could do with some distracting. Cam—'

Nope, enough, no more. She cut Mum off. 'Caaaa—re to meet for a coffee?'

Hazel's features shifted as she thought. Was that a good or bad look? If the garden centre could split in two and swallow her whole, that would suit Louise fine. Maybe the large palm tree could fall in after her, really finish off the job. Ideal.

'Tomorrow? I could do tomorrow.' She focused her attention on Louise. 'Everything okay?'

Louise answered quickly, stopping Mum from meddling any more. 'Fine. Just work stuff.'

'Cool. Well, tomorrow it is then. I'll text you.' Hazel smiled before turning on her heel and heading towards Charlotte, who was studying a pot of heather on the other side of the store.

Louise's stomach flipped with delight. It didn't stop her whacking Mum on the arm. 'I'm going to kill you.'

'What? Why?' Mum's eyes gleamed with devilish delight.

'Why did you make me ask that?'

'What? Can't I look out for my daughter?'

Louise huffed, wandering towards a table laid out with crates of loose bulbs. 'And I appreciate that, but I would like to do things at my own pace, please.'

Mum stopped level with Louise, picking up a large bulb as if to study it, but Louise could tell her focus wasn't on the tulip. 'Sorry. I just got excited. I shouldn't have meddled. If you don't want to meet her, I can think of an excuse for you.'

'It's not that,' Louise said with a sigh. 'It's just, well, Cameron hasn't come up yet and I don't quite know how to broach it.'

'What does it matter?'

'It matters,' Louise quickly interjected and Mum instantly got the gist.

'Right, well. You'll just need to be honest. Can hardly hide the lad.'

'I dunno. Now school's back, I barely see him.' Louise pouted. On the one hand, she wished things could always stay the same. On the other, she was looking forward to the future and all the exciting things that lay in wait. She was forever walking a tightrope of emotions these days.

'This job is doing him good. He said hello to me this morning – usually it's grunts only until noon,' Mum joked.

'I feel like he doesn't need me any more,' Louise

admitted, suddenly filled to the brim with melancholy as much as the crate beside her was filled with crocuses.

'Nonsense. You're never too old to need your mum. Things just shift, roles change. Sometimes things happen out of order. Sometimes things happen quickly, maybe far too fast in some cases. But we adapt. We accept the new and roll with the punches. That's what family do.'

'Embrace the change. Got it. Though it seems easier said than done.'

'It is. So, start with the fun stuff first.'

'Fun stuff,' Louise repeated, looking over her shoulder to where Hazel and Charlotte were talking to Marie. 'I think I can handle that.'

21

L ouise seemed out of sorts when Hazel met her at the statue outside New Look, in the middle of the High Street.

She'd been chewing on her thumbnail as Hazel approached, out of Louise's line of vision, texting someone with a brow so furrowed it would leave crease marks.

After stilted hellos Louise bounced on the balls of her feet, hands stuffed into her gilet's pockets.

'I was thinking,' Louise said with a small smile. 'It might be nicer to get a takeaway, go for a walk up Kinnoull Hill instead? It's a nice day, won't take long for us to get there.'

It was an easy decision: a walk in the fresh air would always win over a dimly lit coffee shop surrounded by other people. And Kinnoull Hill was much more exciting than either of the Inches.

Hazel couldn't remember the last time she'd walked up Kinnoull Hill. She had fond memories of lazy Sundays spent with grandparents. She and Charlotte would traipse up the path, more intent on going off route and into the surrounding forest to jump over burns and rocks in search of red squirrels and roe deer. They never found deer. At that age, Charlotte had been noisier than she was now, believe it or not.

Nan used to drop 10ps on the ground, claiming horse riders must have spilled their bounty, and Hazel and Charlotte would head home, 50p heavier each, feeling like they'd won the lotto.

Twenty years must have passed since she'd last been up.

'Have you been up the hill recently?' Hazel asked as they waited in line at the coffee shop.

'Not for yonks. It's kind of my safe space. The car park.' She waved a hand between them, like it was silly.

'The car park?' Hazel repeated with an amused smile.

Louise's cheeks tinged red. 'Yeah, when I'm feeling overwhelmed, I like to sit in my car in the car park. The forest one, not the one in the quarry. It's nice at night, when no one else is there.'

'At night? Is that not a bit creepy?' Hazel didn't fancy her chances up there at night-time. It was a dense forest; anything could be lurking.

'Don't knock it until you've tried it,' Louise replied, her cheeks getting darker. 'What about you? Been up recently?'

'Nah,' she said, with a quick shake of her head. 'My grandad used to tell me it was an old volcano. Do you think that's true?'

'It's definitely made of lava. I remember learning about it on a school trip,' Louise replied as the barista handed her their two lattes.

They shared stories of school walks and memories of house parties in the surrounding suburbs as they made the thirty-minute walk to the quarry car park, passing by some of Perth's most prestigious houses, finally skirting around the impressive monastery that marked the bottom of the woodland park. They both listened in awe at the calming chorus of the monks that carried on the wind. Sometimes Hazel forgot the monastery was still in use, a hidden gem in Perth's hinterland.

Louise told her more about her night-time visits to Kinnoull car park ('I've not done it in aaaages though!') and how it was her little pocket of zen. Hazel understood: sometimes the world got too much and you had to reset. She'd wished for just that a lot recently; maybe Louise had a point, no matter how creepy it sounded.

Then, Louise filled her in on the other book club members and recounted stories of past meetings, nights out, Jordan's romantic escapades – they weren't in short supply, that was for sure. She joked about finally having someone to walk with; none of the rest liked getting their boots muddy. Unless it was Jordan. She'd been known to suffer worse to meet women.

Time with Louise was easy. If she was a day, she was a Sunday near the end of summer, much like they were enjoying today. No pressure. Like the hours could stretch on forever as Hazel lay in a hammock, eyes closed, sun-kissed and blissed out. Being around Louise made her relaxed.

Except for the weird energy that lay below her surface today, nipping her usual vibes short, like she was holding something back and nervous about it, too.

Donna had said she needed distracted. Louise had mentioned work. Maybe something terrible was going on. She would talk if she wanted to. It wasn't any of Hazel's business.

'You forget how close all this is to the city centre,' Hazel reminisced, as they stood at the bottom of the path that led to the main trail.

Standing on the High Street and looking at the swath of

trees that lined the skyline to the east, most tourists would never guess it contained such an impressive park.

Hidden amongst the beech and pine trees were sculptures, orienteering courses, BMX trails, and bridle paths. It even had its own, custom-built, castle remains.

Hazel took in the path meandering up the hill before them. It was a small summit, heading to a stone table with places of interest carved into it, designed to help you spot landmarks in the valley below. Really, in Hazel's mind, it was a small taste of the majesty to come.

'Will we start on this path then head further in?' Louise asked, weighing up their options. Another twenty-minute walk would take them to an alternative route. But, there was no sense in delaying their time in the trees. Six of one, half a dozen of the other, at the end of the day.

'Sounds good to me.'

They set off, passing a couple that were heading downward.

'Thanks for getting me out the house,' Hazel said, relishing the cold breeze rolling over the hill.

'My pleasure. Anything to carve out a little peace from Charlotte, eh?'

'I'll say.'

Conversation flowed again, Hazel still fully aware of the tension in Louise's shoulders. Even the way she put their coffee cups in a bin seemed laden.

Louise filled her in on the centre's plans for the next quarter: ideas she had for new groups and fundraising. She obviously loved what she did. So, maybe work wasn't the issue after all? Hazel bit her tongue.

Finally, they were deep in the forest, only the hoot of the occasional wood pigeon for company. With the sun blocked out by a thick canopy of trees, it was easy to lose herself in the moment and fully forget the reality of the outside world. Here, Hazel didn't need a job or have an annoying sister waiting at home. She was starting to properly understand Louise's car park ritual.

'Is it not scary when you come up here at night?' Hazel asked. The street lights ended in the quarry car park. The one Louise went to had nothing after sunset. Never mind the darkness between the trees.

'That's all part of the charm,' she replied, with a smile. 'You should join me some time.'

'Only if I can bring a torch.'

Louise laughed. 'I think that kinda defeats the purpose, but whatever would give you peace. I don't get out my car, if that makes you feel better.'

Folk tales boasting men with hooks for hands, and killers on car roofs, danced through Hazel's mind. Time to change the subject, unless she wanted to freak Louise out and ruin her spot. 'I don't remember all these sculptures; they're cool, aren't they?' she said, passing a row of hedgehogs carved into a fallen trunk.

'Amazing, done with a chainsaw apparently. It's fun finding them, little hidden gems in the forest.'

Her brain made a connection between conversations.

'Do you ever remember seeing a car up here?' Hazel asked. They rounded a corner, deeper still into the forest. They were going on muscle memory now: neither had looked at a coloured marker post for ages.

'Oh God, yes. A jeep, wasn't it? In one of the quarries?'

'That's the one,' Hazel said with a grin, happy someone else shared the memory. 'I always wondered how it got there.'

'Me too. I hope it wasn't too grisly. Do you think it's still there?'

'Dunno. We could pass by, have a look. Trees have probably hidden it by now.'

'True. I'd like to see, though.'

They carried on up the hill, Louise only stopping once, taking Hazel by the elbow to point where she thought she'd seen a squirrel. Wee blighter was too quick, though.

'I'm sure it was around here,' Hazel said, hands on hips as she searched the area for clues, having reached another clearing. The quarry and its totalled car were proving evasive today.

'We might need to google this, come back another day.'

'Maybe,' Hazel replied with a sigh.

'Look, come up here,' Louise announced, heading off the path and into the woods before Hazel had a chance to see where she was aiming for.

She ambled after, enjoying the sudden change of the ground under foot. The rocky path had been hard and stable: here was spongy, the moss hiding all sorts of secrets.

Louise stopped on a hummock. 'Didn't realise there was a stream here.'

Hazel looked at the rushing water below. 'Where we headed?'

'Just to that log,' Louise replied, pointing to a fallen tree not far from where they stood. 'Could do with a quick seat.'

Hazel wasn't about to argue with that idea. 'We can jump that, easy.'

Louise scrunched her face. 'Really?'

The other side was a few feet lower, but it looked sturdy enough. The real issue would be getting back, but there would be an alternative route. No point thinking about it now.

'Easy-peasy,' Hazel said and leaped down, landing with a thud. 'Your turn.'

Louise didn't look confident. Her eyes searched the stream's bank, as if sizing up how safe it was.

Hazel held a hand out. 'Come on, I've got you.'

'If I fall in, you're dead,' Louise said with a laugh but Hazel could tell she was serious. 'Here goes nothing.'

Just like that, she was on the bank and Hazel pulled her closer with the hand she'd left extended. 'Ooft, saved your life,' she joked, jolting Louise as if she had in fact stopped her from falling.

The thing was, the universe had other plans.

The ground moved beneath them, mud getting the better of their footing, and soon Louise really was slipping.

Hazel stepped back, pulling Louise close with her, hands on her hips to steady them.

Only their heavy breathing filled the forest.

Two women in the middle of nowhere, inches apart, hands gripped to gilets and biceps.

A moment passed, their breath hanging between them, so super-charged it crackled, before Louise whacked Hazel solidly in the arm, a grin splitting her face. The charge sunk to the forest floor, forgotten.

'You arse! If I'd gone in you were coming with me, I hope you know that.' She walked away with a chuckle, adjusting her clothing to sit right again.

'I don't doubt it for a second.' Something settled low in Hazel's belly, but she chose to ignore it. It was a blip: nothing more than a moment to be boxed away and never thought of again. In fact, this feeling was probably to do with whatever had been bothering Louise today. Something odd lay between them, something that Hazel couldn't quite put her finger on.

Louise plonked herself on the log, stretching her legs

out in front of her. 'I don't think I've walked this much since the fundraiser.'

'That feels like a lifetime ago,' Hazel said, taking a seat by Louise. It had only been six weeks, but it really did seem like years.

They sat in silence for a while, Hazel taking in the woodland surrounding them. She opened her mouth to speak but Louise beat her to it.

'I, erm, I need to tell you something.'

It was a relief, almost, to know Hazel hadn't been imagining the underlying subtext. 'Yeah, what's up?'

Louise tilted her head back, eyes pointed skyward as she released a nervous laugh. 'Urgh, where to begin.'

'The start is usually a good place,' Hazel suggested with a sympathetic smile.

'The start. Right. Gosh, that takes things back.' She took a deep breath. 'I guess it ties into why I was such a dick, so let's start there.'

'Louise, listen, you don't need to. It's fine, let's just have a fresh slate. A new start. This is good, we're good.'

They weren't the Hazel and Louise of the past. They were different people, in different times. It was fresh and weird but also exhilarating. There was no sense rehashing it all, only to bring back bitterness.

'I appreciate that, but there's something that hasn't quite come up and I need you to hear it from me.'

'Yeah?' Hazel's heart stuttered. This didn't sound good.

'When you knew me, I was going through a lot.' Louise rolled the hem of her gilet between finger and thumb. 'Mark, my dad, he was cheating on my mum.'

'Shit.'

She gulped, taking a moment before carrying on. 'I

came home from school one day, skiving off maths, no biggie, and I found him with his assistant.'

'Fuck.'

Louise laughed under her breath, her attention still fixed on her clothing. 'Oh, it gets better. 'He paid me to keep quiet—'

'What?!'

'—which I took. I mean, it was a lot of dosh. The whole thing fucked me up.' She sat straighter, as if a switch had been flicked. A dim light returned to her eyes and she painted on her best smile, albeit weakly. 'So, yeah, life was a bit of a mess.'

'I'm so sorry. I had no idea.'

'How could you? I didn't tell anyone. In fact, you're the first person I've told in years. Jordan, Bex, all my friends, they have no idea.'

'I won't tell anyone.'

'I know.' Her gaze fell to her shoes. 'So. That was that. But the guilt ate away at me. I eventually told Mum.'

Hazel gulped. This wasn't in the ballpark of what she'd been expecting Louise to talk about. Not even the same continent.

'That can't have been easy,' Hazel said, still clueless as to where this was going or why Louise so desperately needed to tell her.

'Nope.' She squirmed, closing one eye as if she was in serious pain. 'This is weird. Sorry. I just, I feel I need to give you the whole picture. You deserve that.'

'It's okay. You don't need to tell me anything if you don't want to. I appreciate you letting me know the truth, though. It explains a lot.'

Louise stared straight ahead, continuing her story as if she hadn't heard Hazel's reassurance. 'The divorce was an absolute shambles. Mum didn't take it well. Neither of us did. To help,' she said, laughing under her breath like it was a private joke with herself, 'I fell in with the wrong crowd at college. I, erm, I drank a lot, took a lot of things I probably shouldn't have taken.'

Hazel was quiet. This was a lot. The air in the forest was heavy and dense, like a thunderstorm was brewing between them. It seemed even the birds had fallen silent to listen to Louise. She let her talk. Hazel's input wasn't necessary; Louise obviously needed this off her chest.

'Mum was so wrapped up in her own stuff she didn't notice how bad things were for me. Which totally isn't a criticism of her,' she corrected, briefly making eye contact. 'Anyway, side note, also had the whole lesbian thing going on.' She added this with a little laugh, but Hazel didn't find it funny. The joke was there, but it was impossible to lighten the mood. Something terrible was coming, Hazel could sense it. 'Common sense has never been my forte, so I dealt with Mark stuff, Mum stuff, gay stuff by sleeping with guys when I wasn't sober.'

'Oh.' Was that it? That Louise had been with men? That was no biggie. Plenty of people found themselves when they were older.

'You don't need to be a therapist to guess what I was trying to do. Feel. Whatever.'

'I get it. But I don't get what that has to do with me?'

'Getting there,' Louise replied, sporting a smile dripping with anxiety. The air still buzzed around them, building to something more. 'I ended up sleeping with this guy at a party in Crieff and, well, I got pregnant.'

Hazel's mouth formed a perfect circle, caught between *oh* and *fuck*.

'Yep,' Louise said, popping her lips together. 'I have a son. Cameron.'

Still her mouth refused to close. In the grand scheme of things this wasn't ground-breaking: plenty of people their age had kids, but it was so left of centre, so beyond what Hazel could have ever imagined Louise needed to tell her, that her brain had completely short-circuited.

In lieu of Hazel's silence, Louise continued: 'I don't speak to his dad. I was lucky in a way. He wanted me to get rid of him. Had no interest, so I got him to sign all his parental rights over to me.'

She blew her cheeks out, finally finding the courage to properly look Hazel in the eye.

Hazel closed her mouth but words wouldn't come. What was appropriate? Congratulations? Sympathy? Something else entirely?

'Say something, please,' Louise urged.

Hazel turned over the options in her head. Finally, she settled on: 'Why the big deal about telling me?'

Louise huffed, releasing a torrent of frustration. The atmosphere was still heavy, as if her revelation hadn't been quite enough to start the storm, diffuse the air.

'It wasn't intentional, not to start with. Then I was worried it would mean you wouldn't like me, or that it would be a problem. I dunno, overthinking, that's all.'

'Wouldn't like you? Why would having a kid stop us being friends?'

It was Louise's turn to open and close her mouth. 'No, like further down the line, future liking, maybe.' Her cheeks burned red as she slowly sliced a palm through the air, as if marking an imaginary horizon. 'I dunno. Ignore me.'

Hazel let the words settle. 'Like you, as in romantically?'

'No, li—'

'Louise, do you—'

'Listen, it's nothing, ju—'

'I'm really not in that headspace just now. I'm a mess. You know that, right?'

'Yeah. It was just . . .' she trailed off, the faintest shimmer to her eyes.

This was too much. 'I think I should go,' Hazel said, standing.

Louise stood too, the forest coming back to life as Hazel walked off. It was like they'd been in their own bubble. 'Hazel, wait,' she called, jogging to come level with Hazel as she tried to find a way back to the path without crossing the stream again. 'That all came out wrong. Can we just talk?'

'I just need a moment,' Hazel replied, not breaking her stride.

'But you know, I wasn't meaning—' Louise cut herself short with a loud groan. 'Can we start again?'

'Bit late.'

'So, you're just going to leave me in the woods?'

Guilt skirted over Hazel but it was quickly replaced by the need to remove herself, get some thinking room. It was like Louise was holding her head under water: there was no space to breathe.

'It's not like that.'

'Then what's it like?'

'Louise,' Hazel snapped.

She didn't need to say any more as Louise fell out of step, coming to a halt as Hazel stomped on.

She couldn't turn around. Louise would find her way home. It was better this way. For everyone.

22

Work had dragged today. Mainly because Louise was intent on checking her phone every ten minutes, torn between wanting Hazel to text her or breaking the silence and reaching out herself.

She'd fucked up. Big time.

Her head was hell-bent on torturing her: replaying the conversation again and again. Every time she thought of Hazel's face she felt sick.

She'd locked herself away in her office this afternoon, feigning a need to catch up on paperwork. The team could handle assisted biking without her. She had a workshop to guide participants to in fifteen minutes, then it was back to scheduled wallowing.

Why had she said that to Hazel?

They could have carried on as friends, no problem at all. There was honesty, and then there was sheer lunacy.

What a stupid, stupid idiot.

Louise leaned back in her office chair, running her hands over her hair. This was too much. She barely knew

Hazel and now she probably thought Louise was halfway to declaring she was in love with her or something.

Nerves had got the better of her and she'd fumbled, screwing the entire thing up, probably irreversibly.

That's why she was running it over in her head: had she really admitted to having feelings, or just floated the notion? Was there more to this than Hazel was letting on? Perhaps Louise had simply given her an out.

Had sharing so much been what really tipped Hazel over the edge? There was a reason why none of her friends knew her full past. She wasn't ashamed: she owned it, the emotional scars were as much a part of her as the physical scar on her stomach from Cameron's c-section. But what she did then wasn't who she was now. Most people didn't *need* to know her life history. Hazel had got hurt in the crossfire, though: she deserved to know why.

What happened with Mark was massive. It was an earthquake of magnitude, so big its destruction ranged for miles, Louise in the centre, fresh fault lines forever ingrained inside her. Some she was never able to patch, so they became part of her, hidden in plain sight.

Maybe Hazel was scared of Louise's mental state, shocked by her drinking and substance abuse, worried she was like Mark.

She wanted to see Hazel, show her she wasn't a mess, prove she was okay now.

The question was: what could she say to bring her round? Louise's fledgling feelings aside, she was enjoying having her as a friend. Nothing else had to come of it. She just couldn't bear the thought of Hazel thinking she was an emotional wreck.

She lifted her phone from the desk, where she'd left it face down, and checked the home screen. Nothing.

What was she expecting? Hazel wasn't going to reach out. This was Louise's mess to fix.

Hazel hadn't wanted to know her to start with; now she had even more reason to steer clear.

There was a knock at the door.

Maybe Hazel had come to speak to her face to face. That would be easier than texting.

'Yeah?' she called.

'It's me.' Cameron.

Louise smiled. This was a welcome surprise. 'In you come.'

The door slowly opened and in poked her handsome son, a cheeky grin on his face, his collar unbuttoned and his school tie hanging skew-whiff. 'Hey.'

'What's up?'

He slumped into the stiff chair on the other side of Louise's desk, and dropped his school bag to the ground. 'It's so hot.'

'Did you come here to give me a weather report?' Louise joked.

He closed his eyes, still smiling. 'Just needing a moment. They shouldn't make us wear uniform when it's like this.'

'I think I'd get done if I let you wear your Speedos to school.'

'Funny,' he retorted, snapping back awake. 'Listen—'

'Uh-huh, here it comes,' she jibed. What was he going to ask for? Staying out tonight? Money? If it had anything to do with taking on extra shifts, it was a hard no.

'My pals are off to the skate park. Can I go too?'

'Of course. So that's why you're in town. Why didn't you just text me, instead of coming in?'

He shrugged. 'You got any juice?'

Louise grabbed her water bottle out of the drawer. 'Just diluting, nothing fizzy.'

'That'll do.' He held his hand out.

'You sure nothing's up?'

He shook his head as he took a long draw of the flavoured water. 'Just thought I'd pop in, see my old mum.'

'Less of the old, please.'

Cameron screwed the lid back on the bottle before passing it back. 'Can I leave my tie with you?'

'No, you'll end up forgetting it tomorrow. Just shove it in your bag.'

'I wanted to leave that too.'

Louise chuckled. So that was the intention. She was the pack horse taking his stuff home. She didn't mind: seeing him was compensation enough. 'Fine. Just pop it down here, by the cabinet. But listen.'

'Yeah?'

'Any problems?'

'Bananas.'

'Exactly, bananas. And I don't want you in too late. I'll see Jordan after work, I can get you on the way home. Sound okay?'

'Deal.'

JORDAN WAS STARTING to get pissed off with work. So, nothing new. Jobs often got called off, her locations changed, rotas flipped. She was coming up for two weeks off though, which wasn't usually how her contractor rolled. Part of her was probably nervous about money and future employment, but she'd never let that slip.

'Bunch of fecking eejits. Couldn't organise a piss-up in a

brewery,' she moaned, sitting under her caravan's awning, a slice of evening sun cutting over her legs.

Louise got comfy in the camping chair opposite. 'No clue when you'll start?'

'No idea. And that's if it ever gets off the ground. There's talk of me going to Berwick.'

'Berwick?'

'I know, right. One minute it's Alloa, next it's Berwick. I'd at least like to know which way to point my hitch.'

'Frustrating.'

'I'll say. Anyway. How was your work today?'

'Good, really good. Great, even.' Louise replied, and meant it. The day had finished with a slow cooker workshop run by a local charity, designed to give women struggling financially a cheaper way to feed their families. As the cherry on top, Louise had managed to wrangle donations from a local supermarket, meaning every participant got to leave with a slow cooker of their own. There had been tears and lots of smiles. It was part of the job Louise would never get bored of.

'So what's got your face looking like a smacked arse then?' Jordan asked and naturally moved back to avoid any retaliation. Louise wasn't in the mood for playful roughhousing, though.

Louise let out a loud sigh. 'Hazel.'

'Christ almighty. I didn't know this woman existed two months ago and now I'm sick of her name,' Jordan joked.

'Sorry.'

Jordan grew serious. 'Hey, no, sorry. I'm just mucking about. What's happened?'

Hux wandered over and dropped a chewy treat at Louise's feet. She gave his ear a good scratch as he lay down to chomp on his bounty. 'I said something to her I shouldn't have.'

'Louise, what did you do?' Jordan asked, arching a brow.

'I told her about Cameron.'

'Right.' Confusion relaxed Jordan's features. 'Why's that bad?'

Louise clicked her tongue to the roof of her mouth. 'It's complicated. Actually, just forget I said anything.' She watched Hux as he chewed on the pleated treat. Oh to be a dog, not a care in the world.

'Lou, come on. You can tell me anything.'

'I guess I made a bigger deal about it than I should have.' She puffed her cheeks, blowing the air out like a steam train struggling to climb a hill.

'Uh-huh.'

'And I might have blurted out that I didn't tell her because I was worried about her liking me.'

'Liking you?'

'Romantically.'

'Shit. Do you actually have feelings for her?'

'No. I don't think so. I mean, I fancy her. But superficial liking is hardly the same as *liking* liking, is it?'

A smug smile ghosted Jordan's lips. 'You're right. You totally are overthinking this.'

'Hey,' Louise whined, finally mustering the courage to swipe at her best friend.

Jordan stroked her chin. 'So, you think she's hot. She knows you think she's hot. She didn't take it well?'

'She ran a mile.' Louise had considered telling Jordan the whole story, but the fallout from Hazel was warning enough. No one else needed to be privy to her past. Not even the woman she would trust with her life.

'You said she was going through a bad break-up, though.

She's probably got a lot on her mind. Plus there's the whole former-arch-enemy thing.'

Louise lolled her head back with a groan. 'I never like anyone. Why is my head, heart, whatever, kicking into action now?'

'Because that's the problem, you never like anyone. You had to break sometime. I have no idea how you live. I get horny after a week without.'

Louise bolted upright, checking the surrounding caravans for life. This was not a conversation to be having in the open. Jordan could be at a dinner party and say worse, though.

'It's not about being horny,' she hissed, keeping her voice as low as possible while still forcing her point home.

'Everything's about being horny when you really boil it down,' Jordan replied, at the same volume as before.

Louise was sure she saw the curtains twitch in the van opposite. 'I'm perfectly fine on my own.'

'I didn't say you weren't. But you like Hazel. So what are you going to do about it?'

'Nothing. Absolutely nothing.'

'So why are you here? Apart from to see my beautiful face?'

'Because, I don't know what to say to her, to make things right, y'know?'

'So, you do want to do something?'

'As in, be friends.'

Hux broke off a huge chuck of his treat with a satisfying crack. 'Friends who maybe like having a little smoochie-smoochie?' Jordan joked, waggling her head and making a kissy face.

'I might go.' Louise wasn't in the mood.

'No, no. Mate, sorry. I'm just trying to lighten the mood.'

She edged forward on her seat, serious once again. 'If you think you've put your foot in it, you need to let her know it's strictly friendship you're after.'

'Right. Yeah, you're right.' She expected an addendum from Jordan but she didn't push it, having finally taken the hint. This was a temporary glitch. She'd found other women attractive before; it didn't mean she had feelings. She thought the woman in Sainsburys was cute. Didn't mean she wanted to date her.

These feelings would fizzle out, just like everything else.

Now it was just a matter of what to text.

23

Hazel laced her fingers together in her hoodie's pocket. Today felt chillier, like the weather was suddenly going to turn from summer to autumn. Yesterday had been boiling, now this. Was nothing consistent anymore?

She'd wanted a quiet walk, to clear her head, but had second thoughts on leaving the house. Usually she would pad around the neighbourhood, enjoying the peace of Perth's residential suburbs, but doing so meant the risk of running into Louise and she wasn't ready to see her.

Which is how Hazel found herself wandering down Perth's busiest road on a Tuesday evening.

A large truck whizzed by, throwing dust and dirt into the air, forcing Hazel to screw her eyes shut.

This was a bust.

But laying in her bed wasn't an option.

Her head was filled with static, her subconscious having nine million conversations at once. Since her break-up, evenings were always the worst. During the day she could busy herself, but after dinner, the vast expanse from food to bed seemed to grow every week, her thoughts taking the chance to spiral.

Usually her mind was preoccupied with Ashley, beating herself up for past choices, worrying about the future. Now a new issue had joined the party.

Adulting was hard. There was no rule book. Just a few flimsy expectations set by other adults who were winging it too.

She'd reacted badly to Louise's revelation, but relationships terrified Hazel: she'd not expected them to be the topic of conversation when Louise invited her out.

Still, there was a little voice, one trying its hardest to be heard over the rabble, that said it wasn't totally repulsed by the idea. Louise was attractive and they got on. Would it be the worst thing in the world?

Her heart had other ideas to her head.

It wouldn't budge: it had already compensated by allowing them to be friends.

Ashley had closed her heart's door and Hazel had swallowed the key, added stronger locks and bolts, invested in alarm systems, moats and a portcullis: the whole hog to stop any unwelcome visitors. Other people only let you down.

Louise would be better investing her time in someone else.

Still, their loose end made Hazel's stomach lurch, like she'd eaten something bad. It didn't sit right.

Weeks ago she would have been glad to finally see the back of Louise; now she wondered if there was a way to just enjoy each other's company again.

Without Louise, her social life was reduced to Charlotte, and even she was on limited time.

She'd started to enjoy hearing her phone buzz, instead

of wondering if it was Ashley, another client cancelling, or a reminder for an invoice she'd forgotten to pay. It was nice to smile again, even if it was just about Jordan and her lack of reading.

Book club could have been good, given the chance.

She couldn't *just* text Louise though, and hope to continue where they'd left things before their ill-fated conversation up Kinnoull Hill. That would be strange. Her words were out there, with no chance they'd stop ringing in Hazel's ears.

Hazel reached the crossroads at the back of the old Cherrybank Gardens. What had once been a beautiful park filled with sculptures and manicured lawns was now row after row of uninspiring, copy-and-paste houses. Funny how things could be so different in the blink of an eye: change often masked as good when really it was anything but.

She sighed, not really knowing where to walk from here. She'd barely gone a mile but her options were limited. Straight on continued on the busy road and headed for town. To her left took her past her old school, which wouldn't be too bad had it not been a series of steep hills leading to even steeper hills. Right took her past the new houses and up to a call centre. Not ideal.

There was a final option. Cross the road and head to the area's only pub.

HAZEL SIPPED her pint of Diet Coke. She'd considered a beer but bad habits were getting boring.

The Beech Tree pub was as old as time and, despite a hefty amount of modernisation, held onto its quaint charm as tightly as a tram to the tracks. Which was handy, since it used to be the old depot back in Victorian times.

Hazel had parked herself in what was affectionately known as The Snug: a small room at the side of the main pub that had enough room for just four tables. It was decorated floor-to-ceiling with dark oak panels, unlike next door, which was firmly in the twenty-first century with whitewashed plaster and a wall of windows offering a panoramic view of the cottages out back.

She's only been here a few times but preferred this part of the pub. It had its own bar, albeit tiny, and usually only housed regulars, unlike next door which all and sundry enveloped on the hunt for cheap booze and pub grub.

She'd texted Yaz, just to check in, but there was no reply yet.

Charlotte had texted, asking where she was off to. It was like living with Miss Marple. Hazel couldn't sneeze without a line of questioning.

She would feel sorry for Charlotte had it not been for the fact that Mum and Dad desperately clung to keeping her informed and included, as if she might forget them and never return from Australia should she not be tagged in every photo, or FaceTimed religiously every Sunday. She might be on the other side of the world, but she'd never missed a beat. She was just as included there as she was right now.

Hazel didn't get the same treatment in Glasgow.

It had bothered her at first, but Charlotte was the baby and being on the other side of the world made things difficult for her parents. Hazel was easy to reach, and with Mum's fear of flying, Charlotte was all but lost. It was easy to take things for granted when you didn't have to work for them.

She couldn't remember if Charlotte was always this clingy, though. This obsessive need to *do* stuff together was driving Hazel bonkers.

She fired off a reply, letting Charlotte know she was out for a walk, then put her phone on the table.

The football was on. No teams she cared about, but the large flat-screen TV mounted on the wall was a nice distraction.

Five-a-side started in a few weeks. Hopefully that would fill a gap.

Her phone screen lit up. A call from Yaz.

'Paaaaterson!' they boomed like a sportscaster.

'Hey, Yaz. How's things?'

'So-so. You?'

Living in emotional limbo, you? 'Not much, just been thinking about jobs.'

'How's that going?'

'Slowly but surely.'

She really wanted to tell Yaz about Louise, but going through the whole story would be tedious and cumbersome. She didn't need to burden Yaz with something that might not even be an issue. Not to mention the two men within earshot. It was one thing to tell Yaz, another to fill two strangers in on her mess of a life too.

'Well, I'm glad it's going somewhere. I was thinking I might pop through soon. That okay?'

'To Perth?'

Yaz laughed. 'Yes, that's where you are, isn't it?'

'Not much to do here. You sure?'

'Of course. I want to see where is so brilliant it stole your heart from Glasgow.'

Hazel held back a groan. There was no heart-stealing of

any kind going on. 'If you insist,' Hazel jested. 'When you thinking?'

'Soon. I need to check some stuff with work. They've got me covering a shit tonne of shifts just now.'

'Okay, well, gimme a text and we'll figure it out.'

Face to face would be so much better but she still wasn't keen on recounting the whole sorry story. Or anything, for that matter. Anyway, by the time Yaz came through there might not be anything to tell them. If there was anything to start with.

Goodbyes exchanged, she put her phone on the table, her eyes back on the football game.

It didn't take long for her phone to rumble but she ignored it, intent on watching the game until at least half-time. There was no sense in getting into a conversation with Charlotte and if she looked at her phone she'd be inclined to reply.

Another rumble distracted her. Charlotte was double-texting now? Or maybe it was Yaz confirming a date; she could handle that.

Yaz was one of those people: you either got instant plans or it was five to ten business days later. There was no in-between. It didn't bother Hazel – they were there when she needed them. That's all that mattered.

The football was boring, so she lifted her phone, crossing everything that it was Yaz who stole her attention first and not multiple messages from her clingy-koala little sister.

It was neither.

Louise: *Listen, the other day everything came out wrong.* Then another text: *Can we just be friends?*

Hazel's insides twisted, knotting around any sensible

answers that might have been formulating in her gut, cutting them off and leaving only one: what the fuck?

She wanted that, but was it fair if Louise was harbouring feelings? She didn't want to lead her on, no matter what the little voice in her head wanted her to believe. Her heart was too strong-willed to concede.

She sucked on her cheek, looking at the TV screen as she held her phone in two hands.

If she was going to cut her losses and leave Louise be, this was the time.

She remembered how good she'd felt on the walk from town to the woods, how a little pop of happiness had settled in her chest and warmed her skin. But this wasn't a second chance for Louise, it was a third. *Totally different*, the little voice in her head piped up, before adding the image of Louise at book club, beaming with happiness at the sight of her and Charlotte. Or how amazing she'd been to listen to Hazel rant when they'd gone for drinks. She didn't want to lose that. *Not to mention how good she looks in skinny jeans.* Her heart jumped up and down on that thought, stuffing it away like a duvet into a too-small bag, screaming *nothing to see here!*

Besides, her head countered: *Third time lucky.*

She replied: *Just friends?*

Just friends.

Sorry for freaking out, Hazel wrote, her cheeks reddening despite the two old men leaning on the bar having no chance of reading her screen.

It's just I'm not in the right headspace for a relationship.

Oh Jesus, Hazel, I don't want that. Friends is fine.

Okay, so, wrong end of the stick maybe? There'd been so much to take in that day. Maybe she'd read too much into Louise's words.

She'd barely had time to take in what else Louise had told her. It was no wonder she was so stand-offish at school. It was no excuse for how she's treated Hazel, but knowing the backstory made a difference. Motive never forgave the crime, but understanding went a long way.

Her dad's actions were so messed up Hazel couldn't get her head round it. And she thought Ashley was bad.

She hovered her fingers over her phone's keyboard. How to reply? *Okay* felt a little redundant.

She couldn't just leave at that though. She had to say something.

A reply from Charlotte dipped onto her screen. She swiped it away: she was too busy for trivial small talk.

This was a crossroads, the power in Hazel's hands.

Leave it and things could be awkward.

Louise had done the hard part by reaching out: she owed it to her to put in a little effort too.

Started on that new book yet?

Three bouncing dots appeared on the screen.

24

S ix days had passed since she'd nearly royally screwed things up. But, in true Louise fashion, she'd excused a handbrake turn just in time.

In fact, she and Hazel had messaged every day since. Conversation was again easy for them and twice this week she'd found herself staying up late just to chat to her. She was aware an issue might be brewing, but fun was outweighing the danger. Jordan was right: why not indulge herself a little? No harm, no foul. No one ever gave her butterflies. Why not ride this wave, before it petered back out to her usual calm millpond of attraction?

Butterflies. Louise snapped the lid shut on that thought and what it might be alluding to. She was too busy for that carry-on.

Today was the centre's annual fundraising event.

Months of organising culminated in six hours of fun for the general public and would hopefully raise some much-needed funds, while bolstering the centre's profile in the community.

It almost sounded easy when you put it like that.

So far, the weather gods had blessed them. Louise had tossed and turned most of last night, worried about a possible spattering of showers predicted at noon, but the hour had come and gone with blue skies.

Of course, she had a back-up plan, but face-painting, Beat the Goalie, and the food trucks all worked better outside and did a grand job of pulling in passers-by who otherwise might not have known the event was on.

She'd set each department a goal for sign-ups and new memberships. Her personal objective was another thirty sigups for Kid Camp in the October holidays. Two weeks of fun were guaranteed, between swimming, kayaking, gymnastics, and a host of other activities. Sometimes she wished there was an adult camp.

Her muscles were finally starting to relax, now that the weather was definitely playing ball, and it was still busy nearly three hours after the event had started. In fact, it felt like it was just ramping up in terms of numbers.

'Sure you don't want a shot?' Billy asked, nodding his head towards the rowing machine they'd set up under a gazebo by the car park. The gym was doing a six-hour row-athon, with staff taking shifts to row non-stop until the event finished. He was still red and sweaty despite his stint ending nearly forty minutes ago. As far as gym managers went he probably wasn't typical in looks: he was just taller than Louise, with a bushy brown beard and the beginnings of a belly. He was damn good at what he did though, even if he didn't always practise what he preached.

'I think I'll leave it to you and the gym crew,' Louise replied, feigning a smile. 'You know I'm better suited to behind a desk.'

'How's your sign-ups going?' he asked, ignoring her reluctance as if he expected it.

'Good, got ten already.'

'Nice,' he said, pride lengthening it to last a few syllables. 'Jane got three new gym members signed. Girl's on fire.'

'No way, that's mega.' Louise beamed. Hopefully everyone else was doing just as well.

'Best be off. Back on the rower in twenty.' He winked and Louise was sure a fresh layer of sweat had formed on his brow just at the thought.

She watched him cut through the crowd, her eyes briefly wandering from his figure to snag something else entirely.

Hazel. Laughing with Charlotte and her parents. Completely oblivious to Louise.

Her stomach flipped.

She kidded on it was because she'd not seen her since their spat in the woods. It was just nerves, nothing else. Plausible. They hadn't physically seen each other, only texted: what if things were awkward? She ignored the way her stomach flipped again at the sight of Hazel's tattoos and dimples as she shared another joke.

Louise gulped before averting her gaze to her clipboard. Maybe it was time to check on the team offering e-bike trials, see if they needed a breather.

Just one last look though.

She lifted her eyes and this time Hazel snagged her gaze, as if she knew she was under surveillance, even from across the plaza and through the bustling crowd. She gave a little wave and Louise's stomach did a full roly-poly as Hazel made her excuses to her family before heading her way.

It was like the world was in slow motion as Hazel cut through the crowd. Louise couldn't take her eyes off her. That was, until her mind snapped into action, warning her she'd not blinked in the last thirty seconds. And what the heck was this smile, making her cheeks ache as she kept it at bay? She looked at her clipboard again, suddenly forgetting how to read but running her eyes left to right regardless.

'Hey,' Hazel beamed, finally standing in front of Louise. 'This place is buzzing.'

'You having a good time?' The words came out as one, running into each other as much as her heart was stumbling over itself.

This was not good.

She'd thought she'd got her head straight after talking to Jordan, but it would seem her heart and her body had latched on to another part of her best friend's advice. Maybe indulging in a little butterfly-chasing was the wrong thing to do after all.

'Yeah, just got here though,' Hazel replied with a mischievous glint to her eye. 'Charlotte wants to chat to someone about Pilates, though I don't know why.'

Louise's brow creased, her heart slowing down now her brain was distracted. 'She still not given you a leaving date?'

'Nope,' Hazel said with a shake of her head. 'Surely we *both* can't be secretly jobless.'

'Not to mention Jimmy.'

'I know, right?' Hazel leaned in conspiratorially and Louise savoured the proximity as much as she did her woody perfume. 'I even had a look on her Facebook. They're still "in a relationship".'

'No you did not,' Louise said with a gasp. 'You really think something's going on?'

Hazel shrugged. 'Dunno. Just seems a bit weird she's hanging about. Mum and Dad aren't asking questions; they'd love her to stay for as long as possible.'

She pursed her lips. 'Weird, but not unusual. She's

maybe been saving up holiday time cause she knew she was coming back.'

'Whose side are you on?' Hazel joked, closing the gap to playfully nudge Louise.

Her heart skipped. She was just about to say something uncharacteristically cheesy when the centre's chairman sidled up, level with them.

'Louise.' He greeted her with a beaming smile. 'Can I steal you for a quick chat?'

'Yeah, course,' she said, internal alarm bells sounding full blast. She shot Hazel a worried look as he led the way.

Was the event not going well? Had she totally misjudged how successful it was? The place was rammed, spilling over with laughter and chatter. How much more could he want?

She racked her brains for anything she might have done wrong in the last few months.

Nothing stood out.

Maybe that said it all, though.

They walked in silence, Louise's thoughts being drowned out by the rabble around them. Finally, when they were safely in the staff-only corridor, beelining for his office, he spoke. 'Event is going well. You happy?'

Was this a trick? 'Yes, so far. Are you?' The second sentence came out almost as a squeak as she wondered mid-question if it was rude to be so direct.

He didn't seem to think so. 'Very! You've hit it out of the park again.' He stopped at his open office door and stepped aside, letting Louise go in first.

She wanted to run. If she didn't know what this was about, she couldn't get hurt.

Sadly, she was too polite to be so brazen.

He let the door close behind him before taking a seat. He looked relaxed, not at all angry: in fact he looked jovial.

Louise braced herself, unconvinced.

'So,' he started, and she wondered if she'd survive jumping out of his window to do a runner after all. 'You'll be aware the community awards are soon?'

Eh, just a bit. It was the highlight of the year. The annual event saw community centres and charities from around Scotland come together to celebrate the best of the best in one star-studded evening of fizz and glitz.

Not only was it a guaranteed good night out, it also counted a heck of a lot to win. It was like the Oscars of her industry.

'Yep, it's not long now.' Her mind ticked into overdrive. 'Has something happened? It's still happening this year, isn't it?'

Chairman Steve's face contorted around a smile, as if he wasn't quite ready to part with it. 'It's still happening, yes.'

Louise cocked her head. 'Is there something going on I should know about?'

'I got a very interesting phone call this morning. I would have spoken to you then, but I knew you were busy launching today's event.'

'Yeah?' Louise replied, feeling about as lost as one of her unruly socks.

He sucked on his lips, building the tension. Louise wanted to shake the words out of him. 'I'm very happy to announce you're shortlisted for the Community Champion Award.'

Louise's brain shut down, like someone had pulled a plug on a TV. She croaked, unable to form a single word.

'I thought this might be your reaction,' he said, finally releasing a grin.

The Community Champion Award was the crème de la crème of the evening. One outstanding citizen scooped the prize each year: deemed to have done the most for their community, having gone above and beyond. It was like being crowned the best of the best.

'I, but . . . I don't understand? Who nominated me?'

'I'd love to say it was just me,' he said, leaning back in his chair, pleased as punch. 'But apparently a few members of the public did too.'

'A few?' Louise said, her voice stuck at an unusually high pitch.

Chairman Steve's smile only grew. 'You deserve this, Louise. I don't doubt you'll win, but whatever happens, I want you to know that the centre, and the people of Perth, are behind you.'

Flabbergasted. That was the only word. 'I, er, wow.'

'Take a while to get your thoughts in order. No need to say any more.'

Good. Because coherent sentences weren't going to happen any time soon.

Chairman Steve stood, signalling their conversation was finished. 'I'd better do the rounds again,' he said, smoothing his council-blue tie against his stomach.

'Yeah, me too,' Louise said, surprised to find her legs could hold her when she rose from her seat.

He opened the door with a smile. 'Congrats again.'

Louise walked the corridor in a daze. Did that really just happen? She didn't deserve that: there were a million other people in Scotland that did more than her. She just showed up to work and did her job.

She pushed open the staff-only door and the noise of the event hit her square in the face, pulling her back towards reality.

Wow, she silently mouthed, her brain trying to quickly catch up and process the news. She was caught between utter bewilderment, wanting to cry, and feeling sick at the thought of the pressure.

She settled on confusion and made her way through the people in the foyer, spotting Charlotte chatting to Penny, one of the yoga instructors.

It was like walking on a cloud. Her feet didn't feel her own: she was watching her life unfold from someone else's point of view.

The cool air helped as she passed through the centre's automatic double doors. She aimed for the edge of the crowd, intent on finding a little breathing space to fully right herself.

She was staring at the top of a nearby tree when Hazel appeared at her side.

'You okay?' she asked, concern clear.

'Yeah, yeah,' Louise replied, still lost.

'You seem a bit, I dunno, dazed.'

'Just—' she turned to Hazel, clarity returning like a whack to the chest. 'I've been nominated for the Community Champion Award.'

Hazel's eyes widened. 'That sounds like a big deal, congrats!'

'It's a *very* big deal. Shit. I have no idea how that happened.'

'Because you're amazing at your job,' Hazel said with a laugh.

'I don't know about that.'

Hazel scoffed. 'I've heard how Mum and her pals talk about you.'

Heat flushed Louise's cheeks. 'I won't win, but being nominated is honour enough.' She checked her surroundings, wanting to make sure no one of importance was within earshot. 'Listen, don't tell anyone. Let's just keep it between us.'

'How come?' Hazel asked with a light-hearted scowl.

'Because then, when I don't win, it's less embarrassing.'

Hazel gave a decisive nod. 'Got it. Your secret is safe with me.' She bumped her hip into Louise's. 'So do you get a crown or something when you win?'

THE EVENT WAS COMING to a close, nearly all stations now fully wound down, and just a few stragglers remaining. Most were friends of centre employees, lingering to enjoy a chat with their mates and help pack up before heading onto more lively pastures to make the most of the weekend.

Louise had smashed her sign-up target and, judging by everyone she'd spoken to, so had the rest of the team.

She was just about to leave when a knock on her office door stole her attention.

Instantly her mind piped up: *it's Steve to tell you there's been a mistake. You're not nominated after all.*

'Hello?' she called, slowly pulling on her jacket.

'Hey, it's me!' a voice answered through the door. It sounded like Hazel. Why would she be back here, though? Or in the centre at all, for that matter? Louise had said goodbye to the Patersons ages ago.

'Come in,' Louise shouted.

'Hey,' Hazel repeated as she popped her head in. 'You alone?'

Louise screwed her face up, a confused smile spreading. 'Yes. What's going on?'

Hazel opened the door wider and stepped inside, a small bouquet of white roses in one hand, a card in the other.

'Now, don't get too excited. These are just from the supermarket, sorry. On a bit of a budget these days.'

Louise shook her head, getting her thoughts in order. 'What? Why?'

Hazel shrugged before holding her gifts out for Louise to take. 'To say congratulations. I figured if I was the only one to know, I needed to make sure you celebrated.' She shuffled on the spot, as if embarrassed.

Louise's cheeks burned hot. 'You're kidding? Hazel! You didn't need to do that. Thank you.' A fresh grin spread across her face as she looked at the flowers.

'Hope you don't mind me being back here,' she said, pulling an exaggerated face of worry. 'Thought it was best to give you these in private though, so I could explain myself. If anyone asks, just say it's for doing a good job today or something.' Now it was Hazel's turn to get red cheeks. 'Well, I'd best be off. Congrats again, Lou.'

'Thanks.' The word came out quietly as Hazel gave a little wave and left the room.

Louise put the flowers on her desk and opened the envelope. Inside was a card covered in copper foil illustrations of shrimp, with the words YOU'RE SHRIMPLY THE BEST in the middle.

She smiled. Can't beat a good pun.

Inside, Hazel had written a message: CONGRATS, LOU! YOU'VE GOT THIS. HAZEL. It was simple, but still, Louise's heart boomed.

Just friends.

Just friends.

Just friends.

25

Hazel led Yaz down Perth's South Street, her skin prickling with unexpected nerves.

It had been a surprise that her best friend wanted to visit Perth, but their presence was welcome. So much had happened in such a short time: she desperately needed to offload.

'So, this is it? One sleepy little side road and a high street?' Yaz commented as Hazel took them towards the city centre. Hazel had met them off the train and even the fact it only took a five-minute walk to reach the centre had amazed Yaz. 'I've lived in Glasgow all my life and never once visited here. I'm starting to see why.'

It was a joke, but annoyance rippled over Hazel. She bit it down, focusing instead on the fact Yaz was here at all.

'It's small, yeah, but it's home,' she replied with a smile, trying to keep things light.

'You're really staying, then?'

'I think so. Fresh start, et cetera.'

Yaz made out they were wincing. 'Abandoned! I never thought I'd see the day.'

'Bet you're glad to get your sofa back though.'

'I'll say.'

Finally, they reached The Victoria Hotel, affectionately known by Perth locals as Vicky's. It had a nice bar and restaurant housed in a conservatory overlooking the River Tay.

When Hazel had been tasked with finding somewhere to take Yaz she couldn't imagine them in any of Perth's small coffee shops or cafes. None of them seemed the right fit. She'd never been nervous to show off her home city before, but suddenly the pressure felt on with Yaz. She didn't want her best friend reporting back to Glasgow that Hazel was living anywhere but someplace brilliant.

Yaz seemed happy with her choice as they took in the view of Perth's iconic Smeaton's Bridge, with its large stone arches spanning the River Tay. 'Starting to see the appeal now,' they said, quietly whistling through their teeth.

Hazel's muscles relaxed. 'What's been happening in Glasgow?'

'Not much. Nora's threatening to break up with Elijah again.'

'Again?' She said the same thing nearly every year. Truth be told, Hazel thought she actually would leave if it weren't for the kids. The guy was a lazy freeloader.

Yaz huffed. 'Won't happen though. Erm, and Chris got a new job. Pen's off to Majorca, *again*. I think that's it.'

She'd barely been away two months. That felt like quite enough. 'Lucky sod,' Hazel said, talking about Penelope. She had more holidays than Hazel had hot dinners.

'I'll say. But, yeah. That's it. What about you?'

Hazel waggled her head from side to side, putting on a show about thinking. They texted often enough, but with nothing exciting happening she kept clear of specifics, focusing mainly on Charlotte drama and (lack of) work stuff. Christ, was there nothing of note in the past month? Time spent with Louise was all that floated to the surface. Thankfully, the waiter interrupted to take their order, giving her more time to think.

Sadly, nothing miraculous or exciting happened to Hazel in those ninety seconds, so she was forced to report her lack of news to Yaz. 'Honestly, nothing. I joined a book club. That's about it.'

'A book club?' Yaz echoed, their brow furrowed. 'That does not sound like you at all.'

'No, it's not,' Hazel said with a little laugh. 'But my friend Louise organises it; she invited me along.'

'Uh-huh. And who's Louise?' Yaz asked, sitting a little straighter.

'It's not like that. We went to school together, that's all.'

'So what was the little smile for?'

'What little smile?' Hazel asked, most definitely smiling now. It was born of awkwardness, not infatuation, though. If she said it enough, she might believe it too.

'You know what I'm talking about.'

'Nope. Not a clue.'

She was enjoying Louise's company, that was all. So they chatted every day? That didn't mean anything. Was Hazel excited about seeing her at book club later in the week? Also yes, but she'd been excited to see Yaz too. Didn't mean she fancied them.

But Yaz didn't send silly selfies when they were bored at work, making Hazel's heart skip with how cute they looked.

Okay. So she might fancy Louise a little bit.

There.

Like hell would she be telling Yaz, though. What was the point when she didn't want it to go any further? She'd thought about it plenty in the last week and concluded there was no denying Louise was hot or how Hazel smiled like a loon when she messaged. But right now a relationship just wasn't on the cards. So she thought she was good-looking and enjoyed hanging out with her? Wasn't the worst combo of the century.

'Let me guess: blonde hair, brown eyes, sunshine to your grumpiness?'

Hazel kept her face stoic. 'A comedian as always, Yaz.'

'Hey now, if your best friend can't read you like a book, who can?'

'I don't have feelings for her,' Hazel said, forcing certainty into her words.

'Would it really be the end of the world if you did? How does she feel about you?'

Christ, had Yaz been reading the Vicky's menu or a play-by-play of the last few weeks? 'She might have feelings for me. I don't know. She did, then she went back on it. We decided to just be friends.'

Hazel's eyes scanned the tables around them, hoping to God she didn't know anyone. In a place like Perth, it wasn't so much six degrees of separation but two. Hopefully, if anyone did know Louise, they hadn't said her name enough to bust Hazel's candid conversation.

Yaz grinned before their smile fell, their face turning serious again. 'You're not still hung up on that boot, are you?'

'Not specifically, no.' The waiter appeared with their drinks and Hazel kept quiet until he'd left. 'Ashley couldn't be further from my mind, *but* I don't want a relationship. Not now. Not ever.'

'You can't say that.'

'Why not?'

'Because Hazel, and I mean this in the nicest way, you're one of those people who are just better in a relationship. I dunno, that goofy smile you just did, it's like you glow. You're different when you're part of a couple.'

'You saying I need to rely on someone else to be happy?' Hazel kept her bitterness to a minimum. She would never admit it, but Yaz had a point. She did always feel more alive when dating someone. It was a horrible trait to have, though, and one she'd wished wasn't true.

'No, I'm saying don't ruin your own chance at happiness because you made a mistake. It's like garlic, yeah?'

Hazel screwed her face up in reply.

Yaz continued: 'Garlic is amazing, possibly one of the best things ever. But add a little lemon and—' They kissed their fingers like a chef. 'It's even better. The flavours complement, bring out the best in each other.'

Hazel's face remained the same, like she'd just sucked on the aforementioned lemon. 'I think you've officially lost it.'

Yaz took a deep breath. 'Look, Ashley was a mistake, but don't cut your nose off to spite your face.'

'That's the problem though. I can't take making a mistake again.' Hazel huffed.

'I get that.' Yaz thought for a moment, their eyes trained on the flowing river outside before returning to Hazel. 'But this Louise: you enjoy spending time with her?'

'Yeah,' Hazel said with a quick shrug.

'Well, do more of that. Chase what puts a smile on your face. And if it turns into more, so be it.'

Hazel could throttle them. 'I don't *want* more. I don't *want* a girlfriend.'

It was Yaz's turn to look exasperated. 'All I'm saying is, take it for what it is. Best case scenario: it's just sex, gets your head back in the game while having a little fun.'

'Just sex,' Hazel blurted, just as the waiter appeared with their food. *Jesus Christ.* Her cheeks turned as red as the tomato in her burger.

Yaz laughed.

Hazel stooped closer, keeping her voice low, still glaring at Yaz for forcing her to embarrass herself. 'Just sex? That's the top advice from an asexual? Get a fuck buddy?'

Yaz bit through a chip, steam rising in a plume. 'No, no. Not one of them. It's called a situationship,' they smirked. 'Keeps things casual, having all the fun of a relationship without labelling it.'

'That sounds ridiculous.'

'Look,' they said, waving the still-steaming chip around. 'You're better in a relationship. But you don't want a relationship. Just call it a workaround.'

Hazel scowled.

'I just want you to be happy,' Yaz said, and popped the rest of the chip into their mouth.

BOOK CLUB ROLLED AROUND QUICKLY and Hazel couldn't wait to get stuck in. She'd never thought a reading group would be for her, but (and no one was more surprised than her about this) she'd enjoyed discussing *The Seven Husbands of Evelyn Hugo* with Charlotte over the last few weeks. Not to mention checking in with Louise at certain pivotal points in the book, seeing if she was there yet and what her thoughts were. It had been great fun.

This time around she had something to bring to the table and was excited to hear what the others thought.

'No Jordan?' Charlotte asked as they took the same seats as last time in the semi-circle, Jordan's chair still empty.

'She's in Berwick,' Tasha informed, pushing her glasses up her nose. 'So we might actually have a proper discussion tonight.' She attempted to jest but her serious undertone seeped through.

'Now, now.' Louise mock-scolded as she entered the room, coffee caddy in her hands.

Hazel gulped, Yaz's words fresh at the sight of her. They'd chatted plenty via text but actually seeing Louise brought the dilemma zipping to the forefront of her mind.

It felt dirty to have even considered it. Like she was taking advantage of Louise. She didn't seem the type to just want sex. Hazel didn't even know if she was capable of it herself.

She took in Louise's messy bun and the way her polo was tucked into her jeans just at the front, hinting at the form that lay beneath.

Could she?

Hazel looked away, deciding to focus on the book in her hands instead.

She'd googled what Yaz had called it: a situationship. *A romantic or sexual relationship that is not considered to be formal or established.* Sounded a lot like a silly word made up by youngsters who were scared of commitment.

It wasn't that Hazel was scared of committing, though. It was the potential hurt that pulled the brakes on any feelings she might be fostering. She'd made the mistake of giving her heart to the wrong person before – stupidly thinking they could get married as well, how wrong could you be?! Her head obviously wasn't to be trusted. What was to stop her making the same mistake again and again?

It would kill her.

Yaz was right though. Being in a relationship did make her happier. She could already feel it with Louise. Waking up to a good-morning text was the right way to start the day.

Then there was the other stuff, the not-so-tangible parts. Having someone in your corner, no matter what. Someone who has your back, no matter how bad your day's going. No longer navigating life as a solo traveller. No longer alone.

She'd looked it up, to see if she was a needy mess or if there was science to back it up. The jury was still out on the first part, but Hazel was pleased to find being in a relationship released 'happy hormones', so she wasn't a total loser for feeling this way.

So there was method to her madness.

Louise made her feel good, so why not pursue it? She deserved to feel good after the crap she'd been through in the last year.

But could you really have all the perks of a relationship without putting a label on the damn thing?

How would she even approach this? *Hey Louise, you fancy me, yeah? Awesome, well, I fancy you too. Let's date but not really, we'll just fu—*

'Hazel? What do you think?' Louise asked, cutting through her thoughts with such force it made Hazel snap to attention, her eyes wide.

'Huh?'

'Do you think it's fair?'

Hazel looked at the circle of women staring at her, searching their faces for a clue as to what the heck she'd missed. Sweat bloomed on the back of her neck.

'Is it fair?' Hazel repeated tentatively, as if she was considering the question.

'That Evelyn tells her husbands' stories when they're not there to defend themselves,' Charlotte whispered, not very subtly.

It was a welcome reprieve though. 'Oh right, yeah. Erm, I think if they were going to do such shitty things they can't really complain. If you don't want your actions discussed, don't do stuff you're ashamed of.'

Tasha nodded, her eyes hooded as if deep in thought. Louise held Hazel's gaze, her head cocked to the side as she turned the words over, analysing them.

'But what if they regretted their actions?' Louise countered. 'Maybe if they were alive they would be able to give further insight, defend their reasoning.'

'They still did it, though. And it's how Evelyn felt, how it affected her.'

Louise opened her mouth to respond just as her mobile vibrated against the desk to her side. She scooped it up, a smile instantly appearing as she read the text. 'It's Jordan. She says *Needed more lesbians.*'

'SOME GOOD POINTS TONIGHT,' Louise said, hanging back to tidy up after the group had finished.

Hazel was lingering too, not quite ready to leave Louise's orbit. 'Thanks. It was a good book. It helped having Charlotte to talk to before today. And you.'

'Glad you enjoyed it.' She paused as if meaning to add something before having second thoughts.

They stood, Hazel painfully aware Charlotte was still here, chatting to Bex as she waited on her sister. Was it obvious she was stalling? Charlotte wasn't daft.

A part of Hazel wanted to ask Louise to go for a drink or something but it suddenly all felt too real. Like she'd dared to indulge in some twisted fantasy and reality was struggling to catch up: it couldn't really happen. She was perverse for even imagining it.

Stupid Yaz and their stupid advice.

'Right, I'd best be off,' Hazel said, checking to see Charlotte hadn't already done a runner.

'Actually,' Louise blurted, stealing Hazel's attention afresh. 'I was going to text you about this but maybe it's best I do it in person, in case things come out wrong again.' She was joking but pink still ghosted her cheeks as she smiled.

'Yeah?' Hazel prompted, goosebumps rising on her skin, unsure where this was going.

'Are you busy next Saturday? In the evening? Well, it'll be overnight, so Sunday too.'

Louise's cheeks darkened. She was cute when she got flustered, no denying it. 'Saturday? I don't think so.'

'Nice,' she replied, her eyes shining with excitement. She ducked closer, lowering her voice. 'The awards are next week and I'd usually ask Jordan but she's in Berwick; not that you're second choice or anything, I just meant it purely as friends.' She cringed. 'Right, anyway, will you come with me?'

Hazel grinned. 'Yeah, sounds good, count me in.'

26

L ouise put her suitcase in the boot of Hazel's car. They were only away for one night but she'd packed enough for a week. It never hurt to have options when it came to outfits.

Hazel obviously didn't share the same reasoning: her duffel bag was about a quarter of the size. Although, Louise had spied a dry cleaner's bag hanging in the back.

She closed the boot with a gentle slam before walking round to the passenger's side door. Her heart had been freestyling all morning. She'd woken at stupid o'clock, her insides plaited with a heady mix of nerves and excitement. Going for a job interview on Christmas Day would probably feel the same.

Coffee and breakfast hadn't gone down easy so she'd pretty much skipped lunch. She'd have to sort that before drinking tonight or there would be carnage.

She took a deep breath and opened the car door.

'Good to go?' Hazel asked with a smile. Louise focused on her reflection in Hazel's sunglasses and not the way the brunette's dimples popped. Her nerves were only just disappearing; she didn't need to rile them up again.

'Let's get this show on the road,' Louise replied, forcing her energy up to a ten.

It had almost been a surprise when Hazel had agreed to come. Lying in bed last night, Louise had wondered if she would have been better to go alone. She'd become a certified entomologist this last week. Her collection of butterflies was now so big, the National Museum of Scotland would likely be in touch soon. When Hazel had sent a post-run selfie earlier in the week, jokingly saying 'bet you wish you'd joined me', a frisson of want had travelled over Louise, the butterfly wings from her stomach fanning across her skin, creating goosebumps.

She should probably start the evening with a cold shower. Get her emotions under wraps.

At least things wouldn't be as steely as the last time they shared a hotel room.

'You nervous?' Hazel asked, and for a moment, Louise forgot she was probably talking about the award ceremony and not sharing a bed.

'A little,' Louise replied as they rounded the corner, leaving Oakbank behind. After passing a few offices on the mini-industrial estate they would be on the motorway: no backing out now.

'You'll be grand,' Hazel reassured. 'Got your big speech planned?'

Louise scoffed. 'As if. Being nominated is enough. There's not a hope in hell I'll actually win.' Still, there was a little bit of paper stuffed in the zippy pocket of her bag. A short list of people to thank, just in case. Was always good to cover all bases.

She watched as Hazel grinned, her eyes fixed on the

road ahead as she negotiated the roundabout. 'I suspect you'll be in for a big surprise.'

'Hopefully.' Her phone buzzed in her gilet pocket.

Cameron: *Don't forget. BANANAS.*

Cheeky wee git.

'Everything okay?' Hazel asked, quickly glancing her way.

Louise laughed quietly. 'Just Cameron being a cheeky sod.'

'Takes after you then.'

Louise exaggerated her outrage, only just remembering she couldn't playfully hit Hazel unless she fancied swerving into the outside lane at speed. 'Excuse me, when have I ever been cheeky?'

'Book club. I'd give you an example but there's too many to choose from. Plus, the other night, you texted me a photo of a potato smiley and said it reminded you of me.'

'That wasn't cheeky, that was endearing. Plus, it really did. I mean, you were always smiling on our walk to Inveroran.'

Hazel chanced a quick look Louise's way and rolled her eyes. 'See.' She paused for a second as she flipped to serious. 'He's okay though?'

'Oh, yeah. We just have this thing. It's silly.'

'Yeah?'

'It's just, if he's ever in trouble, we have this thing where he can just text me *bananas* and I'll come to him.'

'Bananas? Why did you choose that?'

She shrugged. 'It's not really the type of thing you could text by mistake, like with another context. Well, not unless we were doing a shopping list, I guess,' she replied, her brow creasing at the fact she'd never considered that. 'But anyway, it felt the safest choice.'

Hazel nodded, her lips pressed together in impressed agreement.

Louise continued: 'So he texted saying not to forget our safe word, as if I'd need *him* to come get *me*.'

Hazel chuckled. 'You think you'll be getting into trouble tonight?'

Louise watched as Hazel's forearms tensed, her grip steady on the steering wheel. A large dotwork peony flexed as she wiggled her fingers, as if they were getting stiff.

Tattoos had never been a thing for Louise but forearms were always her weakness. She'd apparently found a winning combo as now she was lucky to be sitting down: her legs were like jelly.

'I guess we'll just have to wait and see what happens.' It came out way flirtier than intended, her inner monologue taking control of her tone.

Shit.

'I guess, so,' Hazel replied, her voice just as low.

SHIT.

THE ROOM WAS NICE. Basic but nice.

The awards were being held in a massive hotel just outside of Edinburgh. Despite only checking in twenty minutes ago Louise couldn't remember what the name was. Holiday Inn. Premier Inn. Jurys Inn. Days Inn. She was Inn somewhere, a big chain anyway.

The decor held no clues: stay in one chain hotel, you've stayed in them all. The massive double bed was made with crisp, white linen sheets and big fluffy pillows. An abstract print hung above the bed – was it water or a hillside? Maybe both. And to the right of the bed were two hard armchairs, should you wish to admire the views of the motorway and industrial estate in the distance.

It was just for one night, though. It didn't need to be The Ritz.

'What do you want to do?' Hazel asked, as if they weren't in the middle of nowhere.

That was the good thing about this venue though: the awards were held in the massive event room downstairs. It even had a private bar. They might have had to travel to get here but everything was within walking distance now.

Louise looked at her watch. Two hours to go. 'I say we get ready. Billy usually has us round to his room for a few pre-drinks before the actual event.'

'Community liaison officers can handle their booze, then?'

'Well, I can only speak for myself,' Louise replied with a wink. 'The gym team, not so much.'

'Must be a Perth thing. We did okay in Glasgow.'

'You ain't in Kansas any more.'

Hazel chuckled. 'So who's going first?'

'For shots? Not me.' Louise remembered her empty stomach. 'Actually, do you think they do room service?'

'No, you goose. For the shower? And yeah, they probably do something. I think I saw a menu by the TV. You hungry?'

'Should probably line my stomach. I've not exactly eaten a lot today.'

'So you are nervous,' Hazel said with a wry smile. Before Louise could protest she was standing toe to toe with her, hands on her shoulders, their gazes locked. 'Tonight will be brilliant. You'll be brilliant. Course they're going to pick you. And if they don't? It's a bloody fix; screw em.'

Going by Hazel's expression Louise was meant to laugh here. She forced a chuckle, not having heard a single word.

Her brain was melting at the feeling of Hazel's hands gripping her shoulders, only her thin T-shirt to keep them apart.

Christ. When had things slipped from possible infatuation to this?

They were texting a lot. And Hazel had joined them on the Walkie Talkie this week, having kept Louise company most of the route as Charlotte walked slowly with Marie now her cast was off.

That didn't account for how her stomach was fluttering. Or how her heart lurched at the fact Hazel was only inches from her face.

What a bloody idiot.

'Chips?' Louise blurted, taking a step back as if she was now on the search for the menu.

Hazel's face twisted with confusion but she didn't question the sudden shift in conversation. 'I dunno. I'm trying to eat healthier again. Watch my macros.'

'Mark who?' Louise asked, pausing her quest to locate the room service list.

'Macros. Macronutrients. So, counting the grams of protein, carbs or fat that I'm eating.'

'Sounds serious. Also sounds like chips are not going to fit that.'

'It is a bit serious. It's boring, sorry.'

'No, no, no.' Louise corrected her with an enthusiastic shake of her head. 'Not boring. Important, more like. Especially if you're going to PT again. I never really watch what I eat – maybe you could give me some pointers.'

At that very moment Louise must have passed through a wormhole or something because she could have sworn Hazel's eyes quickly flicked the length of her. 'I don't think you need to watch what you eat. But I'm happy to discuss it if you really want.'

Nah. That wasn't flirty. That was just professional PT talk. Louise made a mental note to learn about macros. If they were important to Hazel, they'd be important to her. For now though, she'd need a little guidance. She found the menu in the folder that was literally staring her in the face. 'There's a salad, does that fit macros?'

Hazel sidled up behind her, looking over her shoulder as she read. Was there no AC in this room? Where had all the air gone? She gulped, hoping to God Hazel didn't touch her or she'd feel her pulse thundering through every vein and muscle.

'Hmm,' Hazel said, the noise a low purr. 'See, the thing with macros is, sometimes you have to weigh up the calories too.' She reached round to point at the salad description, her arm grazing Louise's.

This is how I die.

Hazel leaned closer, her finger still hovering over the menu item, and her chest so close to Louise's back she could feel the heat. The gap between them was hotter than lava.

Another gulp, this time to will her breathing to a normal rhythm.

Hazel continued: 'See, it's got quite a heavy dressing on it, so probably super high in kcals.'

She retracted her arm and Louise could finally breathe again. She allowed herself another breath before attempting to speak. She felt like she'd just run up ten flights of stairs.

This was ridiculous. She needed to text Jordan, get a pep talk off this ledge, back into the friendzone.

'So. No salad, no chips,' she said, finding the courage to swivel and face Hazel. That was a bad idea: now they were nearly nose to nose again. She shifted her weight, beginning to pace as if she was deep in thought. 'What about a sandwich?'

'Bread. Condiments, who knows what else. Chips will be fine. Everything in moderation.'

Which was a fine philosophy for some. Louise's heart, not so much.

GIRLLLLL, you've got it bad, Jordan replied.

Shut up. You helping me or not?

Why's it such a bad thing? You're allowed to like someone.

Not if they don't like me back!!!!!!!!!!!!!!!!

She'd maybe been a bit heavy on the exclamations points there, but whatever, this was serious. Louise scooped a dollop of mayo onto one of her final chips before popping it into her mouth.

Hazel had gone in the shower first and was taking ages. It suited Louise just fine, gave her time to recoup.

Alright, alright. More dots. *You really don't think you can trust yourself?*

It's not that, she quickly typed back. The water had been off for a while: surely Hazel would be emerging soon.

It's just, we'll be drinking. What if I say something stupid? I can't even hold it together sober.

Well then, say something stupid. If she can't take the real you then fuck her. You should never have to hide how you're feeling.

Valid advice but not overly practical. Sometimes sense had to reign supreme: other people's feelings were relevant too. You couldn't go around telling your truth with reckless abandon.

Respect was just as important. Boundaries existed for a reason.

She texted back *okay* and was halfway to stuffing another chip in her mouth when Hazel emerged from the bathroom.

She had on cotton shorts and a sleeveless tee. Louise snapped her attention back to the towel she was tousling over her hair and tried to forget the fact Hazel most definitely wasn't wearing a bra.

Hazel's eyes flicked to the chip suspended in front of Louise's mouth. 'They not cold now?'

'A bit, yeah,' Louise replied, putting it back on the plate. They were fine but her appetite was drowned out by the drumming of her heart, like the organ had miraculously grown twenty sizes in the last ten seconds. 'Is it cool if I go in now?'

'Yeah, sorry for taking ages. Perfection takes time.'

Louise scrambled to the bathroom, almost knocking the chips off the bed in the process.

She whacked the heat down, hoping the cold would wash away these twisted feelings and shock some sense into her.

Rummaging through her toiletry bag a realisation hit: she'd left her PJs in her case. So she'd either have to get fully dressed again or go out in a towel. She'd considered bringing her dress in here but that was overkill. Wasn't worth the risk of getting it wet, either.

She eyed the door. Hazel was probably half naked now.

The mental image flashed through her mind before she had a chance to stop it. She cringed so hard her teeth ached. *Nope.*

A towel would do. Hazel would need to give her space to get ready regardless.

She stripped off and hopped in the shower before she could talk herself into adding a little heat.

A silent yelp escaped as the water hit.

Maybe a little heat. She turned the faucet, bringing it closer to an acceptable temperature.

This was fine.

She squeezed a blob of shampoo into her hair, using her fingers to get a lather going.

Outside, a hairdryer roared to life.

Was this what it was like to have a *crush*?

She'd experienced it fleetingly in high school, but it was different then. Loads of feelings but a small chance of payout. Not that she would have done anything, anyway. Regardless, at that age, in Perth at least, out-and-proud lesbians were few and far between. Plus they were at that awkward age when kissing felt like a huge milestone.

Now they were adults. Both openly gay and both definitely not virgins.

Or at least Louise assumed so. Maybe Hazel was saving herself for marriage. Or maybe she'd had loads of lovers. Louise was somewhere in the middle. She'd slept with one woman. Kissed...she did the maths. *Christ.* Strike that, reverse it: kissing was still a huge milestone for Louise. She couldn't even fill the back of a stamp with women's names she'd locked lips with.

Plenty experience with guys, but—

'Shite.' She winced as shampoo went in her eye.

She let out a ragged breath as she rinsed it clean.

This was not worth getting into a tizzy over. So she had feelings for Hazel? She was human, she was allowed to have feelings. In fact, it was nice to know she was capable after so long.

The fact of the matter was: Hazel didn't like her back. So she had to put on her big girl pants and get on with life. She wouldn't be heartbroken or anything, but it was a waste of time to continue thinking this way.

Dead end. You shall not pass.

She washed the remaining soap from her body and turned the shower off. No more hairdryer. She'd kinda been hoping Hazel would still be using it when she got out, to avoid stunted conversation as she grabbed clothes from her case in just a towel.

She brushed her hair, hoping to look as presentable as possible post-shower.

God, were there not any longer towels? This one barely passed her arse. One wrong move and Hazel would be getting an eyeful.

She yanked at the fluffy white cloth but the laws of physics hadn't suddenly changed, and it stayed the same length.

One final deep breath while maintaining eye contact in the steamy mirror, then it was all or nothing.

Louise opened the door slowly, just in case Hazel was still getting changed. When no screaming of indecency came, she stepped into the bedroom.

'Forgot my clothes,' she said rounding the open door. Her breath caught in her throat, her lungs frozen along with every other muscle in her body.

Hazel stood in front of the mirror, fixing her hair. She was so focused on the task it gave Louise a precious moment to compose herself before they locked eyes.

She had on the most perfect checked suit. Grey with subtle lines of hot pink and summer yellow running through it.

'You mean that's not your final outfit?' Hazel joked, running a hand over her quiff to smooth it.

When she turned and smiled, Louise had to mentally reboot.

The outfit was completed with a matching waistcoat.

The way everything was fitted so perfectly, you could tell it was tailor-made. Hazel looked a million dollars.

No wonder she hadn't packed as many clothes as Louise. When you looked that good, you didn't need back-ups.

Realising she'd been standing still for a silly amount of time, Louise willed her legs to resume their journey to her case.

She'd never been more acutely aware of being nearly naked.

'I'll just, er, I need to grab my . . .' There was no point trying to string anything coherent together. Inside, her mind was screaming.

Hazel said nothing: she just returned to sorting her hair in the mirror.

Louise squatted to her knees, keeping them as locked together as physically possible, all too aware of the breeze she could feel in unusual places.

Her hand was shaking so much, her mind so garbled, that it took her a minute to find her shorts and T-shirt even though they were pretty much sitting on the top of her clothes.

She stood and shot Hazel a thin-lipped smile in the mirror. 'I'll just . . .' she said, holding up the clothes in one hand, the other tightly grasped around the towel.

She scurried back to the safety of the bathroom.

Fuck me, she silently mouthed to the dripping shower.

After rubbing her hair with the towel for a final time she shoved on her clothes, the fabric clinging to her damp body.

Louise swept her hair over to one side, giving herself another glance in the mirror. Aside from the trembling of her lungs as she breathed, everything looked and felt normal. Hazel would never know what was going on in her head.

Take two.

She exited the bathroom to find Hazel now sitting in one of the armchairs, scrolling on her phone.

'You're looking smart,' Louise said, en route to her case.

Hazel slipped her phone into the inside pocket of her jacket. 'Thought I'd better make an effort, since the big prize-winner invited me.'

Louise rolled her eyes with a smile. 'No pressure tonight, eh?' She dipped to her case, needing to find her strapless bra before anything else. With shorts on, she was happy to take her time, although her last rummage had ruined any ideas of keeping her clothes neat.

'After a drink you'll be fine.'

Louise could feel the warmth of Hazel's smile on her back. She was just about to chance another look at her impossibly fine suit when someone knocked at the door.

Not missing a beat, Hazel stood. 'I'll get it.' She peered through the peephole and turned back to Louise, a smile quirking her lips. 'It's Billy.'

Louise grinned. 'Aww, nice. Let him in.' She rose, as Hazel opened the door, and pulled the lid of her case down, not wanting Billy to see her hunched over a sea of underwear.

'Ladies,' Billy said, entering the room in a suit nowhere near as heart-stopping at Hazel's. 'You ready to rumble? Louise, guessing by your attire you might need a mo?'

'Shrewd as always,' Louise replied. 'Hazel, you done?'

'Pretty much, yeah.'

Louise pursed her lips in thought, wondering if her

suggestion would put Hazel on the spot. In for a penny. 'Why don't you go with Billy? I'll be along in thirty?'

She could see the mental calculations fly past Hazel's pupils. *Shit.* Maybe she would have preferred to stay here and watch Louise amble about as she got ready. Seemed silly to confine herself to a bathroom when Hazel could be off having fun though, giving her the entire room. But that involved people she didn't know.

'Unless you'd prefer to stay here?' Louise added, throwing Hazel a lifeline.

'No, no, sounds fun,' Hazel said more to Billy than Louise. She smiled, a flicker of nerves making it droop.

'Just don't take too long,' Billy joked, already heading to the door.

'Me? Never!' Louise said before finding Hazel's gaze and bringing her tone to a more soothing level. 'I won't be long. Promise.'

With a smile, Hazel and Billy were gone, their chatter silenced by the closing door. As it clicked shut, Louise flopped onto the bed, arms wide like she was free-falling.

She was going to kill Jordan. Butterflies were one thing. A whole damn zoo was a step too far.

27

Hazel walked the long corridor with Billy, the busy diamond pattern on the carpet making her head ache a little. Why did hotels always insist on using the most garish motifs?

'So have you known Louise long?' Billy asked, making small talk.

'Since school. Kind of fell out of touch though, but we reconnected when I came back to Perth.'

'Aw, nice. Where were you before?'

Talking to people had never been an issue –she did it every day with her PT work – but she kind of wished she could have come up with an excuse quicker to stay with Louise, maybe have a drink just on their own.

There'd definitely been a moment when she came out of the shower. Hazel had seen how her eyes had trailed the length of her, the way they bugged slightly at the sight of her waistcoat.

It was a good suit. She'd got it for her engagement dinner and it cost a small fortune. It was either donate it or reclaim it: make new memories to fuse into its lining. The latter felt the best option. It was tailor-made. The chances of someone in Perth being her exact same measurements were a million to one. Good suits shouldn't be wasted. Especially not ones that made Louise look like she was wondering what it would be like to pop the buttons on it.

Billy looked at her for an answer, still striding at top speed down the hall. This place was massive. They'd need a map and compass just to get back to the room tonight.

'I was a PT, in Glasgow.'

'Sweet – your own business or working for a gym?'

'My own,' Hazel replied, with a wee shrug as if it was no big deal.

'Living the dream, eh? So you PTing in Perth now?'

Hazel scrunched her mouth from side to side. 'Not so much. Having a wee break. Although I think I'll start again soon.'

She'd pretty much decided it was happening. The enthusiasm to succeed was there. Motivation to start? Not so much.

'We're always looking for new team members if you need something in-between.' Hazel had no time to acknowledge the offer as he came to a halt outside a door. He was already onto a new conversation as he beeped the key card to the handle, letting them inside. He raised his voice as chatter spilled into the hall. 'Don't worry; there's not many of us. Hey guys!' Billy said, stride still unbroken. 'This is Hazel.'

Finally they stopped walking. 'Hey,' she said with a little wave, two guys and a woman staring back at her. They were also dressed to the nines. Hazel was glad she'd made an effort.

'So, this is my partner Helena,' Billy said, pointing to the brown-haired lady perched on the bed. 'And this is Rob and his pal Philip. Steve doesn't converse with the minions. He'll get us downstairs later.' He finished with a hearty laugh.

Rob chuckled as he sprung to life, grabbing a glass off the side table. 'You want a drink, Hazel?'

'What have you got?'

'Vodka and Coke.'

Not her usual choice but it would take the edge off being in a room with four strangers. 'Sure, why not?'

He poured a generous measure before topping it up with mixer. 'There you go, get that down your hatch. Catch up with Helena.' He winked – well, started to. It turned into a grimace when Helena smacked his hip.

Hazel took a sip, making a face. God, that was strong. 'So, are you guys all nominated?' she asked, leaning her bum against the table for support. Sitting down felt too formal, like she'd not know what to do with herself.

Billy nodded. 'Yep, so the two of us have nominations related to our departments. Or, if you're Louise, cause you're a friggin community rock star.' He mimed air guitar as he said it. Hazel couldn't figure out if Billy was always this excitable or if booze had loosened him up. He seemed a nice guy, regardless.

'So what are you up for?' Hazel asked Billy, taking another sip of the potent booze.

'The gym ran a scheme for OAPs to get them using the equipment. It's as much a social thing as it is technical. And Rob is head of kids' activities: his summer swimming initiative is up for an award.'

'Competitive swimming is totally dominated by middle- and upper-class families,' Rob added, clarifying what he did. Passion burned in his eyes, a smile instantly taking hold. 'So we created opportunities for other sociodemographics.'

'Very cool. The centre does a lot for the community, then?'

'Loads,' Helena confirmed, downing the rest of her glass. Which wasn't a small amount, going by the two big gulps it took. 'People just think it's a sports centre but it's so much more.'

Hazel nodded as a quiet descended over the room. Awkward and comfortable all at the same time.

Billy broke the silence. 'So, while she's not here. Louise is totally going to win, isn't she?'

Rob grinned. 'Totally. She's playing it down but we know she's got it in the bag.'

'What was she like at school?' Billy asked, adding more vodka to his glass. She was going to have to pace herself if she was to keep up with these guys. They were here for a good time, no doubt about it.

'Louise? We were in totally different circles,' Hazel replied, keen to put the past to rest. 'She's barely aged, mind.' Always good to deflect with a joke.

'You wouldn't think she had a teenager, would you?' Rob said in awe. Philip was being super quiet: maybe he was as out of his depth as Hazel was. He didn't seem the type to go solo, though.

'You know, I've still not met him,' Hazel said, the rim of her glass resting against her bottom lip. 'I was starting to wonder if he was real.'

'Oh, he's real alright,' Billy replied with wide eyes. 'Boy's a mountain now. I remember a few years ago he was a skinny wee rake of a thing, then woooooof,' he said, zooming a hand into the sky to mark how Cameron towered over him. 'Shot up to be this tall and made of muscle.'

'That's what you get for letting him use your gym,' Helena joked, a wry smile forming before she'd even got her next sentence out. 'You ever thought of joining him?'

'Hey! Two kids have taken their toll on me.'

Helena's smile said it was all in jest but she shot Billy a look anyway, hamming up the joke. He was saved a verbal ticking-off by a knock at the door.

He practically skipped to open it.

Hazel kept her glass to her lip, knowing before she'd even seen the full view of Louise that she was in danger of pulling a muscle as she fought the urge to grin.

She gulped, hoping it would keep her smile at bay as well as making sure her heart didn't leap up her throat and out her mouth.

Louise was beautiful.

And not just in a conventional way.

In a I-would-probably-walk-into-a-lamp-post-if-we-passed-in-the-street kinda way.

The last time Hazel had felt like this was seeing Ashley dressed up for their engagement announcement.

She internally scolded herself for comparing them, but her heart was having a moment, flailing in circles trying to put out a fire it didn't even know it had the matches for.

Louise locked eyes with Hazel over Billy's shoulder as he closed the door, biting her bottom lip as if she was a little embarrassed.

There was absolutely no need to be, though.

She'd straightened her hair, styling it to one side. Hazel wasn't sure she'd ever seen Louise with straight hair. And if she had it would have been years ago. She'd probably been too angry and resentful to take it in.

Her make-up was gorgeous: how she'd managed a smoky eye in that time was beyond Hazel. But mascara took Hazel an age alone; she'd never been one for getting dolled up. A little concealer was as far as Hazel went.

Then there was her dress. WOW. The almost floor-length garment was a stunning emerald green, so dazzling the Wizard of Oz himself would be taken aback by its beauty.

The figure Hazel had admired under polos and jeans was now accentuated in all the right places, as if the dress had been made especially for Louise. Maybe it was.

It was like she'd jumped into an icy lake. Hazel's breath was stolen, her heart rate speeding before slowing; Louise bringing calm into the room while simultaneously putting Hazel on high alert. Her body was in shock but Louise was the saving hand, pulling her from the water, air returning with a jolt as she smiled at Hazel. In a room full of people it could have been mistaken as a universal greeting but it wasn't: the smile was just for her. It thawed her out, warmth settling over her body like a blanket.

'Hi guys,' Louise said, beelining for Helena and the alcohol.

'Hey,' Hazel said as she passed, the word coming out as a purr.

'What you drinking?' Louise asked, peering into Hazel's cup.

The other four might as well have not been here.

'Vodka. And a splash of Coke,' Hazel replied with a conspiratorial grin.

Rob wasn't so courteous for Louise: he stayed seated while she poured her own.

'Everyone got a bevvy?' Billy asked, raising his glass into the air for a group cheers. 'Let's get this party staaaarted!'

THE EVENING skirted on boring all evening.

Thankfully, it never veered off the tracks and into Dullsville, due to present company. Even Chairman Steve was on top form.

Which was more than could be said for the table to their right. Hazel was sure one of the members had been asleep in their chair for the last half hour.

The hall was massive and set out with a few dozen round tables, each decorated with fancy white tablecloths and elaborate floral centrepieces. All eyes were on the stage at the front of the venue, with its large projector screen announcing category names. Swamped in the middle was a tiny plinth with a microphone.

It was the closest Hazel would likely get to the Oscars. Very glam, but thankfully with less paparazzi.

'I'm going for a wazz,' Billy announced to the group.

His voice was lost to the presenter on stage, a guy in a navy suit and red bow tie, introducing the next award. Under-Sixteen Fundraiser of the Year.

'Is yours soon?' Hazel asked Louise, leaning so close her lips almost brushed her earlobe.

'I think so,' she replied with a deep breath.

The table had come with two complimentary bottles of wine. Those, teamed with many trips to the nearby private bar, had taken the edge off the evening no bother. Hazel had watched Louise's shoulders visibly relax over the last couple of hours. Now her time was coming, though, the nerves were creeping back.

The room went quiet as the compère built the tension before announcing the current award's winner.

Hazel glanced at Louise's profile quickly.

Alcohol encased her senses but the memory of seeing Louise walk into the hotel room was still fresh: beer goggles weren't the cause of her new infatuation. Louise was gorgeous. She'd seen it before but tonight had confirmed it. Like a stonemason carving their initials into stone, Louise's beauty was permanently stamped on Hazel's heart.

Maybe she *could* do what Yaz had suggested. Or at least float the idea.

What was it Yaz had said? *You're better in a relationship. But, you don't want a relationship. Just call it a workaround.* That's all it was: a loophole. A technicality. An escape clause.

Ashley had obliterated her heart, but why did that mean she could never be truly happy again? If her head and heart weren't going to agree, then alternatives had to be explored.

Being alone forever was not a viable option.

Applause erupted around her and Hazel joined in, despite having no idea what she was clapping. A gangly teenage boy made his way to the stage, caught between being ecstatic and being a bag of nerves. Hazel would probably feel the same.

'I think I'm next,' Louise shout-whispered as the lad gave a short speech.

She maintained the tiny gap between them, as if waiting for Hazel to respond. Hazel searched her mind for an answer, her thoughts still straying elsewhere. 'Won't be long, anyway,' she finally managed.

'And now,' the compère said with gusto, 'the big one.'

*Ohh*s and *ahh*s popped through the crowd.

'Community Champion of the Year!' he continued. 'And the nominees are—'

Hazel's breath caught in her throat as Louise placed a hand on hers, gripping it tightly on Hazel's lap.

It was no use trying to decipher the names being read out; her brain was too distracted by the raw energy travelling up her arm. Every nerve was alive, tuned to a hundred, gloriously aware of every sensation.

'The winner is,' the compère said, pausing for dramatic effect. Louise gripped tighter. Hazel narrowed her eyes, desperately wanting to hear above the sound of the blood pumping in her ears as her heart went into overdrive.

She focused on the slow rise and fall of Louise's chest before darting her eyes to Louise's face, aware it might have looked like she was checking out her boobs.

'Louise King,' the compère boomed.

There was a split second where Louise did nothing. Soon, her face was flipping through emotions, before settling on utter shock. Her mouth hung open, her eyes already glossy.

'You did it!' Hazel beamed, squeezing Louise's hand with both of hers. 'Go on, do your speech.'

Louise was dazed when she stood, completely blissed out and overwhelmed in the best possible way.

The rest of the sports centre crew roared with delight, clapping louder than anyone around them.

The noise was almost deafening.

Still, Hazel's heart stole the show, thumping louder than the crowd. She watched as Louise made her way through the tables, her hand still deliciously warm from where Louise had held it.

Her chest swelled with pride as Louise took the stage, her glass award cradled to her chest.

'Thank you,' she said, her voice cracking. 'Thank you, I don't know what else to say.'

She held a hand to her brow and shook her head,

smiling so much Hazel's cheeks ached as she returned her infectious joy.

The crowd rippled with supportive laughter.

'Erm, thank you to Steve, our chairman, my team at Perth Sports Centre, all our wonderful staff and visitors. Gosh,' she huffed, interrupting herself. 'I'd written a list but I don't have a bloody clue where I put it.'

Another peal of laughter.

Hazel wanted to stand, scream and shout: *I know her!* Proud didn't cover it. She wanted to lift her up and put her on a pedestal.

Louise rounded her speech off with a few generic acknowledgements before holding the award aloft and getting another gigantic round of applause.

It wasn't long before she was back at the table, the compère now moving on to a round-up of the evening and a slide show of all the wonderful things achieved over the year.

'Did I sound okay?' Louise asked, slightly out of breath as she sat down.

'You were brilliant!' Rob boomed.

'Out of this world,' Billy shouted, complete with rock-on hand gestures.

'Fantastic,' Hazel added, giving Louise's thigh an encouraging squeeze.

Was that too much? She quickly retracted her hand. Louise was too caught up in the moment to even notice, though.

She held her fingers to her temple and grinned. 'Fuck, what the hell. Is this even real?'

'You betcha, baby!' Billy roared, reaching round to pass Louise a full flute of champagne.

'When did you get this?' she asked, confusion knitting her brow.

'Had a hunch. Got it while I was at the bar before.'

'People will be saying we rigged it,' Helena joked.

'To the Community Queen!' Billy toasted.

Hazel kept her eyes on Louise as she drank. Alcohol was fine, but Louise was a greater high.

28

She'd won. She'd actually bloody won.

Two glasses of champagne, a loo break, and a thousand strangers offering their congratulations later, it still hadn't sunk in.

She was half-expecting someone to walk up, take the award back and explain it had been a terrible mix-up.

'Here, finish this bottle off,' Billy said, leaning over her shoulder as he tipped the last of a bottle of white wine into her glass.

All this mixing was going to give her a lethally sore head tomorrow.

That was Future Louise's problem. Tonight, she was enjoying the moment.

She chugged the wine, lifting the empty glass with a whoop. The rest of the table followed suit.

'I'll go to the bar,' Hazel said, half-rising from her seat with a hand on the back of Louise's chair. 'You want the same again?'

She nodded, watching her leave out the corner of her eye.

Hazel's gaze hadn't gone unnoticed.

She'd not been subtle as she dragged her eyes over Louise in Billy's room. Okay, maybe not dragged, but she'd definitely taken Louise in, every inch of her.

It felt good. It had been a long time since someone attractive had checked her out. It felt different when it was someone you found alluring. There was a different weight to it. Hazel's eyes had settled on Louise's body and left a lasting mark, one that would give her a confidence boost for years to come.

Not that she needed someone else's approval to feel good in her own skin. But the thought of those eyes on her naked body would definitely bolster her ego.

Her phone buzzed. She flipped it over.

'Be right back, guys,' she said, getting up from the table with a slight wobble. 'Mum! Hi!' she shouted, putting the phone to her ear.

'You won!' Mum shrieked, making Louise pull it back, lest she go deaf.

'I know!' Would she ever have a conversation again without shouting?

Thankfully, things were a little quieter in the foyer. She passed the queue for the toilets and found an empty corridor. She took root by a pot plant, kicking off her heels since no one could see her.

'I'm so proud,' Mum gushed. 'And Cam too.'

He cheered in the background. 'Well done, Mum!'

'I'm still in shock.'

'I bet.' There was a pause; Louise used it to sink to the floor. 'You having fun with Hazel?'

Louise chuckled. 'Yes, and the rest of the gang.'

'You've not sent me any photos?'

'Of just Hazel, or are you accepting ones of anybody?'

'Har har. You, mostly. I bet you look incredible in that dress.'

It had been a toss between two she'd bought online. Louise didn't usually do green but there was no way she could say no to it once she'd shown Mum and Cameron: they'd flipped. She'd watched herself in the mirror, hands running over the satin gown as she smoothed it, and wondered if Hazel would do the same. As in flip out, not run her hands over her—

'I'll be sure to get you some snaps when I go back.'

'Of course, of course. You go back now, enjoy the party. And Louise?'

'Yeah?'

'Enjoy yourself.'

There was an undertone she couldn't quite put her finger on. It was well-meaning, anyway.

'Naturally.'

*Love you*s and *goodbye*s said, she hung up the phone, but she didn't stand. Her feet were killing her. When you spend the majority of your life in boots and trainers, high heels are a shock to the system.

Round the corner, music blasted. Time for Billy's favourite bit of the evening: dancing.

Good thing she'd had enough booze to cut some shapes.

She shifted herself up the wall, rolling her neck when she was finally upright. Her muscles were no longer tense with nerves: now they buzzed with lingering excitement. She was living in a dream.

Louise slipped her heels on, the balls of her feet instantly protesting, and made her way back to the event room.

She took a moment to grasp the situation.

The tables had been moved to the side to make room for

the dance floor – as was always done each year – but she now had no idea where her friends were.

In a sea of faces not a single one was familiar.

Hands appeared on her waist, but it wasn't like the surprise she'd received in the garden centre.

This time, Hazel glided to face her, hands locked to Louise's body, her palms running over the smooth fabric of her dress, leaving a trail of desire. She might have traced the equator of her hips, but Louise felt Hazel's touch swell in her core.

'Table's way down there,' Hazel said with an enthusiastic smile, her eyes shiny with alcohol. 'Want to dance before I show you where?'

How could she say no? 'Sure, lead the way.'

They lingered for a second, Hazel's hands still on Louise's hips, before Hazel pumped her eyebrows with a smile. It was a challenge, a silent question Louise was meant to decipher.

And if she was correct, alcohol-impaired conclusions aside, Louise was certain she knew what was coming.

An upbeat pop tune blared over the sound system as Hazel led the way, her hand in Louise's.

She never wanted to let it go. Was there a way to make her hold her hand all night?

They weaved through the dancing crowd, avoiding people pulling some serious moves, couples already taking the opportunity to get closer, and a good dusting of shoe shufflers.

Finally, Hazel was happy with where they were. She turned to face Louise, a smile taking over her face. She leaned closer. 'Now we're here, I suddenly feel really self-conscious,' she joked but the way her face was reddening left no doubt.

'It's easy,' Louise assured her, her last mouthful of wine providing just enough courage to be silly. 'Just move your hands and twist your feet.' She did her best rendition of a stiff dad dance.

Hazel's cheeks burst with laughter. 'You're kidding. Is that your best move?'

'What?' Louise exaggerated her steps, making her dancing even worse. She was only just keeping a straight face.

'I can't tell if you're being serious,' Hazel said, making a show of leaning back and watching Louise flail.

She couldn't hold it any longer and laughter spilled out. 'Okay, okay. I've no clue either.'

She looked around, hoping for inspiration on how to stand with Hazel. Anyone else and she would have just gone for it, let her body decide the moves. But with Hazel? The pressure was on.

Thankfully, Hazel took the lead. Ish. 'We could always do the sprinkler,' she joked, holding a hand to her head and stretching out the other. She turned on the spot, executing the move perfectly as she pumped her arms together.

'Or there's flossing,' Louise suggested, pulsing her hands back and forth inside and outside her legs. 'I've seen Cameron do it with his mates.'

'You're so hip.' Hazel pretended to be impressed. 'I guess there's the classic: cardboard box.' She forced her face to be serious and locked eyes with Louise as she did the hand gestures for little box, big box.

Louise creased with laughter. 'Love it! Well, how about this?' She kicked a leg backwards and hooked her ankle with her hand, her other hand on her head as she whipped her knee back and forth.

It was all going so well until someone stumbled into her, causing her to fall towards Hazel.

Her hands caught Louise's biceps, just in time. She looked over Louise's shoulder to check the other person was okay before her eyes found hers.

'You good?'

'Yeah.'

One look was all it took for them to explode with laughter, Hazel still holding on, keeping Louise steady.

'That's what I get for trying to be too cool,' Louise said once they'd calmed a little. Tears lined her eyes: she hadn't laughed like that in ages.

'You, too cool? Never.'

She playfully poked Hazel in the ribs. 'I don't know if that was a dig or not, but it sounded like one to me.'

Hazel wrinkled her nose in response.

Neither pulled apart.

Louise certainly wasn't going to be the one to break the moment but the silence hanging between them needed relieved. 'This is more of a slow dance move, isn't it?' Just to prove her point, she put her hands on Hazel's hips. Over her jacket. She wasn't quite that brave. Yet.

'True. I don't think it quite fits the music,' Hazel agreed.

They swayed together but couldn't quite make it work with the song's tempo. Pitbull's 'Timber' would never be a tune for atmospheric slow dances.

Hazel stepped back, biting her tongue as a devilish smile plastered her face. Their eyes locked, and in a flash, she was robot dancing.

Louise mirrored the moves, happiness washing over her.

29

Tonight had been a blast.

'Think that's me done,' Billy said, slowly patting Hazel's shoulder. Going by his glazed eyes, he'd been done a few hours ago. She wouldn't want to share a bathroom with him tomorrow. Or a bed tonight.

He flashed them both a lopsided grin and sauntered away.

'And then there were two,' Hazel said to Louise.

Chairman Steve had disappeared as soon as the dancing started and the other three hadn't quite made it to Billy's cut-off.

Now only Louise, Hazel, and a few dozen stragglers remained in the event hall.

She didn't want the night to end, but she also didn't want to continue it in the company of strangers.

Blame it on the booze, but the energy between them had shifted tonight. It was almost palpable. There wasn't one magic moment when it suddenly changed, but she could feel it now. The grand sum of a thousand tiny moments.

'I wish there was somewhere to get fresh air,' Louise said. It *was* stuffy.

Hazel pursed her lips in thought. 'Unless we want to wander around a car park, not much chance of that. But how about we go back to our room? Crack a window open?'

Louise smiled. 'I think my feet would prefer that plan, to be honest. These heels are killing me.'

Hazel cocked her head, looking at Louise's feet. 'We're inside. I won't judge you if you take them off.'

'Nah, people will think I'm lame.'

Hazel turned to the almost empty room. 'Hey, everybody!' she called and no one batted an eye. 'Anybody care if this chick takes her shoes off?'

Not a peep.

Louise playfully whacked her arm regardless. 'You've proven your point.'

Their eyes lingered on each other, gazes snagged as lazy, alcohol-laced smiles pulled at their lips. Happiness spiralled between them, an invisible whirlwind Hazel swore she could feel brushing her skin.

It was the same feeling she'd got walking up to Kinnoull Hill, times ten. Her body begged for more.

'Come on, kick those shoes off and let's go home,' Hazel said, her voice as dreamy as she felt.

'Home?' Louise replied with a smirk, shucking her shoes off to the side of her chair.

'Home, room, whatever. You've plied me with a lot of alcohol tonight.'

'Me? You were the one going to the bar every two minutes,' she joked.

Hazel scrunched her face up as she pushed her chair back. 'Had to keep the bubbles flowing for Her Majesty. Shit, actually, don't forget that,' she said, grabbing Louise's award from the centre of the table where Billy had made a temporary shrine of bottle caps and corks for it.

'I still can't believe it,' Louise said, getting to her feet, high heels swinging off her finger.

Hazel draped her jacket over one arm and extended the crook of her other for Louise to take. 'Well, you'd better. You're a muthafuckin' rock star.'

'You've spoken to Billy too much tonight.' Louise jested, looping her arm through Hazel's.

They wandered through the haphazard tables towards the elevators. Hazel pushed the button and they waited, still arm in arm.

Ping. The doors slid open and they stepped into the empty lift.

Hazel desperately wanted to say something but nothing felt right.

In their tiny cube, rising four storeys, there were no words. Just the heavy sensation of two people not doing what they were thinking.

What Louise was thinking remained a mystery.

But Hazel knew exactly what occupied her. She had a one-track mind: how to get Louise on board with a situationship.

She grimaced internally.

That word wasn't going to work for her.

Casual. Keeping things casual. That was better.

First call: ascertain if Louise *did* have romantic feelings.

Louise smiled, as if struggling for the right thing to say too. 'Did you have a good night?'

'Amazing. You?'

'How could I not?'

The elevator doors opened and they exited to the never-ending corridor of room doors.

Hazel would be the first to admit she lacked game. That was how she ended up going to a dating event and meeting Ashley.

Suave was never her style. Subtle could do one. And smooth? Not a hope.

'Billy is going to be rough tomorrow,' Hazel said as they passed his and Helena's room.

'I wouldn't like to be the one driving him home, that's for sure.'

Quiet descended again, and Hazel was acutely aware of how Louise's fingers felt wrapped around her forearm, the pressure of each digit like beacons on her skin.

'I hope Helena's got some plastic bags on hand.' Hazel scolded herself; this wasn't the topic of conversation they should be having. *Quick.* Back on topic. 'Shame we don't have anything in our room. A little nightcap would be nice.'

'You not had enough of my chat tonight?' Louise joked as they arrived at their room. A beat passed before she let go of Hazel's arm and produced the key card.

Hazel held the door open for her.

It was like they were doing another dance move, both skirting around each other, circling what was really going on.

A spark hovered between them. Hazel just had to figure out how to capture it: a lightning bug in a bottle.

Louise flung her shoes into the doorless wardrobe with a thump.

'Where do you want this?' Hazel asked, holding up Louise's award.

'Ohh, give it here,' she replied, extending a hand. Hazel passed it over and Louise clambered onto the bed, holding it above her head. 'Queen of the world, baby!'

'Shhh,' Hazel mock-scolded, finger to her lips after she'd dumped her jacket over a chair. 'You'll get us chucked out.'

Louise hunched her shoulders, pretending to look sheepish. 'Sorry.' She jumped off the bed, losing her footing slightly. Hazel steadied her.

Here they were again. How many more opportunities would the universe give her if she kept passing them up? *Fuck*. What to say? She searched Louise's eyes but came up short.

'I . . .' Louise started, before trailing off.

Even drunk as a skunk, Hazel was floundering. Quick, anything to keep her here, in the moment. Close to her. 'I had a lovely time tonight,' Hazel said, her voice soft. It was an echo of their earlier conversation but the fact bore repeating.

'Me too,' Louise replied, matching Hazel's volume.

She snagged the light in Louise's eyes, watching them twinkle, before flicking her gaze to her lips, then back to her eyes.

Light a match and this room would explode.

And yet Hazel had no clue how to start things.

Her breathing slowed: hopefully time would too.

'You looked beautiful tonight,' she ventured, dipping a toe into unknown waters.

'You looked amazing too.' Louise sucked on her bottom lip, her eyes never leaving Hazel's.

Only inches separated them.

Maybe words weren't the issue.

Hazel closed her eyes and the remaining gap.

For a brief second she imagined Louise had pulled away, then her lips found hers.

There was a moment of hesitation, Louise's muscles

stiffening under Hazel's hands as she placed them on her waist, then her lips moved in time with hers.

Hazel pulled her closer and Louise's lips parted, inviting her tongue inside.

This was a rush like no other.

All of Hazel tingled with an exotic high. Her core pulsed. The hairs on the back of her neck stood to attention.

Her head was swimming with one thought: kissing Louise was amazing.

Hazel gently pushed Louise onto the bed, quickly slotting between her legs.

Louise's brow creased but her eyes still burned with want.

She held a hand up at Hazel's shoulder, stopping her from dipping in for another kiss all the while still pushing down on Hazel's leg, the heat from Louise's centre like a fire on her thigh.

'I thought you just wanted to be friends?' she asked, breathless.

'What's the harm in having a little fun, just for tonight?'

Louise considered it before grabbing a handful of Hazel's shirt and pulling her close, kissing her hungrily.

Heavy breathing filled the room as Hazel pushed her thigh hard against Louise's core.

Her clit throbbed in anticipation.

Never in her wildest dreams had she imagined how good a kisser Louise was.

Her mouth was skilled in ways Hazel had never experienced.

She nibbled Hazel's bottom lip before pulling away, but close enough that their mouths grazed as she spoke.

'You're sure about this?'

'Deadly.'

She kissed her again and Hazel slid a hand along the bare skin of Louise's leg. She groaned in response and Hazel felt her own core harden.

This was going to be quick.

'Fuck,' Louise moaned into Hazel's mouth as her hand found the hem of her lacy underwear.

She dropped her mouth to Louise's neck, just below her ear.

Another desire-fuelled moan filled the room.

Hazel was so focused on the way Louise's soft skin felt against her lips that it took a second to register she'd spoken.

'Wait, stop.' Louise sighed, a hand squeezing Hazel's bum to get her attention.

She stilled, no longer able to take a breath. 'What's wrong?'

Louise pushed into the pillows, creating a little space. 'I just – I'm not sure.'

Hazel sat back, her heart tripping into action. *Shit.* 'Are you okay? Did I hurt you?' A thousand questions raced through her mind, almost as fast as her heart was now beating.

'No, no, it's just,' Louise said as her face fell. 'I'm not sure.'

'Okay.' That was all she could manage. Her stomach swooped as a heavy, sick feeling walloped her in the gut. 'Are you mad?'

'What? No! Of course not, it's just, I dunno.' She swallowed hard, shimmying out from under Hazel. 'I'm going to nip to the loo. Just gimme a minute to think.'

'Okay,' Hazel said for what felt like the hundredth time. *Fuck. Fuck. FUCK.*

Hazel stayed on her knees as Louise rounded the bed to

the bathroom.

This was bad. What had she done wrong? Apart from cross a line she could never take back. Why the sudden change of heart?

The bathroom door clicked closed and Hazel flopped onto her back, hands clasped over her chest, scared her heart would explode outward any minute.

She'd done this all wrong.

Should she leave?

This was going to be awkward.

FUCK.

She said *gimme a minute to think*: maybe that meant things were salvageable?

Hazel wanted to scream.

Why had she listened to Yaz? They'd put thoughts in her head, made her see signs that weren't there. Louise didn't have feelings for her. She'd made a mistake. Again.

She wasn't cut out for this.

Hazel ran her hands down her face, pulling at her cheeks.

Just as she was starting to feel at home in Perth, just as she was starting to feel like her old self again, just as she was starting to think she could maybe, possibly, somewhere in the future have a relationship again . . . she'd fucked it all up.

She wasn't ready for this.

Her heart was too fragile.

It was different when she was holding the sledgehammer, though.

Minutes passed and still no Louise.

Should she knock? No. She needed time; Hazel couldn't rush her.

With a sigh, Hazel closed her eyes and wished the ground would swallow her up.

30

L ouise woke first.

When she'd finally come out of the bathroom, after having a serious chat with herself in the mirror, she'd found Hazel asleep.

She'd been ready to talk last night, set some ground rules, ask some tough questions. But now in the light of day, booze only just ghosting her bloodstream, it all felt too much.

They'd need to address it, though.

Last night happened whether they liked it or not.

And had been good, really good. Louise had all but forgotten the rush of quick and lustful sex.

But she couldn't just go with the flow. Not when so much was at stake.

She slipped out of bed and padded to the bathroom.

Her head wasn't sore and she didn't feel sick. Which probably meant her hangover would hit later. There was no way she could drink as much as she did last night and not have repercussions.

After using the toilet she downed two glasses of water, hoping to at least dampen the severity of what was to come.

Her tongue was still like sandpaper.

She brushed her teeth, to little effect.

What now? Go back to bed and lie awake? Or play on her phone until Hazel woke up?

Probably her phone. She could text Cam, see he was okay. Waste some time on social media.

Distraction sounded like a good tactic. Otherwise she'd just lie there, turning things over in her head.

She quietly opened the bathroom door, aiming to tiptoe to the other side of the room: her bag was somewhere in the area. She could hazily remember dumping it near the chairs.

'Hey.' Hazel's croaky voice was like a gunshot in the quiet room.

'Hey, sorry, did I wake you?' Louise asked, changing her mind and slipping into bed by Hazel. It would be weird if she went on her phone now.

'No, I've been awake on and off all night.' She closed one eye as she rubbed a hand across her mouth. God, her bedhead looked cute.

Louise gulped, knowing it was now or never. 'So, about last night—'

'Hold on, I need to pee.' Hazel said, jumping out of bed.

'Oh, okay.'

With that, Louise was alone.

She pulled her knees to her chest, hugging them through the duvet. Nerves settled in her gut. If she wasn't careful they'd rage out of control and make a mess, jumble her thoughts. She tried to focus on other things. She'd won the award. That was bloody fantastic. And in a few hours she'd be back in her own house, their impending conversation just a memory. She stopped those thoughts from developing. *Award.* She'd won the award.

Thankfully, Hazel didn't take long to return.

She climbed in beside Louise, her stiff reluctance suggesting it was a bed of nails.

'So.' Louise started again and gave Hazel no room to interrupt this time. 'Last night. I stopped because I didn't want to be some drunken mistake, something you regretted in the morning.'

Hazel shuffled closer, propping herself up on her forearm. 'I wouldn't have. Promise.'

Louise shifted to face her, coming down to her level on her elbow. 'You said you just wanted to be friends.'

'And I do.'

'Friends don't do that,' Louise countered, forcing a smile.

'Not usually, but I, er—' Hazel scratched the back of her neck. 'I guess we need to lay everything on the table.' She let out a short huff of air. 'I'm not ready for a relationship, *but* I do find you attractive and I like hanging out with you.'

Louise's heart skipped a beat. This was news. 'So, what? You want to be friends who have sex? F—'

'Don't say what I think you're going to say,' Hazel said, cutting her off with a finger to Louise's lips. 'No. Not that. Just casual. That's the word. Just two consenting adults having fun. Casually.'

'Casually,' Louise repeated against Hazel's finger before she finally removed it.

Casual. Could she *do* casual? It had never been an option before: she'd never had to consider it.

Hazel mistook her silence for rejection. She flopped onto her back, covering her face with her hands. 'Silly idea. Sorry. You must think I'm mad,' she mumbled.

Louise scooted closer, meaning to place her hand on Hazel's stomach to reassure her, aiming squarely for her T-shirt. Instead she found bare skin under the covers where her top had ridden up. Hazel's muscles tightened at her touch but Louise stayed, enjoying the unexpected contact.

'What exactly is casual?' she asked, caressing Hazel's skin with her thumb as she closed the gap further, her body now pressed against Hazel's side.

Hazel lowered her hands, following her cue, looping one arm over Louise's shoulder to place her palm against her back.

'I guess we do whatever we want without putting a label on it.'

Louise smiled, unconvinced. 'That sounds flimsy.'

'Flimsy?' Hazel echoed, trying to sound offended. But her dimples gave her true feelings away.

'Yes. And that's how people get hurt.' Another brush with her thumb. Hazel responded by dancing her digits over Louise's back.

'True. Well, let's just keep doing what we've been doing – texting, hanging out, book club etc. – plus sex.'

'You make it sound so easy.'

'Why can't it be?'

'So, this isn't just a one-time thing, then?'

'Depends; you might be shite,' Hazel replied with a smirk.

'I don't remember you thinking I was shite last night,' Louise retaliated, her voice low as she teasingly closed the gap between their mouths.

'We skipped the most important part.' Hazel pressed her hand against Louise's back, gently encouraging her closer.

Casual.

Why not?

Kissing Hazel *had* been amazing. Sparks of joy lingered on Louise's lips, igniting at the memory. Her core begged her not to overthink this. She was an adult, a little fun was allowed. She knew the score. In fact, she was probably going to regret saying no more than saying yes. Heat pooled between her legs as she replayed the vision of last night in her head. She could feel that again: all she had to do was loosen up a little and take a chance.

Hazel's hot breath ghosted her mouth, pulling the plug on her busy mind. Her centre was in the driving seat now: common sense was overrated anyway.

With a flick of her eyes, taking Hazel in as she silenced the final inner critic, Louise put her lips to Hazel's.

She tasted minty.

Last night was a blur of alcohol and confusion. Now her focus was laser sharp.

She drove the kiss deeper as her mind did cartwheels. If only seventeen-year-old Louise could see her now.

In one swift move, Hazel tumbled them over, putting Louise on her back so they were where they'd left off last night. Her thigh pushed between Louise's legs and her core swelled as she ground down, her clit responding instantly to the pressure.

She moaned, unravelling with Hazel's touch.

It had been a while. She couldn't even remember the last time she'd touched herself.

Hazel's hand glided north, pulling at the hem of Louise's T-shirt. 'Can this come off?'

Louise arched her back, pulling the garment up. Hazel helped shimmy it over her head, biting her bottom lip as her eyes trailed over Louise's breasts. She may as well have been marking their journey with her finger; Louise could feel everything. Her nipples stiffened as Hazel's gaze lingered.

She opened her mouth to speak but had second thoughts, choosing instead to duck her head to Louise's left nipple, taking the taut bud into her mouth and sucking.

Louise pressed harder against her leg, her hands on Hazel's hips for leverage as she found a rhythm.

Hazel flicked her tongue against her nipple with a smile and Louise felt heat ripple through her body, settling between her legs.

The butterflies that had made her their home had fanned the flames inside, which were now spiralling into a twisted inferno, turning faster and faster as the heat ramped up. It was intoxicating. Louise's head was spinning. She closed her eyes, savouring the moment.

With every brush of her tongue Hazel brought Louise closer to the edge, all sensations on overdrive: amplified and exaggerated.

Hazel lifted her head, bringing her mouth in line with Louise's before tracing a line of kisses along her jawline, to just below her ear.

That was the magic spot and why she'd had to call time last night. Hazel's mouth on her neck was pure ecstasy. Last night she'd been seconds away from ripping her clothes off and coming there and then.

With a single kiss, Hazel brought her right back to the moment.

As if sensing her desperation, Hazel yanked at the waist of Louise's pyjama shorts. She lifted her hips and slid them off, kicking them down the bed.

Hazel kept contact with Louise's neck as her fingers skimmed her stomach, only just stopping at her core.

She opened her legs, inviting her in, gasping as Hazel's finger slipped between her wet folds.

Her breath stuttered.

Hazel pulled back, shifting position so she could get a better angle as her fingers found Louise's clit and started tracing lazy circles.

She pushed her head into the pillow. Either it had been a while or she had no real recollection of sex, because this felt like nothing she'd experienced before.

With every pass of her fingers Hazel brought her closer to the edge, desire pooling in her lower abdomen, swelling with each touch. Every time she thought she was going to pop it only served to get bigger.

Her skin tingled with anticipation, a satisfying sweat coating her body.

Hazel coaxed her closer, teasing with a new rhythm. Louise squeezed her hands around Hazel's hips, goading her on.

If this was casual she never wanted to be formal again.

'That feels amazing,' Louise said, torn between wanting this to last forever and finding release.

Jordan had been joking about sex being the answer to her problems but she was starting to see a kernel of truth to her thinking.

She bore down against Hazel's hand, intensifying her strokes.

And just like that, Louise was tumbling, running down a hill with no way of stopping, the only thing to do was lean into the moment, enjoy it for all it was.

She arched her hips, Hazel keeping her hand in place as she bucked, an aftershock shooting through her with a jolt.

It was like everything was falling into place. Hazel had taken her apart and was slowly putting her back together, creating a new, more alive Louise. It was like she hadn't even noticed she'd been walking through life in a hazy dream, and now Hazel had shaken her awake.

Her heart thumped so hard against her ribs that every beat was a pop, reverberating from her belly to her ears. She closed her eyes, focusing on her ragged breathing and the echo of bliss still ghosting her core.

Hazel pressed her hand into her clit, making her shudder.

'You're something else,' she growled, dipping her head to Louise's neck and making her want to do it all over again.

THE DRIVE HOME WAS NORMAL. No unspoken tension or awkwardness.

That was, until Hazel pulled up in front of Louise's house.

What was the etiquette here? Kiss on the cheek? Lips? Nothing at all? They'd had mind-blowing sex three times this morning; a high five wasn't going to cut it.

'So, erm, see you around,' Louise said, undoing her seatbelt.

'Yeah, I'll text you. Maybe we can meet up sometime before the Walkie Talkie. Wednesday?'

'Maybe. I'll need to check.' She paused, still unsure how to properly end things. 'Right, so, bye.'

Hazel smiled. 'This is going to take a bit of getting used to, isn't it?' She extended her arms. 'Come here.'

Louise went in for a quick hug and all uncertainty melted away.

Hazel kissed her on the cheek. 'I had a good time.'

'Me too.' She pulled back and cracked open the car door. 'I'll text you.'

'Okay.' She had one foot out the door when she got lost

in Hazel's dimple-fuelled smile. 'Shit, better get my case out the boot.'

Hazel shook her head. 'Need a hand?'

'Nah, I've got it.' She bounded out the car, shutting the door behind her before quickly grabbing her case. Hazel was putting the passenger side window down when she returned.

'You take care,' she said, flashing a grin that could get Louise into all kinds of trouble.

'And you. Bye, Hazel.'

'Bye.'

She was off.

Louise wanted to punch the air, act out a celebratory montage fit for an American romcom movie. She walked up the drive with a spring in her step: if she'd had braces her thumbs would be tucked under them as she strutted.

When she'd left the house yesterday she was mainly worrying about the ceremony. Now she was walking through her front door, award in her bag and a mind full of memories. Sexy, sexy memories.

Was it just her or was the sun shining a little brighter today?

'Hello!' she called out as she swung the door open.

It took two seconds for Mum to appear in the hall. 'Hello! There's my little award winner.'

Louise grinned. 'I'm going to nip to the shop, get some champers. You want anything?'

If any day called for fizz it was today. In fact, she was in such a good mood she'd let Cameron have a tiny glass too. Why not? Life was for living.

'I'm good, but I might join you, stretch my legs.'

'Okay. Just let me dump my stuff, then we'll go.'

She took the stairs two at a time and plopped her suitcase on the bed to be dealt with later.

She snagged her own gaze in the mirror as she turned. She looked the same but inside she was different: excitement buzzed in her veins, possibilities filled her head.

Casual was fantastic.

31

Hazel put her phone on her bedside table, her cheeks aching from having a permanent smile.

Three days had passed and it was a relief to find their momentum hadn't changed. She and Louise were texting with the same voracity as before, not an ounce of awkwardness.

Plus, flirting was now on the table.

Life was a breeze when you had someone to share it with.

Casually.

Of course.

A knock at her door made her sit up.

Charlotte.

'You got a minute?' Charlotte asked, looking the complete opposite of how Hazel felt. If Hazel was sunshine and clear skies, Charlotte was thunderstorms and rain clouds.

'Yeah, sure, come in.'

Charlotte trudged over before flopping on to Hazel's bed, narrowly missing her feet.

'Fancy going to the Beech Tree?' Was it just that Hazel's mood was head and shoulders above everyone else, or was Charlotte flatter than a pancake?

'With you?' Hazel asked, hoping to pep her up.

Charlotte huffed. 'Sorry. Doesn't matter.' She was only stopped from rising by Hazel's foot. 'Oi, get that stinky trotter away from me.' A smile flickered before being extinguished.

This was odd.

Hazel lowered her decidedly un-stinky foot. 'You okay?'

'Yeah, just got a lot on my mind.'

Hazel narrowed her eyes, sirens sounding between her ears. Charlotte *had* been weird the last few days.

Sluggish. Despondent. Grumpy.

It was like they'd swapped personalities.

Perhaps there was a secret happiness quota in the Paterson house. That would explain a lot.

'Is this about going back to Australia?'

'In part.'

Dad had asked about her return flights over Sunday dinner and Charlotte had nearly choked on her vegetarian Kiev.

Hazel was meant to be meeting Louise, though.

Not even a week in and things were getting tricky.

They'd agreed that the number one rule of keeping things casual meant not telling anyone, especially close family members and best friends. They wouldn't understand. They'd try and get involved, give advice when it wasn't asked for.

Which made finding alone time a squeeze.

Donna had a samba class this evening and Cameron was at football practice. That gave them a free hour at Louise's.

She was meant to walk round in forty minutes. It would be tight if she did something with Charlotte.

'I need to head out,' Hazel said, swinging her legs off the bed. 'But I can meet you after?'

'Where you going?' Charlotte asked, new life in her bones from Hazel's mysteriousness.

'None of your business.' That was too obvious. She added a smile. 'I'm meeting someone, an old PT contact. Nothing serious.'

'Sis, that's exciting. You going to PT again?'

She would never learn, would she? At this rate, her PT biz would be relaunched purely to carry through a lie.

'I don't want to say anything yet.'

Charlotte nodded. 'Okay, I get it. So, how long will you be?'

'His schedule is nuts so it will only be a quick thing tonight. I'll meet you at the pub around 7?'

'Sounds good.'

'WHAT DO you think she wants to talk about?' Louise asked, tucked under Hazel's arm as they lay naked and sated in bed. She lazily traced a finger over the geometric tattoo on Hazel's chest, bringing out a fresh flush of goosebumps.

'Not a clue, but she's being really weird.' She laced her fingers with Louise's, stopping her fingers dance. She had to leave in ten minutes to avoid the Kings: they couldn't risk an encore.

'Pregnant.'

'Huh?'

'Maybe she's pregnant.'

'Nah. She wouldn't tell me first.' Would she? Hazel cast

her mind back. She'd seen Charlotte drink, hadn't she? Nothing stood out, apart from taking her to meet Nina and Stacey. But she hadn't actually seen her have alcohol that night. They weren't the kind of family to have a drink with dinner or share a bottle to unwind in the evening. In fact, she'd not even see Charlotte touch the whisky Mum had got her at Castlehill Farm.

'Dunno, would explain a lot.'

'Wouldn't she want to go home though? As in, back to Oz? That's where Jimmy is.'

'Maybe it's not his.'

'Louise—' Hazel's pretend offence was cut short by an alarm blaring from Louise's phone. 'What's that for?'

Louise untangled herself and silenced her mobile before answering. 'Didn't want us to lose track of time.'

'So you set an alarm?' Hazel smirked.

'Yes. One of us has to be organised.'

Hazel scooped her close, playfully nibbling between Louise's shoulder and the base of her neck. 'Oh, I'll organise you.'

Louise giggled, which only encouraged Hazel to act out more.

'Whoa, whoa.' Louise gasped, still giggling between words. 'Remember the rules.'

'No marks, I promise.' Hazel pressed two fingers to the bottom of Louise's ribcage and a love bite she'd left earlier. 'Not where the public sees, anyway.'

Desire flashed in Louise's eyes and Hazel felt it leap straight to her core. No time: it would need to be saved until their next stolen moment.

'I'd better go,' Hazel said, her voice a near whisper.

Louise didn't argue. Crack their heads open and they'd both be thinking the exact same thing.

She watched as Hazel got dressed.

'Should you not be . . .?' Hazel asked, motioning a hand up and down her top.

'Nah, I'm always swanning about the house naked at half six on a Wednesday evening.' She paused for a beat, a hazy smile plastering her face. 'Just enjoying the show.'

Hazel shook her head, biting her cheek to stop the grin spreading. 'Don't be bad.'

Louise stuck her tongue out between her teeth. 'Never. Now, you'll text me, yeah?'

'Of course.'

'I mean about your sister.'

'Oh, yeah. As soon as I know, you will too.' She ducked in for a kiss and let it linger until the last possible second, any longer and she would never leave. 'Can I get some water before I go?'

'Course, I'll get you downstairs in a sec.'

Hazel strolled downstairs as she checked her phone. Yaz had texted, asking if she'd been up to anything exciting today. If only they knew.

After a few goes she found the glass cupboard and filled one up from the tap. She gulped the ice-cold liquid as if she'd been lost in the Sahara. Sex was thirsty work.

'Mum?' Cameron's voice called from the hall as the door closed.

Hazel froze mid-glug.

The sound of a heavy bag thudding to the floor and shoes being kicked off was the only thing to rival the hammering of her heart.

She swallowed the water in her mouth as quietly as she could, just in case Cameron had supersonic hearing.

Up until now he'd only been a concept in her mind. She'd seen baby photos in the house. His Lynx body wash in the bathroom. A scruffy schoolbag by the door. But nothing concrete.

Didn't matter: a second later he was in the doorway, doing a double take. His T-shirt was covered in blood, the remains of a nosebleed on his face despite obvious efforts to clean up.

'Oh. You're my mum's friend, aren't you?'

Billy hadn't exaggerated: he was tall. He'd inherited Louise's thick wavy hair, only a few shades darker, and by the way it was sticking out at all angles, someone had put him through the wringer at football, which probably explained the blood.

'Hazel,' she muttered, because remaining silent would be weird. Her heart still pumped at an extraordinary speed, taken off by the sudden interaction. She swallowed hard, clinging to her steely demeanour. 'You're home early?'

'Nosebleed. You're a personal trainer, yeah?'

Hazel's shoulders relaxed. Apparently Cameron wasn't fazed: in fact, his eyes were shining with genuine curiosity.

'I am. Well, usually. Between jobs at the moment.'

'So, like, can you do plans for people? Now I've got a job I can't go to the gym as much and, well . . .' He trailed off, as if he'd lost the confidence to continue. He scratched the back of his neck and inadvertently showed off a still-impressive bicep.

'Understandable. You got weights?'

'Dumb-bells,' he replied, the light of excitement back in his eyes.

'Yeah. I can do a plan. Do yo—'

Either a herd of rhinos was coming downstairs or Louise was en route.

Hazel and Cameron looked towards the noise in the hall, just as she flew around the corner, still straightening her top and her cheeks flushed. Hazel sucked on her lips, hiding a smile. *Super subtle, Lou.*

'Cameron, hey, what are you doi—Christ, what happened to your face?' she asked, slipping into mum mode.

'Took an elbow to the face. Stacks drove me home,' he replied, dodging Louise's inspective hands.

'Stacks?' Louise repeated, still pawing at his face.

'Yeah, his parents are rich.'

'I don't get it.'

Hazel smiled as she put her now empty glass into the sink. Didn't matter that Cameron was a head above his mother; he wasn't getting away without being checked over.

'He's got *stacks* of cash.'

'Oh right,' Louise said, not impressed by the ingenuity of the nickname. She gently held her fingers to his nose. 'Do you think it's broken?'

'I'm going to head,' Hazel said, trying to slip by the ducking and diving duo.

Cameron finally broke free. 'Wait, you think you can put something together for me?'

'Yeah, course. I'll give Lou—your mum, a programme to pass on.'

'Yass, thank you.'

She shot Louise a look that said *I'll explain later.* 'Right, best be off.' This was weird. Her limbs felt all wrong, indecision paralysing her. How to say goodbye? She settled on a half-arsed tiny wave. 'Bye, guys.'

Despite the unexpected ending, she thought about Louise the entire walk to the pub, a goofy smile making her lips twitch. Today was a good day.

～

CHARLOTTE WAS ALREADY THERE when Hazel arrived. She'd taken her order and headed to the bar, taking pity on her mopey face and putting her hand in her pocket for the first round.

'Your wine,' Hazel said, placing the glass in front of her sister.

Hazel took a seat as Charlotte took a long, slow sip. Not a word. She'd never been this quiet in her life.

But definitely not pregnant though. It was a start.

'Right. Come on, who are you? Where is my sister?'

Charlotte smiled but as soon as their eyes locked her lip wobbled.

Hazel put a hand on hers and squeezed.

Thankfully, the Beech Tree's snug was empty tonight: they were the only punters here. Even the barman had pushed off next door after he'd served them.

'I'm sorry,' Charlotte squeaked, pushing her fingers into her eyes.

'Charlotte, what's going on? You're scaring me now.' Hazel sipped her Coke even though she didn't really want it. Her stomach was swirling with nerves but she had to do something; she couldn't just sit here waiting for a response, buzzing with anxious energy.

Now finger-free but rimmed with tears, Charlotte's eyes were glossy with emotion. 'I don't really know where to start.'

At the beginning sat on Hazel's tongue, but she washed it away with a glug of Coke. Charlotte didn't seem in the mood for jokes. 'You don't want to go back to Australia? Is that it?'

'A bit.'

'A bit,' Hazel repeated, wondering what was the quickest way to get blood out of a stone. 'What does Jimmy think about you staying here?'

Another wobble of the lip. Charlotte's eyes fell to her wine as she played with the glass, twisting its stem between her fingers. 'We broke up.'

Ah.

Shit.

'Sorry.' A thousand questions floated to the surface, but having been on the receiving end of most of them in the last twelve months, Hazel knew none were appropriate. 'Do you need me to kill him, or did it end okay between you?'

'It was me that ended things.'

Hazel nodded: that changed things. Break-ups still hurt though. 'You don't need to tell me why if you don't want to.'

'No, no, I do. That's why I'm here. I feel like I'm going to explode if I don't tell anyone,' she said, squirming in her seat.

'What about Nina? Or Stacey?'

'I can't tell them. They'll *judge*.'

Intriguing. 'Okay . . .'

'Sorry. I know this is a lot to put on you, but we're family so we look out for each other, yeah? You've always got everything so figured out. I just need a little guidance.'

Hazel tensed her jaw, picking her sister's sentence apart. So much to digest. Was Charlotte talking about the same person?

'You think I've got everything figured out?'

Charlotte waved a hand in Hazel's direction. 'You're modest, I get it. But—' She picked up her half-full glass and downed its contents. 'I need another drink.'

'Sure,' Hazel replied, the word lasting the time it took for Charlotte to stand.

She wanted to text Louise, but *WTF* wasn't enough. She'd barely scratched the surface and already this was weird as heck.

She glanced at her sister as she waited at the bar.

Was this a wind-up? Her mood suggested it was real but the whole thing was so out of character, it couldn't be more off if it tried.

They were still in a relationship on Facebook: she'd seen it when she'd done a little snooping, trying to figure out why Charlotte was staying so long. But maybe they had their reasons for keeping the break-up quiet. Or they'd simply forgotten. Jimmy was never a social media guy; it was Charlotte who lived her life online.

Finally, the barman appeared, serving Charlotte another large white wine. If she tried to down this one, Hazel was going to have to pull the sensible big sister card. She wasn't carrying her home, no way. Mum's leg was still too weak for driving and there wasn't a hope in hell Hazel would risk paying a fine in a taxi for Captain Charlotte Upchuck.

Hazel locked her gaze on the drink as Charlotte wandered back to the table, as if the answers could be found floating in the glass.

She'd barely sat down when Hazel spoke.

'Okay, so. This seems complicated. Why not go back to the beginning? You weren't happy with Jimmy, no?'

Charlotte's face crumpled but she kept it together. 'I was happy with Jimmy. He was a great guy, it's just everything changed.'

'How so?'

She shrugged. 'I've had this conversation in my head so many times but now it's happening it's all garbled.'

'That's okay. Take your time.' Hazel couldn't remember the last time they'd had a serious conversation, if ever.

Once, she'd caught Charlotte crying her heart out over a boy called Timothy Jones at a house party and had to forcibly remove a bottle of White Lightning cider from her grubby little fifteen-year-old paws, but that was it.

'I wasn't happy in Australia for a long time. It was Jimmy's dream, not mine. In fact, I started to hate it.'

Hazel sat back, shock stiffening her shoulders. 'I thought you loved Australia?'

'Nope.'

'All you've done is say how much you love Australia. You can see the confusion, yeah?' Hazel smiled: if this was going to be a serious topic she'd do her best to stop Charlotte sinking too deep.

She forced a smile. 'I could hardly be honest. Mum and Dad would have kittens.'

'True. Well, that's okay. They'll love having you back! Why are you worried about telling people?'

'I'm not finished yet.'

'Ah.'

Suddenly eye contact was impossible. 'I told Jimmy I was unhappy and we tried to make things work, we really did.'

'Uh-huh.'

'He thought maybe some clubs would help, you know, get me back to loving life down under.' She paused, momentarily snagging Hazel's stare. 'I'm sorry for everything that happened with Ashley. I should have been a better sister.'

'You couldn't have done anything, you were on the other side of the world. You don't need to feel bad about anything.'

'I know, but, I was going through my own stuff and lost sight of what mattered.' She took a long draw of wine and Hazel was poised to stop her downing it. She relaxed when Charlotte placed the glass back on the table. 'You've been so strong through it all, it inspired me to take control too,' she continued.

'I don't know about that. I've been a mess.'

'Hardly.'

'I slept on Yaz's couch for three months.'

'Mum said you were sharing a flat.'

'Semantics.'

Charlotte popped her lips together, her eyes narrowed to slits, as if Hazel had just burst a major bubble in her narrative. 'Well, regardless. I thought you had your shit together. I wanted that too.'

'Why did that mean you had to break up with Jimmy? He won't come back to Scotland?'

'He probably would if I asked. He'd be gutted, but he would. For me. Which is why I had to break up with him.'

Hazel scrunched her eyes closed, her mouth hanging open as she tried to find the right words. 'You broke up with him because he loves you so much?'

Charlotte tipped her head back and Hazel didn't know if she was going to laugh or cry. A strange little sound escaped, lodged somewhere between the two. 'I knew I was coming back to Scotland. It kind of became my D-day. My get-out. So I broke up with Jimmy. Well, he thinks we're just on a break.'

That explained Facebook. 'I still don't get why.'

'Getting there.' This time she downed a third of her glass, wincing as she swallowed. 'I, erm, I've been thinking about other *things* a lot recently too. So, the night before I flew out here, I slept with my surf instructor.'

Charlotte held Hazel's gaze as if hoping the rest would follow telepathically. It would never work: Hazel's brain had stalled at the curveball.

'Okay.'

'You know I can't do casual, so I figured that way, there was no chance to get attached. It was just a way to experiment, see if I was right.'

'If you were right?'

'Yeah.'

'About?'

'My instructor, they were, well, their name's Amelia.'

'Amelia. So, like a *woman*?'

'Yeah.'

'So you're . . . ?'

'No idea. But yeah, not straight, that's for sure.'

'Okay, so, like—' Hazel's words came out like a spluttering exhaust pipe. Nothing was gelling together. 'Not liking Australia is one thing, but being gay, where did that come from?'

'I dunno, you're a lesbian?' she said, cheeks fit to burst with laughter. 'Must be genetics or something.'

Hazel chuckled. 'I didn't mean it like that. I meant, have you always felt this way or what?'

'Yeah, I suppose. I mean, doesn't matter either way, does it?'

'Not really. So that's the issue? Or is Australia the issue?'

'Mum and Dad will be fine about Australia. Well, Dad will probably moan about my job prospects and stuff, but whatever. It's the whole Jimmy mess. What do I tell them?'

'Why do you have to tell them anything? You broke up, that's that.'

This was where they were so glaringly different. Charlotte was an open book with Mum and Dad. Hazel was a classic tome, kept behind glass: look but don't touch. They read the page she wanted them to.

'You don't think I should tell them about the other stuff?'

'Not until you're ready.'

Charlotte let out a slow breath through her nose, weighing up Hazel's suggestion. 'And what about the rest?'

'Huh?'

Her eyes drifted to the small window. 'I know you don't think you've handled things well but to me you did. What do I do? I had it all and now I have nothing.'

They might never have really seen eye to eye, but she'd always be her sister. Hazel would die for Charlotte, no questions asked. And the funny thing was: distance and age had only made that feeling stronger. She might get on her tits more than anyone else on Planet Earth but Charlotte Paterson was to be protected at all costs.

'Well, you're pretty caught up on my course of action. Fall apart, move home, live off Mum and Dad.'

Charlotte laughed under her breath, her features finally softening, like the weight of the world was off her shoulders. 'Christ, can you imagine all four of us back under one roof?'

'It's not going to be pretty.'

'I've applied for a heap of retail jobs. Flats are more expensive than they used to be, though.'

An idea flashed through Hazel's mind, but she wasn't ready to say it out loud.

She needed to speak to Louise first.

32

L ouise had only just managed to contain her excitement the next day, when the week's Walkie Talkie rolled around.

Totally normal to be excited to see a friend, yeah?

Hazel had been pretty cryptic about Charlotte but she said it was a lot, better explained in person.

That was probably why Louise's stomach had been churning all day with a fluttering furore.

Cameron's brief interruption aside, they'd not actually been with each other in the company of other people yet. Talk about jumping in at the deep end. Mum had a sixth sense which tingled at the slightest hint of change – if they could pull this off, they could do anything.

Louise mingled with the crowd, catching up with regulars. No new faces today, but every week can't be a winner.

She steeled herself at the sight of Hazel crossing the car park.

Louise put on her best 'listening' face as Veronica told her about her husband's bad ankle. In her head, her own personal highlight reel played as she picked certain points to rewind and replay: Hazel's triceps; the way she looked when she slotted between Louise's legs, grinding their cores together; the line of those glorious PT abs and how they felt under her tongue.

'So, of course he's ended up with a support brace,' Veronica concluded.

'Terrible.'

'And what about you?'

'Me?'

'Any news?'

'Same old, same old. Cameron's working in McDonald's now.' Hazel's eyes caught hers through the crowd and Louise's insides flipped like one of Cam's burgers.

'McDonald's? How do you feel about that?'

Louise knew what she was hinting at. Veronica was one of the more elderly, traditional-thinking walkers who also came from a suburb that probably thought eating with your hands was the height of bad manners, never mind working in a place like that. 'Money's good, it's teaching him some big life skills, and hey, cheap chips if I'm lucky. One min, I just need to do something,' Louise said, quickly scuttling away. She didn't mind talking to Veronica – who gave a rat's tooter what someone else thought of Cameron's job? – but it was almost time to get this show on the road. And the quicker that happened, the quicker she could segue into speaking with Hazel.

She stepped onto the large lip of the nearest concrete planter and clapped her hands together. Sometimes she did a little speech, announced updates or news if needed, but today wasn't one of those days.

'Ladies! Let's get walking!' she shouted and hopped off

the planter, waving a hand as if she was an enthusiastic tour guide.

A few soft whoops came from the back, but mainly everyone just swivelled, continuing their conversations at a pace.

Sometimes Louise felt like a modern-day Pied Piper.

She zipped her jacket up higher. The autumnal weather wasn't exactly on their side today but rain never dampened their spirits.

Louise remained at the front for a short distance before doing her usual and falling to the sidelines, giving the ladies a little space. She was a co-ordinator more than anything. She'd set them off like sluggish greyhounds; now it was their job to work the course.

She took her time, falling further and further back until she was right where she wanted to be.

Hazel flashed her a smile but kept talking to her mum.

All in good time.

In her head, Louise was rushing over, jumping into Hazel's arms and giving her a ginormous hug before yanking her back to the centre for some alone time.

In reality, they were twelve feet apart with a woman loudly discussing haemorrhoids between them.

There was a time and a place, Keira.

The worst part was: Louise had a solution for her. She'd message her later.

She slowed slightly, tuning Keira out.

Hazel matched her step, effortlessly switching to be on Marie's other side.

In one swift motion she crossed the group and fell into step beside Louise.

'Hey,' she said and Louise's knees came close to buckling.

'Hey.'

They shared a moment, a split second where only they existed.

Keira's loud voice ruined it.

Some people were born with a megaphone in their hands, Louise was sure of it.

'How's your week been?' Louise asked, biting back a smile.

'Uneventful. Got in a good workout yesterday, that's about it.'

'Is that so?' Louise's cheeks ghosted red, she would blame it on the weather if interrogated.

'Actually not,' Hazel gushed, dropping her head and tone. She quickly checked over her shoulder before continuing. 'Charlotte dropped a bomb and a half.'

'Come on then. I've been dying all day.'

'You have to promise, and I mean *promise*, not to tell anyone. Okay?'

Louise held a hand over her heart. 'Guide's honour.'

'Charlotte's not going back,' Hazel hissed.

'I kinda guessed that? Why?'

They looked around, assessing their neighbours. No one was close enough to hear but Hazel still dipped closer to Louise, her voice at its absolute lowest. She had to concentrate to hear over the surrounding chatter.

'Lesbian,' Hazel said so silently she pretty much just mouthed it.

Louise's mouth opened in shock. She switched to confusion with lightning speed. 'Really?'

'Well, no.'

Louise playfully slapped Hazel's arm before she could finish.

'Hold up,' she begged, laughing. 'It is kind of the truth.

She doesn't know what she is. But that's the gist of it. I'll fill you in on the specifics later.'

'She's okay though?' Louise had been genuinely worried something bad had happened. It was a relief to know something wasn't wrong.

'Oh, yeah. Just broken up with her boyfriend and hated where she lived. The usual.'

'Oh wow. Still, all things that can be fixed.'

'You're always so positive. How do you do it?'

'Someone's got to, balance out the old grumblers.'

'*The old grumblers.*' Hazel repeated, a glint in her eye. 'Better not mean me,' she jested, making a grab at Louise's side.

She swerved just in time. 'Careful. Remember we've got company.'

'Wish we didn't.'

'I was thinking, I bet when we loop past the centre we could sneak in. They won't miss us for the final lap.'

'No way. They'll totally notice we're not there.'

'Want to bet?'

Hazel pursed her lips. 'You're on.'

They shared conspiratorial glances as they rounded the final corner past the war memorial and finally arrived on the home stretch parallel to Rose Terrace, both keeping quiet as if being silent might make them invisible.

Louise's mind was full of visions of what they might manage, given thirty minutes alone in her office.

They slowed their gate, the centre coming into view.

By the time they got level with it, they were a good twenty feet behind everyone else.

'Will we go now?' Hazel asked, her pinky brushing Louise's as they walked.

'Yeah.'

They walked diagonally until they were at the edge of the path, the centre now a straight line in the direction they were headed. If they ran, they could make it, no bother.

Louise was giddy.

'Okay, now,' Hazel said, taking their walking from a normal pace to a purposeful march.

They got two steps before: 'Everything okay?' Hazel's mum called from the back of the pack.

Louise stopped, looking at the ground, hands on hips. She daren't look at Hazel or she'd laugh. 'Yeah! Thought I saw an earring on the ground.'

Hazel followed suit, pretending to look at the nearest patch of grass. 'It's nothing!' She lowered her voice to a grumble. 'Rumbled.'

'We'd better go back.'

They both kept their eyes to the ground, talking to the grass more than each other. 'They've seen us, they'll know something's up.'

'Nah.'

'Er, yah.'

'Fine.'

THEY'D JOINED the gang and completed the circuit separately. Sometimes you had to cut your losses. They'd had plenty of fun this week. Time to quit while ahead.

'So, when will I see you next?' Hazel asked outside the centre, the gaggle of women nearly fully dispersed.

'Not sure. I don't think I have a free house until Wednesday again.'

'That feels like ages.'

'I know.'

Hazel gulped. Louise was glad she wasn't the only one

feeling it, though. It was like being a teenager again. She ate, slept, lived for her next moment with Hazel. She woke up and Hazel was her first thought. And, drifting off to sleep she was her final vision.

Louise gave a small but decisive nod. 'See you when I see you, then.'

'Mum, I need to pee,' Hazel called over her shoulder.

'What are you doing?'

'You're going to your office, yeah?'

'Yeah.'

'Go on then.'

Louise didn't ask any more questions. She had no idea where this was going but she already liked it.

The giddy feeling was back, swirling in her chest, making her muscles buzz with energy. Walking felt abnormal: she wanted to skip. She would probably be sectioned if she started giving in to her Hazel-guided thoughts.

They quickly marched to the centre. Only one Walkie Talkie-goer in the foyer, using the vending machine to get a bottle of water. Louise gave her a polite smile as they burst through the staff-only door.

Finally, they were at Louise's office.

The door had barely clicked closed when Hazel had her up against the wall, lips crashing together.

Their heavy breathing filled the tiny office, escaping in the moments between pure lust, mouths open, needing more.

Louise's hand slid under Hazel's top, instantly finding her taut obliques. She grabbed, pulling Hazel closer. Her chest heaved.

There was no clear endgame. Her head was screaming

to do it there and then, logic out the window, but reality was a ticking clock.

Delight twinged low in her belly, her core aching for anything, whatever she could get. Even the slightest touch would satisfy.

There was no getting enough of Hazel. Even in bed they never quite felt close enough. Louise always wanted more.

She pressed Hazel closer, desperation replacing every cell in her body. Walking had been silent foreplay, teasing her close to the edge. Look, but don't touch. Want, but can't have. This woman was driving her crazy. Rational thought was impossible; her hunger was too insatiable.

Hazel pulled back, both so out of breath they may as well have sprinted twice around the Inch.

'I don't think we can get away with much longer.'

Louise shook her head, too breathless for words.

'I'll text you when I get in, yeah?'

'Yeah.'

Hazel kissed her, slow, just on the right side of naughty to leave Louise wanting more and not hate her for leaving before she could give it.

THE NEXT DAY, Louise looked at her phone. Again.

Nothing.

She put it back on the arm of the sofa and tried to focus on the film she and Mum were watching.

Some Sandra Bullock ensemble. It wasn't grabbing her attention.

She looked at Mum. She was enjoying it.

Phone again, just in case she missed something.

'I need a glass of water,' she announced, jumping to her feet. Mum mumbled something in response.

She padded to the kitchen. Got a glass. Filled it under the cold tap.

Hazel hadn't messaged all day.

Louise had messaged this morning, just as usual.

Hazel had read it, then . . . nada.

They'd agreed to casual, so maybe this was it. There would be days when Louise was ignored.

Didn't mean anything.

So why had it dictated her whole day?

The morning had been bad enough. She'd felt on edge. Work was a fine distraction, though. There were a lot of final loose ends to tie up for the holiday camps. Most of it involved talking to people or focusing on emails. No room in her brain for Hazel.

By lunchtime she was worried.

This was out of character. Had she done something to piss her off? No, their last texts were normal. They'd said goodnight to each other before going to sleep. She'd not said anything controversial this morning.

She'd considered double-texting but it felt *un-casual*. No sense freaking out at the first hurdle. Hazel would have good reason.

The afternoon was reserved for agitation. What was more important than her? It wasn't like Hazel had a job. God, had something else happened to Marie? She'd checked her Facebook and she'd put up a post about autumn gardening jobs at 2pm. She wouldn't be doing that if something had happened.

Maybe Hazel had just forgotten? But who forgets to reply to a text? Especially someone you're having sex with.

She held back on thinking more. They weren't dating.

But still, if she cared she would reply. Louise would be on her mind. She wouldn't be dicking about, doing a thousand other things that occupied her brain more than Louise.

She'd thought of Hazel all day. That had to count for something.

There was no way she could just forget she existed.

After work she'd busied herself with house jobs, dinner, conversation with Cameron and Mum.

But now? She was frustrated and fucked off.

She'd drafted a text twice, only to delete it.

If Hazel wanted to get in touch she could.

How hard was it to just send a text? It would take two seconds.

Louise didn't mind if she was busy but it wasn't hard to send a quick message: *Hey! Busy today, talk later.*

Then they both knew what they were doing.

She poured the rest of the water into the sink and stuffed the glass into the dishwasher.

Hazel could fuck off.

Maybe this was it. She'd had her fun, now she'd lost interest. They could have steamy office kisses on a Thursday and by Friday Hazel was on to someone new.

Well. Whatever.

She trudged back to the living room.

'You okay?' Mum asked.

'Yeah, why?'

'Dunno, you just seem a little on edge.'

'On edge?'

'Mhmm.'

Mum's attention returned to the TV. Louise faced forward but she wasn't taking in the show. She wasn't on edge. Annoyed, yes. But on edge? Nope.

She crossed her arms.

She needed to keep busy, that was all.

No need for Hazel. A month ago this wouldn't have even bothered her. She'd got suckered into some strange routine and now things were shifting again. No need to panic, just back to the old days when she'd be watching TV and thinking about work tomorrow.

'Did Cam have homework?' she asked, her mouth working of its own accord as her brain busied itself.

'Huh?'

'Doesn't matter,' she huffed, standing up.

Shit, she'd not taken the stuff out of the dryer. She was too preoccupied after dinner.

Louise dragged herself to the utility room, rolling her neck.

Fuck, she'd left her phone in the living room. Why bother, though? A text would be there when she returned, no biggie. There was no rush to reply to Hazel anyway. In fact, when she did bother her arse to reply, Louise would take just as long. No! Longer! Not her usual two minutes or less. Fuck her.

She rammed the clean clothes into her basket.

Any other day and she would have ironed Cameron's work uniform and school shirt for him. She couldn't be arsed today. She just wanted to curl up in bed, covers over her head, and go to sleep. Get this day over with.

She stood, basket resting on her hip.

This was no good.

Since when was her day dictated by one person?

She pulled the uniform from the pile, placing the basket back on the floor.

Board out and iron heating up, Louise retrieved her phone from the living room. Just to look at socials, of course.

She'd just lifted the iron when her phone buzzed.

Sorry, forgot to reply earlier. So much to tell you from today! You okay?

Her heart flipped. A smile spread across her face. Her mood one-eightied.

No worries. I'm good. You?

33

Today was a whirlwind.

Hazel had kept her agenda to herself, though, scared it might fall through. She hadn't even told Louise. Right now, her plans were closer to wishes, and if she dared to utter them out loud they'd disappear into thin air, never to happen.

Charlotte's predicament had sparked an idea, one that could solve everyone's problems. She'd not even told her sister, though. She was liable to jump ten steps ahead and there were too many hurdles to negotiate first.

She plonked herself on the sofa, next to Charlotte. Dad was watching the TV while simultaneously scrolling on his iPad. There was a good chance he'd not even clocked Hazel entering the room.

Mum was in the conservatory, reading a gardening magazine.

Really, Hazel wanted to be at Louise's, spilling the contents of her head, but she'd barely achieved step one of the grand master plan. Excitement only led to disappointment. She had to play it cool.

'Heard back from any of your job applications?' Hazel asked Charlotte, as quiet as possible. Dad wouldn't be able to hear if they were shouting, though. Sometimes his increasing deafness was advantageous.

'Just the two: M&S and a little indie gift shop that's just opened.'

'Nice. Going to go?'

'Yeah, probably. I need the dosh.'

Charlotte was going to tell Mum and Dad tomorrow, with Hazel at her side. All she could do was be honest. In fact, Hazel would wager Mum had probably been secretly hoping she would stay. As long as Charlotte was happy there would be no issue.

Everything was falling into place.

Hazel felt her news settle in the pit of her stomach. She couldn't say, though. Not yet.

She'd tell Louise the entire plan when she next saw her; that would lighten the load a little. Plus, Louise could be trusted not to get carried away or tell anyone else.

Once she got confirmation and things gathered momentum, she would tell Charlotte. There was no way she would have a problem with the next part of Hazel's idea.

It was plain sailing once this part was done.

Hazel had spent most of the day at Perth's Neil Lesley gym. They were a big-name chain spanning most of the UK, owned by some hotshot business man from Edinburgh.

Usually, Hazel preferred to work with indie gyms, but in Perth you had to take what you were given. None of the indie ones had space for her right now, despite extensive enquiries.

Which left council gyms – like Louise's – and Neil Lesley. Unfortunately the council didn't work with independent PTs, so there was one final option.

Surprisingly, when she'd emailed this morning the head of recruitment had called her in for a chat that very afternoon.

It was good to know her previous client list still held a little weight.

It felt like a step back, but they were happy for her to PT using their facilities. And, as an added bonus until her client list got to a more financially friendly level, she was qualified to lead some of their classes.

She'd lose a percentage of her PT dosh to them, but hopefully it would even out in the long run.

This was the start. Things were finally turning around.

Hazel refreshed her email. As soon as her paperwork pinged through it would feel real. The day was just a mishmash of memories otherwise.

Stage two was simple, but she'd need to chat to Charlotte first.

A text appeared from Louise. Talking about book club.

She'd reply in a bit. Her mind was too focused on this email to digest anything else.

Waiting was horrible. Why couldn't they just have given her a copy when she left? Or sent it this afternoon? Amir had said he was on shift until seven and he'd get a formal offer over before that.

He had twenty minutes.

Cutting it fine, Amir.

God, if she had to wait until Monday for this, she'd pop.

'Want to catch a movie or something tomorrow?' Charlotte asked. 'Like in the evening, after *stuff*?'

'Sure. What's on?'

'I'll check.'

Hazel refreshed it again. AN EMAIL!

Argh.

She opened it, skimming the attached document at super-speed. Everything looked in order.

She was a breath away from hugging her phone to her chest and shrieking with delight.

Beside her, Charlotte stared intently at her phone, checking cinema times. To her left, Dad continued to listen to the TV and scroll on his iPad. No one had a clue that her life had just changed.

A new course, one full of shiny, bright possibilities lay ahead.

She'd never imagined being back in Perth, but somehow it just felt *right*.

'*Scream*,' Charlotte said.

'You what?'

'*Scream*,' she repeated, jutting her head forward as if Hazel should know.

'Why?' Did she know?

'The film, you numpty. It's on at Perth Playhouse.'

Oh. 'You don't like horror films.'

'Not usually, but *Scream*'s a classic. More slasher than psychological bullshit.'

Dad briefly looked over his iPad at her. Deaf as a post but he could still hear a swear a mile off.

'Yeah, sure, I'll go see it.'

'Really?' she said, narrowing her eyes.

'Yes,' Hazel replied, drawing the word out. 'Why?'

'You're being unreasonably nice to me these days. What you after?'

'Just in a good mood.' She looked at Dad, who was back to doing whatever the heck he was doing. Probably watching model railway videos. 'Can I chat to you?'

'Of course.'

'Alone.'

'Ah.'

CHARLOTTE LED them to her bedroom. It wasn't a room Hazel was ever really in. It was funny how you could live somewhere and not use every room. The dining room was the same: frozen in time between Christmases. The air always felt different in it, harbouring the same feeling as when you return from a long holiday. It was still and held its own type of silence.

Charlotte's room did not hold silence *or* serenity.

The walls were still a pale pink from when she'd painted it as a teenager and her duvet alone held enough colour to make Hazel's organs wince. Despite only returning with a suitcase, she'd somehow made it full-on Charlotte. Some of it was probably left from pre-Australia days, mind. Either that or Hazel was going to have to quiz Charlotte on her penchant for carrying a Backstreet Boys poster with her.

'So, what's the haps?' Charlotte asked, flopping beside a cushion rimmed with bright pink pom-poms.

Hazel looked for somewhere to sit. She plonked herself on the edge of a green pouffe decorated with Mediterranean fabric and sequins. In her black trackies and T-shirt, this felt like a fever dream.

'I had a meeting today.'

Charlotte stopped playing with the cushion's pom-pom and tilted her head. 'What kind of meeting?'

'You know the Neil Lesley gym? The one in St Catherine's retail park?'

'Yeah?'

'There. I'm going to be PTing, instructing a few classes.'

'Shut up!' Charlotte yelped, sitting straighter. 'That's mega!'

'Thank you.' Hazel was surprised to find herself blushing. She gulped, knowing what was coming next.

When she'd had the idea on Wednesday, she'd kept it to herself. It was crazy. Even a month ago she would have thought she was going insane for even considering it.

But she'd sat on it, let it ruminate. And it still felt like the best option, so it was time to bite the bullet.

The question lodged in her throat. Maybe she should have spoken to Louise about this. A second opinion is always good.

'So, when do you start?' Charlotte asked.

'Next week, hopefully, if the paperwork goes through quick enough.'

'Nice! See, I told you you always had your shit together.'

'Still not sure about that,' Hazel replied with a smile. 'But I was hoping we could help each other out.'

Charlotte's face muddled with intrigue. 'How so?'

'You'll get one of these retail jobs no bother—'

'Hopefully.'

'I was thinking, if we stay here a month or so, save up a little.' She kept her voice steady, her words light, hoping to not make a mountain out of this mole hill, 'Then we could look at getting a flat together?'

Charlotte's eyes sprang out of her head, like she was one of those funny cartoon characters with googly eyes. 'Me? You want to share a flat with me?' She pointed at her chest.

'Yeah, you keen?'

'Ehhh. Obvs. I would love that!' Charlotte leaped to her feet and before Hazel knew it she was enveloped in a vice-like hug. 'Thanks, Haze . . . el.' The last-second name change was noted, and Hazel appreciated it.

She pulled back, stuffing her hands in her pockets.

'Okay, so, we'll get tomorrow out the way, you get a job, and then we'll play the rest by ear.'

'Easy-peasy,' Charlotte replied, shooting Hazel finger guns.

Hazel looked around her kaleidoscopic room for a final time before leaving. Lord only knows what their living room would look like, but dang, things might actually work out after all.

34

Louise flopped onto the bed, pressing the back of her head hard against the pillow as she enjoyed the final flickers of her orgasm.

Hazel turned, her features soft in the orange glow of Louise's bedside lamp. 'That was amazing,' she hummed, pushing a loose strand of Louise's hair behind her ear.

She could only manage a breathy 'Yeah' in return. Hazel's tongue was skilled and Louise was enjoying putting it to good use. Especially when Hazel insisted she sit on her. It had been worth waiting until Wednesday for, and if she had to wait another week the golden-hued memory would last her another seven days, no bother.

It more than made up for her spotty comms. After last week's blip they'd returned to normal, only for her to go AWOL again on Monday.

The lack of conversation didn't bother Louise: how she felt about it was the issue.

She couldn't name a single other friend she messaged so much, so consistently, nor one whom she missed when they didn't reply.

Waiting on Hazel sometimes felt like days, when really only hours had passed. She didn't get so triggered when Jordan failed to reply, and that could take days when she was really busy.

Twice now, Hazel had video called her before bed and Louise had indulged in quiet conversation until they'd given in and succumbed to sleep.

It felt dangerous, with Mum and Cameron so close, but Hazel had been too good to resist.

Was that normal with *just* a friend?

Not at all. She didn't need to be a brain surgeon to know that.

They'd agreed to casual, but maybe Hazel wanted more too? It was too soon to broach the subject. And definitely not now, when Hazel had so much to do with her new job starting soon.

That was another step in the right direction. She'd dropped her anchor in Perth for good now.

Louise would be a fool to think she was the reason, but maybe, just maybe, a tiny part of Hazel had considered Louise in the decision?

A girl can dream.

'What's the time?' Hazel asked, dropping her arm over Louise's waist and pulling her close.

She checked her phone. 'Got twenty minutes left.'

Hazel snorted. 'You and your sex alarm.'

'Hey, if it works, it works.'

She wouldn't need it if they were official.

Yesterday, as she lay awake in bed, trying in vain to sleep, she'd allowed herself to wonder, just a little. Indulge in a what-if. There was no harm.

She could see Hazel and Cameron getting on. He was already enamoured with her workout programme. It was a shame they'd not physically crossed paths since, though. Still, it was a start.

Somewhere down the line: family dinners, all four of them watching a film together, Sunday morning breakfasts.

It could happen.

'Are you free for a coffee or something on Saturday?' Hazel asked.

'I could be. Or, if we're hanging out in the public eye, why don't you come here, watch a film?'

Hazel's face creased. 'Won't your mum and Cameron be here?'

'Cameron is at a party and Mum will be about, but if we're just doing friend stuff does it matter?'

Also, she really wanted Mum to get to know Hazel better. It would be nice to just be the three of them.

'Hmm. Maybe. Can I have a think about it?'

Not the answer she was hoping for. 'I mean, I can totally do coffee. If you'd prefer.'

'No, no, it was just an idea.' Hazel eyed Louise's phone. 'We've got fifteen minutes left, let's not waste it.'

'But the coffee thing—'

Hazel silenced her with a nibble to her neck.

Louise melted into the moment: the feeling of Hazel's breasts pressed against hers as she kissed below her ear was too good to ignore.

She relaxed her muscles, sinking into the mattress. Her mind didn't relax, though. She tried in earnest to focus on the delicate touch of Hazel's lips, marking a trail south before lightly sucking on her nipple.

Louise groaned, a melting pot of desire and frustration. Even as she felt her clit twinge her brain refused to be silenced.

Was Hazel avoiding coming here on Saturday? Had she made it weird?

Hazel smiled against the soft flesh of her breast before her mouth engulfed Louise's nipple once more, her tongue flicking slow and deliberate stokes as her hand wandered to Louise's inner thigh.

She shifted, making room for her.

Couldn't this be enough? Why the need to blur boundaries?

As Hazel's finger ran through her wetness, her mind blanked.

This is all that matters.

It wasn't to last. Annoyance flushed through her veins in an angry torrent, hot and spiky. If Hazel wanted this, she needed to gel a little with Louise's life. Or at least try. She couldn't sneak around forever.

Why couldn't she have waited and asked about a film later? Ten minutes would have made all the difference.

Hazel paused, hovering over Louise, bodies inseparable.

'You okay? You seem a little distracted?'

Louise closed her eyes and took a deep breath, the kind that pooled at the base of her throat and didn't actually provide any air. 'I'm fine, sorry.' Hazel's eyes called bullshit, so she added: 'Honestly, sorry.' Plus a little squeeze of Hazel's bum for good measure.

Time to be present.

Hazel made it easy when she flipped position, now sitting by Louise's side, her back to her as her fingers massaged Louise's clit, her other hand now snaked under her leg, teasing her entrance.

'That feels good,' Louise groaned, knowing talking would stop her brain from pulling her away from how amazing

Hazel's touch was. She slid inside, every pass of her fingers on Louise's hard clit now matched with a thrust, Hazel's outer fingers giving the rest of her core the attention it deserved.

She tried to add further encouragement but words were hard. 'Fuck,' she growled.

'You like that?' Hazel purred.

Desire built with each motion, taking her right to the edge before tugging her back, building, building, building, until she couldn't contain the wave any more, her thighs clenching as release came.

This could be enough. But what if Hazel wanted more too? She'd be a fool to waste time with silly alarms if they could have a normal relationship.

As Hazel turned to kiss her, she knew her patience for casual was running thin.

'How was Samba?' Louise asked Mum when she wandered into the kitchen later that evening.

'Good. I am pooched now. Layla had us doing all sorts.' Mum threw her hands to the side and gave her hips a shimmy.

Louise smiled against the glass of water she'd been downing. She leaned her hips against the kitchen counter as she let out a quiet huff. 'Glad you had fun.'

Mum put her bag on the chair before standing at the other side of the counter to Louise, her eyes searching her daughter's face. 'You're flat this evening. What's going on?'

'Flat? Nah, just tired.'

'You used that excuse the other day.'

Louise rolled her eyes. 'Not an excuse. The truth.'

Mum stood her ground. 'Come on, what's up? Has something happened at work?'

'It's nothing to do with work.' She put the glass into the dishwasher and turned it on. Cameron could empty it when he got home from football.

'Ah, so it is something,' Mum shot back, her eyebrows rising to proclaim *gotcha*.

Louise sighed. She hated hiding stuff from Mum. Usually they shared everything.

She pursed her lips, sucking in short bursts of air as she thought. 'It's nothing.'

Mum followed as she went to the living room, slumping onto the sofa and turning the TV on. A show about a factory making biscuits was on. She didn't have the energy to channel surf.

'Louise, you might be a grown woman with a son of your own, but I'm your mother, and I know when something is up. Spill.' Mum said, joining her on the sofa and not even giving the empire biscuits a second glance.

Louise huffed, lolling her head into the soft cushion of the chair. Mum was a safe space; she wouldn't be taking out an ad in the Perthshire Advertiser to announce the family's secrets. She kept her eyes to the ceiling as she spoke. 'I slept with Hazel.'

The tiniest of surprised tuts was all that came in response. Louise didn't dare make eye contact.

Finally: 'And why is this not a good thing?'

Her skin prickled with irritation. Maybe being honest wasn't the best idea. Hazel had been right: explaining their arrangement was a toughie. 'It is a good thing. I'm really happy.'

'Yeah, you seem it.'

Louise didn't need to look at Mum to know she'd be smirking. 'It's complicated, that's all.'

'How so?'

She shifted, pulling her leg onto the sofa so she could finally face Mum. She let out a long huff, hoping to lose the surplus words which were preventing her from forming coherent sentences. 'Like, how do you know when someone likes you as more than a friend?'

Mum's face pinched together with confusion. 'I would say sleeping together would be a pretty big clue.'

'No, not like that,' Louise replied, waving a hand between them.

'You're going to have to elaborate.'

'Hazel isn't ready for a relationship, so we agreed to keep things casual. Just be friends.'

'Who sleep together?'

'Yeah.'

'Brings a whole new meaning to gal pals.'

'Muuum,' Louise whined.

'Sorry, sorry. Well, okay. So Hazel isn't ready. But you are? Is that the issue?'

'A bit. I know she wants to keep things casual but a lot of things are feeling really *un-casual*.'

'How long has this been going on?' Mum turned the sound on the TV down with the remote. There was only so much chat about runny icing that could be suffered.

'Not long.'

'Still super new then?'

'Yep.'

'Relationships take a while to find their rhythm. Neither of you are going anywhere. Why not just enjoy it for now? Maybe it will naturally progress to something more in time.

It's still so new that if you rock the boat now, Hazel might feel it's too much.'

Mum. Always bang on the money: what a trooper. 'I guess that makes sense.'

'You don't sound convinced.'

'You know patience isn't my forte.'

Mum put a hand on Louise's knee. 'You're right there. I remember the time you had a full-on meltdown in the chippy because you had to wait in a queue.'

'I was three.'

'Exactly. You've only gotten worse since then.'

'Hoi!' Louise put on her best agitated face.

Mum gave a soft smile in return. 'Everything will be fine, Louise. You got your chips in the end, yeah? Good things come to those who wait.'

Louise tapped her fingers against her mouth as she thought. 'You're right, you're absolutely right.'

Now Louise really wanted chips too. Thankfully, there was an app for that. When she'd finished putting her order in she texted Hazel with the same mindset: *I don't want coffee. You're coming to mine instead.*

It never hurt to speed things up a little.

35

Hazel repositioned the cushion behind her on the Kings' sofa. They were watching *Stardust*, Louise's choice. Apparently, she was really into romantic fantasy films, and had already declared *Enchanted* would be on the screen next time.

Hazel had never seen *Stardust* but was totally enthralled by the star-studded cast and their fairytale-esque carry on.

They weren't half as captivating as Louise, though. She had on loose trackie bottoms that hung from her hips in the most delicious way. If only Donna wasn't here.

But that was the point. If they didn't throw in a few 'friend only' excursions they would just be two people having sex, and that definitely wasn't what they were about.

She'd been reluctant at first. The thought of having Donna with them had felt a bit odd, but she was happy to be proven wrong. Louise's mum was good company.

It would be nice to be snuggled up though, instead of two feet apart with fire-fuelled chemistry hanging between them.

Would that go against the casual manifesto though? She

hadn't set out any real ground rules for when they weren't in bed.

Right now, she was just enjoying being with Louise. Yaz was right. She was able to have all the best bits of a relationship without silly, pressure-inducing labels. Problems would only arise if Louise met someone else.

Hazel swallowed, the thought making her stomach clamp.

It didn't sound like Louise was going to find anyone soon; she'd been single for years. Although, it would be just Hazel's luck for Ms Right to appear when she was with Louise.

With Louise.

Was she *with* Louise?

She smiled as the TV briefly stole her attention: the pirate onscreen was dancing to the cancan, wearing a woman's frilly dress, while his crew fought for their lives upstairs. This film had everything. Robert De Niro could do no wrong.

If Hazel had to introduce Louise she would say 'friend'.

It sat weird, though.

Like the word was balanced on an edge, slightly lopsided, and the smallest nudge would send it toppling.

Friends didn't usually make Hazel smile the way Louise did.

Or give orgasms that made your thighs ache for days.

She stole a glance at her profile.

They certainly didn't make your chest hurt from how damn cute they looked, either.

It didn't matter.

That was the whole point really.

They were friends, that's why it worked so well. Enjoying each other's company was part of the parcel.

'Anyone want another drink?' Louise asked, getting up from the sofa.

'Nah, I'm good,' Hazel replied as she passed. Oh, to be able to smack that bum as she sidled between the sofa and the coffee table.

'Mum? Another gin?'

'Yeah, why not. It is the weekend.'

Hazel had stuck to Coke today. If she was going to be PTing again she had to get serious. Mum and Dad didn't really get macros, but they'd understood enough to not be offended she was no longer eating the same meals as them.

Mum's roast dinner would be the true test tomorrow. Those yorkies were irresistible.

Louise returned with a full glass of wine and a gin for Mum. When she sat back down, she was a smidge closer to Hazel than before.

Had that been on purpose?

What would Donna do if she just leaned back, got comfy under Hazel's arm?

Saying that, she'd seen a few *looks* exchanged tonight. Either Donna had a sixth sense or Louise had told her something was going on.

'Fuck,' Louise barked, bolting upright, phone in hand.

'What's wrong?' Donna asked and Hazel could tell by her face Louise wasn't usually the type to swear in front of her. Something was seriously up.

Louise was up and hopping over Hazel's leg before she'd even answered. 'Bananas,' she said, her voice weak.

'Bananas?' Donna repeated with a streak of terror to the word.

What did that mean again? Hazel had a vague memory. It was bad, she could remember that. Although, not a hard guess going by the way her present company had swung into action.

'What's bananas again?' Hazel asked, getting to feet with the need to do something.

Louise had her car keys between her teeth as she yanked on a fleece. 'Cameron's in trouble,' she mumbled.

Oh shit. That's what bananas was.

'You can't drive, you've had wine,' Hazel said, holding up her hand so Louise could spit her keys out. She dropped them into her palm with a clink. 'We'll take my car. Where is he?'

'Are you sure?'

'Course I'm sure,' Hazel replied, stepping into her trainers.

'Do you need me to come?' Donna asked, flying up behind them.

'No, you stay here in case we need anything.'

'Did he say what's wrong?'

'No. Just bananas,' Louise snapped back, already heading out the door.

'He'll be fine.' Hazel reassured Donna as she followed, but she didn't even convince herself.

'So, he's never done this before?' Hazel asked on the main road to Old Scone.

Louise momentarily stopped biting her thumbnail to answer. 'Nope.'

Her leg bounced in the passenger footwell of Hazel's car. She was a nervous wreck and Hazel hated that she couldn't do more than push the upper end of Perth's speed limit.

'And still nothing else back?'

'Nope.'

He was at a party, so chances were he was wasted and just needed to come home, sleep it off. If anything serious had happened, surely he would have called?

Louise said he wasn't the type to get silly drunk.

Bets were, though, that most mums would say the same.

If Marie and Tom had seen half the things she and Charlotte got up to they'd be comatose.

'Do you remember—' Hazel said, before having second thoughts. Maybe stories of their drunken youth weren't appropriate.

'What?'

Or maybe a distraction would be a good idea. Once they got to Old Scone they still had a fair way to go: the village Cameron's house party was in lay miles past it.

'One of Violet Gellar's parties. She had us all playing spin the bottle?'

'God, Violet Gellar's parties were something else. I'm surprised there weren't more teen pregnancies in our year, the things that used to happen there.'

'Oh God, yeah, *that shed*. Anyway,' Hazel said, shaking free the memory of what she caught Henry Fuller doing to Owen Ramsey after one particularly heavy drinking sesh. 'This night, she had spin the bottle. And Jamie Kelleway's spin landed on Charlotte. She was two seconds away from kissing him when she chundered in his lap.'

Louise pulled a face, a hand to her mouth. 'Oh jeez. I'd forgotten about that. Shamila had to spew in the kitchen sink at the sight of it.'

'She definitely killed the mood, that's for sure.'

'Do you want to know a secret?' Louise asked, and Hazel was glad the plan was working; she seemed a little more relaxed now.

'Of course. Who says no to a secret?'

She chanced a quick look at Louise to find her smiling, her teeth holding her bottom lip as she replayed whatever was on her mind.

'I remember that game vividly,' she said, her voice the most level Hazel had heard since Cameron had texted. 'And not because your sister was sick. Because I really wanted my spin to land on you.'

'Shut up,' Hazel said with a honk of laughter.

'No, really.'

'You didn't speak one word to me at that party.'

'I was a complex woman back then.'

'If only you'd been honest, we could have had our own fun in Violet's shed.'

'We wouldn't have worked back then,' Louise bit back, maybe a little more harshly than intended.

Silence smothered the car as Hazel wondered how to respond. The first thing Louise had done when they'd left was turn off the music, saying it was setting her on edge. Right now, Hazel would kill for some over-energetic DJ to be filling the gap between them.

'Sorry, I was just kidding,' Hazel mumbled. It wasn't Louise's fault. She was worried about Cameron, that's all.

'Sorry, that came out wrong,' Louise replied, running a hand over her hair. 'For what it's worth, I'm glad I kept my distance from you then.'

Hazel side-eyed her, unsure how to take that. Her stomach was a yo-yo, dropping quickly before bouncing back into place as a cold sweat flushed over her. Stressed Louise was blunt.

'Okay, that definitely came out wrong,' Louise gushed, twisting so she could put her hand on Hazel's thigh. 'What I meant was: I had so much going on back then, if I'd been honest about my feelings I would have only fucked things up. Then you *really* would have hated me. This way, we could be together now. Well, not together, *together*, you know what I mean.' She twisted back, biting her thumbnail again as if it was damming another torrent of words.

Hazel's stomach settled. She got exactly what Louise meant. Their history was complicated enough: if they'd added anything else to the mix their pasts would have definitely nixed any chance of happiness in the present.

'Still, a little fun in the shed could have been nice,' Hazel said, hoping to lighten the mood again.

Louise sniffed, on the edge of worried tears, and Hazel wanted to hold her close and sap every drop of anxiety from her. Unfortunately, the logistics of driving didn't allow it.

All she got was a weak smile in return as Louise checked her phone again.

'We're nearly there,' Hazel said, no clue where she was on the back roads, but her phone said five minutes to go.

It was surreal that this would be the longest she'd spent with Cameron outside of their brief kitchen chat. And he probably stood a good chance of ruining her back seat's upholstery. What a way to make an impression.

Everything she knew was from Louise. He was sporty and apparently loving the weights programme Hazel had made him. He was smart, but he hated studying. Loved his PlayStation more than life itself. He sounded like a good kid, not one that would be getting into fights or causing trouble. Whatever had happened tonight, Cameron would have good reason for invoking their sacred pact.

'When we get there, I'll need to leave a voicemail,' Louise said, a wobble to her voice. The closer they got, the more her nerves frayed. 'The deal is that it's to look like I'm the one making him come home, get him out of whatever situation he's not happy with.'

'Clever.'

'We came up with this years ago. I never thought we'd actually have to use it.'

They rounded a corner, the beams of Hazel's car lights illuminating a country lane. This really was the arse end of nowhere. A few cars were dotted down the track, the parking more condensed near a cottage in the middle.

Two older boys shared a smoke by a towering hibiscus bush.

Hazel took a space at the end of the track and killed her lights and the engine.

'I'll call him outside, if that's okay,' Louise said, her eyes glassy in the moonlight.

Hazel nodded. 'Course.'

Louise paused as she opened the car door. 'Listen, if he's sick in your car, I'll pay for whatever needs doing.'

'We'll get him home, that's the most important thing. Whatever happens, we'll talk about it tomorrow.'

Louise flashed a tight smile then ducked out of the car.

36

Only a couple of minutes had passed since she'd left the voicemail and Louise's leg had bounced every passing second. If she didn't expel the nervous energy inside her somehow, she would pop.

She kept her eyes glued to the wooden gate at the edge of the cottage's garden, unblinking, her jaw tensed, as she sat in the car.

Would he need to be helped outside if he was really drunk? Should she go and look for him?

House parties weren't usually a problem. Yes, he'd sometimes disappear to his room for the day after, the faint musk of stale alcohol on him, but he was a teenager: she would rather know where he was than him hiding it and doing it anyway. Plus, he had a shift tomorrow. He was going to work whether he wanted to or not. He had responsibilities now.

Louise's stomach gurgled. His friend Wes had picked him up. She knew that much. She'd given up quizzing him on who attended these things a long time ago. There were only so many one-sided conversations a person could endure. Wes was the driver, though: she'd had a few conversations about car safety with Cameron when his mate had appeared in a beat-up Ford Fiesta one Saturday.

Then there was usually Kieren. And Paul. They were a good group, truth be known. But they were at an age where mistakes were easy to make, and sometimes they couldn't always be taken back.

She couldn't see Wes's car. Maybe that was it: they'd fallen out.

A figure appeared at the gate.

'There he is,' she yelped, sitting to attention.

He didn't seem hurt. *Or* drunk.

His hood was pulled tight around his face, his rucksack clutched tightly in one hand, his shoulders slumped.

Someone called out and he turned, flipping them the bird.

He briefly made eye contact with Louise as he passed to the back seat and she searched his face for clues. There was nothing.

'Hey,' he grunted, chucking his bag in before he piled into the tiny space of Hazel's car.

Louise turned, going on her knees so she could fully face him. 'What's up? Are you okay? What happened?'

His eyes quickly flicked to Hazel before returning to his mum's. 'It's nothing.'

'You called me out here for an emergency – it's not nothing.'

'Honestly, it's fine now. Can we just go home?'

'Cameron.' Tension filled the car, one match away from an explosion. Louise was the strike paper. 'What happened?'

'Just give it a rest,' he snapped before turning to face out the window, chewing on his bottom lip.

She couldn't even smell booze on him. He looked fine, no cuts or bruises.

Anger radiated off him like the fire she'd just ignited and Louise was far too close: she stood the risk of getting burned if she pushed any further.

'Let's get home,' she said to Hazel, returning to a normal seated position.

THEY DROVE in silence the entire journey. Like all fires left unfed, his intensity fizzled out, the tension in the car returning to a normal level by the time they got home.

She was embarrassed when he failed to say thank you to Hazel. Instead he was out of the car before it had even really stopped, slamming the door with such ferocity the vehicle shook.

'Thank you,' Louise said with a wince. 'I'm sorry you had to get involved tonight.'

'Don't be daft,' Hazel replied with a small smile. 'I'm glad I could help.'

'Bet you're just glad he never spewed,' Louise joked.

'You know me so well.' Hazel unclicked her seatbelt and her lips were on Louise's before she could register what was happening. It was a soft kiss, quick, but it left a mark of reassurance. Her eyes drove the message home as they snagged Louise's. 'Text me later, yeah?'

'Always.'

She wanted to stay, burrow into Hazel's chest and cry all the worry of the night out.

But Cameron needed her.

There weren't enough words to express her gratitude, so she kept quiet instead. Sometimes it was better to say nothing than fall short.

She closed the car door and didn't look back.

Mum was waiting when she got in the house. She'd texted earlier, but when there wasn't much to report, so she could understand her need for an update.

'He's gone straight to his room.'

'Figured he would,' Louise replied, unzipping her fleece. Where was the wine she'd poured earlier? She needed it more than ever now.

'Still not told you what happened?'

'Nope. I'll go speak to him now.'

She trudged upstairs to find his door closed. He usually only closed it when he was getting changed. She knocked. Nothing. Another knock. 'Cam, can we speak?'

Silence.

There was no way he was sleeping.

She pursed her lips as she thought, hand poised to knock a third time.

She dropped it to her side. Space was the best option for tonight. Maybe sleep would bring some clarity.

Louise was woken by the heavy weight of a man snuggling into her side, lifting an arm to get a proper cuddle.

It took her a second to realise it was her son and not an over-friendly intruder.

He'd not been in her bed for years.

She kissed the top of his head, her brain still waking up.

'Are you mad at me?' he asked, just as she was about to drift back to sleep.

'Why would I be mad?'

'Because you had to get your friend to come pick me up.'

'I'm not mad,' she said into his messy mop of hair. 'Ready to tell me what happened?'

Seconds passed and he said nothing. She wasn't going to push it.

'Hungover today, then?' she asked, hoping at least for some clues as to what had gone on.

'I didn't drink yesterday. I've got work today.'

She stroked his arm, grateful his problems weren't alcohol-based but now more intrigued than ever.

'I'll give Hazel petrol money. I know it costs a lot these days,' he added, still sounding like he was liable to get a telling-off.

Another kiss to the head. 'She won't mind. We're both just glad you're okay.'

He was quiet again and Louise was sure if she put an ear to his temple she'd hear the cogs turning. The air was heavy, what he really wanted to say on the tip of his tongue.

He was here because he wanted to talk. It was her job to find the right words for him.

'Did you get into a fight with Wes?'

He shook his head against her chest. 'Why would you think that?'

'Just guessing.'

No booze. No falling-outs. He definitely wasn't on anything when they'd picked him up.

'Was last night a contained problem, or is there anything I can help with today?'

She felt his jaw tense. He gulped. 'Contained, I think. I'm over it.'

'Good.'

He was lying, though. Louise's bones ached with the knowledge. Time to change tactics. 'Hazel and I were reminiscing about the house parties we used to go to. They could get super messy at times.'

He was quiet, so she continued: 'You know, I was nearly sick on a pony once.'

Cameron sat up, giving Louise a view of his face for the first time. His eyes were stained red. He'd been crying. She tucked the observation away, her focus fixed on getting him out of his funk and ready to talk.

'No you did not. That's gross.' He settled back against her chest.

'It's true. Too much to drink and I leaned over a fence on the way home, didn't realise it was there. Think it got as much of a fright as I did.'

He laughed quietly. 'I can't imagine you drunk.'

'Some things you only do when you're young. Scaring ponies with your hangover is one of them.'

'I'll keep it in mind.'

'You know, you might think I'm old and boring now, but I used to get up to all sorts.' She swallowed an uneasy smile. He didn't need to know the half of it. 'So whatever happened last night, I might be qualified to help more than you think.'

He was quiet as he considered her proposition.

'There was a girl, if you must know. But she kissed someone else, so it doesn't matter now.'

Ah.

Louise's heart broke for him. Who was this idiot that chose someone else over her son? He was better off without her. She obviously had no taste.

'Have you liked her for a while?' she asked, rubbing his back with lazy strokes.

A nod.

'Did she know?'

'Doesn't matter,' he mumbled.

She gave his arm a playful whack. 'Eh! Unless this poor girl is Mystic Meg it matters a lot.'

'Honestly, I'm over it. She kissed Tate, so she obviously doesn't like me.'

He must have really liked her to call Bananas.

'Have you spoken to her since?'

'She texted to ask if I was in trouble.'

'Right. So, she snogs someone else but takes the time to text you later? Mhmm. What did you reply?'

'I didn't.'

'Cameron Leonard King, you text that poor girl back now.'

'As if.'

'Do it or you're grounded.'

He sat up, his tear-stained eyes looking a little brighter. 'You can't ground me for not texting someone.'

'I most certainly can. My house,' she replied adding an authoritative huff to drive her seriousness home.

'Well, what would I say?'

'Ask her round.'

'You've lost it,' he said, rolling onto his back.

It was like the old days when he was eight or nine and they'd watch cartoons in bed on a Saturday morning.

'Trust me. How is she meant to know you like her if you've never said? Maybe she's out there wanting the same thing.'

'Unlikely.'

'What's her name, my future daughter-in-law?'

Cameron rolled his eyes. 'Sienna.'

'Sienna King. Nice ring to it.'

He sucked on his bottom lip, truly fed up with her. 'I can't just ask her round.'

'Sure you can. Say I've grounded you, for last night, and you're already bored out your nut. Because I'm so cool and chill, I said you could have someone round. Does she want to watch a film or something?'

'Urgh, that's so painfully obvious. No.'

'Think about it.'

'No.' His grin said he might, though. His smile dropped and he let out a long, breathy sigh. 'I need to get ready for work.'

'Welcome to adulthood.'

'I don't know why anyone bothers,' he said, slipping out of bed.

'Me neither.'

He was nearly out the door when he turned. 'Thanks, Mum.'

She flashed a smile. 'Just think about it, yeah?'

'Noooo.'

She scooped her pillow closer when he'd left. Maybe she should take her own advice, tell Hazel what she was thinking. Nothing ventured, nothing gained, and no one likes a hypocrite.

37

Hazel resisted the urge to skip along the road to the sports centre.

Her first day at Neil Lesley's had gone fantastically. The gym was way fancier than the one in Shawlands. She could add all sorts to her routines, plus, when she wasn't working or PTing she could use all the equipment herself.

Working with others would take getting used to, but it would be worth it. They were a nice team and hopefully Hazel could use the gym's reputation to her advantage.

It was her win to celebrate but she'd picked Louise up some flowers on the way over, wanting to share the moment.

Hazel grinned, aware she probably looked like a crazy person as she walked along the Inch's path. She couldn't help it, though. Her face was fixed. She wanted to jump for joy.

Charlotte had added to her smile, too.

She'd got her job in the indie gift shop so Hazel had picked her up a bottle of prosecco to toast with later. She was like sapphic Santa today.

Hazel checked her watch; she was a little early for

Louise finishing work. No harm in waiting in the office. Better than being late. She didn't actually know she was visiting today, so any later, she ran the risk of Louise going home, unaware she was en route.

She'd been a little flat since Cameron's predicament at the weekend, and despite reassuring Hazel he was fine there was definitely something that wasn't being said. Hopefully flowers and Hazel's good news would cheer her up.

Finally she was at the sports centre.

A class must have just finished: a crowd of women lingered in the foyer all kitted out with tank tops and leggings, yoga mats slung over their shoulders. Hazel weaved her way through them and pushed open the staff door.

She chapped on Louise's door before poking her head in. 'Hello you.'

Louise's face broke into a grin. 'Hazel,' she chirped, pushing her paperwork away and laying a pen on top. 'What are you doing here?'

'Just finished work, thought I'd surprise you.' She passed the flowers to Louise.

'Well, aren't I lucky? Did it go okay?'

Hazel put her bag on the spare chair before walking round to Louise's side of the desk. 'First things first,' she said, pulling Louise close for a kiss. It didn't matter how many times they did it, Hazel would never tire of Louise's lips.

Louise's eyes were glazed, a dreamy smile playing on her lips as Hazel pulled back. 'So, spill the beans. How did your first day go?' she asked, sounding hopeful as she looped her arms around Hazel, settling them under her bum and pulling her close.

Hazel had wanted to play it cool, ham things up a little,

but now the time had come she couldn't stop the smile taking over her face. 'It was amazing. Really nice bunch, great set-up, seems like a good place to work.'

'So it's going to work, then?'

Hazel bit her bottom lip, failing to keep her composure. 'Yep, even got my first PT client booked in.'

'Get out!' Louise squealed.

'I know, I can't quite believe it.' Hazel chuckled. 'You free tonight, to celebrate? Charlotte's had good news too.'

Louise smiled but it didn't quite reach her eyes. 'I could be. Actually, I wanted to have a chat with you.'

Hazel was on cloud nine and something about that sentence said it would piss on her parade. Maybe there was a way to get Louise on the same wavelength.

'Of course, but . . .' Hazel said, finishing her sentence with a kiss. She hadn't meant for it to go far but before she knew it her hand was on the back of Louise's neck, urging her closer.

She parted her lips and Louise's tongue slipped into her mouth. She groaned, mindful she had to be as quiet as possible. She was at Louise's work, after all.

Louise's lips pulled into a smile and this time her eyes twinkled too. 'You're bad,' she said, her voice husky.

'Me? I've done nothing.'

But they were still kissing, Hazel's knee trying to find purchase between Louise's legs. Louise squeezed Hazel's bum.

She looked at Louise's office door. 'Don't suppose that locks?' Waiting until next Wednesday would be torture after a kiss like that.

'Unfortunately not.' She ran her thumb along the line of Hazel's jaw, her eyes hazy with desire. 'Thankfully everyone knocks, though.'

'Oh really?' She studied Louise's face, wondering if she was joking or not. A flicker in her eyes said she was feeling as daring as Hazel. 'So if I was to do this,' she whispered, running a hand up Louise's inner thigh. 'It would be okay?'

Louise laughed under her breath. 'You're going to get me in trouble.'

'I would hate for that to happen,' Hazel said, her fingers still skirting Louise's thigh. 'But . . .' She cupped her hand to Louise's centre and created a little pressure with her palm.

Louise nibbled Hazel's bottom lip before kissing her. 'What are you up to?' she asked, smiling.

'Nothing.' Hazel teased. She pulled back, sweeping her eyes up and down Louise. The idea was rampant in her mind, the notion an uncontrollable wildfire in her veins. Could she really? She was on a high from work going so well: right now it felt like anything was possible.

Only one way to find out.

She dropped to her knees, ducking under the desk and running her hands up Louise's outer thighs, her hands settling on the waist of Louise's joggers.

This was dangerous. She could already feel her own clit throbbing.

'What *are* you doing?' Louise asked, an unsure but curious lilt to her voice.

'You'll see,' Hazel replied with a mischievous smile. 'But just say stop and I will.'

She stole a quick look at Louise's face. She looked nervous but consenting. Hazel got confirmation to continue when she arched her back, and with a slight tilt of her hips, Hazel was able to shimmy Louise's joggers and pants to her ankles.

'Wait, wait, wait,' Louise urged, almost whispering. 'What if someone comes in?'

'Just pretend I'm not here.'

If anyone did come in they'd be none the wiser. The desk was solid from the front, Hazel safely concealed in the centre.

Louise inhaled sharply as Hazel gently parted her legs and edged her forward, kissing up her inner thigh in the process.

She hovered in front of her core, enjoying the thrill and wanting to make it last. It was also the final chance for Louise to back out. There was no protest, so she was free to do what her heart desired.

Hazel's heart hammered as she ran her tongue up Louise's centre. There was no going back now. She was so wet that this wasn't going to take long.

She ran circles on her clit before sucking gently, Louise's hand now on the back of her head.

Her tongue worked with careful precision, bringing Louise closer to the edge with every stroke.

Her grip on Hazel's head tightened, her fingers tangled in her hair, telling her not to stop.

If only her thighs weren't restricted by the arms of the chair, she could create a little more room, let Hazel inside her. It wasn't to be though, so Hazel settled for her thumb and used the leverage she had to rim the entrance to Louise's core.

Voices near the door made her stop. A man was dangerously close. Hazel could imagine him right on the other side, his fist paused as conversation interrupted him knocking.

'You want me to stop?' Hazel whispered.

'Not yet.' The squeeze of Louise's fingers told her not to worry and teased her back into motion.

She drove the flat of her tongue hard against Louise's clit and her tensed muscles hinted she was close.

The voices outside continued, still as loud as ever. Only a few inches of wood separated Louise from trouble.

Hazel smiled. She'd never done anything like this before. But that's how things were these days. Everything felt brand new.

She opened her mouth to triple-check Louise was still on board, but was interrupted by a knock at the door.

She froze, her breath stolen by her heartbeat. If it drummed any harder their unexpected guest would be able to hear it through the door.

Louise's hand gently ushered Hazel backwards, into the recess of the desk. She put a finger to her lips, telling Hazel to be quiet.

Her cheeks flushed red as they knocked again. 'Louise?' a middle-aged guy shouted again. Hazel knew the voice: Steve the chairman.

Louise's eyes held Hazel's, both frozen to the spot, neither even daring to breathe.

A new voice joined Steve in the hall, a guy Hazel didn't recognise. 'Steve! That you off home?'

'Yeah, was just looking for Louise but she must be off already.'

'Walk with me to the car park? I need to ask you something.'

'Of course . . .' Their voices faded.

Hazel gulped and Louise breathed a sigh of relief.

They marinated in the silence, Hazel's heart rate slowly returning to an acceptable level.

'That was close,' Louise said with a breathy snigger.

'I'll say. Sorry.' A hand on her shoulder stopped her from getting up.

'Where do you think you're going?' Louise asked, her eyes burning wild.

Hazel grinned. 'You want me to keep going?'

Louise nodded.

She licked her lips in anticipation as Louise opened her legs again. She was so wet, just the sight of her made Hazel's core pulse.

She ran her hands along the outside of Louise's thighs as she pulled her close, quickly finding her clit with her tongue.

Louise moved in rhythm with her strokes, her hips rolling with each sweep.

A few more flicks of her tongue and Louise's back arched, her hand holding Hazel in place as she came. A quiet groan escaped, only to be cut off, Louise remembering the need to be silent.

Hazel continued working her tongue until Louise shuddered, releasing her grip.

Only the sound of Louise's heavy breathing filled the room as a new conversation passed by the door. Laughter rippled through the wall.

Hazel pulled back, pulling Louise's joggers and underwear up to her knees so she could wiggle them back on.

'Wow,' was all Louise could say as she pushed her chair back, freeing Hazel. 'I've definitely never done that at work before.'

Hazel ran her fingers around her mouth, the taste of Louise still on her tongue. 'Just a teaser of how I'll be celebrating later,' she said, getting to her feet.

'A teaser? More than that might kill me.' She pulled Hazel close.

'Do you need to work before we go?'

'Nah, it's all done. I was just doing extra stuff for Steve. That's probably why he called by.'

'Sorry.'

'Don't say sorry. I liked it.' She rearranged the papers on her desk into a new order then stilled, as if something was on her mind, battling to get out. 'You're something else.'

'In a good way?' Hazel asked, draping an arm around Louise.

'Most definitely.' She placed the top stack of papers to the side. 'Now, grab my phone. I'll text Mum, let her know my plans, and then we can start the real celebrations.'

She winked and Hazel felt her knees wobble. Today was shaping up to be unforgettable.

38

Louise thought she might implode if she didn't talk to Hazel soon.

She'd rehearsed it in her head so many times she was slowly driving herself mad. But the time never felt right, the setting never quite spot on.

It was getting silly, though, dampening her spirits more by the day. Her thoughts had a chokehold on her mood: the longer she left it, the more they dragged it down like she'd been tied to a weight and chucked in the River Tay. She was sinking. Fast.

She looked at Hazel as she chatted to Marie, the smile she'd been sporting since coming to Louise's work still firmly fixed in place. She'd never seen Hazel so happy.

The way she'd turned up at work, flowers in hand, and then done *that*: she had to be feeling it too, yeah?

Two glasses of prosecco were giving her courage. If she didn't say it tonight, she was only wasting time.

It would be fine. Hazel would probably be relieved, say she was thinking the same and thank God Louise had had the foresight to bring it up.

Her heart skipped, sinking closer to her stomach. Maybe she could just leave it? No. She wasn't bottling out. If she went home tonight, words unsaid, she'd only feel worse tomorrow.

On the flipside, if she took the plunge today, tomorrow she'd be on cloud nine, she and Hazel on the same page, reaping the rewards. They could do something nice this weekend. Hazel could even stay over after. The world would be their oyster.

Hazel popped a crisp into her mouth before joining Louise on the sofa.

'Can we, erm, go somewhere for a chat?' Louise asked, finishing the last of her drink.

Hazel's smile dimmed a little. 'Of course. Let's go to my room.'

Louise followed her through the hallway. She'd never been to Hazel's room before.

Her heart rate intensified with every step.

'You first,' Hazel said, gesturing towards the open door to their right.

It was a simple room, and it was obvious Hazel was only a temporary resident, but it still had marks of her personality. A shelf above a desk had trophies from when she was younger: swimming, football, cross country. A stack of dumb-bells sat in the corner, a yoga mat rolled up and tucked beside them.

On the bedside table there was a framed photo of—

'Is that Jodie Foster?'

Hazel turned beet red. 'I was a *little* obsessed when I was younger.' She snatched the photo up and shoved it into her top drawer. 'So, what do you want to talk about?' she asked, taking a seat on the bed.

Louise joined her, only capable of sitting on the edge.

She wanted to pace, rid herself of nervous energy, calm herself down before talking. Pacing wasn't an option though, especially not before she'd even started talking. Hazel would think she'd lost the plot.

It was now or never.

How had she planned to start this, again?

There were so many thoughts rattling around her head she would sound like a maraca if shaken.

She gulped.

'So,' she said and had to stop, surprised her voice was already cracking. 'This casual thing we've got going.' Hazel's smile slid from her face and Louise lost the nerve to continue. She turned her attention to her hands, wringing them in her lap. She gulped. She'd started: no going back. 'It's brilliant. I mean, the sex is top notch.' God, this was already going off script. Keep it simple. 'But I want more.'

'More sex?' Hazel asked, a confused but surprised lilt to her voice.

Louise laughed nervously. 'Not exactly. Well, I'm never going to say no to that, but no, I want *us* to be more. Like, an actual couple.'

'Ah.'

That was not a sound Louise liked. It was short, sharp, and definitely not positive.

The silence in the room was so loud Louise thought she might hyperventilate. It was like the walls were closing in, pushing the air from her lungs.

She chewed on her cheek, unable to look at Hazel. She couldn't speak: her heartbeat was too powerful, it would smother the words.

'Louise,' Hazel said, her voice soft with pity.

'That'll be a no then.'

'I told you, I'm not ready for a relationship.' She put a hand on Louise's thigh and she yanked her leg free.

'But isn't that what this is?' she snapped, flapping a hand between them. 'We're doing everything but call it one.'

Hazel shrugged. 'So why change things?'

Finally, Louise could look her in the eye. Fury bloomed in her chest, heat whooshing up her neck to her cheeks as her mind kicked into gear. 'You want to keep your options open, is that it?'

'What? No,' Hazel barked. 'Why would you think that?'

'So I'm fine to fuck but not to keep?' Her voice was knife-sharp, her brain working of its own accord, pushing the words out before she had a chance to second-guess them.

'Louise, where has this come from?'

It was the only thing that made sense. Why else would Hazel be happy to have all the bells and whistles of a relationship but not actually want to make it official, go public? How had she not seen it before? 'You're just using me, aren't you?'

Hazel was stunned.

Louise took the chance to continue. 'Is that what it is? This is just sex?'

The muscles in Hazel's cheeks flexed as she tensed and relaxed her jaw. Still she said nothing.

Louise nodded hard. 'Right, okay, that's it. Just sex, got it.'

She stood and finally Hazel came to life.

'Louise, please sit, let's talk.'

'What's there to talk about?' she huffed, throwing her arms out to the side. 'I want more; you're using me as a stopgap until the right girl comes along. Nothing to discuss.'

'Lou,' Hazel begged, reaching out to take Louise's hand. 'You're being ridiculous.'

Wow. She did not. 'Ridiculous?' she repeated,

incredulous. She stopped herself before she really lost her temper. After a deep breath, she spoke. 'Look. You can't have your cake and eat it too. Either this becomes more, or it's done.'

Hazel's brown eyes snagged Louise's, refusing to let her go as she thought. Louise wanted to shake the words from her, get this over with so she could either storm out of the room or hold her tight.

How could Hazel be so nice and not have feelings? Who brings their mate flowers, then fucks them in their office? Who stays on FaceTime until midnight, talking about nothing, when they've spent the day texting? Why give so much if she felt so little?

'I can't, Louise. I'm sorry.'

Louise nodded, stuffing her hands into her pockets. She had one final question, one that if she didn't ask she'd forever regret it. 'What are you afraid of?'

'Getting hurt again.' Her voice was quiet and Louise could see a wobble to her bottom lip, but she was holding something massive back.

'I'm not Ashley. Or is that it? You think having that letter A on your chest makes you her property? Am I just a poor replacement cause you can't have the real thing?'

'I think you've said enough now.'

She was right, but Louise wanted to keep pushing until she hit a nerve, got to the crux of the problem. The whole thing was fucked, anyway: if breaking Hazel wide open got a semblance of truth out of her, it would be worth it.

'Was this some twisted way to get back at me?'

Hazel held her gaze, her chest heaving with anger. 'Is that what you really think of me? You think I would stoop to that? Fake all this as some weird revenge? Is that who you think I am?'

Words she could never take back danced on her tongue, anger begging for them to be set free. Once she snapped there would be no return, though. She swallowed her vitriol, nothing good enough floating to her surface, nothing that could move this conversation forward instead of finishing their friendship completely.

If there had even been one to start.

Tears pricked at her eyes.

'I don't think I know you at all. Not really.'

She left before Hazel could retaliate. If she did eventually say something it was lost to the blood pumping in Louise's ears, angry, loud, and hot.

Charlotte was at the other end of the hall when she rounded the corner, a chocolate biscuit hanging out her mouth as she texted someone.

'Louise, you okay?' she asked, taking the biscuit from her mouth as concern washed over her face.

She ignored her, stomping to the front door as quickly as she could, lest she see any other Patersons.

The cold air as she opened the front door bought her some time, but she'd be lucky if she made it home before the tears fell.

39

Hazel lay on her back, staring at the gym's ceiling as she completed her final round of chest presses.

It had been forty-eight hours since their fight and she'd still not had the heart to text Louise. Nothing felt right. Until she got her thoughts in order, there was no sense in starting conversation.

Louise obviously felt similarly, because she'd not heard from her either.

Hazel dropped the dumb-bells onto the padded mat and sat upright.

The gym was dead. But that tended to be the case when you went at ten o'clock at night.

She scrunched her eyes up, sweat making them sting.

Ever since their fight she'd had a horrible fluttering in her chest, like she was stuck on the edge of panic, one bad decision away from a full meltdown.

Out of the corner of her eye she spotted a red polo, a Neil Lesley uniform, darting between the treadmills. Before she knew it, Ginny, one of the gym workers, was beelining for her, a grin on her face. Hazel matched it. That was the problem with starting a new job. No matter what your mood was, you always had to dial the happiness to eleven. First impressions were everything.

Hazel took an earbud out, pre-empting conversation.

'Hazel! Hey! You're in late,' she said, leaning on the corner of the squat rack.

'Yeah, just getting some reps in.'

Also, can no longer sleep due to being a colossal fuck-up.

'It's my favourite time to come, means there's no waiting on machines. Plus, no one to ask for advice.'

'I know that one. At my last gym, I couldn't walk two feet without someone wanting something.'

Ginny smiled. 'I'll leave you to it. I hate when folk talk to me when I'm working out.'

Ah, Ginny. She might just be Hazel's new favourite. 'See you around,' Hazel said, popping her earbud back in.

She's been tempted to stick on Carrie Underwood but wasn't *quite* at the wallowing stage yet.

It would be an easy fix. Bets were, if she called up Louise and said she wanted to get together, be a proper couple, they probably could just pick up where they left off.

A huge part of her was sorely tempted.

Spending time with Louise was the highlight of her day but the thought of sticking a label on it and making it an actual thing, well, that made her heart stutter and her stomach clench. Think about it too much and the room started spinning.

It was too much. She wasn't ready.

But her brain was screaming that Louise was too good to let go. People like her, connections like theirs, didn't come around often.

Why did she have to complicate things by wanting more?

They had a good thing going.

Couldn't it just continue?

If she wasn't going to get with anyone and Louise wasn't going to get with anyone, why did she have to get all pigeonhole-y? It was a moot point.

Hazel huffed. And that was without considering the hurtful things she'd said.

She got it, though. Why Louise would think that.

Maybe this was a lesson in being more open.

Would be good to be honest with herself, for a start. She didn't have a fucking clue what she wanted.

She stood and wiped the utility bench down. Her heart wasn't in this workout but exercising always made her feel better. When she and Ashley had been on a break she'd pretty much lived at the gym. It was like her brain was working shit out behind the scenes as her muscles did the heavy lifting. Literally.

She'd do some bicep curls next, watch her form in the mirror, focus on something other than the constant back and forth in her head.

She looked at the rack of weights, the dumb-bells lined up in order of size, and let out a slow, frustrated huff.

The problem was: Hazel didn't trust herself. Her intuition wasn't reliable.

She'd made a mistake, paid the price, but her head and heart still weren't on speaking terms. It would seem her heart held a grudge.

She'd worked so hard on forgiving Ashley, she'd forgotten to forgive herself, too. But, in the same way she still considered Ashley's actions inexcusable, her poor judgement was as well. She should have seen the signs, respected herself better than to hang around when it was obviously a bad fit.

If she picked the wrong dumb-bell weight she could put it back, get a new one.

But people were more complicated. It didn't take much to get intertwined, merge lives, blend the fundamentals.

You couldn't just switch them out.

No matter what she did, they'd always hold a little of her heart. And the trouble was: the more she loved the less she had left to give. This final piece was to be protected at all costs. She couldn't throw it away on a whim.

Hazel grabbed an 8kg dumb-bell. The only way she was going to get any inner peace was to make her muscles burn. Flaming biceps were better than focusing on the pain in her chest. She turned her music up full and started her reps.

HAZEL NEARLY JUMPED a mile when she found Charlotte on her bed, reading the latest assignment from book club: *The Midnight Library*.

She'd given up on reading it. Felt a little too deep for her current mental acrobatics.

'You're in late,' Charlotte said, dropping the book to her lap like a disgruntled mother who had been waiting all night for a tearaway teen.

'Why are you on my bed?' Hazel grunted, ignoring her inference completely.

Charlotte pursed her lips. 'What did you say to Louise to upset her?'

Something between a squeak and a cough choked Hazel. She tamped her anger, too tired to make a scene.

She dropped her gym bag at the end of her bed with a loud thump, chewing on her cheek to stop her saying anything she might regret tomorrow.

Charlotte's eyes followed her every move.

'I want to get changed,' Hazel said, motioning for her to get out.

'Tell me what happened and I'll go.' When Hazel didn't speak, she added: 'I want to help. I'm not just being nosy, promise.'

'Why do you think you can help?'

She shrugged. 'Dunno. Problem shared is a problem halved. You helped me.'

Hazel considered it as she took a seat on her desk chair. She'd not used it in about a decade and could feel how stiff the swivel plate was instantly. It squeaked as the greaseless metal ground together.

It would be good to talk to someone.

She'd not told Yaz anything. She'd wanted to keep Louise to herself, see if things worked out before breaking the news. It was the right decision. They already thought Hazel's life was a mess: they didn't need to know she'd found a new way to fuck things up.

'Louise and I—' She took a deep breath. Speaking to Charlotte about this felt *weird*, but what other choice did she have? 'We slept together.'

'Whoa. Okay. So, what's the problem?'

'Louise wants a relationship.'

'And you?'

'Don't.'

'Yeah, real conflict of interest there. And I'm guessing you were a dick about it?' A smile flickered over her lips and Hazel appreciated her adding a little humour to the topic.

'Actually, no. She was. But it was justified.'

Charlotte nodded. 'Were you up front, before you—' She slapped her palms together a few times.

'Yes. I told her I didn't want a relationship.'

'Well. More fool her.'

Hazel's eyes narrowed to slits. 'Is that it? No grand, metaphorical speech?'

'Why bother? You told her what you wanted: she didn't listen.'

Hazel rolled her neck, stiffness from her overly hard workout already kicking in. 'I think part of the problem is, I don't know what I want. I maybe gave the wrong impression with stuff. It wasn't just sex.'

'I don't get what you mean.'

'It wasn't a one-time thing, and between sleeping together we have been quite couple-y.'

'But, you still told her that? That you didn't want a relationship?'

'Yep.'

Charlotte shook her head, disappointment hardening her features. 'This is why casual doesn't work. Someone always falls harder than the other.' She sat straighter, tossing her forgotten book to the side. 'But, you're to blame too. Why did you go all couple-y if you just wanted to smash?'

Hazel winched. 'That's a truly horrible phrase. Don't say it again.' She berated her with a smile. 'Because I like her. And I like being in a couple. I just don't want to complicate it by being a couple.'

'Wow. That's really fucked up, Hazel.'

'Hey, now.'

'Harsh but fair. You're toying with this poor woman's affections.'

Hazel dropped her head backwards with a groan. 'I know.' She lifted her head again, looking Charlotte square in the face. 'How did you know you had to end things with Jimmy?'

'That was different. I just got to a stage where the

thought of being stuck with him made it difficult to breathe. I felt trapped. Like I was on the wrong path. And because I loved him I couldn't drag him along for the ride. I felt like I was wasting his life, too.'

'Maybe I'm just protecting Louise.'

'You're not. It's okay to be selfish sometimes. You're protecting yourself, that's allowed.'

'Protecting myself from what though? That's the question.'

'Guess that's what you need to figure out.'

Christ, since when had her little sister been the voice of reason? Just goes to show, everything and anything can be turned on its head.

40

Louise lay on her bed, trying in vain to concentrate on this month's book. It was a good read: she just couldn't stop her mind wandering elsewhere.

Next door, Cameron's laughter rippled through the wall, followed by Sienna's giggles.

It was nice to hear him so happy. Usually he was holed up in that room with only his PlayStation for company.

He was under strict instructions to keep his door open, though. Louise had enough on her plate without becoming a granny.

She put the book on the bed and picked up her phone. It had now been three days since she and Hazel had fought. Three long days of radio silence.

She couldn't be the one to crack, though. She'd already made a fool of herself.

Instead, she texted Jordan. She was still down south, otherwise a visit to her caravan would have been top of the agenda.

I've fucked things up with Hazel.

It was well after tea time; hopefully she'd see the

message soon. Timing was everything with Jordan. If you messaged during the day she was at work and liable to forget once her shift was over, then a reply came days later. Louise couldn't wait that long.

Another peal of laughter from next door. Louise wanted to pop her head in, offer a plate of choccie biscuits or something, just to see what they were up to, but Cameron would likely kill her for ruining his street cred.

They were watching some horror film. How that was first date material, Louise would never know.

Although, an excuse to cosy up and hide could be nice. She pouted, only just stopping the vision of her and Hazel doing just that.

Part of her was on the constant chastise, wondering why the heck she had to open her big mouth, stop the good thing they had going.

The other half was proud she was honest, had enough respect for herself to be open about what she wanted. A relationship should never be at the detriment of yourself.

Don't forget your own values and needs to make someone else happy. It only leads to resentment. That's no foundation.

Her phone buzzed: Jordan.

FaceTime?

Louise hit call faster than if her life had depended on it.

'Hey,' Jordan said, sitting in the living area of her caravan. Huxley's bum was just in view to her side. 'You okay?'

'Yeah, just having a crisis. How's Berwick?'

Jordan pulled a face. 'Can you not hear the rain? People are nice but I've got fuck all to do in this weather.'

'Have you tried reading the next book club book?'

'Didn't realise you'd switched careers to comedian since

I left Perth.' She changed the topic before Louise could retaliate. 'So, what's happened with Hazel?'

She dropped her voice, aware Cameron and his date were just next door. 'We slept together and it's got messy.'

Louise barely had half her sentence out before Jordan was screeching. 'Louise! What!? I was only joking about having sex. You actually did it? You old dog, you.'

She rolled her eyes, breathing in slowly. 'She initiated it. And to be fair, she told me she just wanted to be friends, but . . .' She trailed off. Saying it out loud only made her feel like an idiot. She had no right to be mad at Hazel. She'd been honest from the start and Louise still decided to go along with it.

'You caught feelings. I get it,' Jordan said, sympathetic.

'To be fair, I think I had feelings way before. So I should have known better. But I never like anyone – I thought I could put that aside and just have fun.'

'So what happened? Why's it gone sour?'

'I told her I wanted more.'

'Louise!' Jordan whined so loudly that Hux twisted round and gave her the stink eye.

'Look, I know, but I had to be honest.'

'Well, she did say she didn't want a relationship. You can't blame her.'

'I know, but it's so hard to explain. Everything she was doing suggested otherwise.' Louise played with the toggle of her hoodie. She'd gone over Hazel's actions a thousand times in her head. She just wanted someone to agree with her, say she wasn't going crazy, that it was okay she'd got her feelings muddled.

'Like what?'

'She brought me flowers. We talked. A lot. We did things together.'

Jordan didn't look convinced.

'I'm not doing it justice,' Louise added. Her brain was fatigued, begging for her to get a new subject.

'So she did all that. Fair enough. What about the rest, though? Did she make an effort to meet your mum? Cameron?'

'Not so much.'

'You can be a nice person and not want more. Everyone is capable of anything. If she liked you, she would make the effort. At the end of the day, if she could, she would.'

'What do you mean?'

'If you like someone you make time for them. You step up. She didn't want to, so she didn't.'

'She did make time for me, that's what I'm saying. She—'

Jordan cut her off. 'I'll be back north soon. Will we meet for a drink? Or you can come to mine for a tea?'

'You think I've fucked it, don't you?'

Jordan breathed out sharply through her nose. 'If you wanted to keep her as a friend you never should have crossed that line. You can't go back to being what you were. And if you had feelings, it's unfair of you to expect more when she clearly said she didn't want anything.'

For once, Jordan was talking sense.

'That's fair. I just hate how it's all ended.'

'So, why not meet with her? Clear the air. Tell her no hard feelings.'

'You're right.'

'What's that? I didn't quite hear.' Jordan jested, scooping her hand around her ear.

'Shut up.'

'Thatta girl. Sounding more like yourself now.'

Goodbyes wished, Louise's finger hovered over Hazel's name. A text would suffice today.

She drafted a message three, four times.

It all felt so contrived.

Finally, she took a deep breath and typed: *Hey, can we meet for a coffee? Clear the air?*

Jordan wouldn't mind Louise stealing her words.

Minute after excruciating minute passed with no answer.

Maybe Hazel would just ignore her.

She regretted saying what she did about Ashley, but in the moment it had been logical. Why else was Hazel holding back?

Finally, her phone buzzed.

Yeah, sure. Tomorrow after work?

Thank God she wasn't going to make her wait until the weekend.

Tomorrow.

Part of her wished Hazel would change her mind by then. There was no way she wasn't missing Louise like she was missing her. You can't talk to someone that much, then not notice the gaping hole they left.

She could do this. Just one sleepless night between now and then.

Just one night to find the right words to make Hazel take a chance.

41

Hazel's stomach swirled with anxiety as she neared the coffee shop they'd agreed to meet in.

Café Oiseau.

Neither had been before. Neutral ground felt important, like she was going into battle.

Which was ridiculous, because Louise was just Louise.

A few weeks ago she would have been looking forward to seeing her. Now she had to keep concentrating on not throwing up.

Louise's biting words still rang in her head. Hazel was nervous in case she'd thought of anything new to add.

That didn't feel like something Louise would do, though. Not now the heat of the argument had gone. Her texts were more apologetic than angry.

Still, she'd played the meeting out a thousand different ways in her head, unable to concentrate on anything else at work. She'd covered the good, the bad, and the downright ugly. It really could go any way.

All too quickly, she was at the coffee shop on the Old High Street. She pushed the glass door open, holding her breath until she'd scanned the six tables to see Louise wasn't here yet.

She was disappointed and relieved at the same time.

It was a funky wee place, with concrete flooring and exposed bulbs sporting orange filaments. Despite its industrial vibes it was cosy, its tiny offering of tables making it intimate in the best possible way.

Hazel walked to the counter, which was decorated with pale pink subway tiles, and was met by a smiley woman with glasses.

'Hello! Just yourself today?'

'Actually, table for two please.'

'No bother, just over here if that's okay.'

'Brilliant,' Hazel said, walking to the small table tucked up the back by a shelf full of succulents. 'Just to check, you are open to seven, yeah?'

'Yep, so plenty time for cake and coffee. Will I wait until your friend arrives to take your order?'

'That would be good, yeah. Thank you.'

Hazel took a seat, her nervous legs thankful for the rest.

She looked at her watch: she was bang on time. Hopefully Louise wouldn't be too late. They had plenty time to chat thanks to the late opening hours, though. It was one of the other reasons they'd picked here. In Perth, late-night coffee spots were few and far between. Late-night anything, for that matter. Sometimes you were lucky if the pubs stayed open past nine.

Hazel nervously bounced her foot.

Not knowing what Louise's thoughts were was bad enough, but she'd still not got her own thoughts in order either.

She missed her. It was strange how someone could become so important so quickly.

Their lack of conversation left an ever-darkening void in Hazel's day.

She'd seen a trailer for a film the other day, some magical realism thing, and instantly thought: *Louise would like that.* She couldn't message her, though. Her chest had ached. It was a little thing, but suddenly a cavern had appeared inside and she'd noticed its presence every day since. In fact, she could swear it was getting bigger.

Something about Louise lit a fire in her chest.

She made Hazel happy in ways no one else could.

But the walls were still there. Like she was on one side and Louise was on the other, ladder in hand, ready to clamber over if Hazel gave her permission. She ached to give the okay.

Lying awake last night, she'd decided it was a lot like weights.

When she'd first started, she'd barely been able to bicep curl 2kg dumb-bells. Now, 10kg was easy on a good day, if she wasn't planning a lot of reps. But that took time, devotion, patience.

Getting her heart back to being relationship-ready would take time, but it was possible.

When she'd realised that, her heart had done a little flutter. She daren't think past the beginning stages, though. No point dreaming of powerlifting when she could barely hold just herself up.

As if her heart had a sixth sense, she looked up, just as Louise was entering the café.

How could someone look so good in a council polo and rain jacket?

Hazel tensed her jaw, completely forgetting everything she'd decided on.

Louise smiled as she and Hazel locked eyes. It wasn't her

usual smile, though. Louise's smile was sunshine: today it was dialled back to match the grey skies outside.

'Hey,' Hazel said, feeling like she should stand up or something. She wanted to hug her, hold her, bring the warmth back to her cheeks and mood.

'Hey,' Louise echoed. 'This place is nice.'

This was fine, no need for it to be awkward. Just two mates, hanging out, probably deciding their entire futures. No biggie.

'It is. Can't believe I've never been.' Hazel scolded herself internally, annoyed her voice was suddenly sounding restrained, not her own.

'You ordered?' Louise asked as she slipped her jacket off. Her skin flushed with goosebumps.

'Nope. You not freezing?'

She smiled, a smidge of her usual self breaking through. 'Baltic. My sweatshirt's in the wash, though, and I couldn't find my long-sleeved top.'

Classic Louise. Probably running around making sure everyone else was sorted before her.

Hazel caught the waitress' eye and they both ordered coffees.

'How have you been?' Louise asked with a gulp.

'Okay. You?'

'Okay.'

Silence fell faster than a bag of rocks. This was stupid.

'Actually,' Hazel said, leaning closer as if it was a secret. 'It's been a bit shit, hasn't it? I hate fighting with you.'

A glint flashed in Louise's eye, a hint that the woman Hazel knew and liked was still inside. 'I didn't realise we'd been fighting. Were we fighting?' she replied, her mouth quirking up at one side.

'I'm sorry,' Hazel said, falling silent as the waitress

brought their orders over. She stirred her flat white, ruining the intricate foam fern on top. 'I think we both could have done a little better at communicating the other day, so let's give talking another shot.'

Louise nodded, also desecrating the art on her cappuccino. 'I lost my temper. I can't take back what I said, but I want you to know I'm sorry.'

'I know.'

'So.'

'So.'

Neither of them spoke. Hazel busied herself by drinking her coffee, Louise by stirring hers again.

She wanted to comment on how nice the plants were, how enticing the cake fridge was, anything but have this conversation. Maybe they could both pretend the other day never happened? If Louise was happy to forgive and forget, Hazel could too. Louise had said stuff in the heat of the moment, who hadn't?

'I don't really know how to start this,' Louise said, with a stupid grin, and Hazel wished she could kiss her right there and then.

'Me neither. But – and believe me, I would really like to just forget the whole thing – I think we need to get stuff out in the open. Like you said, clear the air.'

'Forget the whole thing, as in, you regret it?'

'Oh no, no, no. Not like that. As in, if I could avoid this fucking awful conversation I would. I don't want to hurt you, Louise.'

'Why would you hurt me?' Fear flashed through her eyes and Hazel hated every second of it.

'I already have, haven't I? You wouldn't have said what you did otherwise.'

Louise nodded, as if realising where this might be going.

'Are we still on different pages then?' She pushed her tongue into her cheek, her eyes trained on her coffee.

'Depends. I liked what we had but if you can't do that again I would really like to keep you as a mate.'

'A mate?' Louise repeated like it was the most godawful word in the world. 'I can't just be your mate, Hazel.'

'I was scared you'd say that.' The bottom dropped out of Hazel's world, along with her stomach. 'I've missed you, like *really* missed you the last few days. I don't want to lose whatever's going on between us.'

Louise sucked on her bottom lip as if to steady it. 'But not enough to go any further?'

'I'm just not there yet.'

Louise ruminated on that for a second as the sound of the coffee shop's grinder filled the gap. 'That's fair enough. But I can't be your friend.'

'So, is that it then?'

This suddenly felt very final. No wonder, because it was. Hazel wanted to slap her cheeks, wake herself up. It had to be a bad dream.

'I guess. Perth's small, though. Maybe we'll cross paths again someday.'

The world slowed, the noise of the café dimming. Today wasn't meant to go like this.

Hazel widened her eyes, determined not to cry.

She'd been hopeful she and Louise could find a middle ground. Not this. This was too much. So, she was just meant to walk out of here and never talk to her again?

She didn't want that, but the thought of lying and saying she could do a relationship was worse. Louise deserved better than Hazel. There was a good chance Hazel would never be fixed; she couldn't saddle Louise with someone forever broken. She needed someone strong, dependable, emotionally available. Louise was brilliant. Hazel couldn't match that.

'I just want you to be happy,' Hazel managed. All she could offer was the truth. If Louise attempted a relationship with someone so broken she would only be miserable. She had too much to work through before getting to the stage Louise so desperately wanted. Hazel would drag her down. She couldn't be who Louise wanted her to be. It was like when Dad broke Mum's china robin: all the pieces were there, but no matter how she tried to balance it back together, nothing fitted right.

Not to mention Cameron. Hazel couldn't subject him to her mess.

She searched Louise's face for clues: there had to be something she could say to make this better. But her features were a blank canvas, no magic words, only pain registering in her eyes.

'And I want the same for you. Guess we do have something in common after all.' Louise stood, coffee barely touched, and started to put her jacket on. 'You've done nothing wrong, Hazel. Please don't beat yourself up about this, because I know you will. You're amazing, don't ever forget that.'

Hazel's mind went blank.

Literally nothing but white noise, a complete flat line. It was like watching the scene from someone else's perspective. She was watching the TV, screaming at this stupid twit with the short brown hair to get up, stop the beautiful blonde woman from leaving. Nothing was getting through, though.

What could she say to make Louise understand? This was for the best. What they had was a cushion from who Hazel really was. She'd said she didn't want a relationship from the start – why did it have to be more complicated than that? They could go back to what they'd had if Louise would only give it a chance. Losing Louise wasn't what she wanted: this wasn't fair on either of them.

The thoughts racing through her head didn't slow enough for Hazel to compile a sentence. Or a single word for that matter. Her jaw was slack, useless.

Louise left, and Hazel remained sitting, dumbstruck.

If it had been a TV show she would have turned it off. What a shitty ending.

Hazel blinked, pulling herself back to reality.

She had to get out of here. She pulled a twenty-pound note from her wallet and put it under the salt shaker on the table. She didn't want to suffer small talk with the waitress.

She forced a small smile as she walked the centre aisle between tables, catching the waitress' eye as she served an older couple.

'Money's on the table,' she grumbled.

She got a small smile in return, as if she knew.

Outside, her breathing became a pant. She kept walking, knowing the longer she took to get to her car the more likely she was to have a public meltdown. She didn't know the Neil Lesley clientele well enough yet; anyone passing her could be a patron of the gym. She couldn't face the humiliation.

She took a shortcut through the car park of a nearby church, giving her precious moments of solitude.

This was what she wanted. It was for the best. She had to remember that.

42

'You okay?' Mum asked, kissing Louise on the forehead as she sat on the sofa.

It was a grim day outside. Thick, gunmetal clouds cast a sheet of misty rain over Perth, blocking out the sun and any potential warmth.

Talk about matching her mood.

'Yeah, I'm grand,' Louise replied with a lethargic smile.

Cameron was at work and Mum had been out with friends for coffee, leaving Louise to indulge in a day of housework. She'd quite enjoyed the distraction but would never in a million years let Cameron know cleaning his room had been anything but a pain in her arse.

After resorting to clearing out the tin cupboard she'd been forced to admit, short of putting the shampoo bottles in alphabetical order, that a rest was needed. So mindless channel surfing commenced.

'Can I get you anything?'

'Nah, I'm good.'

Any flatter and Louise would be 2D.

Which could be handy. Cleaning behind the radiators

had been a real chore today.

Mum took a seat, plopping onto the spongy sofa with a little bounce.

'I hate seeing you sad.'

'I hate being sad.'

With nothing more to be said, Mum kicked her shoes off, putting her feet up on their velvety pouffe, and got comfy.

They watched most of a show about walking in Wales in silence.

'Can I ask you something?' Louise wondered out loud. It was something that had been bugging her for the last few days (okay, subconsciously for years, but more so recently) and Cameron was due home soon. She couldn't wait for the trio on screen to reach the peak of Snowdon before asking.

'Yes, of course.'

'Why didn't you date anyone else after Mark?' Mum's face dropped, so she added, 'You don't need to tell me if you don't want to.'

She thought for a while, Louise's throat becoming dryer with every second. It was a valid question but she'd crossed a line, for sure. She seemed to be good at doing that.

'I did, actually.'

'Really?' Louise croaked.

'Yes, I had a few dalliances. They were just never serious enough for me to tell you. Plus, you were so caught up with Cameron, it didn't seem right to say.'

'I had no idea.'

Mum shrugged. 'Does it matter?'

'No. But are you still looking, or . . . ?' She turned to face Mum. All this time she'd assumed Mum was perpetually single. Thinking about it, that was a stupid thing to think. She was a human, after all.

Mum breathed out slowly. 'Not so much. I mean, I wouldn't completely pooh-pooh the idea if the right man came along, but honestly, over time I realised I quite enjoy my own company and other people are a heck of a lot of work.'

Louise chewed on her cheek. Amen to that. 'It's weird, isn't it? How someone else can bring you so much joy *and* so much pain? This time last year I was happy on my own: now it feels like I've had the wind punched out of me.'

Mum pulled her close, giving her a tight squeeze. 'You'll be okay. I thought the world was ending when Mark and I divorced, but I'm fine now. You will be too.'

'Slightly different, though. Hazel wasn't a complete and utter sociopath.'

'Regardless, we'll always have each other,' Mum said with a curt little nod. 'Although,' she added, and Louise braced herself. 'I've always hoped you'll find someone. I'm happy on my own, I won't deny that, but sharing a life with someone is tremendous. Before things got bad with Mark, they were good, really good. That's what hurt the most. But I'm the exception, not the rule. You deserve to be happy. I used to worry you were holding yourself back for me, concerned I'd be on my own if you paired up. I'm glad that's not been the case.'

Louise's eyes misted. 'Of course I think about you, but that's not the reason I've been single. It would seem I'm just super picky.'

'And so you should be. Only the best for my little girl.'

Louise shifted, nuzzling into Mum's chest and getting comfy as they watched the rest of the Welsh walking show. If they shared any more revelations she was liable to become a sobbing mess: better to end the conversation now.

Her mind was a spinning coin just now. One moment

she was resolved to never get in a relationship again, convinced everything with Hazel had been a massive charade to get her into bed or some strange petty revenge. There had to be a reason for being so lovely, so involved, but ultimately wanting nothing to do with Louise.

Then it would flip, and settle on the other side of her internal argument. The side she really wanted to be true. That Hazel was just hurting and she would eventually come around.

She couldn't be her friend until then, though.

They'd crossed a line: how could Louise forget what Hazel's lips felt like? As if she wouldn't be sitting across from her in book club, remembering what it was like to run her tongue around her nipples?

Or, even worse, the thought of second-guessing every text, every interaction. Was she messaging too much? Was she being inappropriate? Would Hazel think she was a fool if she complimented her suit or hair?

Overthinking would kill her.

Even the thought of Hazel with someone else made her retch. What if she met someone while Louise was waiting in the wings? She couldn't be a spectator to that.

She'd gone as far to block Hazel on all social media, certain she'd see something she didn't want to otherwise.

The man on the screen beamed with pride, having finally scaled the mountain.

How dare he be so happy when she was hurting like this.

She wanted to find Ashley, tear her open for ever hurting Hazel. More than that, she wanted to kick her head off for denying Louise the chance at what felt like something real, something solid.

Louise had looked her up on Facebook after a glass of wine last night. She looked annoyingly lovely. Happy, too. In an alternative universe they would probably get on, going by the stuff she posted.

It wasn't enough, though. She was the reason Louise was in a slump, going out of her mind because Hazel was too afraid to commit.

Louise got it, though. Cheating tore families apart: it fucked you up from the inside out. She got why Hazel was so reluctant. A time machine was out of the question, which only left revenge.

But planning the slow, painful death of someone whom she'd never met and was, for all intents and purposes, a wonderful human, wasn't going to solve anything.

She had to respect Hazel's boundaries. She would come around eventually.

Louise had settled on that (coin-flipping aside) because the secret third option, that niggled as she tried to sleep, reared its head in the quiet of 3am or when she'd paused scrubbing the bath to drag the back of her arm across her sweaty forehead, was the doozy she didn't want to give any airtime to, even for a second.

That maybe, just maybe, it was neither revenge nor Hazel's pain holding her back. Maybe Louise just wasn't enough.

She really was only good enough to fuck. Hot enough to be attractive. Good enough company to suffer her mediocre chat.

But not quite enough.

Okay for a fun time, not a long time.

She gulped the thought away, almost choking a little because her throat was still painfully dry.

No.

This wasn't her. It was like Mum said: she would be fine.

A day would turn into two. Then a week. Before she

knew it a month would have passed and she'd feel more like herself.

Maybe they'd meet again in the future, both reach for the same tins of beans. No, beans weren't right. They didn't fit Hazel's macros. They'd bump into each other up Kinnoull Hill, or on the Inch. Or, one day, years in the future, Louise would be out grabbing some essentials and they'd park their cars side by side, Hazel apologising for having her door open when Louise was trying to get out. And they'd go, *Oh, wow, hey, hi! How are you? It's been a while, huh? Will we get a coffee?* And then they'd pick things up, right where they left off. Before Louise made things complicated.

She'd had every intention of fighting her corner when they last met, but seeing Hazel's face, her steely gaze, how steadfast she was on just being friends, had sucked the life right out of her.

She didn't want to guilt Hazel into doing anything she wasn't comfortable with.

For now, her focus was on retaining her dignity and decluttering her wardrobe.

You can't change how other people feel, so there was no sense in putting her case forward. Why waste the energy? Her time was much better spent getting the house in order.

Plus, coming across as a blubbering, delusional mess really put a damper on the whole *retaining dignity* sitch she had going.

Now, if only she could stop checking her phone to see if Hazel had messaged. That would be perfect.

It would happen soon. One day at a time, she would stop obsessing over Hazel Paterson.

43

A little under a week had passed and Hazel felt no better. She was in a constant state of anxiety – chest tight, nauseous, clammy hands, the works – despite her head being totally cool with the whole thing.

Well. Not *totally* cool.

She missed Louise. It was ridiculous, but she did. She had no right to call things off then have the audacity to miss her: she was mad at herself for being such a hypocrite.

Sometimes the greater good didn't feel great or good. But what can you do?

It had stung like hell to realise Louise had blocked her on all socials. Somehow not being able to see her made it worse. It was for the best, though. What was the point in agonising over someone, torturing yourself with their photos? She'd lost the right to that smile when she'd ended things.

Hazel stepped out of the shower, rolling her neck as she looked in the mirror. Even her skin was duller.

She'd still not told Yaz about any of this disaster. Maybe

that's what was causing all this internal affliction: the pent-up truths she was keeping from her best friend.

She just couldn't imagine doing it though. In all honesty, Yaz could be pretty judgemental at times, and she could just imagine them rolling their eyes and saying 'how have you fucked it all up again?'. She didn't need someone else's criticism. She'd disappointed herself enough.

Hazel towel-dried her hair and slapped on some moisturiser.

Tonight should have been book club, but that was off the table now. Walkie Talkies too.

Nothing was left but work.

Which was actually going really well. Ginny had invited her for a run on Sunday. She seemed lovely. Her boyfriend worked at the chip shop on the Old High Street and preferred his Xbox to a quick 5k. Hazel had no idea how that worked, but relationships were a complete mystery these days.

Maybe Ginny could give her some advice between laps.

Hazel hung her towel on the radiator and put on her comfies: an old hoodie and tatty joggers. Tonight was reserved for watching bad TV; she didn't need to dress up.

The sound of Mum and Dad's cooking show blared through the hall as she made her way to her bedroom. She didn't have the heart to sit with them tonight. Bed was the only place for her. She quite liked listening to the rain battering off the windows as she lay cosy inside.

She padded through, clicked on the TV in passing, and flopped onto her bed.

Hazel had barely made it through one episode of *Superstore* before Charlotte appeared in her doorway, her coat dripping.

'Fucking mental out there,' she said, as if Hazel had no eyes or ears.

'Book club good?' Hazel watched in disbelief as Charlotte sat on her bed, wet coat still on. 'Eh, take that off, please. You're soaking my bed.'

'No, listen. This can't wait.'

'What?' Hazel asked, now on high alert. Although, it would take two seconds to take that bloody thing off.

Charlotte's face grew serious and Hazel's stomach flipped.

'Louise wasn't at book club and Jordan said it's the first one she's missed, *ever*.'

'Shit.'

'Jordan was going to see her after but she'd fobbed her off with some excuse about being busy.'

'Maybe she is busy.'

Charlotte tilted her head. If looks could kill, Hazel would be on the floor. 'You've been a mess since you guys broke up.'

'Hardly.'

'I heard you crying the other night.'

Embarrassing. 'I'll be sure to keep my emotions to myself from now on, sorry.'

'I'm not saying that to be mean. Hazel, please.'

'Please what?'

'Just give her a chance? You were so happy.' She smiled weakly. 'We can't both be saddo singles.'

She had been happy, but life wasn't a set of balance scales, happiness outweighing everything else. It had to factor with the rest, be part of the bigger picture.

'I'm just not ready for a relationship,' Hazel said, tired of this broken record. But it was all she had.

'What bit aren't you ready for?' Charlotte huffed, a spray

of raindrops coming off her like a wet dog. 'The part where you get to spend the rest of your life with someone who loves and supports you? Always having someone in your corner? Being happy? What do you think will happen? You'll wake up one day and magically feel different? A physical switch will click, telling you you're ready to be with someone? There's no hard and fast rules here, Hazel. You're not going to suddenly feel like a new woman and life is transformed to something shiny. It takes time: things will change without you ever noticing. Would you not rather do it with Louise at your side? People like her don't come around often.'

Charlotte's eyes burned into Hazel's, powering home her speech.

'Why do you care so much?' Hazel asked, trying not to sound dismissive. It was a real question.

'Because. You've got a shot at something real here and I would be a shithead of a sister if I stood on the sidelines and let you pass it up. I couldn't be there when that arsehole Ashley was breaking your heart. I'm not going to let you down again.'

'You've never let me down.'

'Let's agree to disagree. It's a cliché, but don't let your past ruin your present. Otherwise you're only letting Ashley fuck you over twice.'

She had a point. 'I get the sentiment but I just can't risk it, Charlotte.'

'Risk it? Risk what?'

'Getting my heart broken again.'

She groaned. 'You really think Louise would do that? From what I can see you're the one breaking your own heart by being a stubborn arsehole.'

'Steady.' She forced a smile but Charlotte was touching a nerve: the pain seared hot across her chest.

Charlotte smirked. 'Tell me I'm not right? That poor woman is out there breaking her heart because you can't trust yours. Put a bet on yourself. Have some faith for once.'

Hazel considered it. Louise had lit her up in ways no one else ever had: she'd snuck in under the radar, and now Hazel was lost without her. Every day felt like a stopgap until she got her act together and was ready for Louise. No one else had crossed her mind. She was in training, Louise the main event.

If Louise deemed her good enough, who was she to argue? She had herself on the bench for no reason.

'She wasn't at book club?'

'Nope,' Charlotte replied with a widening grin.

'Maybe it wouldn't hurt to have another chat.'

Charlotte looked like her face was about to split. 'Thank fuck. If you hadn't said that I was going back out to drag Louise here. I can take my jacket off now.'

'So kind of you to soak my bed in the meantime.' Hazel jested, getting to her feet to locate her boots.

'Hey, if your talk goes well it'll have a night to dry out. You won't need it.'

THE RAIN WAS EVEN HEAVIER when she reached the Kings' house. It had gone from raining angry, bullet-like drops to being a full-on deluge, as if she was driving through a waterfall. Her windscreen wipers did nothing; thank God it was just a short drive.

Hazel pulled her jacket's hood as tight as possible and took a deep breath before leaving the car.

It was tough not to close her eyes as she ran from the

pavement to Louise's front door: the icy cold water was like a slap in the face.

She shook herself, stabbing twice at the doorbell, hoping to make a point: be quick.

Suddenly the reality of the situation hit, even fiercer than the slapping rain. She was going to have to do some serious grovelling. Her heart raced into action and she gulped any fear away.

After what felt like an age, the shape of Donna appeared through the frosted glass.

She gingerly opened the door a crack, her face awash with surprise. 'Hazel, hi. You okay?'

Hazel bounced on the spot, her joggers clinging tightly to her legs, already soaked all the way through. 'Yeah. Louise in?'

Donna shook her head. 'She's been at book club, then away to see Jordan, sorry.'

Shit.

'Forgot it was book club tonight. Tell her I popped by?' Her teeth chattered as she spoke. Couldn't have been a dry night, could it?

'Of course. She forgot her phone or I would have said just to call her.'

Double shit.

'No worries, bye Donna.'

Hazel shuffled top speed back to the car, hands shoved in her pockets, determined to expose as little as possible to the elements.

She slapped into the driver's seat with a squelch.

Louise hadn't been at book club. She wasn't going to see Jordan. Where the fuck was she?

Hazel rested her head against the seat and closed her eyes.

Where was Louise?

Her heart hadn't returned to a normal pace since standing on the doorstep but now it thundered for another reason: worry.

The thought of anything happening to Louise cemented Hazel's feelings. She had to find her tonight, make things right. She couldn't lose her. It didn't matter what happened in the future: not having Louise *right now* would be worse. She couldn't go another day without her. Her heart thumped a little harder. With Louise by her side she needn't worry. Her heart was stronger with her, not without.

She turned her key in the ignition, bringing the car to life.

Her head and her heart had finally aligned. She knew exactly where Louise would be.

But first, she needed to find a shop.

44

Louise listened to the rain. It had been heavy when she'd left, now it had skipped torrential and gone straight to monsoon.

It was comforting, though.

Hazel had called her ritual creepy when they'd first come up Kinnoull Hill together all those weeks ago. Well, she'd called the setting creepy. And maybe it was – the pitch black evening had grasped the car, enveloping it as Louise killed the lights – but it was exactly how she wanted it. Doors locked, this was her little bubble. Just her, the rain, and the still air of the car.

She took a deep breath, eyes closed.

The rain relaxed her, so heavy she couldn't see out. No one could see in. She had all the time in the world.

Her brain had spun like the waltzers ride at the summer fair today. She wanted nothing more than to never think of Hazel again but her mind was rabid, intent on torturing her.

She'd boiled it down to two options: get blind drunk or come to her spot.

The former didn't seem all that productive and she'd

only hate herself tomorrow. She had a session booked with twelve OAPs to teach them how to use iPads. She couldn't handle their inane questions hungover.

This car park had saved her sanity a dozen times before. Its track record gave her faith: it might take a few goes to get her brain to calm down, but it was possible.

The first time she'd come here was out of pure frustration. Barely twenty years old, with a baby that hadn't stopped screaming for more than a few minutes that day, she'd told Mum she needed a break and got in the car with no idea where she was going. Her sanity had been so brittle, she was on verge of snapping, but as soon she'd pulled into the car park on that muggy July night, she could feel the stress leaving her body. She'd driven up Kinnoull Hill in a daze, her body knowing what she needed before she did.

Here, it was just her and the trees. How could you feel boxed in when surrounded by nothing but pine and beech trees?

She released a staggered breath then swallowed. This place was like a full body massage, brain included.

When Hazel had first returned to Perth, Louise longed to right the wrongs of the past, show her that she'd changed. Now, she wondered if it had been worth the effort. Hazel had changed the chemistry of her mind. Regardless of what Hazel wanted from her, or what her intentions were, she'd teased out parts of Louise she didn't know existed. And now they were free, they couldn't be hidden again.

She didn't want to spend her life alone. She'd had Cameron to focus on, the ugly scars of Mark and Mum, a career to forge. Somewhere along the way she'd subconsciously convinced herself being single was the best choice, denying a piece of herself in the process. Mum was right: sharing your life with someone was brilliant.

But Mum's words had dislodged a new truth. Any more and she'd need to live in this car park full time.

As she'd lain in bed last night, dissecting Mum's wisdom, she'd realised: her future was Hazel-shaped. She didn't want just anyone – she wanted the gorgeous brunette with stupidly cute dimples, the one who danced like a robot and could run circles around her. Literally. And that wasn't even considering the abs.

There were no ifs, no buts. Only Hazel would do. It was impossible to deny. The sooner she admitted that the better. Because then she could work on getting her head straight.

Who she wanted and who Hazel was were poles apart.

It was a fantasy and could never be more than that.

She was spiralling again.

Louise took another deep breath and focused on the rain battering the windscreen.

Headlights sliced through her bubble of calm.

She checked her doors were locked. It wasn't often she got company up here. Not at this time of day.

Unable to sleep last night, she'd weighed up the option of texting Hazel, saying she could return to casual. She winced at the thought. Having Hazel in some capacity would be better than her current turmoil, but she couldn't keep it up. What if Hazel *never* wanted to take it further?

Better to get the pain out of the way now, rather than prolong it.

Everything was a mess.

Could she have done anything to avoid it?

Logically, she could have pushed Hazel away in that hotel room, stopped it from going further. But the pull was too strong: it was inevitable. There was a reason Louise had only ever seen Hazel in a room full of people when they were teenagers. Even then she'd felt it.

Maybe there was a King curse. First loves were always destined to fail.

She stiffened. Letting the word sink in. Love.

Fuck.

She was just about to rest her head on the steering wheel, stomach leaden with despair, when someone knocked on her passenger window.

Her heart jumped out of her chest, instantly whizzing to go at a thousand beats per minute.

She clenched her jaw, stiffened her muscles. The heavy rain would hide her. Perhaps if she ignored it, whoever it was would go away.

No such luck: they hammered another time.

Shitting fuck, why did she leave her mobile at home? Her need for a little peace was going to get her murdered.

'Louise!' a familiar voice shouted.

'Hazel?' Her voice wavered, unsure if this was her imagination or not.

'Can you let me in?'

She paused. Could this be a trick? They'd have to be a bloody good mimic. But why was Hazel here?

'Louise!'

'Yeah, sorry,' she said, leaning over and pulling the handle of the passenger door, automatically unlocking it as it swung open a little.

In plopped a very wet, very disgruntled Hazel. Her eyes shone as they met Louise's, a grin taking over. It faltered, dying back to an unsure smile as she closed the door with a thud.

She was soaked. If Louise hadn't known better she'd think Hazel had gone for a dip, fully clothed, in a swimming pool. The rain had gone right through her hood, wetting her hair. A big blob of water ran down the centre of her face before dripping off the end of her nose.

'Is it raining?' Louise asked with a twitch of her lips. She wasn't ready to smile yet. Not without knowing Hazel's intentions.

'No. What makes you think that?'

They held each other's gazes for a beat, a poor substitute for actually holding each other.

'What's going on?' Louise finally asked, her voice nearly drowned out by the never-ending rain.

Hazel ran a hand through her hair, scrunching her eyes shut as the move released a fresh river of water across her brow. 'I, er.' She searched in her pocket, eventually producing two small, bruised bananas. She held them out to Louise. 'I'm in trouble and I need you to save me.'

Her lip trembled as she spoke and Louise could have sworn a single tear joined the rain on Hazel's cheek.

She looked at the bananas being held above her handbrake. She gulped: if Hazel was crying, she was sure to as well. She never could see someone upset without joining them.

'Huh?' was all she could muster.

Hazel put the bananas on the centre console. 'That's the deal, isn't it? Bananas means you drop everything and come no matter what? Well, I'm in trouble, Louise.' She shrugged, adding her next sentence as a rambling mumble. 'You left your phone at home, so I had to improvise.'

'How do you know I left my phone?'

'I went there first.'

Louise felt like she'd come into a conversation halfway through with no chance of catching up. 'I'm so confused.'

Hazel sucked on her bottom lip, eyes now set on the

bananas. 'It felt right at the time. Now I'm not so sure. You get the reference, yeah?'

'Course I do, it's just . . . can you start from the beginning?'

Hazel nodded slowly. 'So, my mum broke her ankle, meaning I had to come back to Perth, and—'

Louise held a hand up, finally allowing herself to smile. 'I think you can start a little closer to the present,' she said, gesturing her hand as if to usher Hazel forward.

'Really? You don't want a full recap?' Her dimples winked at Louise, her dark eyes snaring her very soul, even in the darkness of the car park.

'Only if it helps you get to the point.' If Hazel could be cheeky, so could Louise. Anything was better than fighting.

Hazel's gaze dropped to her hands as she flicked her thumbnails together. 'Third time lucky for a chat?'

Louise's heart skipped a little. She wouldn't come all this way just to talk about being friends again, surely? 'Depends, I guess.'

'Depends on what?'

'If you've changed your mind or not.'

'I've not changed my mind.'

Louise's heart and stomach dropped to her boots.

Hazel continued, 'I think I always knew the real answer, so I've not changed my mind, no. Just decided to be fully honest with myself.'

'I'm lost again.' She took a deep breath but the air didn't quite reach her lungs.

'I was so scared of getting hurt, I never realised how scary it would be to not have you.'

Louise's heart slowed, giving her brain space to catch up. 'So you—'

'Need you, yes,' Hazel interrupted, cutting Louise off.

All the twisted thoughts she'd held over the last week, the messy jumble swirling inside her, settled. Like someone had flicked a switch and turned the tornado off, letting its contents fall in perfect order. 'I can't,' she said, as surprised as Hazel was, going by her face. 'This isn't what you wanted. I don't want this if you don't really want it.'

'But I do!' Hazel barked, just as the wind whipped up, throwing a hard splash of rain against the side of the car.

'You've told me twice you don't: what if you change your mind again?'

Hazel's face crumpled, her eyes brimming with tears. 'I won't.'

Louise's own lip wobbled, matching Hazel's. 'How can I be sure?'

In a blink Hazel had her door open, the rain quickly infiltrating the inside of the car. Where was she going? This conversation was far from over. 'Hazel!'

She didn't stop. Louise had no choice but to join her. She gasped as she opened the driver side door, thick, heavy rain soaking her in a moment. She ran to Hazel's side of the car, only just stopping her from storming off.

Fuck, it was cold.

Her chest heaved as if she'd just jumped in a frozen loch. 'Hazel,' she said again.

She stepped away, her back now against Louise's car. 'What's the point?' she shouted, throwing a hand up. 'I've fucked this up, just like I fuck everything up. I'm sorry I dragged you into this.'

A strand of soaking hair slapped Louise in the face, sticking to her cheek. She ignored it. 'Can't we just talk?' She extended a hand towards the car.

The wind whipped through the trees, providing an eerie whistle to mask Hazel's silence.

Hazel crossed her arms and sniffed, tears streaming down her cheeks, so heavy they couldn't be hidden by the rain.

Words were getting them nowhere.

Louise stepped forward, her boots squelching in the mud, and scooped Hazel into a fierce hug. After a second, her arms wrapped around Louise's waist as she nuzzled her head into her shoulder, Hazel's body lurching as she cried.

She held her until Hazel settled, lighter from releasing whatever had been pent up inside. She loosened her grip but maintained the hug, forgetting the driving rain as she dipped her head to rest against Hazel's neck. She stayed for a while, hoping Hazel could feel what she was thinking or at least how much she cared for her.

'Look at me,' Louise eventually said, drawing back.

It was almost pitch black in the car park, but Louise could see the sincerity in her eyes. Her gaze was piercing; it cradled Louise's heart and told her everything she needed to know.

She gently brushed her nose against Hazel's, her arms now looped around her neck. Louise stilled, their noses still touching, as she closed her eyes, their breath mingling as one.

'I'm sorry,' Hazel whispered, her words at one with the weather.

'Me too.'

That was enough talking. Louise pressed her lips to Hazel's, the rain making them slide together before locking in place.

They were slow, tentative kisses at first, as if sussing each other out. Light; lips barely grazing. Each one a silent apology. Louise smiled as Hazel gently bit her bottom lip, the nibble a full stop on their inhibition. They crashed together, the fervour of the last few months spilling out as sloppy, messy kisses. This wasn't the time for perfection. The only priority was proximity. But nothing was enough. Louise parted her lips to find Hazel's tongue, a fresh hunger coursing through her, forcing a leg between Hazel's thighs and pushing upward, her hands gripping what she could, desperation driving her to claim every inch of Hazel she could.

Louise pushed Hazel against the car, hair and clothes still clinging tightly between them, unable to hold a single drop of water more.

'Let's get out of the rain,' she panted into Hazel's mouth.

45

There was so much Hazel needed to say, but breaking this moment with Louise wasn't an option. They could talk later. Right now, the most important thing was *showing* Louise how she felt.

She reached over and opened the back door of Louise's car. 'You first.'

They tumbled in together, Louise whipping around to face Hazel as she slotted between her legs, the weight of her body pressed firmly down, exactly where it needed to be.

The whole drive here, she'd wondered about the best way to apologise to Louise. What to say to truly make her believe.

But actions spoke louder than words.

And right now, screaming *I'm sorry* wasn't going to do anything: pressing her lips to Louise's neck and making her groan was going to change the world.

'The door,' Louise mumbled.

'Shit,' Hazel said, leaning backwards and swinging it shut. Louise held her thighs, stopping her from falling backwards.

Typical Louise. Always looking out for her.

The door closed, their cocoon now sealed. As it clicked shut, everything slotted into place: her mind, body, and heart were in alignment. Her chest felt lighter, the weight of indecision gone.

Hazel allowed herself a moment to study Louise. The sparkle was back in her eyes, the dark cloud from the café a distant memory. As were the lines of indecision that had bracketed them. This was Louise. Her Louise. Back to full beam.

Hazel dipped back to her neck. She pressed her lips to the soft skin just below her ear and hoped her kisses conveyed everything Hazel was thinking at that very moment.

She'd been swimming in a wild sea, lost, hope a distant memory after Ashley had cut her loose. She'd been so blinkered, she'd not seen Louise pull her boat alongside, giving her the strength to keep treading water. She couldn't tread forever, though, and instead of taking Louise's hand to salvation, she'd chosen rejection, sinking under. There was comfort in what you knew, but sometimes you had to close your eyes and step into the unknown.

Hazel weaved her hand under Louise's wet hoodie, making her jump at the contact.

'Sorry, cold hands,' she said as Hazel stilled.

'Sorry.' She pulled it back, finding Louise's hip instead.

It wasn't the biggest car in the world and Hazel was forced to sit on her knees, unable to bend into the position she really wanted. Louise's thighs lay either side as Hazel contemplated what to do.

Ideally, they would be at home, have all the room in the world. But Hazel couldn't wait that long.

'You're beautiful,' she said, as if seeing Louise for the first time.

Finally, with her blinkers off, she could see Louise for what she really was: this was never just casual, some meaningless fling, a physical means to an end. It had always been more.

Her defences were so heavily fortified no one else in the world could have infiltrated them. Although, Hazel suspected Louise had held a key all along, avoiding her defences all together. She'd strolled in like she owned the place, Hazel none the wiser.

Louise pushed herself up on her forearms, a hazy smile rounding out her cheeks. 'So are you.'

Hazel wasn't so sure. She could still feel water running down her face.

She rubbed her hands together before blowing on them, trying to inject a little heat.

As warm as they could ever be, she fluttered her fingers to the button on Louise's jeans and popped it open before undoing the zip. The fabric clung to Louise's thighs, highlighting the beautiful curve of her body. Even soaking wet, hair plastered to her brow, this would be the moment Hazel's heart replayed on a loop. Her emerald dress had been dazzling but right now, Louise couldn't be more perfect.

She leaned forward, her lips finding Louise's as Hazel snaked her hands into her jeans, skipping her underwear and going straight to where she needed to be. Heat pooled underneath her fingertips as she cupped Louise's centre.

She smiled against Hazel's mouth. 'You're not hanging about, are you?' she purred.

'Wasted enough time as it is.'

Seconds were precious with Louise. She grabbed the

next one with gusto and used a finger to part Louise's wet heat, trailing it north to find her clit.

She'd been so close to losing everything: now was the time for showing Louise she was going nowhere. She might have wanted to protect herself from making any more mistakes of the heart, but by doing so, she'd nearly committed the biggest one of all.

Louise groaned, collapsing as far back as she could against the car door, using a hand on the back of Hazel's neck to pull her closer.

Despite the proximity, Hazel craved being closer. She couldn't wait to get home and rid Louise of her wet clothes, feel their bodies pressed together.

Her fingers worked Louise's outer core as Hazel's middle finger ran circles on her clit.

'That feels so good,' she moaned into Hazel's ear, kissing now apparently a sensory overload as she relaxed back, focusing on the pleasure growing between her legs. She gripped Hazel's neck as she nuzzled into her shoulder blade.

Hazel burrowed against her wet hair, tied up but still so unruly. God, she loved Louise's hair.

She pushed her thigh harder against Louise's core, adding a little pressure as she brought her closer to the edge.

It might have been pitch black in the car park, but with every passing moment the world shone a little brighter. Louise had that effect on things.

Whatever happened next, Hazel was stronger with Louise. No matter what, they would tackle things together, side by side. Finally she was where she belonged, no longer drifting. Louise had tethered her in place, triple-knotted. Probably using some fancy technique she learned through one of her community courses. Hazel was going nowhere.

Louise stiffened under her touch before bucking her hips upward as she came undone. Hazel kept her hand in place, riding the wave with her before bringing her to the edge once more. Quivering under her touch, Louise gently placed her hand around Hazel's wrist with a hearty chuckle.

'Wow,' she breathed, eyes fixed on the roof above.

Hazel watched as her chest heaved and a smile pulled at her lips as she found Hazel's eyes.

'What?' Louise asked, looking a little embarrassed but still on cloud nine.

Hazel shuffled into the gap beside her. On the tiny back seat of her car there was hardly room for one person, never mind two, but they didn't need much. Besides, the closer the better. She rubbed her nose against Louise's. 'Just really happy, that's all.'

'Yeah?' Louise's tone was light: she could feel it too. It might be raining outside, but in the car it was blue skies for days.

'I'd kinda forgotten what that felt like.'

She hadn't said it for pity but soon Louise's arms were wrapped around her, holding her tight. She squeezed her as safety and security washed over Hazel, a flush of warmth settling in her chest, as if Louise's arms would always be around her, even when they were apart.

Louise kissed Hazel's forehead. 'You'd better get used to it.'

Hazel smiled. 'That's what I was counting on.'

'But,' Louise added, a hand now cupping Hazel's jaw. 'Any problems or niggles, we sort them together. I've got your back, and you've got mine.'

'I was counting on that too.' Hazel planted a kiss on Louise's lips that left no doubt.

She hadn't realised how exhausted she was from

berating herself every day since Ashley left. It was second nature, but now the habit was broken, she could feel every muscle in her body relax as she sunk back into Louise's embrace.

Just as she was close to drifting off, another gust of rain shook the car. Louise sat up on her elbows. 'Think it's – oh shit. Look how muddy my car is.'

Hazel squinted in the darkness. Even in this light there was a clear mess at the other end of the car. 'I'll clean it. I think it's the least I can do.'

Louise opened her mouth in mock horror. 'Least you can do?' she repeated, incredulous. 'And the rest.' She playfully grabbed at Hazel's stomach, making her laugh. 'What I was going to say was: do you think it's safe to drive?'

'Probably, if we go slow. We can't stay here all night.'

Louise pursed her lips. 'Will you come to mine?'

'Three for three. I was counting on that too.'

'Good. But I need to do a wash. Cameron got tomato sauce on his uniform and he's struggling to get it out.' She rolled her eyes.

Hazel grinned. This is what she wanted: normality. No sneaking about or stolen moments, just two people living their lives in tandem.

Louise pouted. 'Sorry. We've had this amazing evening and now I need to put a bloody wash on.'

'Don't say sorry. It's real life. And I can't wait to keep doing it with you.'

She pulled her in for another kiss, getting lost in each other while the rain battered outside.

A few months later

'That's the last box,' Cameron said after he put it on the floor in the hall. He wiped the sweat from his top lip as he plonked himself on the armchair, opposite Hazel on the sofa. Moving boxes was hard work, even with the chill of winter still in the air.

Hazel flashed him a smile as she waded through the box in front of her, looking for three mugs. Louise had been put in charge of finding the TV leads. She was standing beside a tower of boxes, the one full of plugs and cables sitting on top. How did they manage to tangle themselves? They obviously went to the same school of nuisance as Christmas lights.

The sofa was at an angle in the middle of the room, a sea of boxes enveloping every available space. Louise usually hated moving – the thought of unpacking everything made her skin itchy – but today was filled with so much excitement and hope she couldn't possibly hold any negative feelings.

'Ta-dah!' Hazel proclaimed, fishing out a paper-wrapped mug.

'And the kettle?' she asked. They'd bought a new one but Lord knows where it was now, in this guddle.

'It's somewhere. I'm dying for a cuppa.' She grinned.

'Me too.' Cameron groaned. 'Those boxes were hella heavy.'

'You been doing those hammer curls to Arnold presses I showed you?' Hazel asked, unwrapping the third mug.

'I have no idea what you just asked,' Louise replied with a smirk.

Cameron chuckled. 'I have. Can you not tell?' He flexed his muscles with a grin.

'We couldn't have done today without those guns, that's for sure. Cuppa then?' Louise asked, going to grab the mugs off the table.

'Actually,' Cameron replied, with a stretch. 'I'd better meet Sienna if I'm coming back for the footie. Sure you'll have the telly set up by then?'

'Of course, if your mum can find the cable,' Hazel replied, shooting Louise a smirk.

'Hey! I'm trying. They all look the same to me,' Louise said with a quiet laugh.

He stood, rolling his shoulders in the process. 'Hazel will keep you right. As always. So, quarter to eight?'

'Well, it starts then. You'd better come just before to be safe,' Hazel suggested.

The two of them were tight. No surprise, given their shared love of football and fitness. There was even talk of him going to college to study sports fitness alongside his McDonald's job. It never hurt to keep your options open, and Louise was happy whatever he did, but for now, seeing him excited and focused was a dream come true.

'And I can have a beer, yeah?'

The question was aimed at Hazel more than Louise, but she still answered anyway. 'A small one. You've earned it.' He was eighteen in less than a month. How the hell had that happened?

He grinned. 'Right, see you later.' He turned to Hazel, holding a hand to his mouth as if to hide his words but not reducing his volume a jot. 'Text me if she mucks the cables up. I can just buy a new one.'

Hazel shook her head, smiling. 'I'll keep her straight.'

He waved goodbye and with a click of the door they were alone.

Louise took less than a second to join Hazel on the couch, putting her arms around her waist, careful not to touch her chest, and dragged her closer, toppling them over in the process.

She kissed Hazel's neck, deciding she'd earned the right to a little lie down after all that heavy lifting.

Charlotte wouldn't finish her shift for a few hours, but that was the hardest part done. She could help move the big stuff when she got home, then tonight was all about takeaways and relaxing with a glass of wine or two as they unpacked, football on in the background if she managed to locate this bloody lead.

From what Louise had seen as she helped unload Hazel's hire van, it was going to be an eclectic flat for sure. She'd even spied a luminous pink toy monster, nearly hip-height if she was to hazard a guess. Louise would put money on it not being Hazel's. She couldn't wait to see how it all came together. Or co-existed in the same walls, at least.

It had been brilliant to see Hazel come into her own the last few months. Business at the gym was booming and she was soon to hit the milestone of her first full month of PT bookings. At this rate she'd have no free sessions until Christmas soon enough.

With Charlotte being kept on after Christmas in the gift shop there was no point wasting time – or her parents' sanity – and soon they'd both signed a lease on a charming little flat on Charlotte Street. A coincidence which Charlotte liked to point out as often as physically possible.

Hazel got closer to following through on her threat of smothering the flat in hazel trees every day, just to even things out.

Louise loved seeing their relationship develop. She'd often wished for a little sister and now she'd got one. A damn good one, at that. One that even remembered to pack the teabags in with the mugs.

'What's the time?' Hazel asked, her back still pressed into Louise's chest.

She checked her watch. 'Three thirty. How come? When's the van to be back?'

'Not until tomorrow. Our mums want to go to IKEA, remember?'

'Aw, yeah.' Louise suspected it was more for meatballs and chattering than actually needing anything.

'I was wondering if we had time to christen the place, while we're alone? If you get my drift.' Her voice dropped an octave for the final sentence.

Louise pumped her eyebrows. Hazel always had her priorities straight. The only other thing on their agenda was prepping for tomorrow's dinner. Cameron was bringing Sienna. She'd been at the house plenty of times, but tomorrow felt a big deal. Their first formal meal together. Louise'd had trouble sleeping last night, nervous butterflies stopping her from relaxing: there was so much to do this weekend.

But the move had gone well. Tomorrow would be fine too. Hazel was handling most of the cooking but there was still the pressure of making a good impression. God knows how it would feel when she finally had to meet Sienna's parents. She took a deep breath at the thought. Her, Hazel, and the McEwans. It would be fine. Hazel always brought it.

'You okay?' Hazel asked, shifting to face her. 'Don't stress about tomorrow, I told you. One mouthful of my potato dauphinoise and she'll be smitten.'

'You sure that's okay with your macros? I still feel bad.'

Hazel made her face look extra stern. 'It's a very special occasion. Don't you give it a second thought. Besides, I'm quite looking forward to cooking such indulgent food. It's nice to be naughty sometimes.'

'Speaking of which: bedroom?' Louise asked with a wry smile. 'I'll be extra careful, promise.'

Hazel hovered her hand over her chest, as if just remembering she was sensitive there. 'It's healing fine. I think it should be okay to touch now.'

Louise had given Hazel a tattoo voucher for Christmas and she'd had her booking last week. A cover-up. Gone was that ghastly letter A, but Hazel was yet to tell her what it was. She'd been so busy packing all week they'd had no serious alone time.

She stood, holding a hand out to Louise before helping her up. She interlaced their fingers and led her to what would eventually be Hazel's bedroom. Right now, a bed frame leaning against the wall and a mattress on the floor were the only hints at its intended future.

Hazel pulled Louise onto the mattress, slotting between her legs, instantly making her core pulse as they kissed. There were no in-betweens with Hazel: it was one hundred per cent all the way.

Louise grasped the hem of Hazel's T-shirt, smiling as they kissed a final time before she pulled back. 'Ready to show me, then?'

Hazel smirked, sitting upright, Louise now straddling her thighs. She crossed her arms ready to pull her T-shirt over her head. 'Close your eyes.'

Louise did as told, her heart racing with anticipation. She had no clue what it was going to be. You could hardly turn an A into an L, could you? She'd scolded herself the first time she'd thought that, as if it was a crazy notion to think Hazel would want her initial on her. It wasn't that they weren't going to last, but Hazel had made the mistake once: she would have to be dead certain to repeat anything similar. Tattoos were a big deal.

She could feel the weight of Hazel's stare and desperately wanted to open her eyes. As a substitute she moved her hands forward, finally finding Hazel's taut stomach.

Louise could touch Hazel's body a million times and never tire of it.

'Okay, open your eyes.'

She looked at Hazel's face first. How could you not, with a smile like that?

Then her eyes drifted south. Her breath caught in her lungs.

'Is that? Are they?'

'Bananas,' Hazel said, smile a mile wide. Sure enough, two bananas now covered the infamous initial.

Louise swallowed, hoping she could keep the tears at bay long enough to kiss her girlfriend. It didn't matter either way. Hazel would love her regardless.

AUTHOR'S NOTE

Hazel got her happy ending, finally!

I owed it to her, having put her through the wringer with Ashley. It all worked out in the end though. Sorry for causing so much heartache along the way, Hazel. Not to mention that tattoo.

This story takes us to Perth, where I grew up. I can't believe after all this time it still doesn't have an official LGBTQ+ bar. Maybe I should invent one and fictitiously fill the gap until the real Perth gets its act together.

If you guessed each book club member would be getting a book: you're right! And Charlie too. Who will they end up with...you'll have to wait and see!

To be kept in the loop with new releases and to receive free stories, please join my reader's group via email or connect with me on Instagram at @alliemcderidauthor.

Will you leave me a review?

I hope you enjoyed If She Could. If you have a moment I would really appreciate an honest review on Amazon and / or Goodreads. Reviews help me grow as an author and help new readers know what to expect. The more people that take a chance on my books, the more books I can write. It doesn't need to be anything fancy, a few words will do. Thank you.

Allie McDermid is a lesbian romance author. Her debut novel, Love Charade, was published in July 2022.

Born and raised in Perth, Allie now lives in Glasgow with her ever-growing gang of cats. She is partial to a good scone.

ALSO BY ALLIE MCDERMID

Want to know what happened at the first ever Lovefest?

LOVE CHARADE

Holly Taylor didn't expect to return to Glasgow. And she certainly didn't expect her parents to enter her into a dating competition on her first day home.

Jen Berkley is happily single. Having vowed to never date again after her horror ex broke her heart, no one is more surprised when her best friend convinces her to take part in a dating contest.

Jen wants to win the money. Holly wants to regain the trust of her parents. Will they get what their hearts desire or will the charade fool no one?

Set in Glasgow and full of Scottish charm as well as lashings of delicious desire, smouldering sexual tension and even a few laughs, buy Love Charade today and find out if some things just can't be faked...

Printed in Great Britain
by Amazon